Praise for

DIANE
CHAMBERLAIN

"Diane Chamberlain is the Southern Jodi Picoult."
—*New York Times* bestselling author Mary Alice Monroe

"Chamberlain lays out her latest piece of
romantic suspense in a shattered chronology that's
as graceful as it is perfectly paced…engrossing."
—*Publishers Weekly* on *Before the Storm*

"[A] fast-paced read that explores the psychological
complexity of a family pushed to its limits."
—*Booklist* on *Secrets She Left Behind*

"Exceedingly talented author Diane Chamberlain has a truly
masterful way of constructing compelling, multilayered stories
that are rich with drama and emotion."
—*RT Book Reviews*

"Diane Chamberlain is a marvelously gifted author!
Every book she writes is a real gem."
—*Literary Times*

"Chamberlain skillfully plumbs the nature
of crimes of the heart."
—*Publishers Weekly*

"Chamberlain manages plot with great skill…
Ripe storytelling that deserves a prominent place
in the beach bag."
—*Kirkus Reviews*

DIANE CHAMBERLAIN

Summer's Child

MIRA®

Recycling programs
for this product may
not exist in your area.

ISBN-13: 978-0-7783-2841-4

SUMMER'S CHILD

This is the revised text of the work, which was first published
by Harlequin Enterprises Limited in 2000.

For questions and comments about the quality of this book please contact us
at Customer_eCare@Harlequin.ca.

www.MIRABooks.com

Printed in U.S.A.

First Printing: January 2000
10 9 8 7 6 5 4 3

This story is dedicated to the memory
of my grandmother, Susan Chamberlain,
my inspiration and comfort.

Summer's Child

Prologue

On her eleventh birthday, Daria Cato became a hero.

A deep hush had fallen over the Sea Shanty after the savage weather of the night before, and Daria woke very early, as usual, when the sky outside her bedroom windows held only a hint of dawn. She opened the window above her dresser to let the breeze slip into the room. The sound of the ocean was rhythmic and calm, not like the angry pounding of the night before, and she breathed in the smell of salt and seaweed. The sunrise would be spectacular this morning.

Quickly, she slipped out of her pajamas and into her shorts and tank top, then quietly opened her bedroom door and walked into the hallway. She tiptoed past her sister Chloe's room, and past the room where her cousin, Ellen, slept. Ellen's mother was asleep in the downstairs bedroom, and Daria's parents were in their room on the third story. Her father would be getting up soon for early mass, but her mother, Aunt Josie, Ellen and Chloe wouldn't be up for at least another hour. They didn't understand the early-morning allure of the beach, but that was fine with her. She preferred solitude as she watched the sand and sea change color and texture each morning. This morning would be special, not just because of the storm, but because it was her birthday. Eleven. Kind of a dull number, and still two years away from being able to call herself a teenager, but definitely better than ten.

Daria padded quietly on bare feet down the stairs, trying to avoid the step that always squeaked. Would anyone remember her birthday this year? She was certain it would be nothing like the year before, when her mother had arranged a party for her with all the other kids on the cul-de-sac. No, this year was destined to be different, because her mother was different. She'd changed over this last year, and this first gloomy, overcast week of summer in Kill Devil Hills, North Carolina, had done nothing to lift her dour mood. Daria's mother slept late almost every day and moped around the cottage once she did get up. She barely seemed to remember her daughters' names, much less their birthdays. Chloe wouldn't care, of course. She was seventeen this summer, the brainy one in the family, already finished with her freshman year at college and inter- ested only in boys and what color nail polish she should use to paint her toes. That's when their mother started changing, Daria thought, when Chloe went off to college. "I'm losing my little ones," Daria had overheard her mother say to her aunt just yesterday.

And, of course, the kids on the cul-de-sac would balk at coming to the birthday party of an eleven-year-old this year, now that they were all teenagers. Every single one of them except her! It was a good thing she didn't mind being alone all that much, she thought as she opened the front door and walked onto the Sea Shanty's broad screened porch, because that was obviously the way it was going to be this summer.

From the porch, Daria could look directly across the cul- de-sac and see Poll-Rory, Rory Taylor's cottage. Even Rory, who had been her summertime buddy for most of her life, was now fourteen and pretty much ignoring her. He seemed to have forgotten all the hours they'd fished together, crabbed together and raced against each other while swimming in the sound.

There were no lights on inside Poll-Rory. She looked at the upstairs window she knew to be Rory's bedroom and felt a prickly pain in her heart.

"Who needs you, anyhow," she muttered, pushing open the screen door and descending the steps to the cool sand. She began walking toward the beach, where she could see the sky just beginning its silent, peach-colored glide toward sunrise.

All six cottages on the cul-de-sac were built on stilts, like most of the oceanside structures in the Outer Banks. The Sea Shanty, built by her father and uncle the year Daria was born, was only the second cottage from the water, so Daria quickly reached the low, grass-covered dune overlooking the beach. She glanced at the cottage where Cindy Trump lived, the only home on the cul-de-sac directly fronting the ocean, to make sure it had not been damaged by the storm. It was perfectly fine. She envied Cindy and her brother for living right on the water, but her father said the beach was narrowing in Kill Devil Hills and Cindy's cottage would one day plunge into the sea. Still, Daria thought it would be neat to be able to look out your bedroom window and see nothing but water below you.

The beach was beautiful! The storm had washed the sand clean, and the tide had left behind a deep, wide row of shells, waiting for her to sift through them. The sun was already a thin sliver of copper on the horizon above the water, which was so calm it looked more like the sound than the ocean. Nothing like last night's turbulent, frothy waves. She sat down on the dune to watch the sun's rapid ascent into the iridescent sky. The sand was cool and damp, and she dug her bare feet into it.

Large, brown, orb-shaped horseshoe-crab shells dotted the beach, an eerie spectacle in the coppery light. They looked like something from another planet. She had never seen so many of them at one time, but they only held her interest for a moment or two before she began thinking again about the social dilemma facing her this summer. Although the Catos had been at the Sea Shanty for less than a week, Daria could already see how this summer was going to shape up, and the picture wasn't pleasant. She went over the cul-de-sac kids in her mind, wishing she'd made a mistake in figuring out their ages. Chloe was seventeen and Ellen, who'd be with them for most of the summer, was fifteen. Cindy Trump was sixteen, her brother, Todd, thirteen. There were seventeen-year-old twins, Jill and Brian Fletcher, in the cottage next to Poll-Rory. Next door to them was that really quiet girl, Linda, who was fourteen and always had her nose stuck in a book. An old couple, the Wheelers, lived next door to Daria, and their three children were so grown-up, they were married. Last year, Daria had oc-casionally played with Rory's sister, Polly. Polly was fifteen, but she had Down's syndrome, so it was like playing with someone much younger. But even Polly seemed to have moved far beyond Daria this summer, at least in terms of physical devel-opment, if not interests. She had breasts that Ellen and Chloe were talking about with envy.

Once the sun was fully above the horizon, Daria set out for the inviting line of shells. Her shorts had deep pockets, so she would be able to carry whatever treasures she found. Her bounty would annoy her mother, who now complained about her collecting buckets of "useless" shells each summer, even though she'd never said a word about it before.

The sand was deliciously cool beneath her feet as she walked along the line of shells. She had progressed only as far as the Trumps' cottage when she spotted the largest horseshoe-crab shell she had ever seen smack in the middle of the broad strip of shells. The shell looked odd to her, raised up a bit, as though perhaps the crab might still be inside. Curious, she extended her leg, and with her sandcovered toe, kicked the brown globe onto its back. Daria blinked in disbelief. A bloody baby! She shrieked before she could stop herself, then took off across the sand, screaming and waving her arms, wishing now that she were not all alone on the beach.

She'd run the distance of several cottages when she stopped short. Had it really been a baby? Could it have been a doll, perhaps? She looked back over shoulder. Yes, she was certain it had been a real, human baby. And in her memory, she imagined the small, almost imperceptible movement of a tiny, blood-covered foot. Surely that had not actually happened. She stood rigidly on the beach, staring back at the shell. Okay, maybe it really *was* a baby, but it couldn't possibly be alive. Very slowly, she walked back to the overturned shell. The ocean was so quiet that she could hear her heartbeat thudding in her ears. Standing above the shell, she forced herself to look down.

It *was* a baby, a naked baby, and not only was it stained with blood, it was lying next to what looked like a pulpy mountain of blood. And the baby *was* alive. There was no mistaking the tiny movement of its head toward the sea, no mistaking the weak, mewling sound escaping from its doll-like lips.

Fighting nausea, Daria took off her tank top and knelt in the sand. Carefully, she began to wrap the shirt around the baby, only to pull away in horror. The bloody mountain was attached to the baby! There was no way to leave it behind. Gritting her teeth, she wrapped the shirt around everything— baby, mountain and half a dozen shells—and stood up, cradling the bundle in her arms. She walked as quickly as she could up the beach toward the Sea Shanty. She stopped once, expecting to be sick, but she felt the trembling of the small life in her arms and forced her feet to continue walking.

Once in the Sea Shanty, she laid the bundle down on the

kitchen table. Blood had soaked clear through the tank top, and she realized there was blood on her bare chest as she ran up the stairs to her parents' third-story bedroom.

"Mom!" She pounded on their bedroom door. "Daddy!"

She heard her father's heavy footsteps inside the room. In a moment, he opened the door. He was tying his tie, and his thick, usually unruly, black hair was combed into place for church. Behind him, Daria could see her mother, still asleep in their double bed.

"Shh." Her father held a finger to his lips. "What's the matter?" His eyes widened as he saw the red stain on her chest, and he stepped quickly into the hall, grabbing her by the shoulder. "What happened?" he asked. "Did you get hurt?"

"I found a baby on the beach!" she said. "It's alive but it's all—"

"What did you say?" Her mother sat up in bed, her brown hair jutting from her head on one side. She looked suddenly wide-awake.

"I found a baby on the beach," Daria said, pushing past her father to reach the bed. She tugged her mother's hand. "I put it on the table in the kitchen. I'm afraid it might die. It's really tiny, and it's got a lot of blood on it."

Her mother was out of the bed more quickly than Daria had seen her move in months. She pulled on her robe and slippers and raced down the stairs ahead of both Daria and her father.

In the kitchen, the baby was just where Daria had left it, and the bundle was so still that she feared the baby might now truly be dead. Daria's mother did not balk for an instant at the bloody sight, and Daria was impressed and proud as her mother lifted the crimson tank top away from the infant.

"Dear God in heaven!" Daria's father said, taking a step

backward. But her mother was not repelled. With the practiced hands of the nurse she had once been, she began moving efficiently around the kitchen. She filled a pan with water and put it on the stove, then wet a dish towel and began cleaning the baby with it.

Daria leaned close, made less afraid by her mother's matter-of-fact handling of the situation. "Why is it so bloody?" she asked.

"Because it's a newborn," her mother said. "*She's* a newborn."

Daria looked closer and could see that the baby was indeed a girl.

"Where exactly did you find her?" her mother asked.

"She was under a horseshoe-crab shell," Daria said.

"Under a horseshoe-crab shell!" her mother exclaimed.

"She was with all the shells washed in from the tide," Daria said. "Do you think the storm last night washed her up on the beach?"

Her mother shook her head. "No," she said. "She would have been washed clean then. And she would have been dead." Her lower lip trembled and her nostrils flared with quiet rage. "No, someone just left her there."

"I'm calling the police." Daria's father headed for the living room and the phone. His face had gone gray. Aunt Josie passed him on her way into the room.

"What's going on?" she asked. "Oh my God!" Her hand flew to her mouth as she saw the baby lying on the kitchen table.

"I found her on the beach," Daria explained.

"All by herself?" Aunt Josie asked. "Where on the beach?"

"Right in front of Cindy Trump's cottage," Daria said. She saw her mother and aunt exchange glances. People always did that when they talked about Cindy Trump, but Daria didn't have a clue why.

"The placenta is attached," Aunt Josie said, peering closer, and Daria knew she must mean the bloody mountain still lying next to the baby.

"I know." Daria's mother shook her head as she rinsed out the wet cloth under the faucet. "Isn't this just unbelievable?"

Daria thought of Chloe and Ellen still asleep upstairs. They shouldn't miss this. She started toward the kitchen door.

"Where are you going?" her mother asked.

"To get Chloe and Ellen," Daria said.

"It's not even eight o'clock," her mother said. "Don't wake them yet."

"Teenagers sleep the sleep of the dead, I swear," Aunt Josie said.

Chloe and Ellen would probably blame her for not waking them, but Daria thought it best to be obedient just then. She stepped close to the table again and watched as her mother slipped the blades of the kitchen scissors into the boiling water for a moment, then snipped the cord coming from the baby's belly button. Finally, the baby was free of the horrible, pulpy mass. Aunt Josie brought a towel from the downstairs bathroom and Daria's mother wrapped it around the newly bathed baby and lifted the bundle to her chest. She rocked the baby back and forth. "Poor darling little thing," she said softly. "Poor little castaway." Daria thought it had been years since she'd seen so much life in her mother's eyes.

The policemen and rescue squad arrived within minutes. One of the rescue-squad workers, a young man with long hair, nearly had to pry the infant from Daria's mother's arms. Still wearing her robe and slippers, she followed the baby to the ambulance. She stood watching the vehicle as it drove away, and she stayed there for several minutes after the ambulance had turned onto the beach road from the cul-de-sac.

Meanwhile, the policemen were full of questions, mainly for Daria. They sat with her on the screened porch of the Sea

Shanty and went over and over the details of her discovery until she herself began to feel guilty, as though she had done something terribly wrong and would be hauled off to jail any moment. After questioning her for nearly half an hour, they sent her inside while they spoke with her parents and Aunt Josie. Daria sat on the wicker chair in the living room, the one right next to the window that opened onto the porch, so she could listen to whatever the grown-ups had to say.

"Can you tell us what teenage girls live on this cul-de-sac?" one of the policemen asked.

Aunt Josie began ticking them off. "That cottage there on the beach," she said, "There's a fast girl lives there. Cindy Trump. I've heard the boys call her Cindy Tramp, because she's easy, if you know what I mean."

"Oh, you shouldn't say that, Josie," Daria's mother scolded.

"But I saw her yesterday," Daria's father said. "She didn't look pregnant to me."

Daria leaned her cheek against the wicker back of the chair, positioning herself to hear better. This was fascinating talk.

"I saw her, too," Aunt Josie said. "She had on a big white shirt, like a man's shirt. She could have been hiding anything under there."

Daria could almost hear her father's shrug of defeat. Aunt Josie had been married to his brother, who had died five years ago, and she always seemed to get her way with Daria's dad.

Aunt Josie began speaking again. "There's that girl Linda, who—"

"She's only fourteen," Daria's mother protested. "And she's so shy. Why, she can't even talk to the boys, much less..." Her voice trailed off.

"We'd still like to know what girls are on the cul-de-sac," one of the policemen said. "Whether you think they could be the mother of that baby or not. How about in this cottage? Any girls besides Supergirl? Daria?"

Supergirl? Daria grinned to herself.

"Yes," Daria's father said, "but they're good Catholic girls."

"My daughter, Ellen, is fifteen," Aunt Josie said. "And I can assure you she was not pregnant."

"Same for our daughter, Chloe." Daria's father sounded insulted that Chloe might be considered a suspect. "She goes to Catholic University. Got in when she was only sixteen, so you can guess she spends most of her time hitting the books."

Daria wasn't so sure about that. Chloe was smart enough to get good grades without doing much studying.

"Anyone else?" one of the officers asked.

"In this cottage?" Aunt Josie asked. "No, but there's a couple more girls on this block. There's Polly across the street."

"Oh, for heaven's sake, Josie," Daria's mother said. "She's mentally retarded. Do you really think—"

"She's right to tell us," one of the policemen said. "Who else?" He and Aunt Josie sounded like old buddies.

"I think the only other one is that Jill girl," Aunt Josie said.

"She's the Fletcher girl." Daria's mother's sounded resigned. Every girl on the cul-de-sac was going to be on that list, whether she wanted them to be or not.

Daria saw Chloe descending the stairs from the second story and put her finger to her lips. Chloe frowned as she reached the living room. She walked over to her sister on bare feet.

"What's going on?" she whispered, trying to peer out the window onto the porch.

"Don't let them see you!" Daria grabbed a fistful of her sister's wild black hair to pull her head down.

"Ouch." Chloe extricated herself from Daria's grasp. "Why are the cops here?"

"I found a baby on the beach," Daria said.

"You found *what?*"

"Shh," Daria said. But before she could explain further, their father stepped into the room.

"Chloe, good, you're here," he said. His hair was mussed now. He could never keep it looking neat for long. "I was just coming in to get you. You and Ellen need to answer a few questions for the police."

"Why?" Chloe looked surprised. Her usual olive complexion had a waxy cast to it in the pale morning light, and Daria guessed she was nervous about having to talk to policemen.

"It's all right," Daria said. "I talked to them for a long time. They're pretty nice." *Of course, though, I'm Supergirl.*

"Get Ellen," her father said to Chloe, who rolled her eyes and offered him a look of disdain before stomping up the stairs. That defiant attitude was brand-new. Chloe had been away at college all this year, only joining the family at the Sea Shanty a few days ago, and Daria had not yet adjusted to the change in her sister. Chloe had always been her parents' pride and joy, with her straight-A report card and adherence to their rules. Suddenly, she was acting as though she didn't need parents at all.

"And you." Daria's father looked straight at her, and she knew she'd been caught eavesdropping at the window. "You go on upstairs now. You must be tired. It's already been a long morning for you."

Daria did not want to go upstairs; she wanted to hear what the police would say to Chloe and Ellen, and she should be able to. She was eleven now, not that anyone seemed to have remembered. And if it hadn't been for her, this whole commotion wouldn't be happening at all. But her dad had that stern look on his face that told her she'd better not argue.

She passed Ellen and Chloe on her way up the stairs. Ellen

wore the same pale-faced look as Chloe, and they said nothing to her as she passed them. But when she was nearly to the second story, she heard Chloe call out to her.

"Hey, Daria," she said. "Happy birthday, sis."

When she reached the upstairs hallway, Daria sat down on the top step, trying to remain within hearing range of the voices downstairs. She could tell who was talking, but little of what was said, and her mind began to wander. She thought about what she'd told the police, playing the interview over and over in her mind. If you lied to the police, could you be arrested? Would they arrest an eleven-year-old girl? She had not actually *lied,* she reassured herself. She had simply left out one fact—one small, probably insignificant piece of the story: the baby was not all she had found on the beach that morning.

1

Twenty-two years later

DARIA'S THIRTY-THIRD BIRTHDAY WAS NOT MUCH DIFFERENT from any other early June day. Life was slowly returning to the Outer Banks as vacationers trickled into the coastal communities, and it seemed the air and sea grew warmer by the hour. Daria spent the day with her co-worker and fellow carpenter, Andy Kramer, remodeling the kitchen of a house in Nag's Head. She installed cabinets and countertops, all the while battling the melancholia that had been her companion for the past month and a half.

Andy had insisted on buying her lunch—a chicken sandwich and fries at Wendy's—as his birthday gift to her. She sat across the table from him, nibbling her sandwich while he devoured his three hamburgers and two orders of fries, as they planned their work agenda for the afternoon. Despite Andy's appetite, he was reed slender. His blond hair was pulled back in a ponytail that reached the middle of his back, and a gold hoop pierced his left earlobe. He was only in his mid-twenties, and Daria figured that was the reason he could still eat as he did and never gain an ounce.

"So," he said to her as he polished off the last of his burgers, "are you going to party tonight?"

"No," Daria said. "I'm just going to have some cake with Chloe and Shelly."

"Oh, right," Andy said. "It's Shelly's birthday, too, isn't it?"

"Uh-huh. She's twenty-two." Hard to believe. Shelly still seemed like a child to her.

Andy drank the last swallow of his soda and set the empty cup on the tray. "Well, I think you and Shelly should go out on the town tonight and do it right."

"I have to teach a class at the fire station," Daria said, as if that was the only thing keeping her from "going out on the town."

"You do?" Andy looked surprised. "I thought you weren't—"

"I'm not working as an EMT," Daria finished his sentence for him. "I still want to be an instructor, though. This will be the first class I've taught since…in a while."

He had to know she meant it was her first class since April, when the seaplane went down in the ocean and changed everything in her life, but he wisely said nothing. Daria was anxious about teaching again. Tonight would be the first time she'd faced the other emergency medical technicians since turning in her resignation from the volunteer force, and she knew she had left them confused—and short-handed—by her sudden departure. She feared she had lost credibility with them, as well.

She left the restaurant with Andy, wondering how *he* felt about her quitting. Andy longed to be an EMT. He'd failed the exam twice, and Daria knew it was unlikely he would ever pass it, although he seemed determined to keep trying. He had been at the plane crash back in April, though, and he surely understood how horrendous that situation had been for her. But even Andy didn't know the entire story.

★ ★ ★

The class at the fire station that evening proved that Daria had been right to be nervous about teaching again. No one seemed to know what to say to her. Were they angry with her for leaving so abruptly, or just disappointed in her? Most of them probably thought she had left because her fiancé, Pete, had resigned, and she allowed them that misperception. It was easier than telling them the truth. A few of them, those who had known her for many years, were aware that her leaving had something to do with the crash of the seaplane, but even those people did not understand. After ten years as a volunteer EMT, with a reputation as the "local hero" who possessed exceptional skills and steely nerves, it was unthinkable that one failed rescue attempt could flatten Daria to that extent. As she stood in front of the class that evening, she couldn't blame any of them for their confusion or sudden distrust of her. After all, she was teaching them to perform tasks she was no longer willing to perform herself. She wondered if she truly had the right to be teaching at all. Walking out to her car after the class, she was painfully aware that no one was following her to ask questions or even to chat. They all hung back in the classroom, probably waiting until she'd left the building to begin talking about her.

It was a bit after eight o'clock as she drove home from the station. Although it was only Thursday night and still early in the season, the traffic on the main road was already growing thick with tourists. She knew what that meant: accidents, heart attacks, near drownings. Shuddering, she was glad she was no longer an EMT.

She pulled into the driveway of the Sea Shanty, parking behind Chloe's car. As of this week, all the driveways in the cul-de-sac were full. Seeing the cars, Daria suddenly missed the isolation of the winter months, when she and Shelly had the cul-de-sac entirely to themselves. They'd lived in Kill Devil Hills year-round for ten years, and usually she looked forward to the cul-de-sac's coming to life in the summer. But there was too much explaining to do this year. "Where's Pete?" everyone would want to know. And "Why did you quit being an EMT?" She was tired of answering those questions.

Chloe was sitting in one of the rockers on the porch, reading a book by the porch light. "I've got an ice-cream cake in the freezer," she said. "Now all we need is Shelly."

"Where is she?"

"Out on the beach, where else?" Chloe said. "She's been out there for a couple of hours."

Daria sat down on another of the rockers. "I don't like her to walk on the beach at night," she said.

"She's twenty-two years old, sis," Chloe said.

Chloe didn't get it. She was only with them during the summer months, when she directed the day-camp program for kids at St. Esther's Church. She wasn't with Shelly enough to know how poor the young woman's judgment could be. Shelly could pick up some stranger on the beach, or some stranger could pick her up. It had happened before.

Daria brushed her hand over a spot on her khaki shorts, where glue from the installation of the countertops had found a permanent home. One more ruined pair of shorts. She must have sighed, because when she looked up, Chloe was staring at her. The extremely short haircut Chloe was sporting this summer made her huge brown eyes seem even larger, the dark velvety lashes longer. For a second, Daria was mesmerized by her sister's beauty.

"I'm a little worried about you, Daria," Chloe said.

"Why?"

"You seem so down," Chloe said. "I don't think I've seen a smile on your face since I arrived."

She hadn't known her unhappiness was that obvious. "Sorry," she said.

"You don't need to apologize," Chloe said. "I just wish there was something I could do to help. I don't understand Pete, frankly. Does he ever call you?"

Daria stretched her arms out in front of her. "He's called a couple of times, but it's definitely over," she said. On the phone, Pete sounded relieved to be away from her, and the few times they'd spoken, he'd lectured her about putting herself first for once. It was painful to hear from him, and while part of her wished he would call again, she knew prolonging that relationship would only hurt her in the long run.

"Can you tell me why he broke off the engagement?" Chloe asked gently. She had avoided that question so far, probably hoping Daria would provide the answer on her own.

"Oh, a bunch of reasons," Daria said evasively. "Shelly was part of it." Shelly was all of it, actually.

"Shelly! What did she have to do with it?"

Daria drew her feet up onto the seat of the rocker and wrapped her arms around her legs. "He thought she needed more supervision than I was giving her," she said. "He thought I should put her in some sort of home or something."

Chloe's eyes were wide with disbelief. "That's crazy," she said. She leaned toward Daria, covering her hand with her own. "I'm so sorry, honey. I had no idea Shelly had been that taxing on your relationship with Pete."

Shelly had always been an issue between her and Pete, but after the plane crash it had come to a head. Daria didn't want to discuss that with Chloe. There was no one she could discuss it with.

"It's Pete's problem, not mine." Daria got to her feet. "I'm really tired," she said. "I'm going to lie down for a while. Call me when Shelly gets here and we can do the cake, okay?"

Upstairs, she lay on her bed, but didn't sleep. She stared at the dark ceiling, listening to the night sounds of the ocean and the shouts of the Wheelers' grandkids from the yard next door. Since the summer she turned eleven, every one of her birthdays brought back memories of the day she'd found the infant abandoned on the beach. She closed her eyes, saying a quick prayer that Shelly was safe out on the beach, then let herself remember the day twenty-two years ago—the day that had shaped the rest of her life.

The baby had been the talk of the neighborhood all that day, and for many days to come. The police had questioned everyone on the cul-de-sac, as well as people on neighboring streets and the other side of the beach road, but Daria had been aware only of the little world on her street. As the police made their rounds that afternoon, Daria had sat on the porch with Chloe and their cousin, Ellen, pretending to play with her bug-catching kit while listening to them talk about all the girls in the cul-de-sac. Ellen and Chloe sat in the rocking chairs, their long, bare legs stretched in front of them, their bare feet on the molding beneath the screens of the porch. Daria sat at the picnic table, hunched over her microscope, pretending to be absorbed in studying the wing of a dragonfly. She understood only bits and pieces of the conversation between her sister and cousin. They were talking about sex, of course. She knew that if she asked questions, they would stop talking completely, so she kept her mouth shut and feigned great interest in the dragonfly.

"The cops are in the Taylors' cottage now," Ellen said.

Daria braved a glance across the cul-de-sac at Poll-Rory, the Taylors' cottage.

"I am so white," Chloe said, examining her legs. Her legs were hardly white; like Daria and Ellen, Chloe was of Greek descent and had inherited the trademark thick black hair and olive skin of the Cato side of the family. Nevertheless, Chloe would complain all summer long about her inability to tan, even as she grew darker week by week.

"I don't know why they're bothering to talk to Polly," Ellen said. "I mean, who's going to get a mongoloid pregnant?"

"Well, she *is* fifteen now," Chloe said. "But I really don't see how she could hide being pregnant from Mrs. Taylor. Polly's always with her."

"Well, I'm fifteen, too," Ellen said. "And I'm a whole lot better-looking than Polly, but I'm still a virgin."

Chloe laughed. "Right," she said, "and I'm the Queen of Sheba."

Daria knew what a virgin was. The Virgin Mary had gotten pregnant with baby Jesus without ever having had sex. It had never occurred to her that Ellen or her sister or Polly or any of the other teenage girls on the cul-de-sac could be anything other than a virgin. She lowered her eye to the microscope again to keep the shock from showing on her face.

"What makes the cops so sure it was a teenager, anyhow?" Ellen asked.

"They're probably pretty certain it's Cindy *Tramp's* baby," Chloe said, "but they don't have enough evidence to force her to have an examination. I bet they're hearing all about her at every cottage they go to. She's been doing it since she was twelve."

"Twelve?" Ellen looked astonished.

"Twelve," Chloe said with certainty. "Just one year older than Daria." Both of them looked at Daria, and she raised her head from the microscope, feeling color blossom on her cheeks.

"I don't know what you're talking about," Daria said, although she did. She could not imagine having sex one year from then. She looked across the street at Poll-Rory, thinking of Rory inside that cottage. He was the only boy she could imagine kissing, but even with Rory, she couldn't picture doing anything more than that. She wasn't certain exactly how it was done, anyway.

"I know who it was!" Ellen said excitedly. "I bet it was that girl, Linda." She laughed, as though she'd said something wildly amusing. Chloe laughed, too, and Daria laughed along with them, pretending to understand.

The police suddenly walked out Poll-Rory's front door, with Rory close on their heels. Rory was yelling at them, and Daria leaned closer to the screen, as did Chloe and Ellen, trying to hear.

"...just confused her!" Rory shouted. "What was the point?"

The policemen kept walking toward the street, ignoring him.

"Don't come back again!" Rory yelled after them, a threat in his voice. The sun shimmered on his blond hair, and after only one rainy week at the beach, he was already tan. His voice was deeper than it had been a year before. Yelling at the policemen, Rory suddenly seemed more like a man than a boy, and Daria was both enticed and humiliated, seeing at once how ridiculous she was for hoping he might still want to hang out with her this summer.

"Rory!" Mrs. Taylor opened the screen door of Poll-Rory and called to her son.

Rory did not turn around. He stared after the policemen as they walked down the street, and even from across the cul-de-sac, Daria thought she could see the daggers in his eyes.

Mrs. Taylor came out of the cottage and into the sandy yard, where she spoke with him softly, putting her arm around his shoulders. Finally he turned and walked with her back into the cottage.

"Rory is looking hot this summer," Ellen said, fanning herself with her hand.

"He's only fourteen," Chloe scoffed. "Though I guess that's about right for you."

Daria's mother came out onto the porch. She had on a dress, unusual attire for Kill Devil Hills. "We'll go out for pizza tonight," she said, stroking her hand over Daria's hair. The touch felt nearly alien. It had been a while since her mother had touched her that way. "For your birthday, Daria," she added. "And then to the miniature-golf course. Would you like that?"

"Yes," Daria said, pleased that her mother had not forgotten her birthday after all. Chloe and Ellen looked at Sue Cato as if she'd grown two heads.

"And right now—" Daria's mother smoothed her hands over the skirt of her dress "—I'm going to the hospital in Elizabeth City to visit the baby."

"Why?" Chloe asked. "It's not yours."

"That's true, but right now she doesn't have anyone," Sue said. "No one to hold her and rock her. So that's what I'm going to do."

"Can I go, Mom?" Daria stood up, the dragonfly forgotten. "I found her."

Her mother tilted her head, as if considering. "Sure," she said. "I think you should."

The nurse instructed them to wash their hands with a special soap and put on blue gowns before they could walk into the nursery where the baby was lying in a plastic bassinet. They were not allowed to pick her up, however. They were just allowed to stare. And stare they did. Daria barely recognized the tiny infant lying in front of her. The baby was so small. Had she really been that small when Daria found her on the beach? Her skin was very pale, almost translucent, and her hair was little more than a dusting of fine blond glitter on the top of her head. She was attached to several monitors by long wires taped to her chest.

Daria was surprised to feel tears fill her eyes as she looked at the baby. This baby was alive because of her. She moved, she breathed, because of her. It seemed unbelievable.

Daria's mother took her hand, and Daria held on tightly, something she had not done in years. She glanced up at her mother's face to see tears streaming slowly and silently down her cheeks, and Daria knew that for each of them, this baby was more than a small bundle of flesh and bone. This baby was already changing their lives.

"We're going to stop at St. Esther's," her mother said once they were back in the car and driving across Currituck Sound toward Kill Devil Hills.

"To light a candle," Daria said with conviction, proud she was able to read her mother's mind.

"Yes," her mother said. "But also, we're going to pay a visit to Father Macy."

"Why?"

"Because." Daria's mother stared at the road and clutched the steering wheel firmly in her hands. "Because if the mother doesn't come forward, I believe that baby should be ours." She turned to face Daria. "Don't you? After all, she's alive because of you, my sweet Daria."

It had not occurred to her that they might be able to keep the baby, but instantly, Daria could imagine no other outcome. A little sister! She was going to do something a bit evil when she lit her candle: She was going to pray that the identity of the person who left the baby on the beach was never discovered.

St. Esther's was nothing like the church Daria's family attended during the rest of the year in Norfolk, Virginia. The church in Norfolk was dark and cold and musty-smelling, and always made her shiver with a strange mixture of fear and awe. But St. Esther's stood near the sound in Nag's Head, a large wooden rectangular building that felt clean and new inside. It was open and airy, with huge windows near the high ceiling and pews made from light-colored wood. There was stained glass in some of the windows, a kaleidoscope of translucent glass cut into abstract shapes that sent beams of bright colored light through the air of the church.

St. Esther's was empty that afternoon, and Daria thought their footsteps were entirely too loud as she and her mother walked across the hardwood floor to the tiers of candles in the corner. Daria's mother took a long wooden taper from the holder, slipped it into the flame of one of the candles and used the lit taper to light a candle of her own. She handed the taper to Daria.

It did not seem quite as magical and mysterious to light a candle in here as it would have in their dark, cavelike church in Norfolk, but nevertheless Daria lit a candle in the bottom tier and knelt next to her mother to say a prayer for the baby.

Dear God, let that little baby live and be healthy, she prayed. *And let her be ours.*

When they had finished praying, Daria and her mother walked out the side door of the church to the small attached building that housed the offices of the priests, as well as some classrooms where children attended day camp. They entered the building and began walking through the wide, cool hallway, its hardwood floor gleaming in the light from the skylights. Father Macy was just walking out of his office as they approached.

"Why Mrs. Cato. Daria," he said with a smile. "What brings the two of you here?" He was wearing a Hawaiian shirt, and his hair was the color of the sea oats on the Kill Devil Hills beach. He was a good match for St. Esther's, as approachable and cheerful as the church itself.

Daria felt her mother put an arm around her shoulders. "Go ahead and tell him, honey," she said.

"I found a baby on the beach," Daria said.

Father Macy's brown eyes grew wide. "A baby?" he repeated.

"Yes," her mother said. "Daria had the courage to pick her up and bring her home to us, even though she was a newborn with the, uh…afterbirth still attached." She squeezed Daria's shoulder. "We would like to talk with you about her, if you have a minute."

"Of course," Father Macy said. He stepped back into his office. "Come right in."

They followed him into the small room. A massive desk stood in front of the one large window. It looked out toward the sound, and in the distance, the grand, golden dunes at Nag's Head. The priest sat casually on the edge of his desk, and Daria and her mother sat in two armchairs on the opposite side of the room. Father Macy's easygoing demeanor irritated her father, Daria knew. "He's too informal," he had said, and she doubted that the Norfolk priests ever sat on the edge of their desks. But Father Macy was very young; it was his third year being a priest and his second year at St. Esther's. Even Daria thought he was handsome, with those large, brown eyes and long eyelashes. He had an easy laugh that made her feel relaxed around him.

"So tell me more about this baby you found, Daria," he said.

"I was on the beach very early this morning to watch the sunrise and to beach-comb," Daria said. "And I kicked over a horseshoe-crab shell, and underneath was the baby." She didn't want to tell him about the blood.

"And obviously, it had been born quite recently?" He looked at Daria's mother for confirmation, and she nodded.

"Someone had simply given birth to her right there or very nearby, and left her to die," Daria's mother said.

"My, my." Father Macy looked gravely concerned. "Is the baby...alive?"

"Yes, by the grace of God, she is," she said. "She's at the hospital in Elizabeth City. We just visited her and she's doing well, and in a few days she should be able to go home. But she *has* no home, and that's why I'm here." Daria's mother looked uncomfortable for the first time since they'd entered the priest's office. She looked into her lap and played with the clasp of her purse, and Daria wished she would just get to the point.

"My husband and I would like to adopt her," she said finally. "That is, if no one claims her. And I was wondering if you could help with that. If you could intercede on our behalf."

Father Macy looked thoughtful. "Do you realize what a miracle this is?" he asked. "That Daria found this baby in time to save her? That the baby was found by someone who belongs to a family as devout, as holy and blessed as the Cato family?"

For the second time that afternoon, Daria felt close to tears.

"Yes," her mother said softly. "Yes, we're very aware that the Lord selected us."

"I'll be in touch with the hospital," Father Macy said, standing up. "And I'll be in touch with the state adoption agency. I'll do whatever I can to plead your case. I can think of no better home for that little one."

One week later, the baby arrived at the Sea Shanty, and became the instant celebrity of the neighborhood. Everyone from the cul-de-sac stopped by to stare at the little blond-haired infant and to shake their heads over her rude beginning in life. Daria's mother named the infant Michelle, calling her Shelly for short. The irony of that name had seemed lost on everyone except Daria, who had delighted in how fitting a name it was.

People often commented, though, on the other irony: that this tiny, blond, brown-eyed child was now part of the dark-haired, Greek Cato clan.

All that summer, Daria's mother would sit on the porch, rocking the tiny baby in her arms and telling all who approached that Shelly was her gift from the sea.

"Daria?"

Daria started at the sound of Chloe's voice. She sat up on the bed, freeing herself from the memories.

"Shelly's back," Chloe called from downstairs. "Come have some cake."

"Coming!" Daria called, relieved that Shelly had returned safe and sound. She ran her fingers through her hair and headed downstairs to hug the young woman who was both her joy and her heartache, her blessing and her burden.

2

THE PLANE CAME TO A STANDSTILL AT THE GATE, AND RORY unfastened his seat belt and stood up to reach into the overhead bin. He pulled out the backpack and handed it to his son, who was still buckled into his seat and looked disinclined to leave the plane. Zack stared out the window, tapping out an imagined drumbeat on his knee. He was fifteen years old and annoyed at the prospect of spending the entire summer with his father on the East Coast. It had been a painful flight, at least for Rory, who had vainly tried every ploy he could think of to get his son to talk to him.

"Come on," Rory said. "Let's go find our rental car and get on the road."

With a loud sigh, Zack unbuckled his seat belt and followed Rory down the aisle.

"Welcome to Norfolk, Mr. Taylor," the flight attendant said as Rory passed her to leave the plane. She'd chatted with him off and on during the flight from Los Angeles, telling him how *True Life Stories* was her favorite show on TV. He doubted that was true, but as host and producer of the popular show, he was accustomed to the adulation. Women tended to know him from television, men from his days on the football field. Either way, he attracted attention, and even that seemed to irritate Zack. "We can never go anywhere without people staring at us," he'd said when the third or fourth passenger on the plane had approached Rory for an autograph.

"Welcome to Nor-fuck," Zack said now, under his breath, and Rory pretended not to hear him.

They checked in at the car-rental counter, and there was a subdued flurry of excitement between the two female clerks as they recognized their customer.

"You reserved a Toyota FJ Cruiser," one of the clerks said as she checked his reservation.

"You did?" Zack sounded incredulous.

"Sure," Rory said. He'd specifically requested a Cruiser. It would give them room for their considerable luggage, plus, he knew a Cruiser would please Zack. If Zack was pleased, though, the boy was determined not to show it.

The Cruiser was cobalt blue and looked new. Rory spread his map over the steering wheel and studied the route they would take to the Outer Banks. "It's an easy drive," he told his son, who said nothing in reply.

It was only an hour and a half from Norfolk to Kill Devil Hills, and Zack was no easier to talk with in the car than he had been on the plane. Rory gave up after a while, deciding to simply enjoy the scenery on this much-changed road, with its antique stores and vegetable stands. Zack pressed the scan button on the car radio, hunting for a station that was not too "pitiful."

Rory had his hopes pinned on this summer. He'd been divorced from Glorianne, Zack's mother, for nearly two years, and he and Glorianne had joint custody of Zack. Technically, at least. Rory was supposed to have Zack for weekends, holidays and summers. But several months ago, Glorianne had married the movie producer with whom she'd been having an affair during her marriage to Rory, and she now had a house in Beverly Hills, along with every other material possession she could desire. Rory found himself unable to compete with the glitzy, seductive new life-style Zack was enjoying in Glori-anne's home. Zack was at that age where possessions and grandeur mattered. He was slipping away from his father, and Rory hoped that this summer would bring him back. Rory knew that behind his son's offensive, defensive adolescent facade, Zack was still hurting from the divorce and angry with both his parents for letting it happen. Intellectually, Rory understood all that. He just didn't know what to do about it.

"So," Zack asked dryly as he poked at the scan button, "are we there yet?"

"Another twenty minutes, I'd guess," Rory said. "This road we're on used to be narrow and sleepy, with just a few vegetable stands along it."

"It still looks narrow and sleepy to me," Zack said. He was a true Southern California kid. Anything tamer than the San Diego Freeway was going to look sleepy to him.

Rory didn't bother to argue. He knew Zack hated hearing about the way "things used to be," and he supposed he hadn't cared for that sort of conversation, either, when he was Zack's age.

"I miss L.A. already," Zack said, gazing out the car window.

"Well, we haven't reached the Outer Banks yet."

"I still don't get why we had to come here," Zack said.

Rory thought he'd explained his reasons for spending the summer in Kill Devil Hills to his son, but either Zack hadn't heard them or they hadn't been persuasive enough for him to remember.

"Well, you know I spent my summers here when I was a kid," he said.

"Right. And it's got some kind of nostalgic pull on you or something."

"That's true." Rory tried not to sound defensive. "It was a very special place for me. I still own my family's old cottage there, and I haven't seen it since I was seventeen."

"You mean the cottage has just been standing there, empty all this time? Won't it be rotted out by now?"

"I sure hope not," Rory said. "I've had a real estate agency looking after it. They've rented it to people visiting the beach, and supposedly they've taken care of the upkeep, as well. I guess we'll see about that soon." That was something he was worried about.

"You could have come back for, like, a week or even just a couple of days to check on the cottage," Zack said. "Instead we have to stay here the whole stupid summer."

"I have a good reason for wanting to stay the summer," Rory said, glancing at his son. This part of his plan he had not told him. "There's an old incident I want to research here for *True Life Stories.* Want to hear what it is?"

Zack shrugged.

"When I was fourteen, a baby was found on the beach close to my cottage. She was a newborn. The little girl across the street found her early in the morning and brought her back to her cottage. The police got involved, of course, but they were never able to figure out who had left the baby there. A few months ago, I received a letter from the baby, who's grown up now, of course."

"What did she want?" Zack actually sounded interested.

"She said she knows I try to solve old mysteries on *True Life Stories* and that I'd lived near where she was found. She said she always wanted to know who her mother was and asked if I could try to figure it out." He glanced at Zack again. "The more I thought about it, the more I wanted to do it," he continued. "I'd always wondered about that incident, especially lately. You know how we've been hearing about all these teenage girls having their babies and trying to flush them down toilets or leave them in Dumpsters as if they were nothing more than a Popsicle wrapper? Doesn't it make you angry when you hear things like that?" He didn't wait for a response from Zack; he didn't expect one. "It's impossible for me to imagine that sort of cruelty. When I hear those stories on the news, it makes me remember that baby. Shelly, her name is."

"So, where does this…Shelly live?" Zack asked.

"She was adopted by the family of the girl who found her, and apparently she still lives in the house on the cul-de-sac." He tried to remember the name of that cottage, but failed. "At least, that was the return address on the envelope." Shelly had given him very little information. It had been a short letter— more of a plea, actually. "She was only about three years old the last time I saw her." Rory remembered a slender little girl with long platinum hair and large, brown eyes. Even as a teenager, he'd thought it was odd to see that leggy little waif living in the midst of the dark, exotic-looking Cato family. He'd forgotten her name until receiving the letter, remembering only that it was Sandy or Shelly, something to do with the beach. "I never wrote back to her," Rory said. "I thought I'd surprise her, instead."

The long bridge across Currituck Sound was directly ahead of them, and Rory felt a rush of excitement. "Kitty Hawk is on the other side of this bridge," he said to Zack. "And right next to Kitty Hawk is Kill Devil Hills."

After crossing the bridge, Rory spotted one of the milepost markers along the road and smiled. "People here locate things by the milepost markers," he said. "Watch the side of the road, there. The next marker should be 3. Our cottage is between milepost 7 and 8." He was secretly glad of the markers. He wasn't sure he could remember where to turn, especially since the landmarks had changed drastically since he'd last been here.

"There's 3," Zack said.

"Uh-huh." Rory could not help but feel some disappointment at what he was seeing. This portion of the Outer Banks was overgrown. The landscape was dotted with the trademark cottages on stilts, the main road was littered with shops and restaurants, and there were far too many people and cars.

"What's that?" Zack pointed ahead of them in the distance and Rory saw the obelisk jutting up from one of the hills after which Kill Devil Hills was named.

"It's the Wright Brothers' Memorial," Rory said. "This is where they took their first flight, over a hundred years ago."

"That's cool," Zack acknowledged, as if finally admitting there might be some small reason to like this place.

After passing milepost 7, Rory turned the Cruiser toward the ocean and drove a short distance to the beach road. He turned right, hoping that was the correct choice, and in a moment he saw the cul-de-sac on his left.

"Here we are," he said, turning into the short, broad cul-de-sac. After the jarring sights on Route 158, he felt enormous relief. The cul-de-sac looked the same as it had when he was a child, and nostalgia washed over him. The same handful of cottages was there—less one. The cottage at the end of the cul-de-sac, the one built right on the beach, was gone. Cindy Trump's cottage. He could picture her even more readily than he could her cottage. She'd been a couple of years older than him, with sun-bleached hair, a killer tan and the skimpiest bikini in Kill Devil Hills.

His eyes were drawn to his old summer home, the last of the three cottages on the right. He laughed. "Well," he said to his son, "looks like we now own beachfront property. There used to be one cottage between ours and the beach, but that's gone."

"Gone where?" Zack asked.

"Into the sea, I'd imagine," Rory said. "Probably went in during a storm."

Rory pulled into the driveway of his old home. The cottage looked the same, except cleaner, freshly painted. The rental agency was doing a good job taking care of it.

"Poll-Rory." Zack read the sign above the front door. "Was that you and Aunt Polly?"

Rory looked at the sign himself. It was not the same old wooden sign from his youth; this one had white lettering on a blue background. But it surprised him to see any sign at all after so many years.

"That's right," he said. "My parents named the cottage after us." He felt a pinprick of pain in his heart. Staying here was going to bring back many memories of his sister.

Looking across the cul-de-sac at the Catos' cottage, he saw that a sign still hung above their porch door as well. The Sea Shanty. *Yes.* That had been the name of their cottage. It was no shanty, though. It was the largest cottage on the cul-de-sac, rising three stories above its stilts, and stained a light taupe color. Above the third story was the widow's walk, where he and Daria used to play when they were small.

"God, we're right on the beach," Zack said, opening the car door. "I'm going to go check it out." He took off toward the water, and Rory let him go.

Getting out of the Cruiser, Rory noticed the two cars in the Sea Shanty driveway and wondered who they belonged to. Were Mr. and Mrs. Cato still living? How did they feel about Shelly's desire to track down her roots? Would Chloe be around? Growing up, Chloe had been clearly out of his league. She'd had a bunch of boyfriends, all of whom Rory, in his adolescent yearning, had envied. Three years older than him and in college by the time she was sixteen, Chloe had been knockout gorgeous, with dark eyes and long, wavy black hair. All the Cato girls had that same thick, dark hair. Ellen—she was the cousin, if he was remembering correctly—had been pretty as well, but her cute facade had hidden a mean-spirit-edness that had scared him at times. He suddenly remembered an incident he hadn't thought about in years. He'd been about thirteen, sitting with Ellen and a group of kids on the beach. He was watching an attractive girl walking along the water's edge, when Ellen saw fit to point out to the rest of the group that he had an erection. He'd rolled rapidly onto his stomach, hating Ellen and her big mouth. Even now, he cringed remembering that moment.

Then there had been Daria, his little buddy, the girl who could run faster, swim better and catch bigger fish than he could. She'd been three years younger than him, but she'd been his competitor, nevertheless. He'd always pretended that he was letting her win at whatever they attempted. Inside, though, he'd been filled with admiration for her. He wondered what had become of the three Cato girls.

He opened the back of the Cruiser and pulled out two of the suitcases. He carried them up to the porch, then took a moment to look toward the ocean himself, breathing in the still-familiar scent of the beach he loved. It would be a good summer. He was in one of the finest places on earth, about to delve into an intriguing story, and he had Zack with him. Zack would come away from this summer with a healthy tan, sun-kissed hair and his good values restored. And with, Rory hoped, renewed love for his father. He could hope for the moon, couldn't he?

3

THE LAUNDRY BASKET WAS FULL OF DARIA'S CLEAN WORK clothes—several pairs of shorts and a dozen T-shirts—and she dumped them onto her bed and began folding. She had the windows wide-open, and a warm ocean breeze lifted the blue and white curtains and sent them floating into the room like the wings of a tired gull. It was the sort of early-summer day that used to make her feel light and carefree, but she no longer seemed capable of experiencing those feelings.

She carried the stack of folded shirts across the room and set them on top of the dresser. Pulling open the dresser drawer, she took out the photograph she kept tucked beneath her T-shirts. She stepped closer to the window to study it, as she did nearly every time she opened that drawer. The picture was of Pete. He was leaning against a split-rail fence at a friend's house in Manteo, a beer in his hand, a five-o'clock shadow on his face, and he was grinning at her, the photographer. His dark hair, as smooth and straight as hers was full and wavy, fell over his forehead. It was torture to look at the picture, and yet she did it anyway, over and over again. He'd been a part of her life and her future for six years. Now he was only a part of her past, and it was taking her longer than she liked to get used to that fact.

She replaced the picture, then lowered the stack of T-shirts on top of it and returned to the bed and the laundry basket, but her mind was still back with the photograph. Pete and his callous feelings about Shelly were linked together in her mind with the night of the plane crash, the night the young female pilot died. For two months now, Daria had been visited by that pilot's last moments in her nightmares. She could not seem to free herself from the young woman's pleading gaze.

That morning, she'd received a call from her old Emergency Medical Services supervisor, a call she'd half expected but had hoped would never come. They were pulling her off CISD duty, he said, and she'd winced as though he'd slapped her in the face. She'd worked as a critical incident stress debriefer for five years. After traumatic incidents anywhere in the county, she'd be called in to help distraught emergency technicians cope with what they'd endured. Now *she* was the distraught technician. Her supervisor summed it up for her when she begged him to reconsider. "If you can't manage your own stress," he said, "how do you expect to be able to help someone else with theirs?"

She was finishing folding the shorts when her gaze was drawn through the window to the cottage across the cul-de-sac, where this week's vacationers were moving into Poll-Rory. Something made her move closer to the window, brushing aside the billowing curtain, to stare hard at the newcomers. A man and a teenage boy were unpacking a blue SUV in the driveway. Even from that distance, and even though she hadn't seen him in nearly twenty years, she knew the man was Rory Taylor. She'd watched every game the Rams had played on television when he'd been with them, and she'd watched him on *True Life Stories* for years. She had given up on his ever returning to Poll-Rory, though, especially now that both his parents were dead. He probably had more glamorous vacation spots in which to spend his free time. Yet here he was. Most likely, that was his son with him. She had read he'd gotten a divorce.

For some reason, the first memory that came to mind was of a hayride they'd gone on with some of the neighborhood kids. Her father was the group chaperon, and Rory, who must have been about twelve and full of early-adolescent bathroom humor, told joke after joke that Daria had felt unable to laugh at because her devoutly religious father was along. Rory, of course, understood her predicament and tortured her with ever more raucous stories. The memory made her smile. Rory had been her best friend during the summers of her childhood. When she was ten or eleven, that friendship began turning into a genuine crush, on her part at least. But that's when he began to snub her in favor of the older kids. She knew that she had never truly lost that attraction to him. When she watched *True Life Stories,* she was not simply excited by the fact that someone she had known had become a celebrity; she was excited by Rory himself.

Rory carried a suitcase across Poll-Rory's sandy yard and up the front steps to the porch, and Daria noticed the slight limp in his gait. She remembered that he'd been injured playing football. That's what had ended his career.

She watched until Rory and the boy disappeared inside the cottage for the last time, then she walked downstairs to the screened porch. Chloe was sitting in one of the three blue rockers, reading a book titled *Summer Fun for Kids 5-15,* and Shelly sat at the blue-painted picnic table, stringing shells for a necklace, her long, blond hair falling over her shoulders.

"Did you see who just moved into Poll-Rory?" Daria asked, more to Chloe than to Shelly. Shelly knew that the host and producer of *True Life Stories* was someone who used to live on the cul-de-sac, but she had been very small the last time she'd seen Rory, and it was unlikely she remembered him.

Chloe glanced across the street. "I wasn't really paying attention," she said. "Was it a man and a boy?"

For a moment, Daria wondered if she'd only seen what she wanted to see. But she remembered the man's limp, the breadth of his shoulders, the sandy color of his hair.

"It was Rory Taylor," she said.

"Really?" Shelly asked. "*True Life Stories* Rory Taylor?"

Chloe said nothing. She stared across the street.

"I'm sure it was him," Daria said.

"Why would he come here?" Chloe asked.

"Well, he still owns the cottage," Daria said.

Chloe stared at Poll-Rory a moment longer before lowering her gaze to her book. Rory's return was probably of little interest to her, Daria thought. Chloe had been older than Rory; she had not known him well. She had not looked forward to spending time with him every day during the summers of her childhood.

"Let's go say hi to him." Shelly started to stand up.

Daria felt instantly intimidated. He probably would have little memory of her. How full his life had been since the last time she'd seen him, while here she was, still firmly rooted in Kill Devil Hills.

"Let's give them a chance to settle in first," she said, glancing across the street once more before walking into the cottage to finish folding her laundry.

4

DAYLIGHT WAS FADING, AND RORY FELT THE PINCH OF A mosquito bite. If he and Zack stayed on the deck much longer, they would need to light the citronella candle. They'd eaten dinner on the rear deck, which jutted from the second story of the cottage and gave them a view of the ocean to the east as well as the sun falling over the sound to the west. Between Poll-Rory and the sound, though, were many, many cottages. Far more than Rory remembered. Still, little could ruin his pleasure at being in Kill Devil Hills.

They'd eaten carryout North Carolina barbecue for dinner—one of those culinary delicacies he'd been craving ever since deciding to make this trip.

"Let's have takeout every night," Zack said, closing the disposable box and lifting a can of soda to his lips.

"Well, a few times a week, anyhow," Rory said. The truth was, he loved to cook, and two years of cooking primarily for himself had grown old. He was looking forward to spending time in Poll-Rory's rudimentary kitchen this summer.

"This is crazy," Zack said, looking above him at the darkening sky. "I'm never going to get used to East Coast time."

"You will," Rory said, although they had eaten dinner very

late because their stomachs still thought they were back in L.A. "Tomorrow morning, we'll have breakfast at nine, and then we'll be on track."

"Nine? Forget it. It's summer. I'm sleeping in."

"Okay," Rory said. This was not worth arguing about. "You can sleep as much as you like." He slapped a mosquito on his thigh. "I'm going across the cul-de-sac to see the neighbors," he said. "Want to join me?"

"I saw some kids over on the beach before you got back with dinner," Zack said. "Think I'll go see if they're still there."

Well, at least Zack wasn't shy. Or maybe he simply wanted to get away from his father for a while after this long day of togetherness.

"Okay," Rory said. "I'll see you later."

Rory walked down the steps from the deck, through the cottage, and out to his sandy front yard. The warm, humid air smelled strongly of the sea, and he couldn't shake a sudden bittersweet wave of nostalgia as he walked across the cul-de-sac. The screened porch light was on at the Sea Shanty, and as he neared the cottage, he saw a blond-haired woman inside, sitting in one of the rocking chairs, engrossed in something on her lap. She stood up when she spotted him and walked to the porch door.

"Hi," Rory said. "Are you Shelly?"

"Sure am." The woman pushed open the screen door. "And you're Rory," she said.

"Right." Still standing in the sand, he put his hands on his hips and cocked his head to study her. Her smile was wide, her teeth straight and white, and she was very pretty. Her long hair was a silky, pale blond. "You were about three years old the last time I saw you."

"Well, you were about thirty-five the last time I saw *you*."

She grinned. "I saw you just the other night on *True Life Stories.*"

He laughed. "Thirty-six," he said.

"I don't remember you from when I was little," Shelly said. "Daria and Chloe remember you, though."

"Who are you talking to, Shelly?" A female voice came from the living room, beyond the porch.

"Are they here?" Rory asked. "Daria and Chloe?"

"Yes, they're inside. Come in." She stood back to let him walk past her onto the porch, and he noticed she was tall— nearly as tall as he was. "Did you get my letter?" she asked in a near whisper.

"That's why I'm here," he said.

"Oh, thank you!" She gave him a quick, sideways hug, then led him into the living room.

"Rory Taylor's here," Shelly announced to the woman who was sitting on the couch, a book on her lap.

It took him a minute to recognize the woman as Chloe. She rested the book on the couch and stood up. "Hello, Rory," she said.

She was still beautiful, although she looked quite different from the last time he'd seen her. Her hair was very short, capping her head in dark curls. She looked like a Greek goddess.

"Hi, Chloe," he said. He wanted to move forward to give her a hug, but her stance, stiff and uninviting, kept him rooted near the door. The sound of an electric saw came from somewhere in the cottage, and he wondered if Mr. Cato was still building furniture in the Sea Shanty's workshop.

"It's been a while," Chloe said. "You remember Shelly, I guess?" She looked at her sister.

"Very well," he said. "Although I can't say I would have recognized her."

"I'll get Daria," Chloe said, heading for the door to the porch. "She's down in the workshop. Shelly, why don't you get Rory something to drink?"

"We have lemonade or iced tea or soda pop," Shelly said once Chloe had left the room. "Orange, ginger ale or Coke."

"Orange sounds good," he said.

"Be right back. Don't go away!"

He watched her disappear into the kitchen. It was strange to be in this cottage again. The furniture was different—of course it would be, after all these years. Poll-Rory's furniture, purchased for him by the real estate agency, was the boxy wood and nubby upholstery type that would hold up to the abuse of renters. The Catos' furniture, with its blues and yellows and traditional lines, had a homier feel to it. The walls were lighter, and he noticed that the wood paneling had been painted a soft cream color. Were Mr. and Mrs. Cato still living? he wondered once again. Daria was in the workshop, Chloe had said. Was she with her father down there? He remembered that workshop. It was on the ground floor, built into a space among the stilts, and it smelled of wood and metal. He recalled that every time a major storm came through, the Catos would have to pack up the tools and carry them up to the first or second story of the cottage to get them out of harm's way.

"Rory!" Daria strode into the living room and over to him, wrapping him in a welcome hug. "I can't believe you're in Kill Devil Hills."

He drew away to look at her. She'd probably been about fourteen the last time he'd seen her. He guessed she'd been pretty back then, but now she possessed the rare, exotic sort of beauty that had once attracted him to Chloe, with those dark eyes and long, thick, unruly black hair. Unlike Chloe, though, she still had the body of a tomboy—tight, small-breasted, compact and tan in her shorts and T-shirt. Her hair was barely contained in a ponytail and there was something pale and feathery scattered through it. Sawdust?

"I'm happy to see that you guys are here," he said, glancing at Chloe, who stood in the doorway, arms folded across her chest, a small smile on her lips. "I was hoping you would be."

Shelly walked into the room and handed him a glass of orange soda. "We're *always* here," she said.

"How long are you staying?" Daria asked.

"All summer," he answered. "My son is with me."

"Well, sit down," Daria said, motioning toward one of the chairs.

He took a seat. Chloe and Daria sat at opposite ends of the sofa, while Shelly sat on the floor, her back against one of the other chairs in the room. She was wearing a deep purple sundress, and her long, slender legs looked very tan against the pale carpet.

"So, bring me up to date," he said. "Your parents? Are they…?"

"Mom died fourteen years ago," Daria said. "And Dad, just last year."

"I'm sorry to hear that," Rory said. "I guess you know I lost my parents."

"Yes," Daria said. "The real estate agent who handles your cottage told us. What about Polly? How is she doing?"

"She died two years ago."

"Oh, I'm sorry, Rory," Daria said.

"Me, too," Chloe added. "Polly was truly special."

"Mmm, very," he said.

"I read about your divorce," Daria said.

He laughed. His life was open to the public. "I guess I have no secrets," he said.

"That must be strange," Daria said. She sounded sympathetic. "But the news just reports the facts about a celebrity.

So and so got divorced. So and so landed in a mental hospital. They don't say how so and so feels about what happened to him."

"Good point," Rory said. "Well, I can sum up my feelings about those events pretty quickly. Losing my parents was the pits—they were too young. Losing Polly was even worse, as you can imagine."

"I bet," Daria said.

"My divorce was…difficult, but a relief in the long run. And my son is the best thing that ever happened to me, although he hasn't figured that out yet."

"Who is Polly?" Shelly asked.

"My sister," he said.

"Why did she die?" Shelly asked.

"She had Down's syndrome," Rory said. "It affected her heart."

"She was so fair," Daria said. "I remember she'd always burn, every summer, no matter how much lotion your mom put on her."

"That was Polly," Rory agreed. "She wasn't much of a beach person." He looked at Chloe. "So," he said, "now all of you know what I've been up to. How about the three of you? Chloe? You were so smart. You were in college before I could even spell the word. I remember you were studying history, right? You wanted to be a teacher. Is that what you are?"

The three women laughed, and he raised his eyebrows, surprised. "I'm wrong, I take it?" he asked.

"Well, no, you're not wrong," Chloe said slowly, coyly. "I teach history and English at a Catholic school in Georgia during the year."

Shelly giggled. "Chloe is really Sister Chloe," she said.

"Sister Chloe?" he repeated, confused.

"I'm a nun," Chloe said.

"Oh!" He knew he couldn't prevent the shock from showing in his face. Chloe Cato was a nun? He suddenly remembered that the Cato family had been very religious. Mr. Cato had gone to church early every morning, and he and his wife had been very strict, requiring Daria and Chloe and their cousin, Ellen, to come inside as soon as it got dark, while the other kids were still playing on the beach. Still, this was hard to believe. Chloe's *head* might be telling her she was a nun, but her body and beauty were doing their best to deny it. He still remembered how she looked in a bikini: those large breasts, tiny waist and narrow hips. The boys on the beach had followed her around with their tongues hanging out. He remembered everyone ruling Chloe out as a suspect in the deserted-baby incident because, except for those breasts, she had been notoriously thin. Anorectic, almost. Yet that body was hidden now beneath long, loose shorts and a baggy T-shirt.

"I think you've rendered him speechless," Daria said to Chloe with a laugh.

"I just…hadn't expected that." He laughed himself. That explained Chloe's reserve in greeting him. "So, do nuns get the summer off? Is that why you're here?"

"I'm working at St. Esther's, the Catholic church in Nag's Head, for the summer," Chloe said. "I've been doing that the past few summers, running a day camp for kids."

"Well, I'm almost afraid to ask what you're doing, Daria," he said.

"I'm a carpenter," she said.

Rory laughed. "I should have guessed," he said. "For real?"

"For real," she said. "I probably have sawdust in my hair right now."

"I was wondering what that was," he said. "I thought maybe it was a new Outer Banks trend."

"It's just a Daria Cato trend." Shelly grinned.

"I was working on a bookshelf for a cottage in Duck when Chloe told me you were here. There's always a lot of building going on in the Outer Banks."

"Are you living here year-round?" he asked. Despite the fact that Shelly's letter bore the Kill Devil Hills return address, it was hard for him to imagine anyone living here year-round. For him, the Outer Banks had always meant summer and the beach.

"Uh-huh," Daria said. "Shelly and I have lived here for the past ten years."

"Wow." He wondered what it would be like to live smack on the beach during the winter.

"Daria's also an EMT," Shelly said. There was pride in her voice.

"An EMT?" he asked. "Emergency medical technician?"

"Well, I was," Daria said. "I'm taking some time off."

"A lifesaver." Rory studied her with admiration. "You started that avocation early, didn't you?" He looked at Shelly. "She was only ten years old when she saved your life."

"Eleven," Daria corrected.

"I know," said Shelly. "People around here call her Supergirl."

"I remember!" he said, flashing back to the newspaper articles that followed Shelly's discovery on the beach. "They still call you that after all this time?"

"'Fraid so," Daria said. "I'll be sixty and they'll still call me Supergirl."

"It's because she's kept on saving people," Shelly said. "She's the local hero."

"I'll never forget that day." He wondered if he should tell them now that Shelly's letter had prompted his visit to Kill Devil Hills this summer, but he had more catching up to do first. He set his empty glass on the coffee table. "Is there anybody else left on the cul-de-sac from the old days?" he asked. "I noticed Cindy Trump's cottage is gone."

"There was a bad storm more than a decade ago," Daria said. "The ocean swallowed their cottage in one gulp. It did a lot of damage to the Sea Shanty, too, but your cottage was spared."

"The Wheelers are still around," Chloe said. "Do you remember them? They live next door."

"Still?" He remembered a quiet older couple who often strolled on the beach in the evening, hand in hand. "They're still living?"

"They're only in their seventies," Daria said. "Their cottage is filled with their grandchildren all summer long."

"Did he know Linda and her dogs?" Shelly asked.

"Yeah, you knew Linda, right?" Daria asked.

He narrowed his eyes in concentration, picturing a mousy young girl lying on the beach with her nose in a book. "I think so," he said.

"She lives in that same cottage with her partner, Jackie," Chloe said. "They raise golden retrievers. Linda is a lesbian."

Chloe revealed that fact as easily as if she'd said that Linda was a teacher or a swim coach. Rory had had little experience with nuns, but he'd assumed that Chloe had become moralistic and judgmental. He hoped her matter-of-fact description of Linda meant that she had not.

"Well, you never can tell how people are going to turn out, can you," Rory said. "What about your cousin? Ellen? What's she doing?"

"She's married," Chloe said. "She comes down every few weeks or so with her husband and kids."

"Not this summer," Daria said. "I mean, Ellen and Ted will be here, I guess, but not her daughters. They're traveling in Europe as part of a high-school exchange program," she explained to Rory. "Ellen's a medical technician. She does mammograms all day." Daria and Chloe laughed at that. "I don't know if you remember what she was like, but that job suits her perfectly."

Rory smiled. "She had a bit of a…sadistic streak, if I recall," he said.

"You've got it," Chloe said.

"What about the twins who lived next door to me?" Rory asked. "Jill and…her brother. I can't remember his name."

"Jill and Brian Fletcher," Daria said. "Jill is still around."

"The bonfire lady," Shelly said.

"Yes." Daria looked at Rory. "Remember the annual bonfire we had on the beach near the end of each summer?"

He had forgotten, but the memory slipped back easily. The huge, roaring fire. Great food. The sound of the ocean. Willing girls and the sheltering darkness. He nodded.

"Well, Jill has kept that tradition going," Daria said. "She has to get special permission each year, because bonfires are no longer allowed on the beach. She has to make the fire closer to the water, but she's fanatical about it. She's got a couple of teenagers, and her husband comes down on the weekends. I don't know what happened to Brian, her brother." Daria looked at Chloe, who shrugged.

"Haven't seen him in years," Chloe said.

Rory was pleased to hear that some of the old residents were still around, although he was disappointed that Cindy Trump was not one of them. He'd always thought that Cindy somehow held the key to the mystery of the foundling.

He looked at Shelly. She was a striking young woman, with large, light brown eyes, that long blond hair, a willowy body and perfect tan. Sitting there on the floor of the living room, she was all legs and arms and gossamer hair. She'd been wearing the same ingenuous smile since his arrival, and he realized that she had a childlike way of speaking, a simplicity about her. He'd lived with Polly long enough to recognize it, and he wondered if Shelly's rude introduction to the world had left her with some brain damage.

"How about you, Shelly?" he asked. "What are you up to?"

"I work at St. Esther's Church as a housekeeper," she said proudly. "And I design shell jewelry."

"Shell jewelry?" he repeated.

"Uh-huh." She stood up and walked out to the porch for a moment. Back inside, she handed him a choker, a small, gold-plated starfish set in the center of a strand of tiny shells. He was impressed. He'd expected shell jewelry to be a bit on the tacky side, but this was certainly not.

He looked up at Shelly. "It's beautiful," he said. "Was this a real starfish?"

"Yes," she said, taking the choker back from him. "I collect the shells on the beach. It's hard to find a starfish that size, though."

"It's wonderful, Shelly," he said. "What do you do with the jewelry after you've finished it?"

"I sell it at the gift shop on…" She looked to Daria for help.

"Consignment," Daria said.

"Pretty cool, huh?" Shelly said, grinning at him.

"Yeah, it is." He felt the broad smile on his face. Something about Shelly touched him. Reminders of Polly, perhaps, or maybe it was just the simple joy that emanated from her.

"Tell us about your son," Chloe said.

"Oh." Rory looked out the window at the darkening sky and wondered if Zack had made any friends on the beach. "He's a California kid," he said. "He doesn't want to be here. But—" he stretched and sighed "—I'm hoping he'll adjust to it. He's a good kid, just screwed up a little from the divorce." He wondered what Chloe thought about divorce—or the phrase "screwed up," for that matter. Did he have to watch his language around her?

He leaned forward abruptly. "Well," he said, getting down to business, "I received Shelly's letter a few months ago, and I've decided to follow up on her request to find out who left her on the beach twenty-two years ago. I plan to make it an episode on *True Life Stories*."

Dead silence filled the room. Chloe and Daria looked at each other, and Rory didn't miss the disapproval in their faces. Shelly wore a sheepish smile, and Rory suddenly realized she had written the letter without her sisters' knowledge.

"That is so cool!" Shelly said finally. "Thanks, Rory."

Daria looked at her younger sister. "You wrote to Rory?" she asked.

Shelly nodded.

"I wish you'd told me that, honey." Daria's voice was disapproving, but not unkind. Even so, he instantly felt sorry for Shelly.

"I thought it was a wonderful letter," Rory said quickly. "A wonderful idea. And if I can't uncover the answer during my research, Shelly, maybe someone watching the show will know what really happened and contact me."

Chloe tucked her legs beneath her on the sofa. "I don't think this is such a good idea, Rory," she said. "Why dredge up something that happened twenty-two years ago?"

"Chloe's right," Daria said. "I'm sorry to put a damper on your idea, but Shelly's a Cato, Rory. She has been, right from the start. Of course, she's always known what happened to her, but she's one of us, an integral part of us. Who her birth mother was doesn't matter."

For the first time since his arrival, Shelly lost her smile. "I know I'm a Cato," she said to Daria. "But I'm also something else. I've always wanted to know what that something else is."

Daria looked surprised. "You never said anything about it, Shelly. Nothing at all."

"Because I figured there was no way to ever find out," Shelly said. "But I was watching *True Life Stories* one night, and I knew Rory lived here when I was found, and he always can figure out those mysteries, so…if he wants to try—" she shrugged "—I want him to."

He had not expected resistance. It was understandable, though, that Chloe and Daria would find his plan unsettling if they hadn't known about Shelly's letter. Was he being intrusive? Was Shelly's plea enough reason for him to tamper with their lives?

"Well," he said, standing up. "I guess I'll have to give this some more thought." He saw Shelly bite her lip. A crease formed between her eyebrows. "And right now, I'd better go home and see what my son is up to."

"Good seeing you, Rory," Chloe said. She did not stand up, but Daria did. She walked him to the porch door.

"Don't be a stranger, Rory," she said.

"Thanks," he said. "I won't be."

"I'm sorry Shelly bothered you about…"

"It's not a bother at all," he said.

Daria brushed a few flakes of sawdust from her hair, and in the porch light, Rory saw a world of worry in her eyes. "I think it would be a mistake to pursue the story," she said.

"Well," he said, touching her arm, "we'll talk about it again, all right?"

He left the Sea Shanty and was halfway across the cul-de-sac when Shelly caught up to him.

"Rory, wait a second," she said.

He stopped walking and turned around. Poll-Rory's porch light lit her face.

"What's up?" he asked.

"Please, Rory. I still want you to try and find out who my real mother was," she pleaded. "I really want to know."

He hesitated. "Your sisters have some genuine concerns," he said.

"Yes, but I'm the one who counts, right?" Shelly asked.

He studied her face. She was a stunning young woman with hope in her eyes, and he couldn't help but smile at her. "That's right, Shelly," he said. "You're the one."

5

DARIA'S MOOD WAS LIFTING. SITTING IN HER PARKED CAR IN the Sea Shanty driveway as she waited for Shelly and Chloe to join her for the drive to Sunday mass, she felt a lightness she had not known for the past two months. She'd felt it when she'd awakened that morning and found herself getting out of bed with a smile on her face. She only had to look across the street at Poll-Rory to know the reason for her altered mood. Her lightness was tempered, though, by Rory's desire to pry into Shelly's past. Nothing could be gained by that…and too much could be lost.

The Wheelers—seventy-something Ruth and Les—were getting into their van in the driveway next door. A few of their grandchildren climbed into the van with them, and Daria knew they were going to St. Esther's for mass, as well. She waved, and Ruth Wheeler called out a greeting.

Chloe and Shelly walked down the wooden front steps of the Sea Shanty. Shelly got into the front seat of the car, Chloe the rear.

"St. Christopher," Chloe prayed as Daria backed the car out of the driveway, "guard and protect us on our journey."

For as long as Daria could remember, Chloe had uttered

that prayer every time she got in a car—even after St. Christopher had been desainted. Chloe had a bit of the rebel in her.

"There's Rory Taylor." Shelly pointed toward Poll-Rory, where Rory and his son were crossing their yard, carrying beach chairs and towels under their arms.

Daria tapped her horn. Rory waved at the car with a smile as she passed them. Rory's son reminded her of the boy she had known many years ago—the handsome, blond-haired boy with the broad-shouldered build that would later serve him well on the football field. She remembered what a strong swimmer Rory had been and how she'd liked to watch him swim far out into the ocean until the lifeguards whistled at him to come in. He'd been a lifeguard himself one year, and he'd rescued an elderly man caught in the undertow. He'd been seventeen then, and by that time he'd definitely forgotten she existed. The local newspaper printed his picture after he rescued the man, and she'd carried that picture around with her for years, even after he'd gone off to college and stopped coming to Kill Devil Hills.

"Your cheeks are red, sis," Chloe teased from the back seat of the car.

"Are not." Daria tilted her chin to look at her reflection in the mirror. She feared Chloe was right: she could feel the flush rising from her stomach all the way to her ears.

"What do you mean?" Shelly studied Daria's face. "Why would her cheeks be red?"

"'Cause Daria has a thing for Rory," Chloe said.

Shelly lit up at that news. "You *do?*" she asked.

"I don't know what Chloe's talking about," Daria said.

"A new man for you!" Shelly exclaimed.

"Oh, no," Daria protested. "No way." She glanced over her shoulder at Chloe. "Thanks a lot," she said.

Chloe laughed.

"I'm not interested in Rory Taylor that way at all," Daria said to Shelly. "Chloe just remembers back when we were kids, and it's true, I did have a crush on him then, but that was a long time ago, so don't get your hopes up." She knew that Shelly had been worried about her ever since Pete fell out of her life. Shelly didn't know how much of a role she'd played in his leaving, of course, and Daria intended to keep it that way.

"I think he's really nice," Shelly said.

"Yes, he is," Daria agreed. She'd been particularly touched the night before by the warm and easy way Rory had related to Shelly. That was a sure way to Daria's heart.

St. Esther's was packed with the summer crowd. The church had expanded physically since that day Daria and her mother had lit candles for the infant abandoned on the beach, but the atmosphere inside was the same—clean and light and filled with the scent of the sea. Daria knew she could be considered part of the summer crowd herself, since she rarely attended church any other time of year. Shelly went most weeks, either walking or riding her bike or catching a ride from a fellow parishioner. But in the summer, Daria felt a need to attend mass out of respect for Chloe. She'd somehow missed out on the devout genes that had coursed through her family for generations. Perhaps Chloe had received her share.

Communion was a problem for her this summer. Although she'd left behind church dogma and ritual, she still felt guilty about receiving communion when she had not confessed the truth about the plane crash. Yet she received it, anyway. Otherwise, Chloe would have known she was carrying around some sin in her heart. Daria told herself she had done her best the night of the crash. Everyone had done their best. No one had any intent to harm. Nevertheless, she had covered up their human failings. That was her sin.

A group of children mobbed Chloe—*Sister* Chloe—in front of the church after mass, badgering her with questions about what they would be doing in day camp the coming week. Daria liked watching Chloe with the kids. Her sister was animated and affectionate with them, unlike the nuns Daria remembered from her own Catholic school childhood.

Sean Macy approached them as they were walking to the car, and the three of them turned to greet him.

"Hi, Shelly, dear," the priest said when he'd caught up to them. "Sister." He nodded at Chloe, then looked at Daria. "Good to see you at church, Daria," he said. He had a teasing twinkle in his eye, and Daria smiled at him. All of the Catos had a special place in their hearts for Father Macy, since he'd helped Sue and Tom Cato adopt Shelly long ago. He'd also gotten Shelly her housekeeping job at the church, and he worked side by side with Chloe in the day-camp program.

"I need a moment with Daria," the priest said to them. He took Daria by the arm and led her away from the car, and she waited for him to speak again. "I've been asked to talk with you, Daria," he said.

She raised her eyebrows. "What about?"

"About resuming your EMT duties."

She groaned. Someone at the Emergency Medical Services must have been bending Father Macy's ear. "Who told you to speak with me?" she asked.

"Several people, actually," the priest said. "You are sorely missed. And the community suffers without you, you know."

"Thanks for the guilt trip," she said.

"Seriously, Daria." His face lost its smile. He was handsome, his hair still that wheat-blond color, but when he didn't smile, he looked tired. "I don't know what demons you're grappling with," he said, "but I want you to know that I'm here, if you ever want to talk about it."

"Thanks, Father," she said. "But I really have nothing to talk about. I just needed a break for a while."

"I can understand that," he said. The smile was back again. "I feel that way myself sometimes." He squeezed her hand warmly, then told her goodbye, and she turned and began walking, slowly, toward her car.

She had certainly considered counseling. That's what she would suggest for anyone else who'd suddenly relinquished their EMT duties. But counseling wouldn't help. She'd lie to the counselor, so what would be the point?

In the car, she found that Shelly was now in the back seat, Chloe in the front. She started the engine.

"What did Father Sean want to talk to you about?" Shelly asked.

Daria pulled out of the parking lot and turned onto the road. "He just wanted to see if I could help out with the charity auction this year," she said.

"Oh," Shelly said, satisfied, but Chloe gave Daria a dark look.

"With a lie like that," she said under her breath, "you'd better go to confession before you receive communion next Sunday."

Daria thought she was only half joking.

6

GRACE SPOONED A DOLLOP OF WHIPPED CREAM ON THE mocha latte and handed the cup across the counter to Jean Best, one of the regular customers at Beachside Café and Sundries.

"How are you doing, Grace?" Jean asked. Her eyes bore concern, and the question was sincere, but Grace busied herself cleaning the espresso machine.

"Just fine, Jean," she said. "Thanks for asking." She knew she should ask Jean how things were going with her elderly mother and the house she was trying to sell, but she didn't want to engage her—or anyone, actually—in conversation.

"I'm glad to hear it," Jean said, taking her cue from Grace's reticence and backing away from the counter. "Thanks for the coffee." She carried her coffee to one of the small tables near the window overlooking Pamlico Sound, and Grace was relieved to see her go.

Beachside Café and Sundries was small, cramped and popular among locals and tourists alike. She and Eddie opened it eight years ago with money Eddie's mother had left him. They carried a few staples, but they were most beloved for their coffee and sandwiches, which ran the gamut from avocado and cheese to Italian subs, something for everyone. The shop had been a labor of love, a *reflection* of love, and people used to comment on the warm, supportive relationship she and Eddie still enjoyed after twenty years of marriage. No one was commenting on it now, though.

Grace made a couple of sandwiches for a man and woman she didn't recognize. She was more comfortable these days with the strangers, with people who didn't know her and know all she'd endured these past few months. She didn't want pity. She didn't want sympathy. And most of all, she didn't want to talk about it. Because if she talked, she would disintegrate into little pieces. And that she couldn't afford to do.

She knew her regular customers worried about her. They worried about how much weight she'd lost and how fragile she seemed to be, both physically and emotionally. They commented about her pallor and her inability to concentrate on what anyone was saying. A few weeks earlier, she'd overheard a conversation between two of her customers, one of whom said, "Grace just isn't herself these days." That had become her mantra. Whenever she found herself thinking or doing something out of character for her—which was often, lately— she heard that voice inside her head: *Grace just isn't herself these days.*

She could hear Eddie in the small office behind the counter area, typing on the computer, and she wondered how many of the regulars knew that things had fallen apart between the two of them. It had to be obvious. The jovial atmosphere that had once existed in Beachside Café was gone, and now there was a palpable tension between Eddie and herself. Several customers even knew that Grace had moved into the above-garage apartment she and Eddie used to rent to tourists in the summer. How they'd found out, she didn't know, but the year-round population in the Outer Banks community of

Rodanthe was small, and it wasn't hard for people to learn each other's business. And, of course, everyone knew the reasons for the change in Grace, as well as for the change in her marriage.

"Grace?" Eddie poked his head out from the back office of the café. "Phone."

Grace wiped her hands on the towel hanging below the counter and walked into the office. She took the phone from his hand.

"I'll watch the front for you," he said as he left the office.

She nodded, avoiding his eyes. Once he was out in the café, she lifted the receiver to her ear. "Hello?"

"Hi, Grace, it's Bonnie."

"Bonnie!" There was only one person Grace could handle talking to at that moment, and it was Bonnie, her oldest, dearest friend. But Bonnie rarely called. She lived in San Diego and sent an occasional letter or e-mail once or twice a month. A phone call was rare, and it worried her. "Is everything okay?" she asked.

"Everything is fine here," Bonnie said. "I'm more interested in how things are going there."

"Oh, you know." Grace sat down on the desk chair and ran a hand through her hair. "It's been rough."

"Well," Bonnie said, "I wish I could do something to help you, and I'm worried that my reason for calling might just make things worse for you. But I wanted you to—"

"I don't see how you could make things worse, Bon," Grace interrupted her.

Bonnie hesitated. "Do you know who Rory Taylor is?" she asked finally.

"Of course. *True Life Stories.*"

"Right," Bonnie said. "Well, I was reading one of the L.A. magazines and there was this tiny little blurb—I almost missed it. It said that he's going to be in Kill Devil Hills for the summer."

Grace frowned, trying to figure out why that would be of any significance to her. "So?" she asked.

"He's there—" Bonnie let out a long sigh "—to look into that baby that was found on the Kill Devil Hills beach twenty-two years ago. He wants to do a story about it for his television show."

Grace was silent, a chill racing up and down her spine. "For what purpose?" she asked. Her voice sounded tremulous, she thought, even though she was struggling for control.

"I don't know, specifically," Bonnie said. "But he's usually trying to solve some sort of mystery. Like, who the baby's mother was."

Grace shut her eyes. "You know," she said softly, "that baby has been on my mind a lot lately."

"Of course she has," Bonnie said. "Of course she would be."

"Why now?" Grace asked, a bubble of anger forming in her chest. "Why, after all this time, does somebody have to delve into that—"

"I know," Bonnie said. "It's the wrong time. Not that there ever was a good time for it. Gracie, how are you doing otherwise? What does the doctor say?"

Grace ignored her question. "You know who I hate?" she asked. "Who I despise? Even after all these years?"

Bonnie hesitated a moment before asking, "Who?"

"The nurse," Grace said. "Nurse Nancy. I would love to get my hands on that woman."

"I know," Bonnie said, her voice soothing. "So would I. Look, Grace, I'm worried about you. Maybe I shouldn't have told you, but I didn't want you to find out some other way. Do you want me to come to North Carolina to be with you? Maybe I could help out somehow?"

"No, no," Grace said. "I'm all right."

"I know Eddie would be there for you if you'd let him," Bonnie continued. "But he said you're freezing him out."

"He froze himself out," Grace said, although that was not the truth and Bonnie probably knew it. Eddie *would* be there for her, but right now she couldn't even stand the sight of him. She could hear his voice, a deep voice she had once found mesmerizing, coming from the café. He was laughing with one of the customers. *Laughing.* She pressed the phone more tightly to her ear to block out the sound.

Bonnie uttered more words of concern, more words of comfort, but Grace barely heard her. She was too absorbed by the thought of Rory Taylor hunting for clues to how that baby came to be on the beach. And by the time she hung up the phone with her old friend, Grace had a plan.

7

THE SUN WAS SLIPPING INTO THE SOUND AS DARIA DROVE into Andy Kramer's driveway.

"You have an incredible view, Andy," she said to her co-worker, thinking of how he must enjoy this spectacle every evening.

"I know," Andy said, opening the car door. "I'm a lucky guy. Now if I just had a decent van." His van was in the shop again, the third time in the past few months.

Daria spotted the boat tied to the pier behind Andy's cottage. "I didn't know you were into boats," she said. "Is that new?"

Andy laughed, his earring glowing a vibrant rose color in the muted sunlight. "Brand-new," he said, "but it's not mine. I share the pier with my next-door neighbors, and it's theirs. Raises my property value, though, having it behind my cottage."

She could see his neighbors, a man and woman and a little boy, on the side deck of their cottage, grilling their dinner. She could even smell the steak. "Well, I hope they at least take you out in it sometime," she said.

"Me, too." Andy got out of the car and shut the door, but

bent over to look in the window. "Thanks for the lift," he said. "And have a good soak in your tub tonight."

"I plan to." She pulled out of his driveway, already thinking about spending a leisurely half hour in the whirlpool tub later that night. The tub was the one extravagance in the Sea Shanty, but it was truly a necessity after a day like this one. She and Andy had spent the day building wall-to-ceiling bookshelves in a huge house in Corolla, and her shoulders and arms ached. Before she could take a bath, though, there was something she needed to do.

She drove the mile and a half across Kill Devil Hills to the cul-de-sac, where she parked in the Sea Shanty driveway. But instead of going inside the cottage, she walked across the street to Poll-Rory.

Rory answered the door in shorts, sky-blue T-shirt and a handsome grin that threatened her resolve. She had to keep the purpose of this visit firmly in her mind.

"Come in, neighbor," he said, pushing open the screen door for her.

Daria stepped into the living room and took off her sunglasses. She had been in Poll-Rory many times over the years, so the changes in its interior were no surprise to her. She imagined they had been to Rory, though. The furniture, the new paneling on the walls, the artwork and knickknacks had all been selected by the real estate agent handling the property.

Daria spotted a computer on the table in the dining area. Papers and books were strewn across the table's surface.

"Looks like you're working," Daria said.

"Working and playing," Rory said. "That's my plan for this summer." His hands were on his hips, and she felt him appraising her. She probably had more sawdust in her hair. She knew she had paint on her white T-shirt and a smudge of varnish on her cheek.

She looked at him squarely. "I need to talk with you about Shelly," she said and felt the apology forming on her face. Rory had come all the way across the country to get to the bottom of Shelly's story, and she planned to make him stop that search before he'd even begun.

He must have seen the concern in her eyes, because his grin faded. "Well," he said, "this looks like a serious, sitting-down kind of conversation. Let's go up on the deck."

She followed him out the back door and up the stairs to the small deck, with its view of both ocean and sound. Nearly as good a view as from the Sea Shanty's widow's walk.

"I'd offer you something to drink," Rory said, "but all I have right now is water and milk. Zack already drank the soda I bought. I'd forgotten how much food he can go through."

Daria sat in an Adirondack chair and slipped her sunglasses on again, even though the sun had fallen well below the horizon. Rory's green eyes were uncovered, and she wished that were not the case. There was something about his eyes that had always made her weak-kneed, even when they'd been kids.

After a few moments of chatter about Zack and the view and the changes that had taken place in Kill Devil Hills during Rory's absence, she got to the point of her visit.

"I know Shelly asked you to find out about her past," she began, "but it's really not a good idea. You don't understand Shelly. She's not—" Daria hunted for the right choice of words "—like everyone else," she said. "I know she seems perfectly fine. I know she's beautiful, and a wonderful person, but—"

"I think I *do* understand," he said. "I picked up on what you're saying when I met her. Did she suffer some brain damage when she was born?"

Daria was surprised that he'd grasped that fact; she hadn't thought Shelly's problems were that obvious. She nodded.

"Yes, that's what they figure. Her IQ is in the very low-average range, but on top of that, she has some learning disabilities that kept her back in school. Plus, she has a seizure disorder and, although she's on medication for it, it's not under very good control. She's not allowed to get her driver's license because she's never been seizure free for a year, and that's the requirement." She glanced toward the Sea Shanty, but the only part of the cottage she could see from back here was the widow's walk. "She's a bit phobic," she continued, "and very dependent on me. After Mom died, she became my responsibility. She was only eight, and I was just nineteen. Now she gets scared when I'm not around."

"Why was she your responsibility?" Rory looked puzzled. "What about your dad? He was still living then, wasn't he?"

"Yes, but Shelly was too much for him to handle. She really needed a woman. A mother."

"What about Chloe? She was the oldest. Why didn't she help?"

Everyone asked that question, and Daria was ready with her answer. "Chloe was already a nun," she explained. "She was living in Georgia, and there really wasn't much she could do."

"What did you mean about Shelly being phobic?" he asked.

"She's afraid of a lot of things—earthquakes and snakes, for example, even though she's never encountered either. But mostly, she's afraid of being away from the Outer Banks. *Pathologically* afraid." Daria wasn't sure how to explain this. She'd tried over the years to describe Shelly's fears to doctors and teachers, but no one really seemed to understand. "Shelly is only happy on the beach," she said. "When she was little, we came to the Sea Shanty for the summers and spent the rest of the year in Norfolk, and we began to notice that she had a sort of…split personality. She'd be anxious and down in the winter, and relaxed and up in the summer."

"Well, aren't most kids that way?" Rory smiled. "I sure was."

"Yes, but for a different reason," she said. The light on the deck was fading, and she took off her sunglasses. "At first, we thought it was because she was in school in the winter and free in the summer, the way it is with most kids. But gradually we realized it was the beach itself that made her calm and happy. One time, when she was only about seven years old, we came down at the beginning of the summer. Dad had just pulled the car into the driveway—he hadn't even come to a stop— when she jumped out and ran to the beach, right to the exact spot where I'd found her, although there was no way she could have known that. She sat down there and watched the ocean, all by herself, all afternoon. It was as if she could finally relax."

Rory actually shivered. "That's a little spooky," he said.

"It was," Daria agreed. "But after all these years, I've just come to accept that about her. She needs the beach. Period. After Mom died and I realized how happy Shelly was here, I started bringing her down on weekends. Just Shelly and me. Dad was…" She remembered her father's years as a widower as one long fall into a life barely lived. "Dad withdrew after Mom died. He never dated or did things with friends, even though he was only in his fifties. He spent more and more time at church. Chloe and I used to say that he and God were dating." She laughed at the memory. "He loved Shelly and me, but essentially, we were on our own. So, anyhow, Shelly had to settle for weekends at the beach. But then, when she was twelve and went on a field trip with her class to a museum in Norfolk, she disappeared. We didn't know if she'd been kidnapped or what." Shelly had been kidnapped once before, but she didn't want to get into that.

"The police looked for her," Daria continued. "The next day, when she was still missing, I called Chloe in Georgia to tell her about it. Chloe wondered if Shelly might have gotten here to Kill Devil Hills somehow. It seemed impossible, but it turned out that's where she was. We never did find out exactly how she'd managed to get here—some combination of buses and hitchhiking, I guess. She'd broken one of the Sea Shanty's windows to get in and had pretty much set up house for herself. I decided that was it—we'd move here." She glanced at the widow's walk again. "I still don't know if it was the right thing to do for her. Maybe she should have been forced to tough it out somewhere else, because—to be honest—I think she's even worse than she was. Whenever we have to go to the mainland now, to visit someone or to see a doctor, she gets panicky. But I *love* her." She looked directly into Rory's eyes and saw sympathy there. "To see her miserable tears me apart," she said. "To see the total joy in her face when she's safe on her beach makes it all worthwhile to me."

"Maybe it *was* the right move for her," Rory said. "She's able to hold a job here, it sounds like. Would she be able to do that if you lived back in Norfolk?"

"I don't think she would have been able to get out of bed in the morning if we'd stayed in Norfolk," Daria said. "And she's very responsible about her work. But frankly, there really isn't much she can do to earn a living or to allow her to live independently. Sean Macy—the priest at St. Esther's—and the others who supervise her give her a lot of direction in the housekeeping she does. Sometimes I think they keep her there out of pity. She probably wouldn't be able to hold a job anywhere else." Daria suddenly felt as though she had painted a one-sided picture of her sister. "She *does* have skills, though. She's very kindhearted and likable. She's creative. Her jewelry is actually in demand. She's a terrific swimmer. Physically, she's very graceful."

"Yes," Rory said, "I noticed that."

"She can't work, but she sure can play volleyball." Daria

smiled. "She excels at just about everything that's fun. She just can't do the serious things in life very well."

Rory laughed. "Maybe we should all take a lesson from her," he said. Then he leaned forward, his face now sober and not far from hers, and she saw the fine lines around his eyes. "I understand what you're saying about Shelly and why you'd be concerned about her," he said. "But she certainly knew what she was doing when she wrote to me about *True Life Stories.* She understood what the show is about and how it might be able to help her."

Daria felt tears of frustration form in her eyes. He still didn't get it. "Shelly is so vulnerable," she said. "She's fragile. She needs protection. People take advantage of her very easily. She'll do anything if she thinks it's helping someone else."

"Are you saying she's only enthusiastic about me telling her story because she wants to help me out? To give me an episode for the show?"

Daria shook her head. "No, that's not what I mean. She really does seem to want you to do it, I can't deny that. But I think it would be a mistake to unearth that sordid mess, or to make her face the reality of the woman who...who essentially tried to kill her."

Rory leaned back in his chair again at that, and Daria continued.

"Shelly feels secure with us," she said. "She knows she's loved, she knows she's been loved from the very first day. Why tamper with that? I don't know what it would do to her to have the truth come out."

"Maybe the truth would be positive, though," Rory argued. "Maybe her birth mother regrets what she did and would love to know that Shelly is alive and doing well."

"You're fantasizing a happy ending, Rory," Daria said. She felt a twinge of anger at his perseverance.

"You know, I understand better than you think," Rory said. "The way you feel about Shelly was the way I felt about Polly."

She had forgotten his devotion to his sister. "I can still picture Polly perfectly," she said. Polly'd had a short, boxy build, white hair and the almond-shaped eyes of a Down's syndrome child. She remembered how Rory had defended her against the teasing of other children and taken time out from his own activities to play with her. Seeing him with Polly was one of the reasons she'd been attracted to him.

"Remember the incident with the fish hook?" Rory asked with a laugh. "When you said you were an EMT, that's what I thought of."

She'd forgotten about that, but the memory came back to her instantly. Polly had managed to get a fish hook stuck through her toe. Neither Rory nor his mother seemed to know what to do to get it out, and Daria, then only twelve, had performed the feat.

"You knew exactly what to do," Rory said. "It makes sense that you got involved in medicine."

"Dad had told me how to extract a fish hook in case I ever got stuck by one," she said simply. She didn't want to discuss her EMT work and answer the inevitable questions about why she was no longer doing it, so she changed the subject. "I don't remember Polly and your parents ever coming to Kill Devil Hills again after you went off to college," she said.

"That's right," Rory said. He let out a long sigh and stretched. His T-shirt strained across his chest, and she looked away for the sake of her own sanity. "They stopped coming," he said. "That's when I realized they'd bought the cottage primarily for me, so I could get to spend time on the beach in the summer. But my parents never sold Poll-Rory. I'm sure they were hoping I might use it for my own family one day. Until this summer, that just wasn't possible."

"Why not?"

"Glorianne. My ex-wife."

"She didn't want to come here?"

"An understatement. She and I were very different. She was…" He looked toward the ocean for a moment, as though carefully selecting his words. "When I first met her, she was very young and shy and…unassuming. Her parents had been killed in an accident. They'd had little money and left lots of debts, so Glorianne had essentially nothing. She needed me, and I liked being needed. She changed over time, though. Once we had money, it was as though it all went to her head. I'd always wanted us to live in a middle-class neighborhood, with Zack attending public school and experiencing the sort of down-to-earth upbringing I'd had. Glorianne thought we should live in Beverly Hills and send Zack to a private school, since we could afford it. I didn't want Zack to think that being famous and having money was more important than being honest and having good values."

Rory paused before continuing. "So, the upshot was that we did live in a very nice upper-middle-class neighborhood and Zack did attend public schools, but I had to compromise. And that compromise took the form of where we vacationed. I would have loved to have spent all our summers here in Kill Devil Hills, but Glorianne hated the beach and she didn't like the East Coast altogether. She always wanted to travel during the summer, and said that if I was going to limit Zack in what he could be exposed to during the year, then the least we could do was take him to Europe for the summer." Rory looked perplexed, as though he was still amazed that his simple, unassuming wife could have changed so much. "So, that's what we've been doing," he said. "Till now, anyhow."

"This summer with you should be good for Zack."

Rory laughed. "He doesn't seem to think so," he said. "At

least he's doing a lot of complaining about it. But I do have hope. I think he's already making some friends. He's out on the beach right now."

"Is that what ended your marriage?" she pried, curious. The article she'd read had claimed irreconcilable differences as the cause, and she'd always wondered. "Your disagreements over where to live and how to raise Zack?"

"And a million other things," he said. "Actually, Polly turned out to be a big reason for the demise of my marriage," Rory said.

That surprised her. "Why?" she asked.

"Well, after my parents died, I took Polly in. I moved her from Richmond to California to live with us. I wanted Zack to get to know her," he said. "I wanted him to understand that people with Down's syndrome were still lovable and valuable. And I think that really did work. Zack got along well with Polly." Rory looked up at the darkening sky, as if searching for the words. He returned his gaze to Daria. "But having Polly there put a terrific strain on Glorianne and me," he said. "We were already shaky enough to begin with, and Glorianne always felt as though Polly was an intruder in her family. And Polly never really adapted to living on the West Coast or to losing our mother. Plus, she had cardiac problems and needed a lot of medical care, and making sure she took her medications and running her to doctors' appointments just wasn't Glorianne's thing."

"That must have been hard on you," Daria sympathized, moved by the way Rory talked about his sister. She was struck by the similarities between Rory's situation with his wife, and her situation with Pete. At least Glorianne had allowed Polly to move in with them. "I know by the way you talk about Polly that you understand how I feel about Shelly," she said. "You must understand why I want to protect her."

He nodded. "Of course I do, Daria," he said. "But Shelly is very different from Polly. Shelly is still able to analyze a situation and make up her own mind as to what she wants."

He was right, though only to a degree. She sighed. "I haven't succeeded in getting you to change your mind, have I?" she asked, standing up.

"I'll think about what you said," he promised, "although I think the decision is ultimately up to Shelly." He stood up as well and followed her to the stairs. They were quiet as they walked through the cottage.

"Is there a gym around here?" he asked when they neared the front door.

"There's a health club," she said. "A nice one. I go there a few times a week." She told him where it was located and suggested he check into the summer fees.

They walked onto the porch. "Do you still beach-comb every morning like you did when you were a kid?" Rory asked.

Daria laughed. "I have to be on the job early in the morning these days," she said. "And those mornings I'm not working, I'd rather sleep in."

She looked through the screen door at the Sea Shanty. It was Shelly who loved the beach at dawn now. Shelly who sifted through the shells and basked in the sunrise, taking her energy from the sea. Daria could not, would not, let Rory or anyone else harm her sister's world.

8

RORY SAT ON THE PORCH OF HIS COTTAGE, LISTENING TO THE breakers swell and collapse in a sleep-inducing rhythm as he watched for Shelly to leave the Sea Shanty. He planned to begin his research by talking with her. He felt almost as if he needed Daria's permission to do so, especially after his conversation with her the day before, but Shelly was twenty-two years old, for heaven's sake.

A golden retriever sat next to him on the porch, her massive head resting comfortably on Rory's knee. Rory buried his fingers in the dog's thick coat, scratching her neck and behind her ears. He didn't know where the dog had come from—she had simply appeared after Rory sat down on the porch—but he was glad for her company.

From the porch, he could see the ocean, but not the beach. He knew the beach would be crowded, though, and he knew Zack was part of the crowd. Zack was out there with his new friends. He'd had little to say when Rory questioned him about who he had met and who he was hanging out with. Zack was not about to admit that spending the summer in Kill Devil Hills might not be such a bad idea after all.

Rory thought he saw some movement on the Sea Shanty's

front porch, but no one emerged from the cottage. Since Daria's visit, he'd considered her concerns, wondering if he should indeed go forward with his exploration of the past. He knew his motivation was mixed. Shelly had felt strongly enough to write to him about the situation, and given his link to her and his memory of the event, he had a personal desire to pursue the story. There was no doubt that the tale of a beautiful foundling would make a great episode on *True Life Stories*. Plus, the person who left the baby on the beach might finally have to face what she had done. He often wondered about that young woman. Had she just blindly, guiltlessly, gone on with her life? He knew he had a hostile attitude toward her, perhaps too much so. He was not ordinarily a punitive sort of guy, so that feeling surprised him, but the cruelty of her actions seemed unforgivable to him. Especially now that he had met Shelly and knew how close she had come to losing her chance at life. But what if the woman was remorseful and had been able to make a normal, healthy life for herself? What right did he have to disturb that?

Despite Daria's protestations and his own misgivings, he felt that Shelly had the right to make the final decision. He needed to make sure she understood what she was getting into, though; that's why he wanted to talk with her today. If Shelly still wanted him to pursue the story, he hoped Daria would eventually come around. He respected Daria and treasured the remnants of the childhood bond they'd shared. He would hate to spend the summer as her enemy.

The dog spotted Shelly first. The golden retriever lifted her head and stared in the direction of the Sea Shanty, and a few seconds later, Shelly appeared in the side yard. She must have come out the rear door of the cottage, and now she was headed for the beach. Rory stepped off the porch, the dog at his heels, and walked quickly toward her. She was cresting the low dune at the edge of the beach as he neared her. There was an otherworldly quality about her as she stood there among the sea oats, and he stopped to simply stare at her. She wore a white bikini, set off by her tan. The bikini bottom was covered by a gauzy white skirt wrapped around her waist. The breeze blew her long, pale blond hair away from her face. What a perfectly stunning creature she was. *The Foundling.* That's what he would call the episode on *True Life Stories.*

"Shelly?" he called, taking a step closer.

She turned and smiled at him. "Hey, Rory," she said. "I see you've got one of Linda's dogs with you."

Rory looked down at the retriever, now leaning against his leg. "She seems to have adopted me," he said. He'd met Linda briefly on the beach the day before. She'd introduced herself to him; he would never have recognized her otherwise. She was now an attractive, big-boned woman with short blond hair and round glasses, and he could not get it through his mind that she was the cul-de-sac's bashful bookworm from twenty-two years ago.

"Can I join you for a walk on the beach, Shelly?" he asked.

"Sure," she said. "But Melissa's not allowed. Go home, Melissa!"

The dog performed an obedient pivot and trotted off down the street.

"Which way do you want to go?" Shelly asked as Rory joined her on the beach.

He pointed south. "You must know that dog well," he said as they started walking.

"And you must like dogs a lot, because Melissa is Linda's unfriendliest dog."

"I didn't know there were any unfriendly golden retrievers," Rory said.

"That one is. Though not to me. And not to you, either, I guess."

They cut through a sea of blankets, beach chairs and umbrellas and began walking along the water's edge. "I wanted to make sure of something," he said. "I know that Daria and Chloe worry about me looking into how you came to be on the beach that morning when you were a baby. I need to know that you really want me to do this."

"Yes, I absolutely do," Shelly said.

"What if I uncover...if I find out something that would be very painful to you? I might find out, for example, that your real—your biological mother—doesn't want anything to do with you. She might even wish that you had died that day. How would you feel if I learned something like that?"

Shelly looked down at the ground, where the water rose and fell over her feet with the rhythm of the waves. For a moment, he wondered if she had heard him—or understood him. Then she turned toward him, a small smile on her lips. "Well," she said, "that would be the truth, and what I really want to know is the truth."

"Okay," Rory said, relieved. "But if you change your mind at any point, you just say the word, and I'll back off, okay?" He hoped it wouldn't come to that.

"Okay."

"Well, then," Rory said, "tell me what your life has been like."

"Oh, I've had a wonderful life," Shelly said. "I've—" A beach ball suddenly flew across the sand in front of them, and a little boy of about three ran after it, wailing. With a couple of long strides, Shelly grabbed the ball and returned it to the child, patting the top of his head as she sent him back up the beach to his parents. She fell into step once more with Rory.

"Isn't he adorable?" she asked, turning back to look at the boy. "Isn't the beach the best place?" She raised her arms out from her sides and tipped her head back to breathe in the salt air. Then she looked at Rory. "I always want to live on the beach," she said. "It's where I was born and it's where I want to die."

"Isn't it kind of nasty here in the winter?" Rory asked.

"Oh, I don't mind the winter at all," she said. "The only time I ever mind the weather here is when one of those bad storms is coming and they say we have to evacuate. I hate evacuating." She shuddered at the thought. "I hate going to the mainland."

"Why is that?" Rory asked.

"I don't know why," Shelly said. "All I know is, I feel like I can't breathe when I'm away from here. I can't breathe, I can't sleep, I get real jumpy. Nothing's right until I get back to Kill Devil Hills."

He wanted to put a fatherly arm around her shoulders and give her a hug. She was indeed fragile, as Daria had said.

"It's really windy here, though," Shelly continued. "Especially in the winter, but really all the time. Daria doesn't like that, because she says she has bad wind hair. I have good wind hair, though. That's what I mean. It's like I was designed to live here."

He wasn't sure what good and bad wind hair were, but he got her point.

"There's Jill!" Shelly said.

He followed her gaze to a heavyset woman sitting on a beach chair, reading a book.

"Jill, from the cul-de-sac?" Rory asked, although the woman looked nothing like the Jill Fletcher he'd known as his next-door neighbor.

"Yes. Let's go say hi to her." Shelly was walking toward the woman in the beach chair before he had a chance to say a word.

"Hi, Jill," Shelly said when they were right in front of her.

The woman looked up, shading her eyes with her hand. She smiled. "Hi, girlfriend," she said, then looked past Shelly at Rory. Her smile broadened. "Rory Taylor," she said. "I heard you were here for the summer."

He wouldn't have recognized her any more than he had Linda. She'd been a couple of years older than him and had hung around with a different crowd, but he'd seen her nearly every day during the summers of his youth. He remembered her as a little on the skinny side, with very straight, dark hair. Her hair was almost entirely silver now, and it was short and thick and very becoming on her. She was no longer skinny, however. She had to be at least forty pounds overweight, and her breasts formed a deep cleavage above the neckline of her one-piece, black bathing suit.

He leaned over to shake her hand. "Hi, Jill," he said. "It's good to see you again."

Jill laughed. "Just don't go telling me I haven't changed a bit," she said.

"You look great," he said, and he meant it. Despite the weight, she was an attractive woman. She still had those enormous blue eyes rimmed with dark lashes.

"I've already met your son," she said.

"You have?" He glanced around him at the surrounding bodies, slick with tanning lotion, wondering if Zack was nearby.

"Uh-huh. He's about fifteen, right? Same age as my son, Jason. They met on the beach a couple of nights ago and have been hanging around together. Although I hear your son already has his eye on one of the Wheelers' granddaughters."

He did? Rory was definitely out of touch with Zack.

"Probably Kara," Shelly said. "She is so cute."

"Daria said you're in charge of the bonfire this year," he said.

"This year and every year," Jill said. "Those bonfires have always been my fondest memory of the summer."

"They were great," he agreed.

Shelly suddenly unwrapped her gauzy skirt and dropped it on the sand. "I'm going to take a quick swim," she said to Rory. "I'll be right back. Don't go on without me!"

"I'll wait."

"Isn't she something?" Jill asked as they watched Shelly run toward the water. She offered him a towel to sit on, and he accepted, lowering himself to the sand. "She's out here every day, walking along the beach like a breath of fresh air." She looked at him. "I heard you're planning to feature her on your show," she said, and he tried unsuccessfully to read the tone of her voice.

"Well, she's asked me to do a little digging into how she came to be abandoned on the beach when she was a baby," he said.

Jill kept her gaze on Shelly, who was swimming straight away from shore with long, easy strokes. "I hope she doesn't come to regret asking you," she said. "I've watched her grow up, summer after summer, and she is a dear, dear soul. Her mother used to call her a gift from the sea."

"You can't blame Shelly for wanting to know the truth," Rory said. "I just need to be sure she's ready to hear whatever I might uncover."

"Right," Jill said. "I'm never sure exactly how much she understands about any given topic." Jill changed the subject to his sister, and they were still talking about Polly when Shelly returned to the beach, her hair slick over her shoulders. Jill tried to hand her a towel, but Shelly waved it away. "I'm fine," she said, lifting her skirt from the sand and tying it around her waist. "The sun will dry me off." She turned to Rory. "Ready to walk some more?" she asked.

"Sure." He stood up, his knee a bit stiffer than when he'd sat down.

They said goodbye to Jill and began strolling along the water's edge again. Shelly stopped to speak to a woman who was hesitantly dipping her toes into the chilly water. "It will feel warm and wonderful once you're in," Shelly said.

For the first time, Rory understood, and maybe even shared, some of Daria's concern for her sister. Shelly was open to everyone, friend and stranger alike, and that could indeed leave her vulnerable to being taken advantage of.

"Did you hurt your leg?" Shelly asked when they started walking again.

"I hurt my knee a long time ago, when I played football," he said.

"Is it very painful?"

"Not too much," he said. "It's a chronic pain, so I'm used to it."

"What does chronic mean?"

"It means ongoing. Not like banging your toe into a table leg. That's a bad pain, but it's over in a few minutes, usually. Chronic means it goes on and on."

"Yuck," Shelly said, and he laughed.

Shelly reached down to pick up a shell. She examined it, then dropped it on the beach again. "I have a secret friend," she said abruptly.

"Who might that be?" he asked.

"I'll never tell," she teased. Her gaze was still riveted on the sand in front of her. "Daria's been pretty sad lately," she said in another rapid change of topic. The way she flitted from subject to subject with no thought of censoring herself reminded him of Polly.

"She has?" he asked. "Why is that?"

"Because Pete—he was her fiancé—broke off their engagement."

"Oh."

"I never liked him very much," Shelly said. "He was one of those he-man types, you know what I mean?"

Rory laughed. "I think so. You mean, sort of macho?"

"Right. He had tattoos on his arms, one of a sea horse." She wrinkled her nose. "But Daria loved him, and she was really, really upset when he said he wouldn't marry her. They'd gone out together for six years. He moved away to Raleigh."

"Do you know why they broke up?" He felt a little uncomfortable, as though this might be information Daria would not want him to know.

"Daria would never tell me," she said. "She said it was personal, so I figure it must have something to do with sex."

Rory laughed again. "There are personal issues that don't have anything to do with sex," he said.

Shelly looked at him coyly. "Daria likes you," she said.

"Well, I like Daria, too." He hoped Shelly was not implying that there might be a romantic relationship between Daria and himself. "She was a good friend when we were little kids," he said. "I'd like us to be good friends again."

"You know what, Rory?" Shelly said. She raised her gaze from the beach to look at him.

"What?"

"I have chronic pain, too."

"You do? Where?"

"No one knows about it," she said.

"Can you tell me about it?" He felt some alarm. Was she ill?

"Only if you promise not to tell Daria or Chloe. It would upset them to know."

"I promise," he said.

"Well, it's not an arm or a leg that hurts," she said. "It's actually all of me. My body and my head and my heart. They all hurt from not knowing who my real mother is."

Rory looked at her, at those beautiful brown eyes, filled with hope and sadness, and this time he did put his arm around her and gave her a hug. He truly had her permission now.

9

THE HEAT IN THE CAR WAS ALMOST INTOLERABLE. THE DAY WAS not all that warm, and Grace had the windows open, but after sitting in the parked car for nearly two hours, she was beginning to wilt. She'd parked the car at the end of the cul-de-sac, close to the beach road and just two lots away from the cottage she'd learned belonged to Rory Taylor. She'd driven past the cottage before parking and saw the sign: Poll-Rory. Who or what did the "Poll" stand for? she wondered.

She was nervous. She'd been nervous since leaving her tiny apartment in Rodanthe that morning. It had taken her half an hour to drive from Rodanthe to Kill Devil Hills, yet it had seemed an eternity. She knew she was doing something crazy; she almost felt as if she was doing something illegal. *Grace just isn't herself.*

Suddenly, the front door to Rory Taylor's cottage opened, and her heart kicked into high gear, skipping a beat or two, alarming her. Had she taken her medication that morning? She couldn't remember, and now there was no time to worry about it. The man emerging from the front door was almost certainly Rory Taylor. She knew what he looked like; everyone did. He was carrying a beach chair, and she grimaced as he headed toward the beach. *Damn.* She'd been hoping he would get in his car and drive out of the cul-de-sac so that she could follow him. She'd pictured him driving to the nearest grocery store, where she could "accidentally" bump into him in one of the aisles. But things were not going her way. Nevertheless, she'd prepared for this possibility as well. She wasn't supposed to be in the sun, but what did a rash or a sunburn matter at this point? Grabbing the beach blanket from the back seat, she got out of her car.

Rory had just finished the first chapter of the paperback he was reading, when a woman spread her blanket on the sand near his chair. He tried to keep his attention on his book, but he couldn't help staring at her, and he hoped his dark glasses would prevent her from noticing. The woman was very attractive, tall and slender, with light brown hair that reflected the sunlight. Her one-piece, high-necked navy blue bathing suit made her shoulders look sexy. She was very pale, though, as if she hadn't spent much time on the beach so far this summer. She lay facedown on her blanket, took off her sunglasses and closed her eyes.

She's going to burn to a crisp, he thought.

It was a weekday, and the beach was strewn with sunbathers, but not really crowded. He could see Zack sitting close to the water, sharing a blanket with a few other kids his age. Zack already had the sort of tan it took most people a summer to acquire, and his hair was several shades lighter than it had been when they'd first arrived. Had Rory tanned that quickly, looked that good when he was Zack's age? If he had, he'd never known it.

He returned his attention to his book and was in the middle of chapter three when the woman lying near him suddenly let out a yelp and jumped up from her blanket.

Startled, Rory looked up at her. "What's wrong?" he asked.

The woman laughed, her cheeks coloring. "I think something bit me," she said, brushing her hand over her arm. "Probably just a horsefly." She had deep bangs that framed her face and accentuated her chiseled features, and she was older than he had first guessed. Late thirties, or maybe even early forties.

"Oh, yeah, there are a few of them around," he said, although to be honest, he hadn't seen any yet this summer.

The woman suddenly stood perfectly still, staring at him, and he knew that he'd been recognized.

"You're Rory Taylor!" she said.

"Guilty." He rested his book facedown in the sand, glad to have an entrée to talk with her. "And you're...?"

"Grace Martin," she said. She sat down again, brushing her hand over the invisible bite on her arm as she smiled at him. She had one of those wide, straight smiles that was impossible to observe without smiling back.

"I live down in Rodanthe," she said, lifting her sunglasses from the blanket and slipping them on. "I was visiting a friend up here in Kill Devil Hills, and the day was so beautiful that I decided to relax on the beach awhile before heading back." Her hands were still shaking from her run-in with the fly, and even her voice sounded a bit tremulous, but the flush remaining in her cheeks made her look very pretty. Her sunglasses were see-through blue, and he could still make out her brown eyes behind them. There was something needy about her, and he felt an unexpected desire to comfort her by taking one of those pale hands in his own.

"What's the beach like in Rodanthe?" he asked, although he didn't particularly care about the answer. He just wanted to keep her talking.

"Oh, about the same as this. Not as many people, though."

"Must be nice," he said.

"So, why are you here?" she asked. "We don't usually get movie stars in the Outer Banks."

He laughed. "I've never been in a movie," he said. People made that mistake all the time. "But to answer your question, my family has had a cottage here ever since I was a kid, right behind us on that cul-de-sac." He pointed behind him. "I haven't been back to it in a long time, but recently I've been thinking about an incident that happened here many years ago that might make a good episode on the show I produce."

"*True Life Stories,*" she said.

"Right."

"What is the incident?" She cocked her head, and he wondered if she was coquettish or merely curious.

"Well, a long time ago, a newborn baby was found on this beach," he said, "right about where we're sitting. A little closer down to the water." Right where Zack was sitting, actually, he realized.

Grace leaned forward, eyes wide behind the glasses. "You're kidding?" she said. "*How* long ago?"

It was genuine curiosity, he thought now, and it was gratifying. He'd wondered if the story would capture the interest of the general public. "Over twenty years ago," he said. "I was fourteen the summer it happened. My neighbor, a little girl who lived across the street from our cottage, found the baby early one morning."

"Who'd left it there?" Grace asked.

"No one knew," he said. "They never found out. So I thought, even after all this time, it would be interesting to try to find out who that might have been. Who did it, what prompted her to do it, how has she lived with herself since then. That sort of thing. And I thought that her answers might lend some insight into the reasons for the rash of abandoned newborns we're seeing these days."

"It must have been terrible for the little girl who found the baby," Grace said.

"Oh, I don't know. She was a pretty tough little kid," he said. And a tough grown-up as well. "Her name is Daria, and she was considered a hero. There were articles in all the papers about her. Were you living in the Outer Banks at that time? Maybe you remember reading about it?"

"I was living in Charlottesville twenty years ago," she said. She looked perplexed. "Why was the girl considered a hero if the baby died?" she asked.

"Oh, the baby didn't die," he said. "That's the exciting part of the story. She—the baby was a girl—would have certainly died if Daria hadn't found her, but she survived, and Daria's family adopted her. She suffered some mild brain damage, but she's beautiful and—" he searched for a word "—charming."

Grace looked astonished, and he knew the story was even more captivating than he had thought.

"So…where is…I guess the baby would be a young woman by now…" Grace seemed to have trouble putting her thoughts into words. "Where does she live?" she asked finally.

Rory turned and pointed behind them at the Sea Shanty. From where they sat, only the white widow's walk was visible above the sea oats. "Right there," he said. "She and Daria live together in that cottage."

"Right there," Grace repeated. She stared at the widow's walk as if lost in a daydream.

Rory spotted Zack walking toward him across the beach. "Here comes my son," he said with some pride, and Grace slipped out of her daydream to turn toward the boy.

"Hey, Dad," Zack said as he neared him. "Can I have some money?"

Rory should have guessed Zack was not coming over to him for some father-son conversation.

"Zack, this is Grace," he said. "Grace, meet my son."

"Hi, Zack," Grace said.

"Hi," Zack said without really looking at her. He was waiting for Rory to answer his request.

"I don't have any money on me," Rory said. "My wallet's in the cottage if you want to help yourself to a five."

"A five? Don't want to leave you broke or anything, Dad." Zack grinned, glancing to his left, and Rory noticed that a teenage girl was waiting for him a few yards away. She was as tan and blond as Zack, and wore a skimpy green tankini and some glittery thing in her navel.

"Make it ten," Rory said.

"Thanks." Zack nodded to the girl, and both kids headed up the beach toward Poll-Rory.

"He looks a lot like you," Grace said once Zack and the girl had disappeared over the dunes.

"He's too much like me for his own good," Rory said. "Do you have any children?"

"No." She looked down at her arms, and he wondered if she realized that she was starting to burn. Should he tell her? She spoke before he had a chance to decide.

"I read about your divorce a couple of years ago," she said. "I'm recently separated. I guess I'll be divorced myself soon."

"I'm sorry," Rory said, feeling instant sympathy for her. "It's hell to go through, isn't it?"

"Just kind of…hard to get back on my feet again," she said.

He remembered what that was like all too well. The loneliness, the roller-coaster of emotions. He could almost see the pain of starting over etched on Grace's face. He wanted to know if her husband had been the one to leave. Had there been an affair? Had she, too, suffered that agony?

"Well, I had my work to keep me active and prevent me from thinking too much about it," he said. "Are you working?"

She nodded. "I own a little shop in Rodanthe. I'm usually there, but my partner is handling things while I'm away today." She glanced at her watch. "I didn't realize it was so late," she said. "I really should call my partner and tell him I got delayed. Is there a pay phone nearby?"

"My cottage is right next to the beach," he said. "You're welcome to use the phone there." Her partner was a *he*. It was crazy, but that disappointed him.

"I hate to put you out," she said.

He got to his feet. "No problem. Come on. I should check on my son and his friend, anyhow. Probably shouldn't leave them alone in the cottage for too long." He held out his hand to help her up from the blanket, and it seemed to take some effort for her to stand. Her shakiness had to be due to more than a fly bite.

"Are you all right?" he asked, not wanting to embarrass her, but her unsteadiness begged the question.

"Oh, I'm fine," she said, brushing the sand from the rear of her bathing suit. "I've been ill recently, but I'm okay now." She lifted her blanket from the sand, and he helped her fold it. Her shoulders were quite pink; she would suffer later.

As they walked over the dune to the cul-de-sac, he wondered what illness had left her so tremulous, weak and pale. She walked smoothly across the sand, though, with a fluid ease. Her eyes were on the Sea Shanty.

"You said you've met…the woman who was found on the beach?" she asked.

"Yes. She's a very sweet person."

"What about the brain damage you said she has?"

"It's mild. Just makes her seem more childlike than someone her age." He stepped into his front yard. "This is my cottage," he said.

"How cute!" Grace said as they neared the front steps. Zack and the girl were just coming out of the door.

"Were you coming to chaperon us?" Zack grinned. The girl punched his arm, obviously embarrassed. "Maybe we'd better stay to chaperon *you*," Zack added.

"Very funny," Rory said. "Grace just needs to use our phone."

Inside the cottage, Grace made a quick phone call, while Rory put on his shirt and busied himself emptying the dishwasher. It relieved him to hear nothing intimate in her voice when she spoke to her partner. She hung up and turned to him.

"Well, I'd better get on the road," she said. "Thanks so much for the use of the phone."

"Where are you parked?" he asked.

"Just at the end of the street."

"I'll walk you." He closed the dishwasher and left the cottage with her.

"So," she said, glancing toward the Sea Shanty, "will you take…what do you call it? Footage? Will you take footage of the Sea Shanty? Will you have the grown-up abandoned baby on the show?"

They walked side by side down the cul-de-sac toward her car. "I don't know what shape the story will take yet," he said. "But I'm pleased that you seem intrigued by the idea. I want to make sure it's a story that will appeal to the masses."

Grace laughed, and he realized it was the first time he'd seen true levity in her face. "Well," she said, "I'm not sure I'm representative of the masses, but I certainly think the story of a foundling is interesting." She pointed to the sedan parked on the side of the road. "This is my car," she said.

He couldn't let her drive away without knowing if he might get to see her again. "Do you visit your friend in Kill Devil Hills often?" he asked.

"No," she said. "She was just down for the week. She's leaving tomorrow."

"Well, now you have a new friend to visit in Kill Devil Hills." It felt strange to be that forward, yet she looked pleased.

"Why, thanks," she said, smiling that wide, engaging smile again.

"May I have your phone number?" he asked.

"Sure." She rattled off the number. Neither of them had anything to write on, or with, but he memorized it. As she drove away, he saw her turn her head to look again at the Sea Shanty, and he knew he had a winner of a story on his hands.

10

"So," ANDY SAID, "IF YOU TAKE CARE OF THE WALL UNIT, I'LL make the pantry they wanted for the kitchen. Deal?"

Daria barely heard him. She and Andy were sitting on the Sea Shanty porch, going over the designs for a house in Corolla, but her eyes were fixed on Rory. He and a woman had walked from the beach into his cottage. They'd been in there ten minutes or so, and now he was walking her to her car. He'd been bare-chested from the beach to Poll-Rory; now he wore a broadly striped white and blue short-sleeved shirt. The woman was tall and slim and had the gait of a model. Her dark bathing suit was cut high on her shoulders; her long legs probably bore no trace of cellulite. *Damn.*

"Earth to Daria," Andy said. He stood up and slipped the drawings into his portfolio.

Daria smiled at him. "Sorry," she said. "Yes, I'll do the pantry."

"No, you'll do the wall unit," he said. "I knew you weren't listening to me."

"Was too," she lied. "I was just teasing you."

Rory touched the woman's arm, and Daria felt a strangely familiar sense of loss, the same loss she'd felt when she was eleven and he started hanging around with the older kids. She was losing him again, and she'd never even had him to begin with. She'd be the first to admit this obsession of hers was nuts.

"Do you teach your EMT class tonight?" Andy asked.

"Uh-huh."

"Wish I was in it."

She smiled at him again. "I wish you were, too," she said.

"See you tomorrow?" He pushed open the screen door.

"Okay."

Rory was walking back toward his cottage now, but when he spotted Daria sitting on the screened porch, he waved and turned in her direction.

"Good luck," Andy said to her with a grin as he closed the door behind him.

God, everybody knew she was in heat.

Rory and Andy exchanged a greeting as they passed each other in the Sea Shanty's front yard, then Rory opened the screen door and stepped onto the porch. He stopped short and smiled.

"I walked in here just like when I was a kid, without knocking first," he said. "May I come in?"

"Of course," Daria said, motioning toward one of the rockers. "Have a seat." She knew he had taken a walk on the beach with Shelly a few days earlier, and she wanted to be irritated with him for it. She *should* be; he had intentionally discounted her concerns. But how could she be angry with him when he'd sent Shelly home in such excited good spirits? Shelly had talked of nothing else that night other than Rory this and Rory that and how she felt certain he could find her mother. This yearning for her birth mother was brand-new…at least to Daria. If Shelly had been feeling it, she'd kept it to herself all these years. Daria had talked with her sister about the possibility that Rory might fail to uncover anything new—a very real possiblity, since Daria was going to do her best to make sure that was the case. Shelly had merely shrugged. "What will be, will be," she'd said. It was an expression she'd picked up from Chloe, and Daria wondered if Shelly truly understood its meaning.

"So," Rory asked as he sat down in the rocker, "was that someone you're seeing?"

Daria was not certain what he meant at first. Then she understood and laughed. "No, that's Andy. He's a bit too young for me." She wasn't certain exactly how old Andy was, but he couldn't have been more than twenty-six or -seven. "He's a carpenter. We work together."

"Ah," Rory said.

His question had given her the invitation to be equally as inquisitive. "And how about the woman you just walked to her car? Is she someone you're seeing?"

"Not yet," he said. "I met her on the beach. We talked for a while, and I think we hit it off. She's recently separated from her husband and seems pretty distressed about it." He looked in the direction the woman's car had taken, his interest in her so apparent that Daria felt intrusive for witnessing it. "Do you think I'd be making a mistake going out with someone who's newly separated?" he asked.

Yes, she thought. *Big mistake, when you have me, ready and willing, living right across the street from you.*

"Depends," she said. "Does she have a lot of emotional baggage?"

"Don't we all?" Rory asked with a smile.

"Speak for yourself," she said, although she knew she had a truckload all her own.

"I think she probably does," Rory admitted with a sigh. "She seems…wounded. Like she needs to be taken care of."

"You always were the caretaker type," she said, annoyed at the glib tone her voice was taking.

Rory groaned. "I wish you hadn't said that. That's exactly what the marriage counselor told me. He said that when I met Glorianne, she seemed helpless and needy and that I felt sorry for her and wanted to rescue her. Then when Glorianne got strong, I no longer felt needed. I don't really buy that interpretation, though. I think as she got stronger, her strength and mine clashed because our values were so different. I don't think I'm really a caretaker."

Daria grinned at him. "Remember that kid everyone used to pick on because he never caught any fish?" she asked.

Rory groaned again.

"You stuck a bunch of your own fish in his pail," she said. She had thought it was a typical Rory Taylor kindness at the time. Now she realized he was a pathological rescuer. A strong woman didn't stand a chance with him, and that suddenly irritated the hell out of her.

"So?" He looked defensive. "Was that a crime?"

"And Polly. You were always rescuing Polly."

"And you're always rescuing Shelly."

"Okay," she said. "The rescuing of sisters is hereby excluded from this discussion. Back to the woman."

"Grace," he said.

"Grace." She nodded. "If you go into it with your eyes open, I suppose it would be okay to go out with her. Just realize she's probably not too rational at the moment."

"Are you speaking from experience?" Rory asked.

"What are you implying?"

"I don't want to bring up a sore subject," he said, "but Shelly told me your fiancé broke up with you a couple of months ago."

"We are discussing *you* right now, Rory, not me." She laughed as if she was teasing him, but the fact was, she was in no mood to discuss Pete and her failed attempt at love. Rory saw through her, though.

"I have a feeling I hit a nerve," he said, sober now, his intense green gaze on her face, and she felt herself seduced by his sympathy. The spell of the caretaker.

"Let's talk about Grace," she said, although Grace was the last thing she wanted to discuss. Still, Grace seemed to be Rory's new favorite subject, and so they talked about her until Daria had to leave for her class. And as she drove away from the Sea Shanty, she knew she had drifted into a role she did not want: that of Rory's summertime confidante.

11

SHELLY BENT OVER THE LINE OF SHELLS IN THE SAND AND picked up a piece of turquoise glass, washed smooth by the sea. She examined it, then slipped it into the fabric bag tied around her waist. Smooth glass was a find, and once she polished it, it would make a beautiful necklace or ring. She'd seen man-made tumbled glass, but it always had an unnatural look to her. The sea did a much better job.

It was very early in the morning, the sun peeking out from a purple cloud above the horizon, and she had this stretch of beach to herself. A few people and a couple of dogs were in the distance both north and south of her, but this area near the cul-de-sac was her own. *Thank you, God, for this beautiful morning.* There was never a morning on the beach that she didn't feel close to God. How could she not? His creations were all around her.

Bending over the shells once again, she heard a voice behind her.

"Watch out, Shelly!"

Shelly turned to see a golden retriever racing toward her. The dog leaped at her joyously, nearly knocking her to the ground, and she laughed. She caught her balance and looked up to see two more dogs bounding toward her, followed by their owner, Linda.

"Sorry," Linda said as she walked closer to Shelly. "They saw you and just started running."

"That's 'cause they know I love them." Shelly dropped to her knees to cuddle all three of the dogs.

"Are you finding some good shells this morning?" Linda asked. She was barefoot and moved closer to the water so that it rushed over her feet after each break in the waves.

"Lots of colored glass today," Shelly said. Standing up, she reached into the bag at her waist and pulled out the turquoise glass to show her.

"Pretty color," Linda said. She threw the red plastic bumper she was always carrying into the water, and two of the dogs chased after it. The remaining dog, the one whose name Shelly couldn't remember, jumped up on Linda, his paws nearly to her shoulders, and she stroked its back. "You know," she said, "Jackie's birthday is coming up in a few weeks, and I would love to commission you to make one of your sea-glass necklaces for her."

"What does commission mean?" The word was familiar to her. It had something to do with the way she sold her jewelry in the shops, but she didn't know what Linda meant, using it the way she did.

The dog jumped off Linda and ran into the ocean, where the other dogs were fighting over the bumper. "I mean, I'd love you to make a necklace that I could buy specifically for Jackie," Linda said.

"Oh, sure, that would be easy," Shelly said. "Come over to the Sea Shanty and pick out a piece of glass and the style of necklace you would like, and I'll make it."

"Great," Linda said. Melissa dropped the bumper at her feet, and she picked it up and threw it into the waves again. "Isn't it amazing that Rory Taylor's on the cul-de-sac for the summer?" Linda asked.

"Yeah, it's great," Shelly said. "Melissa hangs out with him sometimes."

Linda looked at her dogs, who were jumping over the breaking waves to get to the bumper. "So that's where she's been," she said.

"Daria and Chloe knew him when he was a kid," Shelly said.

"Yes, so did I. Although I don't think he remembers me. I was pretty shy and quiet back then."

"Oh, yeah, I think he remembers you," Shelly said. "Daria and Chloe were telling him who still lived around here, and he knew who you were. I don't think he knew you were a lesbian, though."

Linda laughed. "Even *I* didn't know it back then. I just knew I was different."

"Like I know I'm different," Shelly said. She hoped Linda didn't think she meant that she was a lesbian. She knew for a fact that she was not. It was hard for her to understand how a woman could want to be the lover of another woman, but she liked Linda and Jackie, and if that's what they wanted to do, that was okay with her.

"You are *wonderfully* different, Shelly," Linda said. She called to one of her dogs, who was sniffing at the overturned shell of a horseshoe crab, and the dog trotted obediently to her side for a biscuit she had hidden in her shirt pocket.

Shelly wanted to tell Linda that Daria was madly in love with Rory, but knew her sister would not appreciate her blabbing that fact around the neighborhood. It was so wonderful, though, to see some life in Daria's eyes again… even if Rory had not yet gotten the message that she was beautiful and available. Shelly hoped he would figure it out soon, or else she would have to bop him over the head with it. Daria had seemed almost dead since Pete broke off their engagement and she'd stopped being an EMT, and Shelly longed to see joy in her sister's face. She would do anything for Daria, no matter what the cost.

"Do you know what Rory is here for?" Shelly asked.

"What?"

"He's going to try to find out who my real mother is."

Linda took a step away from Shelly, her eyes wide behind her round glasses. "And how, pray tell, does he expect to do that?" she asked.

"I don't know, but that's what he plans to do. He wants to tell my story on *True Life Stories.* You know, about Daria finding me on the beach and all."

Linda was quiet for a moment, doling out treats to her dogs, but not really paying much attention to them. Her lips were pursed in thought. "Do you want to know, Shelly?" she asked finally. "I always thought of you as just a member of the Cato family."

"Yes, I want to know." Shelly felt her eyes burn. Why did this surprise everyone? "It was my idea. I wrote to him and asked him to help me. Wouldn't you want to know who your real mother was?"

"Yes, I guess. But what if your…real mother turns out to be a person you despise?"

"I don't despise anyone," Shelly said. Except maybe Ellen, she thought, and felt guilty for even thinking it.

One of the goldens relieved himself near the horseshoe-crab shell, and Linda bent over to scoop the mess up in a plastic bag.

"Well," Linda said as she knotted the bag and set it near her feet on the sand, "what if she turns out to be someone you feel no respect for and don't want to spend time with or have anything to do with? How would you feel then? I mean, maybe it's best to leave things the way they are."

"You sound just like Daria and Chloe." Shelly was exasperated. "The only one who wants me to find out who my mother is is Rory. I'm so glad he's here."

"I think Daria and Chloe…and I…are just trying to protect you from being hurt."

"Well, I'm already hurt. Somebody dumped me on the beach when I was a baby, and my brain never got as good as it should have. So, now I'd like to meet the woman who did that. I'd like to understand why she did that to me."

"Could you ever forgive her for doing that?"

"I can forgive anyone for doing anything," Shelly said with certainty. Father Sean always said that forgiveness was the most important quality a person could possess.

Linda shook her head, a smile on her lips. "I wish I could be a little more like you, Shelly," she said. She whistled for her dogs, and they ran up to her. She gave them treats, then picked up the full bag. "I'll stop over in the next couple of days to pick out a piece of glass for the necklace, okay?" she asked.

"Okay. Is it a surprise? Should I be careful what I say around Jackie?"

"Please do," Linda said. "And…tell Rory not to make you agree to anything you're not comfortable with."

Shelly rolled her eyes. "Right, Linda."

She watched as Linda and the dogs walked up the beach toward the cul-de-sac, then she continued her own slow and purposeful journey. It was hard to concentrate on the shells, though, after her conversation with Linda. She wished everyone would lighten up about her trying to find her real mother. Maybe it came as a surprise to them that she even cared. She'd always known that expressing interest in the identity of her birth mother was somehow forbidden, as if that meant she hadn't appreciated all the Catos had done for her. But suddenly Rory was giving her the freedom to say that she did indeed care. He was the best thing that had happened to her in a long time. If only he would be the best thing that happened to Daria, as well.

12

"LET'S GO UP TO THE TOP," RORY SAID TO ZACK. THEY WERE standing in the small parking lot near the Currituck Lighthouse, looking up at the red brick structure. Rory started walking toward it, but Zack didn't budge.

"Come on," Rory said to him.

"Is there an elevator?" Zack asked as he fell into step next to Rory.

"No, but the stairs in the lighthouse are really neat," Rory said, trying to be patient and well aware that the word *neat* would make Zack roll his eyes. "It's a spiral staircase. Gets tighter and tighter till you reach the top, and then you have a terrific view."

"I'll stay down here," Zack said. He had spotted a bench in the small, green courtyard surrounding the lighthouse, and he walked over to it. With a sense of defeat that had been mounting in him all day, Rory entered the lighthouse alone.

He paid the entry fee to the young woman sitting at the table inside the lighthouse, then began climbing the stairs. This was not what he'd had in mind when he invited Zack to tour the Outer Banks with him that morning. He'd wanted to share the area with his son, to instill in Zack a love of the Barrier Islands. But so far, his plan had not worked. They'd visited the Wright Brothers Memorial and Museum. Zack had sighed repeatedly, twisting and turning in his seat during the lecture, and he'd trudged about twenty paces behind his father as they walked up the grassy hill to the memorial itself. Zack saw no point at all in visiting the wildlife refuge and he had no interest in taking a boat ride to see the dolphins. Rory was afraid that what was really boring Zack was his company. Around his newfound friends on the beach, Zack was lively, active and perpetually smiling—nothing like the somber kid Rory was dragging from one attraction to another.

Rory had purchased memberships for both Zack and himself at the health club where Daria belonged, but even there, he'd felt distanced from his son. Zack liked the fastpaced classes—the cardio-kickboxing and the spinning class on the bikes. Rory and his knee could handle neither.

He was winded by the time he reached the balcony at the top of the lighthouse. The view was stunning: curlicues of land and water for as far as he could see. He spotted Zack sitting on the bench far below him, and he would have waved at him, had Zack been looking up, but that was not the case. Rory had the balcony to himself. He leaned against the railing and looked out to sea, and for the first time that day, let his mind drift away from his son to the woman he'd met on the beach. Grace. He'd called her that morning. She said she'd been hoping he would call, and those words raised his spirits. He asked if he could come down to Rodanthe to see her, but she said she would prefer coming to Kill Devil Hills. They made plans for the following day.

He'd thought about her often over the past few days, remembering the many questions she'd asked him and her genuine interest. It had not been the sort of fabricated, calculated interest women often showed in him, which he knew was meant to entice him. Since his divorce, he'd met many women who were interested in him primarily because he was Rory Taylor. He had not felt that way with Grace. Her questions had not been about fame or fortune, but about his ideas, particularly his idea for the foundling episode on *True Life Stories.*

There were two ships far out in the ocean, tiny white specks in the distance, and he imagined what it would be like to have been a lighthouse keeper back in the old days, trudging up these stairs, making sure the huge lens was clean and the light inside burning. But his mind only rested on those images for a moment before returning to Grace.

He'd wanted to call her sooner, and the newness of her separation and Daria's warning about his being too much of a caretaker were only part of his hesitation to do so. It was Zack who stopped him. How did you date when you had a fifteen-year-old son to set a good example for? He'd dated since his divorce, but not on the weekends and holidays when he had Zack with him. Of course, Glorianne had not only dated someone else, she had married him as well, and Zack had survived that upheaval in his life. Glorianne had not, however, set a good example for their son. Not by a long shot. That had to be Rory's primary concern. Yet he wanted the chance to get to know Grace better.

He looked down at Zack, who was now stretched out on the bench, arms folded across his chest, and possibly even asleep. He was most likely thinking about the Wheelers' granddaughter, Kara, that pretty little flirt who'd been glued to Zack's hip since their arrival in Kill Devil Hills. Maybe *that* was how he could connect with his son: women. He'd tried sharing his memories of his own adventures at each of the sites they'd visited, and that had elicited only more of the eyerolling and yawning. He might as well try some guy talk about women. He descended the circular staircase inside the lighthouse quickly, primed for his new approach.

Zack had indeed fallen asleep on the bench, and Rory nudged his shoulder. "Ready to go?" he asked.

"Yeah." Zack got up and walked with Rory to the parking lot.

"Well," Rory said as he and Zack got back into the car. "Where to now?"

"How about Poll-Rory?" Zack suggested.

"Oh, come on, Zack," Rory said. "One more spot. Why don't we go down to the dunes in Nag's Head? We can watch the hang gliders." He realized his son had not yet gotten a good look at the dunes. Nor had he, in twenty years, although at one time they'd been the most alluring, most tantalizing part of the Outer Banks for him.

"Whatever," Zack said.

They drove in silence for a couple of miles, Rory trying to find a way to begin the conversation. "So, tell me about Kara," he said finally.

"Like what?" Zack asked.

"Anything."

"There's nothing to tell," Zack said.

"How old is she?"

"Fifteen."

"Where does she live in the winter?"

"Philadelphia."

"How long has she had that pierced navel?" Why did he ask *that*?

"Awhile, I guess."

"Does she have any hobbies?"

Zack rolled his eyes. "I don't know," he said.

"Well, she seems very nice," Rory said lamely. He had no idea if she was nice or not. She hadn't said a single word to him, and surely Zack knew that.

Silence fell between them once again. For some reason, Rory

remembered carrying three-year-old Zack around Disneyland on his shoulders. He remembered how Zack would try to emulate his every move when they played softball at the local playground or kicked the soccer ball around the backyard together. He remembered Zack wearing little-boy pajamas, giggling when Rory tickled him, laughing at Rory's goofy jokes.

Rory kept his gaze steady on the road, but he felt a wholly unexpected desire to cry, and the sensation took him by surprise. He was not the crying type. He'd shed a tear or two when Polly died, and came close when he found out Glorianne was having an affair, but why now? He swallowed hard and stared at the road. Zack was all he had. Why couldn't they have a warm, amiable, father-son relationship? What was he doing wrong? He'd already lost today's battle; unless something changed soon, he was going to lose the entire war.

The massive gold dunes rose in the distance, and he felt Zack perk up next to him at the sight.

"They're the tallest dunes on the East Coast," Rory said.

"Pretty cool," Zack admitted.

"When I was little, developers were just about to demolish the dunes to make room for new homes," Rory said. "Some woman stopped them and turned the area into a state park."

"Check out the hang gliders," Zack said.

Rory turned into the crowded parking lot. "Let's go see them close up," he said.

They got out of the car and began walking. Gradually, the sand grew steeper until they were climbing up the slope of the first dune. People were scattered across the face of the dunes, some of them perched on the crests, and children rolled and tumbled down the sandy hills. Above them, a couple of hang gliders floated in the air; a few more were poised for takeoff on the side of the tallest dune—the dune Zack was most intent on climbing. He charged ahead of Rory, whose bad knee gave a warning twinge as he neared the crest, and he was breathing harder than he had in years. Either the dunes had grown a lot taller over the last twenty years or he'd grown a lot older. He never remembered being winded when he climbed them as a kid.

He had so many memories of these dunes. He'd been one of the small children who rolled down the sand hill, standing up dizzily at the bottom, only to scamper up the slope again. He'd been a wild preteen, flinging himself from the top of the dunes into a slide to the bottom, where he'd have to empty pounds of sand from his shorts and sneakers. And he remembered being a teenager out here, in the daytime with the sun and the heat. At night with the stars.

A string of people were seated along the crest of the dune, watching the gliders, and Zack and Rory joined them. The sun beat down on them, but there was a soft, refreshing breeze that blew grains of sand gently against their cheeks. From where they sat, they could see both sound and ocean, and the cottages down by the beach were so minuscule, it was like viewing them from a plane.

"I think those people are just learning how to hang-glide," Zack said, pointing to a group surrounding a hang glider, which rested on the sand.

Rory tapped the shoulder of the young woman sitting next to him. "Do you know if that's some sort of class?" he asked.

"Uh-huh," the woman answered. Her blond hair blew across her face and she brushed it away with her hand. "It's a beginners' class. My cousin's in it."

"Which one is your cousin?" Zack asked.

"The guy that just landed," the woman said. "Or, I should say, the guy that just got dragged across the sand on his face."

The woman's cousin, who looked quite young from this

distance, appeared none the worse for wear from his rough landing. All of the would-be pilots were wearing harnesses and helmets. Rory and Zack watched a few more takeoffs and landings, and no one seemed to get terribly high in the air or fly for very long, but the smooth glide a dozen feet or so above the sand was inviting.

Zack was clearly mesmerized. Finally, something besides the beach and Kara was getting a rise out of him.

"Why don't you and I take a lesson one day?" Rory suggested.

Zack looked at him, disbelief etched on his face. "A hang-gliding lesson?"

"Sure."

"Are you talking about here? This summer?"

"Why not?" He could do this, he thought. It looked safe enough. He'd watched enough of the beginners crash-land on the cushion of sand and get up unscathed to feel confident that he and Zack could handle this. He did wonder how his knee would fare; it was still aching from the walk up the dune. But this was finally something they could do together.

"I can't believe you're serious," Zack said. "I just can't see you—"

"I was at one time a professional athlete, you know." Rory felt quite the old man at the moment.

"Let's do it," Zack said. "When?"

"Well, how about I…" He stopped himself. He should give this responsibility to Zack. "How about *you* call the school and find out when they have beginners' classes. You can sign us up."

"You probably think I won't call," Zack said with a grin.

"I hope you will," Rory said sincerely. "I'd really like to do this with you."

The emotional edge to his voice must have been a little too

much for Zack, because he stopped talking, turning back to watch the gliders sail off the dune. And Rory turned to his own thoughts, his own memories. Did teenagers still climb these dunes at night, he wondered, after the park was closed and it was not allowed? He remembered one particular night out here. The dunes may have shifted over the years, but that memory was planted firmly and forever in his mind.

It was one memory he would never share with his son.

13

"Should I leave this blind open for you, Father?" Shelly asked. "Or is the light in your eyes?"

Sean Macy looked up from his desk. Shelly was dusting the blinds in his office, while he pretended to straighten papers, shuffling them from one side of his desk to the other. Shelly had been chattering to him, but he had no idea what she'd said until this question about the blind.

"Leave it open," he said, although the sun was indeed in his eyes. "It's fine."

"So, anyway," Shelly said as she moved on to the next window with her duster, "I think they'd be perfect together."

Perfect together? Who was she talking about? Whoever it was, he couldn't think about it now.

It was almost three o'clock, almost time for him to hear confessions, but he was so preoccupied with his own thoughts that he didn't know how he would be able to focus on the sins of his parishioners. He was in deep trouble—with God and with his own conscience. He looked down at his hands where they rested on top of a sea of unfinished paperwork. His hands were large, well shaped and swept with delicate gold hair. They were the hands of a sinner.

"Did you know him?" Shelly asked. "It seems like everybody knew him. Except me, 'cause I was too little."

"Know who?" he asked, struggling to catch up with her one-sided conversation. He couldn't seem to give her his attention today. Usually when he was troubled, he found Shelly's presence a comfort. He would share his concerns with her, enjoying her sympathetic ear—and the fact that she did not easily put two and two together. He could safely share things with her that he wouldn't dare tell another soul. Being able to speak his problems out loud was somehow cathartic and helped him think through his options. He never named names, of course, and was always careful to tell her that she must keep what he said to herself. He was confident that she did. Shelly was nothing if not honest. Besides, the relationship was symbiotic: he was the keeper of her secrets, as well.

"Rory," Shelly said. She turned away from the windows, grinning at him with the devil in her eye. "I don't think you've been listening to me, Father Sean," she said.

He tried to return the grin. "You're right," he admitted. "I'm sorry, Shelly."

"It doesn't matter." Shelly sat down in the chair near the window, the blue duster resting on her knees. "But I didn't tell you the best part yet," she said.

"What's that?" He leaned back in his chair, determined now to give her his attention.

"Rory's going to find out for me who my real mother is." The expression on Shelly's face was childlike. Ingenuous. Expectant. And Sean felt the floor of his office give way beneath his feet.

"I don't understand," he said, completely attentive now. "Who is...do you mean Rory Taylor?"

"Yes! He wants to tell about me on his *True Life Stories* program. Isn't that cool?"

Sean played with a pen on his desk, rocking it back and forth with his big, golden sinner hands. "And what do your sisters think about this?" he asked.

"I don't care what they think," Shelly said, and Sean thought it was the first time he'd ever seen that look of stubborn rebellion on her face. He knew that the Cato sisters would not approve of Rory Taylor's tinkering with the past. No way.

Shelly suddenly groaned. "I almost forgot," she said. "Ellen and Ted are coming tonight."

"Who?" He was momentarily confused by her abrupt change of topic, although after twenty-two years of knowing Shelly, he was certainly used to it. "Oh, your cousin Ellen," he said.

"Yes. And I still don't really like her, Father. I keep trying, but I just don't."

"You're making a sincere effort, Shelly, and that's what matters." He looked at his watch. "I'd better get back to this paperwork," he said. "And you to your dusting."

"Right!" She jumped up from her seat and began working at the blinds once more.

Sean looked at the papers spread out in front of him, then shut his eyes. *Rory Taylor.*

His hands trembled as he put the top on the pen and rested it on the desk. He would never be able to concentrate on hearing confessions now.

14

DARIA AWAKENED HUNGRY THAT SATURDAY MORNING. THE sunlight poured into her bedroom, where everything was white and blue and clean and bright, and she felt the blissful realization that she did not have to go to work or teach a class or do anything other than goof off all day. Perhaps she would go to the gym. Perhaps Rory would go at the same time. Then, suddenly, she remembered that Ellen and Ted were in the cottage, and her mood plummeted.

They had arrived the night before, and Daria had instantly felt her spirits sink when their car pulled into the driveway. She hadn't had to deal with her cousin since the summer before, and only now did she realize how heavenly the year had been without Ellen's opinions and interference. Daria had greeted the two visitors, then pleaded exhaustion and went to bed, feeling a little guilty leaving Chloe and Shelly to provide hospitality.

Ellen, along with Aunt Josie, had spent all of her summers at the Sea Shanty until the year she married Ted. Since then, she and Ted and their two daughters came down on occasional summer weekends. They never waited for an invitation. Ellen would simply call and say they were coming, and after all these years, Daria felt unable to tell her no. Anyway, Chloe would never let Daria turn their cousin away. Chloe was able to view Ellen from an entirely different perspective. "We have to understand why Ellen is the way she is," she would say. "Her father died when she was little. Aunt Josie wasn't exactly the warmest, most maternal human being on earth. We need to have sympathy for Ellen. We need to show her love and compassion." But it was hard to show someone love and compassion when all you received was sarcasm and insensitivity in return.

Trying to recapture her good feelings, Daria got out of bed and pulled on shorts and a T-shirt. She glanced out her window at Poll-Rory, wondering if Rory was up yet. Then she walked down the stairs to face her guests.

She found Ellen on the porch, pouring orange juice into glasses on the picnic table. A platter of waffles and sausages rested in the center of the table, and Daria knew that Shelly had busied herself cooking that morning, probably to escape from Ellen.

"Well," Ellen said, looking up from her task, and Daria noticed that her cousin's hair was strewn with silver now. The color was actually pretty, especially in the sunlight pouring through the porch screens, but it looked as though a five-year-old had cut her hair with dull scissors. "You look a little more with it this morning."

Already, Daria felt her skin prickle. "I'm sorry I crashed so early last night," she said, sitting down in one of the rockers. "It had been a long day at work."

"Well, no one held a gun to your head when you picked such a physical career," Ellen said. She set the pitcher down on the table and arranged the glasses by the individual place settings.

"Guess I'm just a masochist," Daria said, unwilling to get

into a fight. *Better than being a sadist,* she thought, remembering the mammogram she'd had the year before. A small cyst
had appeared in her breast and her doctor had ordered the test
to rule out anything serious. The mammogram had been
simple, quick and painless, but she imagined the experience
would be entirely different if a technician like Ellen were responsible for tightening that cold plastic vise.

Chloe walked onto the porch and glanced at the table.
"How come there are only four place settings?" she asked.

"Guess," Ellen said. "Ted's going fishing."

As if on cue, Ted walked onto the porch, fishing pole in
one hand, bucket in the other. "What's been biting lately?"
he asked Daria.

Daria tried to remember the latest fishing report. It was impossible to live in the Outer Banks and not be aware of what
was biting.

"Croaker, I think," she said. "Spot. Bring us home some
dinner, okay?" She didn't dislike Ted. He was overweight,
with a belly that protruded farther over his waistband every
year. He had kind brown eyes and a receding thatch of gray
hair. He was bland, reticent and a doormat to his wife, but
there was little offensive in his own demeanor. For as long as
Daria had known him, Ted would take off for the fishing pier
first chance he got, and she didn't blame him for wanting that
escape.

He gave Ellen a peck on the cheek. "See you tonight, honey,"
he said. "Be ready to fire up the grill when I get home."

"Why?" Ellen asked. "Are you picking up some steaks on
the way back from the pier?"

"Very funny," he said as he left the porch to walk out to his
car.

Shelly carried a bowl of fruit onto the porch. "Let's eat,"
she said, and the four of them sat down at the picnic table.

"How are your girls doing in France?" Daria asked Ellen, scooping some of the fruit onto her plate.

"Oh, they're loving it. It sounds like they're doing more shopping and manhunting than studying, though." Ellen laughed.

"I'm going to miss not having them around this summer," Daria said honestly. Ellen's daughters were nothing like their mother, and they always tried to include Shelly in their activities, despite the fact that they were five years younger.

"I can't say that I miss them," Ellen said. "It's finally peaceful at our house. No loud music. No teenagers running in and out of the house day and night." She suddenly looked at her watch. "How come you're not working today?" she asked. "You always used to do your EMT work on Saturdays, didn't you?"

"Yes, but I'm taking a break from it," Daria said.

Ellen looked surprised. "Supergirl's getting too old for that regimen, huh?" she asked.

"Something like that," Daria said, taking the easy way out.

"And where's Pete?" Ellen asked. "Feels strange not to have him hanging around here."

"We broke up," Daria said.

"You're kidding." Ellen looked genuinely sympathetic. "You were so perfect for each other," she said. "He was your type, I always thought. You need that supermasculine sort of guy, you being the athletic type yourself. You only look feminine next to a man like Pete."

"Well, it just wasn't meant to be," Daria said, thinking that Ellen had even managed to turn her condolences into an insult.

Daria heard the slamming of the porch door across the cul-de-sac and instantly turned in the direction of the sound, as if she'd been waiting for it. Rory was walking across his yard to his car. Daria extracted herself from the picnic-table bench and opened the porch door.

"Hey!" she called. "Do you want to go to the athletic club later?"

Rory stopped to look at her, his car door half-open. "I have company coming today," he said.

"Oh, okay. See ya." She closed the door and took her seat at the table again, trying to mask her disappointment. She wondered if "company" meant Grace.

Ellen was staring across the cul-de-sac. "Is that...?"

"Rory Taylor." Shelly finished the sentence for her.

"Well, my, my, my," Ellen said. "After all these years."

"He's going to find my real mother," Shelly said.

"He's going to try, hon," Daria corrected her. "You know he might not be able to."

"Well, that's an asinine waste of time," Ellen said.

"What does asinine mean?" Shelly asked.

"Oh, come on, Shelly, you know that word," Ellen said. "Stop playing stupid."

"I *don't* know it," Shelly protested.

"It means, what on earth is the point in him trying to find your mother?" Ellen said. "What will you do with her once you find her? Take her on some tell-all reality show so you can yell at her for screwing up your life?"

"Ellen." Chloe made a very un-nunlike face. "Be kind."

"I wouldn't do that," Shelly said.

Daria knew that when her younger sister's voice took on that tinny edge, she was two seconds away from crying. "We would all rather Shelly didn't pursue this," she said to Ellen, "but it's important to her."

Shelly looked surprised at her sudden support. "Thanks," she said.

"Well, good," Ellen said. "Shelly's finally being allowed to make a decision on her own. After twenty years of you telling her when to blow her nose."

Daria could think of no suitable retort that would not upset Chloe, so she kept her mouth shut. Ellen had always complained about Daria's overprotectiveness toward Shelly. Right from the start, she'd tried to change Daria's approach with her. Shelly should have been in regular public-school classes, she'd argued. She would have learned to keep up eventually. She should be forced to live on her own and get a real job like everyone else. Daria babied her too much. Shelly had never learned to stand on her own two feet. And on and on.

Ellen had no sympathy for Shelly's fears. Even at Sue Cato's funeral, when Shelly was beside herself with grief and battling a whole new crop of fears precipitated by the loss of her mother, Ellen saw fit to torment her. After the funeral, everyone went back to the Catos' house for a dinner of sandwiches and salads. Shelly was sitting on an overstuffed chair in the living room, and Ellen, knowing full well her cousin's irrational fear of earthquakes, snuck up behind the chair and shook it, sending eight-year-old Shelly flying out of the room in terror. Daria, then nineteen, had smacked her older cousin across the face, starting a brawl that left few physical injuries but plenty of hard feelings.

Chloe suddenly stood up. "I have to go over to St. Esther's," she said. "Do you mind cleaning up?" She was looking at Daria.

"No problem." She thought Chloe was rather brave to leave her there with Ellen, when she had to know Daria was ready to rip her cousin's throat out. But she managed to get through the washing and drying of the dishes without incident, and then she escaped to the athletic club, alone.

RORY HANDED GRACE THE GLASS OF LEMONADE, THEN SAT down in one of the other chairs on Poll-Rory's porch. They had the cottage to themselves. Grace had arrived just as Zack left for the water park with Kara and her various siblings and cousins. Rory had felt nervous about this meeting between Zack and Grace, when it would be apparent she was there for some purpose other than to borrow the phone. Zack had merely mumbled a greeting to Grace, then left the cottage with Kara. He seemed truly indifferent to whatever Rory wanted to do. Maybe he was even pleased that Rory had someone to keep him occupied and off his back.

Grace was wearing an emerald green sundress, sandals and the blue see-through sunglasses. Her light brown bangs were long and sexy. He liked looking at her.

"Well," Grace said, "tell me more about the child who was found on the beach."

He was hoping she would ask that question. They'd talked about the shop she ran in Rodanthe—it was part sundries and part café, she said—and they talked a bit about Zack, and he began to wonder if his story about Shelly was not all that compelling after all. But now she seemed interested, her gaze focused on the cottage across the cul-de-sac.

"What would you like to know?" he asked. "What do you think people would want to know about her?"

"What her life has been like," Grace said. "What she looks like. You said she's beautiful?"

"She's a beauty, all right," Rory said. "Tall and blond."

"And brain-damaged." Grace pursed her lips as though this fact made her angry.

"She's just a little…" He didn't want to say *simple*. Somehow that word was not appropriate. "She's…ingenuous, if you know what I mean. I don't know her well, I've only spoken to her a few times, but she seems very trusting in an innocent sort of way."

"Was she treated well by her adoptive family?" Grace asked.

"She's loved," he said. "Her mother died when she was eight, though, and one of her sisters took over her care."

"Oh…" Grace frowned. "Poor little thing. She lost two mothers."

"I think Daria took terrific care of her, though."

"What about…holding a job? Can she work? How did she do in school? What about socially? Did she—"

"Whoa." Rory laughed, pleased. He should be writing down her questions so he'd be sure to address them in the program. "One question at a time. I think she had some special classes. I guess I'll have to find out more about that. And she works as a housekeeper at a Catholic church, but Daria—her sister—told me she needs a lot of supervision. Shelly is pretty dependent on her."

"The brain damage…what do they attribute that to?"

"Something to do with her birth, I guess, or with the time she spent abandoned on the beach. I don't know. I don't know if anyone really knows."

"I don't see how you can possibly find out who left her on the beach after all this time," Grace said. "I mean, I'm a little worried about you being disappointed. It seems like an impossible task."

He was not worried. All he had done so far was sift through the police records, but he was making a list of people to talk to, including the detective involved in the case and everyone on the cul-de-sac. He didn't feel rushed. He had the whole summer.

"You'd be amazed the things we've found out through researching incidents for *True Life Stories*," he said. "Sometimes the mysteries are solved during the research itself, like the time we figured out who had murdered a little boy, even though the police and FBI had been on the case for years and had turned up nothing. Our researchers brought a different perspective to the case and were able to uncover the real murderer." He guessed that Grace was not a regular viewer of *True Life Stories* or she would have known the incredible success the program had had in solving the unsolvable.

"That's amazing," Grace said. "But how exactly will you try to find out who the baby's mother is?"

"By questioning people. Sometimes people remember things now that didn't seem important enough to report to the police at the time. And they'll disclose those things to me. Another way we've solved mysteries is by presenting all the details of the story on the show, and then people come forward with the truth. You'd be surprised at how often that happens."

"How sure are you that you'll be able to solve this one?" Grace asked.

"I have a feeling about it," Rory said. "Probably whoever abandoned Shelly confided in someone over the years. Or maybe she's suffering from having made that decision. Maybe she would want to be reunited with her daughter after all this time."

To his delight, the door to the Sea Shanty opened and

Shelly walked out into the yard. She was wearing her white bikini, her gauzy skirt. She turned in the direction of the beach.

"Speaking of Shelly," Rory said, nodding in the direction of the Sea Shanty.

"Is that her?" Grace leaned forward in her chair. She lifted the sunglasses off her nose for a better look.

"It sure is," he said. "Would you like to meet her?" He was anxious for another opportunity to talk with Shelly himself, but she had already disappeared over the dune. "We can catch up to her," he said, and glanced at Grace's fair skin. "I have some sunscreen in the cottage you can use."

Grace stood up. "I already have some on," she said.

They began walking toward the beach.

"I used to be a sun worshiper," Grace said. She held her arm out in front of her as they walked, and studied the pale skin. "I guess that's hard to believe right now."

"Well," Rory said, "at least you won't get skin cancer." He winced. That had been an insensitive thing to say. Maybe she'd *had* skin cancer, or some other form of cancer, and that was her problem. He wanted to ask her about her illness, but it felt too much like prying.

"Hey, Shelly!" he called as they crossed over the dune.

Shelly turned at the sound of her name and waved to him as she started walking toward them. The breeze tossed her blond hair into the air and blew her skirt against her long legs, and he wondered if Grace was as captured by the sight of her as he was.

"Hi, Rory," she said.

"I just wanted to introduce you to a friend of mine," Rory said. "This is Grace."

Shelly smiled and held her hand out to Grace. "I'm Shelly," she said. She wore small, rose-colored sunglasses, and Rory had to smile. They certainly suited her view of the world.

Grace shook Shelly's hand, but said nothing.

"Can we walk with you awhile?" Rory asked.

"Sure," Shelly said. "Down by the water, okay? I want to get my feet wet."

Once they began walking, Grace was no longer quiet. She bombarded Shelly with questions. What was her job like? What did she like best about it? What did she like least? What was growing up like for her? Did she have friends? Shelly answered every question with the sort of childlike honesty Rory was coming to expect from her.

"Rory told me about...how you were found on the beach," Grace said. "Did you always know about that? Did you always know that you were adopted?"

"Oh, yes," Shelly said. She giggled. "It was pretty obvious, anyway. I mean, everybody else in my family has really dark hair, and they're not very tall. And there I was, this skinny, blond string bean."

"But it sounds like your adoptive family took great care of you, right? Maybe it was for the best that your mother... deserted you, and you ended up with a good family."

"Absolutely," Shelly said. "I got a really good family."

"Were you always very tall?" Grace asked. "I mean, were you the tallest girl in your class when you were growing up? You're nearly as tall as me."

"Yup," Shelly said. "And I think, actually, I'm taller than you." She looked at the top of Grace's head, measuring. "The beach is slanted, and it's hard to tell."

"Kids always teased me when I was young," Grace said. "They said I looked like Olive Oyl. Did you get teased a lot?"

"No, hardly at all. Daria wouldn't let anybody tease me."

"Daria is her sister," Rory explained, in case she'd forgotten.

Grace nodded. "Yes. The one who found her...found Shelly."

"She's Supergirl," Shelly said.

"You mean…because she saved you?" Grace asked.

"Me and a lot of other people. She's an EMT. Well, she was, anyhow."

"She sounds like an amazing person," Grace said. "I'm so glad she's taken such good care of you."

Rory was beginning to feel superfluous to the conversation, but he didn't mind. He was taking mental notes, trying to ascertain from Grace's questions what aspects of Shelly's life would be of interest to his viewers.

"Rory said you make necklaces out of shells," Grace said.

"Not just necklaces," Shelly said. "All kinds of jewelry."

"I'd like to see your jewelry sometime," Grace said.

This was Grace's natural style, Rory thought: passionate interest in others. He liked that about her very much. He wondered if she would be able to draw Zack out with her questions, the way she was doing with Shelly.

"You know," Grace began slowly, "sometimes when babies have a rough start in life, as you did, they develop health problems. Do you have any special health problems?"

The question struck Rory as odd. Intrusive and leading. Was she trying to get Shelly to admit to the brain damage? What on earth was Grace's purpose in that?

But Shelly did not seem the least bit put off by the question. In fact, she embraced it.

"Yeah, actually, I do," she said, a look of surprise on her face. "How did you know that?" She looked at Rory. "She's really smart," she said, nodding toward Grace, who wore a tight smile.

"I guess she is," Rory said.

"I get seizures," Shelly said. "Do you think it's because I was left on the beach?"

Grace touched her arm in comfort, and Rory was moved by the gesture. It seemed as if it had been the right question to ask, after all, and he thought that Grace was an amazing woman. Intuitive, curious and kind. Why on earth would her husband have left her? Of course, he didn't know if that was the way it had happened. And anyway, Glorianne had left him.

"Perhaps, but not necessarily," Grace answered Shelly's question. "Some people are born with that problem. You probably would have the seizures whether your mother left you on the beach or not. How often do you have them?"

"Not very often," Shelly said. "But I've never gone a year without one, so I can't drive. Which is annoying." Shelly made a face. "Daria or somebody has to drive me everywhere. Although I walk a lot. I can walk to St. Esther's if the weather's not too bad. Anyhow, I take medicine, and that helps me not have them as much."

"Rory told me he wants to tell your story on his TV show. What do you think about that?"

"I think it is extremely cool," Shelly said, grinning. Then she instantly sobered as she looked at Grace's shoulders. "Your shoulders are burning," she said.

Rory saw she was right. The skin next to Grace's green sundress was turning pink. "We'd better go back," he said. "Or you'll be sore tonight."

They stopped walking and Grace glanced at her shoulder, scowling.

"You have to start out really slow getting a tan in the summer," Shelly advised. "And use lots of 15."

"Thanks." Grace smiled at her. She looked up at the sun, as if wishing it might go away. Then she sighed. "Yes, I guess we'd better go back."

"I'm going to keep walking for a while," Shelly said. "It was nice meeting you, Grace."

"And you, too, Shelly," Grace said. She watched as Shelly took off down the beach, then began walking next to Rory.

"What a delightful young woman!" Grace beamed.

"You were great with her," Rory said.

Grace looked surprised by the compliment. "I just talked to her, that's all. She's quite easy to talk with. I see what you mean about her being...ingenuous. Someone could take advantage of her way too easily."

"And I don't want to do that," Rory said, instantly defensive.

"Oh, I wasn't suggesting you would."

"Sorry. I'm a little sensitive about it because Daria thinks I shouldn't delve into Shelly's past. But Shelly wants me to. You can tell that, can't you?"

"Yes, she does," Grace said slowly. "But maybe she doesn't know what's best for her."

They walked in silence for a while, and Rory wondered how Zack would respond to all of Grace's questions.

"Would you like to go out to dinner with my son and me tonight?" he asked as they climbed over the diminutive dune to the cul-de-sac.

"Oh, thank you," she said, "but I have to work."

Although she seemed far stronger today than she had the first time he'd met her on the beach, she was once again tremulous as he walked her to her car in his driveway.

"Do you need a glass of water or anything before you go?" he asked.

"No, thank you."

"You seem shaky all of a sudden," he said.

"I just..." Grace looked toward the cul-de-sac as she got into the driver's seat. "I guess I'm just thinking about Shelly. I feel sorry for her. For what she's been through."

Rory nodded. "I know," he said. "She's had a good life with the Cato family, but I still get angry every time I think about that woman who abandoned her on the beach. Shelly came—"

he held his thumb and forefinger a quarter of an inch apart "—this close to dying."

Grace stared through her car window toward the beach. "Maybe you shouldn't be too quick to pass judgment on that woman without knowing the circumstances, Rory," she said. "Who knows what she was going through?"

16

DARIA SAT ON THE BEACH UNDER AN UMBRELLA SATURDAY afternoon. The beach was crowded, but she'd managed to find a small patch of sand near the sea oats for herself. She was reading an architectural magazine—or at least she was trying to. Guilt was taunting her, sapping her concentration. Her old Emergency Medical Services supervisor had called her that morning, telling her they were desperately short-staffed, begging her to come in. *They must think I'm being stubborn,* she thought. They didn't know it was fear and shame that kept her from climbing into the back of an ambulance and rushing off to the scene of an accident.

"Let's go crabbing." The voice came from behind her, and she turned to see Rory approach her chair. He had on a gold T-shirt, black shorts and a straw hat that made her laugh.

"Crabbing?" she asked. "I don't think I've done that since we were kids."

"I was thinking the same thing," Rory said. "We spent half our time crabbing back then, and I didn't even like the way crabs tasted. But I do now, so how about it? I even got some bait in anticipation of you saying yes."

Daria thought of the old crab net and traps gathering dust

in the Sea Shanty's storage shed. She looked up at him. "You deserted me back then, do you know that?"

"Deserted you?" He looked like Huck Finn in that straw hat.

"Yeah. You dumped me for the older kids."

Rory studied the horizon, as though pondering what she'd said. "Yeah, I guess I did. I remember that hanging around you began to seem like a liability, 'cause I was trying to fit into a different group. Never did succeed, anyhow." He smiled at her. "Sorry."

"You're forgiven." She stood up, deciding to leave her chair and umbrella right where they were. "Let's go crabbing," she said.

"Great! Should we drive?"

"How about bike?" she suggested. She knew that he and Zack had rented bicycles for the summer, and she had one of her own.

Rory got the bait from his cottage, while Daria gathered the old equipment from the storage shed. She met him in the cul-de-sac, where they split the equipment between her bike and his, and they set off across Kill Devil Hills for the soundside pier.

She rode behind him, trying to focus on the cars instead of the way he looked on his bike. They'd had a few conversations over the past few days—on the beach and at the Sea Shanty and once at the athletic club—and every conversation had the same focus: Grace or Zack. Rory had seen Grace several times now, and Daria wondered how far that relationship had gone. He talked about being enamored of her, but not about the intimate details Daria both longed to know and hated to imagine. She'd met his adorable son, Zack, who looked so much like Rory at that age that she'd had a hard time looking him straight in the eye. While riding on her bike behind

Rory's, she had to admit that she had herself one more good male friend. Great.

The pier was remarkably empty for the time of year, but the day was so splendid, that Daria imagined everyone was at the beach. They carried their equipment to the end of the pier, put a fish head in the trap and lowered the trap into the water. Rory tied a second fish head to a string and dropped it over the side of the pier. He wiped his hands on a rag with a grimace. "Been a while since I've had fish head on my hands," he said.

"You might as well just give in to it," she said. "No way you can crab all afternoon and not go home smelling like the sound."

He sat next to her on the pier, their legs dangling above the water. The sound was littered with Hobie Cats and waverunners and windsurfers, and in the distance, a parasail soared above the water.

"Weird," Rory said. "For a minute, I felt like I was a kid again, sitting here with you. Then I looked down at our legs and saw these grown-up legs and it gave me a jolt."

She smiled. So he'd looked at her legs and seen grown-up legs, nothing more. She guessed he preferred Grace's long white legs to the tanned, muscular ones she possessed.

Rory had a beach bag with him, and he opened it and handed her a can of Coke.

"Thanks." She took the can from him and popped it open.

"So," Rory said after taking a swallow of the soda, "What do you remember about the morning you found Shelly?"

Daria felt a deep disappointment. In the conversations they'd had over the past week or so, Rory had not brought up this topic, and she'd been pleased that he seemed to be letting it go. Now she felt betrayed. Was this why he wanted to spend time with her today? To pick her brain about Shelly for his show?

"I don't want to help you with this, Rory," she said. "You know I'm not happy that you're looking into the story. I think it's a big mistake."

He was quiet for a moment. "I was just making conversation," he said.

"You were not."

"Was too. I was just remembering how you became Supergirl. An eleven-year-old hero. I didn't know any other kid, myself included, who could have picked up a blood-covered baby and carried it home. I would have run home and gotten my mother. And by that time, the baby probably would have been dead."

She felt as though she'd been a bit harsh with him and decided to open up, if only a little. "Finding Shelly changed my life," she said. "In a whole lot of ways. I learned the facts of life overnight. I didn't know what the placenta was—I was disgusted by it—but when my mother explained how the baby was nourished by it, it fascinated me. I decided then that I wanted to become a doctor, probably an obstetrician. It had been an amazing feeling, having that little life in my hands, and I wanted to experience that again." Daria had not thought about this in a long time, not consciously, at any rate, but it seemed that the memory of carrying the newborn infant, when she had been little more than an infant herself, was still inside her after all these years.

"So, what happened?" Rory asked. "Why didn't you become a doctor?"

"I really wanted to," Daria said. "I was passionate about it. I took premed courses in college and everything. But Mom got sick. She had a fast-moving colon cancer. I quit and came home. Mom was terrified of dying, not because of dying itself, but because of leaving Shelly. She made me promise to take care of her, which was what I would have done, anyway. She told me I was like Shelly's mother. She said it was me who truly gave her life, and it used to blow me away to realize that if I hadn't gone out on the beach that morning, Shelly would never have been part of our family. Mom always let me help with her. Shelly was so beautiful and so…spirited, right from the start. A real smiley baby. She brought joy back into our house. My mother had been going through a depression before I found Shelly. I didn't realize it then, but of course I do now. Shelly brought her back to life."

"You sound as though you think there's something almost… magical about her."

She smiled at him. "Don't you?"

"Yeah," he admitted. "She's definitely out of the ordinary."

"But she needed a ton of supervision back then," Daria said. "I know you think I'm exaggerating when I tell you she can easily be taken advantage of, but it's true. Right before Mom died, Shelly was kidnapped by this guy who was preying on young girls in our neighborhood. She didn't even realize she was in danger, just got out of the car when he stopped at a light. She knew she wasn't supposed to go off with strangers, but the man told her he wasn't a stranger, so she went with him."

"But, Daria, she was only eight then. We all did idiotic things when we were eight. You don't have to protect her to that extent anymore."

"I'm aware of that," she said defensively. "She still doesn't have good judgment, though. Trust me on it."

Rory didn't argue. He pulled up the string, looked at the untouched fish head and dropped it into the water again.

"Didn't you feel some resentment about having to take care of her, since it meant you had to give up your dream of being a doctor?" he asked.

"None at all," she said honestly. "I thought taking care of

Shelly was my life's calling, the way religious life was Chloe's."
She remembered talking over her decision with Chloe back
then. Chloe had cried; she'd wanted Daria to be able to finish
school. Once Daria had reassured her that she was doing what
she wanted to do in taking care of Shelly, Chloe seemed to
accept her decision more readily. "I got more carpentry
training. Do you remember how I used to make furniture with
my father?"

"Yeah, I do."

"Well, I loved building things, and I found an outlet for my
medical interest by becoming an EMT. I have no regrets."

"Why aren't you an EMT now?" he asked.

"Ten years was long enough. I really loved it, though." Her
throat closed up on that last sentence, and she began pulling
the trap from the water, hoping for a crab to help her change
the subject. She was lucky. "Look," she said. "We've got two
of them." She pulled the trap onto the pier and emptied the
two large blue crabs into the bucket.

Rory extracted another fish head from the bait box and put
it into the trap. He was less vigorous in wiping his hands on
the towel this time, and Daria lowered the trap back into the
water.

"You said that Shelly can't leave the Outer Banks," Rory
said. "Does that mean you plan to live here forever?"

She hadn't allowed herself to think that far ahead. "I don't
know," she said, although she did not see how her situation
would ever change. "Right now, though, Shelly needs to be
here, and I love it here, so there's no problem."

"But it's so sparsely populated. How do you meet people?
How do you meet men?"

Daria laughed. "There are men here," she said. She had
dated numerous men on the Outer Banks, but dating had
never played the critical role in her life that it seemed to play

for other women. She'd been different: she raised her sister, wore sloppy clothes, worked as a carpenter. Chloe had told her she lacked the "primping hormone," and she guessed that was the truth. That didn't mean, however, that she didn't have longings. And the man she longed for most was sitting right next her at that moment. "Men tend to see me as their pal," she said.

"I don't understand that," Rory said. "You're attractive and smart and athletic and interesting."

"Thanks." She felt herself glow despite her attempt to conceal how much those words meant to her.

"But in a way, it makes sense," Rory recanted his first statement. "You're straightforward and don't play games. Not like a lot of other women. And I fear Grace is one of them," he added as an aside. "So, I could see how guys might treat you like you're one of them."

"Well, I haven't been totally antisocial," she said, wanting to correct any warped image of her he might be getting. "I've had a few…love interests," she said, for want of better words to describe the men she'd dated. She remembered the man to whom she'd lost her virginity at the age of twenty. Several days after that momentous occasion, he'd dumped her for a pretty, prissy eighteen-year-old, and Daria feared it had been her performance in bed that led him to leave her. For a couple of years after that, she was afraid to make love. She would not tell Rory about that particular guy.

"I had a long-term relationship with someone," she said. "I met him when I was twenty-three, right after I moved here, and we dated for a couple of years. He wanted me to quit my carpentry job and wear a dress and red lipstick, and needless to say, we fought a lot. He finally moved away. Then when I was twenty-seven, I met Pete. The infamous fiancé Shelly mentioned to you. He was a carpenter and an EMT, so we saw eye to eye on most things and got along great for a long time."

"What happened?"

"Shelly was a problem for us," she said. "Just like Polly was a problem for you and your ex-wife. Pete said I let Shelly run my life and that I should just—" Daria shook her head "—cut ties with her, I guess. Or at least let her fend for herself."

"I can't see you doing that."

"You're right, there was no way I would. It wasn't an issue at first. Shelly was only sixteen when Pete and I started seeing each other, so it was a given that I was responsible for her. But as she got older, he wanted me to place her somewhere."

"Place her? She doesn't really need that, does she?"

Daria had never thought so, but ever since the plane crash, she was not sure exactly what Shelly needed. She thought of telling Rory about that incident. It would be so good to tell someone, and she was certainly doing her fair share of gut-spilling here. But she didn't want to burden him with that, or to color his positive feelings about Shelly. She still wondered what the family of the pilot had been told about how she had met her death. Whatever they'd been told, they'd been lied to.

"No, I don't think she needs a placement," she said. "But she does still need *me*. Pete was offered a job in Raleigh, and he wanted me to go with him, which, of course, meant leaving Shelly behind, and I couldn't consider that. Even if Shelly would have been willing to move to Raleigh, Pete would never have allowed her to live with us." Saying this out loud, reliving it, made her angry with Pete all over again.

"He doesn't sound like a very sympathetic sort of guy," Rory said.

"Not when it came to Shelly, anyway."

"You're right. It does sound like our problem with Polly, although in retrospect, Glorianne and I had drifted apart on a lot of other issues as well. I don't like thinking about it," he said with a shudder. "It was a terrible time, with Polly getting stuck in the middle. That's when she died, and I can't help but think that the stress of living with me and Glorianne contributed to that."

Daria touched his arm. "I think it was better that she was with you, no matter what the circumstances, than to be left alone after your parents died. Don't you?"

"I think so," he said. "I hope so." He looked out to sea, and she saw sailboats reflected in the lenses of his sunglasses. Two small lines creased the skin above his eyebrows, and she wanted to touch them, erase them.

"You're a good person," she said softly. "I wish you weren't so hot on digging into Shelly's past, but I'm still glad you've come to Kill Devil Hills this summer."

He smiled. "Me, too."

"I *do* worry about Shelly's future, though," she said. "Is she going to clean the church for the rest of her life? The jewelry she makes has given her an ego boost, and she really needed that, but it hardly earns her a living. I know she should really be in some sort of vocational training program, but there is no such thing here."

"Can she leave the Outer Banks at all?"

"Her doctor is in Elizabeth City," Daria said. "But she freaks out when we go to see him. He always thinks she needs tranquilizers, because she's such a mess when she's at his office. He doesn't realize that she's completely calm and peaceful when she's back here."

"What happens when there's a hurricane and you have to evacuate? Shelly said she hates that, but it's mandatory sometimes, isn't it?"

Daria laughed. "She hides," she said matter-of-factly. "I found her in the storage closet once, and just a couple of years ago, she hid out in one of the neighbor's cottages that had already been evacuated."

"Poor Shelly," Rory said.

"She's still a little girl in so many ways," Daria said. "She's not even interested in men, and I'm really glad about *that*. Otherwise, I'd have birth control to worry about, too."

Rory frowned. "Even Polly was interested in men and sex," he said. "Are you sure about Shelly?"

"Oh, a few years ago she went through a couple of boyfriends, but they were not the nicest fellas. I was afraid they were using her." She remembered one of them talking Shelly into buying him a television set. "I broke them up. Shelly was angry with me at the time, but I think that now she's frankly relieved that she doesn't have to worry about dealing with a boyfriend."

"So," Rory said, "in your heart of hearts, who do you think abandoned Shelly on the beach twenty-two years ago?"

She stared at him, incredulous. "You're incorrigible," she said.

"Seriously," he persisted. "Do you think it was someone on the cul-de-sac, or—"

"I'm certain it was Cindy Trump," she interrupted him. "If you must know, that's who I think it was. I found Shelly on the beach right in front of her cottage. Cindy could have just walked out her back door, dropped the baby close to the ocean, expecting the waves to wash it out to sea, and walked back into her cottage. Job done."

"So, where is Cindy?" Rory asked.

"I don't know, and I don't want to know. Shelly is a Cato, Rory," she said. "Cindy, or whoever Shelly's mother was, didn't want her then. She doesn't deserve to have any part of her now."

Her eyes were suddenly drawn to a woman walking toward

the bay, a short distance from the pier, and it wasn't until Daria spotted the three golden retrievers with her that she recognized the woman as Linda. The dogs splashed in the water. Linda threw a stick far into the bay for them to swim after.

"That's Linda," she said to Rory.

Rory turned to look at the woman. "I met her already," he said. "And one of her dogs has a thing for me. She sure has changed."

Daria could barely remember the timid girl from the old days on the cul-de-sac. This Linda was a tall, impressive-looking woman with short frosty-blond hair.

They watched Linda and her dogs play together for a while. Daria was glad to be off the topic of Shelly and Cindy Trump. But then Rory brought up an even less pleasant topic: Grace. Daria knew that Grace had been at Poll-Rory at least twice in the past few days.

"I introduced Grace to Shelly," he said.

She knew. Shelly had said that Grace asked her many questions. "She told me," she said.

"She has—or had, I guess—some sort of illness. Do you think it would be crude of me to ask her what it was?"

Daria looked at the crabs in the bucket. One of them raised his claw at her in an angry fashion, but she barely noticed. Rory didn't even know what Grace's serious illness was? Exactly how intimate could they be?

"If you ask her in a supportive way, I don't see why not," she counseled, hating herself as she slipped willingly into the role.

"You can sympathize with what she's going through, with her divorce," he said, "since you and Pete were together so long. All three of us have been there. Except you're much stronger than Grace."

His marriage counselor had been right when he'd called Rory a caretaker. He was.

The sun had grown huge and orange by the time they packed up their equipment, stuck the bucket of crabs in the basket of Rory's bicycle and headed back across the island. They rode directly to the Sea Shanty.

Shelly and Chloe were discussing what they should have for dinner when the crabs arrived, and they immediately got into the spirit, digging the crab steamer out from the dark recesses of the cupboards, filling it with water and putting it on to boil. They got out two sticks of butter, hammers, crackers and picks. Laughter filled the kitchen, along with easy chatter, and Daria had to admit to herself that she and Rory were no more than a couple of good friends, cleaning crabs together on a Saturday night.

17

BOB MYERSON HANDED RORY A BOTTLE OF BEER AND TOOK a seat in the wicker chair. The trees outside Bob's living-room window dripped with pale, purply Spanish moss, and Rory's gaze was drawn to them as he told the retired detective the reason for his visit.

"I think you're going to be disappointed," Bob said.

"Maybe," Rory said. "But I have to try. You were closer to that case than anyone else. I've read the police reports, but I'd like to hear it firsthand from you. What do you really think happened?"

The detective's house was located deep in the woods of Colington Island. Although the island was only a few miles from Kill Devil Hills, Rory had gotten lost and was running late. He was supposed to meet Grace at Poll-Rory at six, and they were planning to go out to dinner with the Cato family. Even Zack was going, although that had taken some arm-twisting. Rory thought he'd be able to squeeze in this meeting with the detective first, but between getting lost and the man's enthusiasm for discussing football, time was getting short.

The detective sighed. "We didn't uncover much, I'm afraid," he said. "There were a bunch of teenage girls in the area at that time, and every one of them, it seemed, pointed her finger at someone else. But we couldn't subject anyone to a physical examination without more evidence to go on. So, if it was one of those girls, well, she got away with it." He shrugged his thick shoulders, and Rory imagined the detective had been formidable in his college-football days, of which he'd already heard too much. "But, to be honest," Bob continued, "I don't think it was any of them."

"Who do you think it was, then?"

Bob took a swallow of his beer and rested the bottle on his bare knee. "There were a couple of women who'd been reported missing around that time," he said. "One of them was from North Carolina, inland a ways, and the other from Virginia. Neither of them was ever found. My best guess is that one of them was Shelly Cato's mother. The family of the North Carolina girl thought she might be pregnant, although they didn't think she was that far along. What I think is that the girl was more pregnant than they figured, and she was despondent and scared. I think she delivered the baby right there on the beach sometime that night or early morning, then walked straight out in the ocean and drowned herself."

"But wouldn't her body have washed up, then?" Rory asked.

"Oh, you can't really predict what the ocean's going to do with a body." Bob took another swallow of his beer.

"Where can I get information on the girls who were missing?" Rory asked.

"Their names should be in the police report."

Rory vaguely remembered something about a missing girl or two. He would have to reread those reports.

Bob raised his now-empty bottle of beer in the air. "Ready for another one?" he asked.

"No, thanks," Rory stood up. "I'd better be going. I'm meeting some people for dinner."

Bob walked him to the door. "You're neighbors of the baby's family, aren't you?" he asked. "The Catos?"

"That's right. That's who I'm having dinner with."

"Well, tell that Supergirl Cato…what's her name?"

"Daria."

"Right. Tell her to get back to work. I've heard they miss her over at Emergency Services."

"I'll tell her," Rory said, although he doubted he would. There was something Daria was not telling him about why she'd quit her EMT position. He'd sensed that each time she talked about it, and he figured she would not take kindly to anyone pressuring her to return to work.

Rory spotted the Catos on the crowded deck behind the soundside restaurant.

"There they are," he said to Grace and Zack as they walked onto the deck.

Daria and Shelly sat at a large round table with a man and woman. The woman was Ellen, Rory figured, and the man was probably her husband. Chloe was missing.

He waved, and Daria saw him and stood to wave back. The sound was behind her, still and slate-blue below the setting sun.

"You found us," she said. She looked scrubbed clean and pretty, no makeup on her tanned face. She wore a sleeveless white dress, and her thick hair was pulled back in a ponytail. No sawdust in it tonight.

"Hi, everyone," Rory said. "This is Grace. I guess only Shelly has officially met her. And this is my son, Zack." He put his arm around Zack and tried to draw him forward, but Zack remained stiff.

"I've already met them," Zack said.

"Well, you've met Daria and Shelly, but not Ellen and her

husband, right?" Rory tried to keep good cheer in his voice. "Ellen, hi," he said, then lied politely. "You look great."

"Hello, Rory," Ellen said. "Long time no see." Ellen had put on quite a bit of weight. Of the three Cato girls he'd known from his youth, she had changed the most. The flesh on her face was looser. Her hair had grayed markedly and had lost its healthy sheen. Chloe and Daria were aging far more gracefully, he thought.

"This is Ted," Ellen said, gesturing toward her husband.

Ted stood and gave Rory a bone crusher of a handshake, yet he was a soft-looking man, with friendly eyes and a spare tire around his middle. "Honored to meet you," Ted said. "I'm an old Rams fan."

"Me, too." Rory smiled.

"Have a seat, Zack," Daria invited, and with a sullen shrug, Zack sat down next to Shelly. Rory held out the chair next to Ted for Grace, then took his own seat between Grace and his son.

"Where's Chloe?" he asked.

"At a vespers service," Daria said.

"At St. Esther's," Shelly added.

"Ah," he said.

"What a lovely view from here," Grace said.

"Surpassed only by the food," Ted added, and although Rory didn't look at Zack, he could imagine him rolling his eyes at the banality of the conversation. He knew Zack would far rather be with Kara tonight than at this table filled with adults.

Grace, on the other hand, had accepted the invitation with delight. She wanted to meet the Catos, she'd said, and she'd love to see Shelly again. Rory was feeling some disappointment in Grace, though, and it had taken him several days to recognize the reason for his subtle dismay: Grace had shown little interest in Zack. She'd asked the boy virtually no questions, and did not even talk to Rory about him. Rory had brought up the subject several times, trying to get Grace's input on the relationship problems he and Rory were having, but Grace barely seemed to listen as he spoke. Her indifference came as a surprise and a letdown. Especially after the interest she'd shown in Shelly. He'd expected too much of her, he knew. She had her own trials and tribulations to grapple with.

"Hey, Dar!" A good-looking man walked by their table on the way to his own, stopping to bend low and kiss Daria's cheek.

"Hi, Mike, how are you doing?" Daria asked.

"Just great," he said, giving her bare shoulders a squeeze. "We miss you."

"I miss you guys, too," Daria said.

Mike winked at Shelly, nodded to the rest of the table, then walked across the deck where he joined a woman and another couple.

"One of your pals?" Rory teased Daria.

She wrinkled her nose at him. "Exactly," she said. "Fellow EMT."

They ordered their dinners. At first Zack said he wanted nothing to eat, but Shelly insisted he try the crab cakes.

"They're the best in the universe," she said, and Zack ordered them, probably to stop Shelly from bugging him.

Conversation was superficial but swift. Ted wanted to talk about fishing and football, Ellen, about the shopping spree she had planned for the following day. Grace suggested shops Ellen might try farther south. Rory and Daria joined in the chatter wherever they could, but Rory was keenly aware of Zack's silence. He wished there was some way he could bring his son into the conversation without it looking obvious and contrived, thereby earning Zack's wrath.

Shelly suddenly whispered something to Zack, and Rory realized that he was not the only person at this table aware of the boy's shyness amidst the adults. She whispered again, and a smile crossed Zack's lips. He whispered something back to her, and she giggled. The adult conversation still surged across the table, but Rory listened in on Shelly and Zack to the best of his ability.

"Which one?" Shelly asked Zack.

"Kara," Zack said.

"She is so cute," Shelly said.

"Yeah," Zack said.

"Did you have a girlfriend in California?" Shelly asked.

Rory leaned a little closer to his son, curious to hear his answer.

"A couple," Zack said. He looked at Rory, letting him know he was on to his snooping, then turned his back on his father and continued talking with Shelly in private. There were more giggles and, on Zack's part, some outright laughter. Rory smiled to himself, grateful to Shelly. She knew exactly what she was doing, he thought. She'd seen Zack's discomfort and made the effort to bring him out of his shell.

Their food was served, and halfway through the meal, Shelly asked Zack, loud enough for everyone to hear, "Have you gone to watch the hang gliders yet?"

"Yeah," Zack said, "and my dad and I are going to take a hang-gliding lesson soon." He glanced at Rory. "Right?" he asked.

"Right," Rory said, pleased to have a chance to draw Shelly and Zack's private chat into the conversation of the adults. "We watched one of the classes. It looked pretty easy."

"Well," Ellen said to Rory, "I hope your will is up-to-date."

"Oh," Shelly said, "I think it would be wonderful. I always wanted to do it, but I was afraid to, because I might have a seizure. But Father Sean hang-glides all the time."

"*Father* Sean?" Zack asked. "Is that a priest?"

"Yup," Shelly said.

"A priest who hang-glides?" Zack asked in amazement.

"I hope Father Macy's piloting skills are better than his preaching skills," Ellen said.

The insult seemed to go over Shelly's head. "He's been gliding ever since I can remember," she said. "And he even won a contest a few years ago. Right, Daria?" She looked at her sister for confirmation.

"That's right," Daria said. "He won the summer competition. It's held every year. The next one's in a few weeks, and I bet he'll be in it again."

"If it wasn't for Father Sean," Shelly said, "I wouldn't be sitting here with you all today."

Ellen laughed. "No," she said. "You'd probably be sitting with a nice, normal family somewhere. Maybe even a wealthy family. Look what you missed out on."

"Ellen," Ted said in a voice too small for his size. "Shelly has a perfectly fine family."

"Why wouldn't you be sitting here?" Zack asked Shelly. "What did Father Sean or Macy or whoever he is have to do with it?"

"Sean Macy—the priest—helped my parents adopt Shelly when she was an infant," Daria explained. "So we all have a special place in our hearts for him."

"Dad said Daria found you on the beach when you were a baby," Zack said to Shelly.

"Yes, but I don't remember it."

Rory's mind drifted for a moment. Maybe he should have a talk with Sean Macy, since he'd been involved in Shelly's adoption. He wouldn't know anything about Shelly's parentage, of course, but still, it would be interesting to hear his memories of that time. And the priest certainly sounded human and approachable.

Grace reached for her water glass, and Rory noticed that her fingers were trembling.

He leaned close to her, whispering, "Are you all right?"

"Fine," she whispered back, then suddenly looked across the table at Shelly. "Do you see what I have on?" she asked, touching her fingers to her throat, and Rory leaned forward to see. Grace was wearing a shell necklace, probably one of Shelly's, and he was surprised. She had said nothing to him about it.

"I made that," Shelly said.

"Yes, I bought it at the Shell Seeker, that little store in South Nag's Head," Grace said. "How did you ever make it? It's so delicate."

"Oh, it's easy, once you know how," Shelly said. "It looks very nice on you." She turned suddenly to Zack. "Have you gone crabbing yet? Your father and Daria went crabbing the other day. They said they used to go all the time when they were kids."

Rory was certain Shelly hadn't meant to be rude, but she'd practically cut Grace off midsentence. He felt Grace grow quiet at his side. He reached for her hand beneath the table, and was relieved when she allowed him to take it. Their relationship had been platonic so far. They had seen each other several times, but only during daytime hours, which didn't lend themselves to any sort of physical intimacy. They'd spoken on the phone, but Grace was always straightforward, simply wanting to make plans rather than get into prolonged conversations. And so far, she had vetoed the idea of him coming down to Rodanthe to see her, saying she preferred coming up to Kill Devil Hills. Grace always seemed to keep her distance from him, physically and emotionally. He'd been ready for rejection when he took her hand and was pleased she hadn't balked.

The waitress cleared away their dishes, then took their dessert orders. Grace ordered nothing.

"God, Daria could sure beat you at swimming, couldn't she?" Ellen was speaking to Rory, and he turned his attention to her.

"I let her win," he said simply.

Daria smiled at him. "We'll have to have a rematch," she said.

"We'll see," he said. He'd worked out with her at the athletic club once this past week and feared she could probably still beat him.

"Do you remember that time," Ellen continued, "when Daria stuffed toilet paper in her bathing-suit top and it got wet and started coming out in the water?"

Zack laughed at that, and Daria groaned. "I tried to forget that, Ellen," she said.

"I don't remember it at all," Rory said.

"That's because you were ignoring me by then," Daria said.

He did remember the time Chloe lost her entire bathing-suit top when she was bodysurfing, though. He was about to mention that, but then wondered if it was in poor taste to tell such a story about a nun.

"Daria said you've got some crazy notion that you can uncover the secrets to Shelly's past," Ellen said.

"Well, I'm trying to, anyway," he said. "As a matter of fact, I met with the police detective who covered Shelly's case this afternoon." He caught Daria's dark look, and knew he probably shouldn't talk about this with her present. She still disapproved, but it was hard for him to keep quiet about the topic when it was so much on his mind, and Ellen had given him the invitation to speak.

"What did he say?" Grace asked. "What were the police able to find out back then?"

The waitress brought their desserts, and Rory leaned back to let her set his chocolate mousse on the table in front of him. Grace let go of his hand then, and took a sip from her water glass.

"Not a whole lot, I'm afraid." Rory looked apologetically at Shelly. "The detective I spoke with thinks that Shelly's mother was probably one of two teenage girls who had been reported missing at that time and who were never found."

"It seems strange that no one saw what happened on the beach that morning," Grace said. "Aren't people usually out early to beach-comb or watch the sunrise?"

"There'd been a huge storm the day before," Daria said. "No one had been on the beach for at least twenty-four hours. I think I was the first person out there. Or, at least, the second."

Ted leaned toward Rory, his soft facial features suddenly creased with concern. "Chloe and Daria think you should leave the past alone," he said quietly, obviously not wanting Shelly to hear. "You shouldn't disrupt Shelly's life."

Ellen dismissed her husband with a wave of her hand. "Let Rory find out for himself that it's pointless," she said. "The police did a thorough investigation back when Shelly was found and they didn't come up with a thing. Nobody is going to find anything twenty-some years later." She looked at Rory, false contrition in her eyes. "Sorry, Rory. I just think you're on a wild-goose chase."

"Could be," he admitted, more to ease the tension than to agree with her.

A pager beeped on the other side of the deck, and although the sound was barely audible where they were sitting, Daria jumped. She looked across the deck, and Rory saw her friend, Mike, raise a small cell phone to his ear. Daria pretended to return her attention to her dessert, but Rory knew she was still focused on Mike, and he wondered if she was interested in him as more than a "pal."

Mike got up from his table and walked directly across the deck to Daria. He put his hands on her shoulders and leaned close to her ear, but he spoke loudly enough to be heard across the table. "There's an accident on 158, around milepost 8," he said. "Two cars and a bicycle. Come with me."

Daria shook her head.

"We're short, Daria," Mike sounded insistent. The skin on Daria's shoulders was white from the pressure of his fingertips. "Please," he said. "We need you."

She shook her head wordlessly, her gaze on her key-lime pie, and Mike straightened up and left the restaurant. No one else had stopped talking, and a moment later, Daria raised her head again, smiling, joining in the conversation once more. Everyone chattered as though nothing out of the ordinary had just occurred, and Rory guessed he was the only person at the table to notice the tears in Daria's eyes.

18

DARIA PULLED INTO THE SEA SHANTY DRIVEWAY AROUND
ten that night, a good hour after leaving the restaurant. She'd
sent Shelly home with Ellen and Ted and driven to milepost
8 and the scene of the fiery, deadly accident. She couldn't say
what drew her there. Perhaps she thought she would be able
to help, but that was not the case. Oh, they needed her help,
all right. But she'd merely lurked around the edge of the
scene, just like the other curious onlookers, unable to make
herself walk over to the ambulance to help her former EMTs
deal with the havoc. The sense of being frozen in place, con-
cealed by darkness, made her feel cowardly and useless, and
she'd driven home in tears.

Getting out of her car, she was surprised to see Rory sitting
alone on the front steps of the Sea Shanty. Her heart filled at
the sight of him. She'd figured he would still be with Grace.
He'd been so solicitous of her during dinner. Walking toward
him, she hoped it was too dark for him to tell she'd been crying.

"Hi there," she said, making her voice light and cheerful.
She sat down next to him. "What are you doing here?"

"Waiting for you to get home," he said.

"Oh," she said, pleased. "Well, here I am."

"Ellen said you went to check on that accident," he said.

"Yeah, I did. One car swerved to avoid a cyclist and crashed into another car. The cyclist was hit, anyway. I think someone in one of the cars was killed. Both cars were on fire." She recounted the scene in a flat tone to avoid feeling anything as she spoke.

Rory winced. "Sounds horrible," he said.

"It was." She knew she'd have another of her nightmares that night. Even though she'd hung back, even though she was not even certain if the cyclist was male or female, she knew the pilot would be back to haunt her.

"I really admire you," Rory said. "I can't imagine doing that sort of work. And the fact that you do it on a volunteer basis makes it even more impressive."

"*Did* it," she said. She didn't deserve the credit he was giving her. "I wasn't there to help. I only watched."

"I don't understand," Rory said. "It was obvious you were upset when your friend, Mike, tried to persuade you to go with him. I figured you and he had some sort of…" His voice trailed off.

It took her a moment to understand, and she laughed. "Mike? No. Not at all."

"Then what was holding you back?" he asked. "And if you went over to the accident, why didn't you help?"

"It's a long story," she said. "And not very interesting." She needed a change of topic. "So, how was your evening?" she asked.

Rory hesitated, as if deciding whether to allow her this abrupt switch in the conversation. Then he gave in.

"Well, I have to say I don't really understand Grace," he said. "She seems to want to be with me, yet she doesn't seem particularly interested in me…in a romantic sense, if you know what I mean."

Daria tried to mask her relief. "No, I'm not sure what you mean." She wanted to hear more.

"Well, she seems pleased when I call her. She's pleased when I ask her to do things with me. But she doesn't…I don't get the impression she wants to be in a relationship. Not with me, at any rate. Tonight at dinner was the first time I've even held her hand."

"You're kidding," Daria said.

"No, I'm not. And when I brought her back to Poll-Rory, she darted out of the car before I could attempt to…get any closer. Don't you think that's a little strange?"

"Not really," Daria said. What she *did* think was that Grace was completely out of her mind. "Her marriage just ended. She probably needs some time to get used to the idea of being with someone else."

"Maybe," Rory said. "It's just not what I'm used to. Women usually come on to me. I don't mean that as a brag. I know it's because of my celebrity, not necessarily because of who I am as a person. But that just makes Grace more interesting to me. She's so…fragile. Did you pick that up?"

She had, indeed. She'd noticed a tremor in Grace's hands, and a couple of times, in her voice, as well. It was the first time she'd really seen Grace up close, and she was truly beautiful, in a pale sort of way.

"Yes, I did, Mr. Caretaker," she said. "Did you ever ask her about her illness?"

"No. I figure she'll tell me when she's ready to."

"You two need to talk," she said. "It doesn't sound like there's much communication going on between you."

Rory didn't answer. He looked down at his hands, as if studying them in the Sea Shanty's porch light. Daria wanted to touch one of them, to slip her fingertips beneath his palm and trace a line up his wrist.

"Zack seemed to hit it off with Shelly," Rory said suddenly.

"He did," Daria agreed.

"Shelly was so good with him," Rory said. "As soon as we got home, though, he and Kara took off for the miniature-golf course." He shook his head. "The two of them worry me."

"Why?"

"I don't now. Kara looks a little fast to me."

Daria laughed. "What does a fast girl look like?" she asked.

"Oh, you know. The way she dresses. The pierced belly button. Too much blond in her hair. Too much eye makeup."

"Do you think Zack is still a virgin?"

Rory looked at her with wide-eyed disbelief. "Of course," he said. "He's only fifteen. Give me a break."

"Fifteen-year-olds are a lot different than when we were kids," Daria said.

Rory said nothing.

"Have you talked to him about it?" Daria asked. "I mean, do you ever have frank, father-son talks?"

"I wish." Rory groaned, lowering his head to his hands. "I guess I need to give him the sex-and-responsibility talk. I was hoping I wouldn't have to get into that yet. He and I can't even talk about what to have for dinner, much less sex."

"You probably need to talk with him while you're doing some activity together. You know how men are more comfortable relating through sports or whatever."

"Is that how you are, since you hang out with guys all the time?"

"I *am* still a female," she said, thoroughly insulted.

He smiled at her. "I've noticed that," he said. "Especially tonight at the restaurant. You clean up good."

"Thanks," she said wryly. She figured that might be the best compliment she would get out of him.

"You raised Shelly," Rory said. "Was she ever rebellious? Did you have any problems with her when she was Zack's age?"

"Shelly was easy," Daria said. "The only time she and I ever butted heads was when I made her break up with those guys several years ago. She screamed at me. She'd cry and mope. But that was about it for Shelly's rebellion."

Headlights turned into the cul-de-sac, and they watched a car approach the Sea Shanty.

"It's Chloe," Daria said. "She must have stayed late at St. Esther's."

Chloe pulled into the driveway and got out of the car. Daria and Rory watched her approach the porch steps, and she stopped in surprise at finding them there.

"Oh, hi," she said. Her face was unsmiling, and Daria knew that was due to Rory's presence. Chloe wished Rory had stayed in California. But she took a seat on the steps next to Daria, anyway, and worked at a smile. "How was dinner?" she asked.

"Great," said Rory. "Some terrific restaurants have opened up here in the last twenty years."

"Yup," Chloe agreed. "You won't go hungry."

Chloe's voice was flat, and Daria could almost feel her sister's discomfort. It was more than Rory that was upsetting her. Daria put her hand on Chloe's arm.

"What's wrong?" she asked quietly, but Chloe simply squeezed her hand in reassurance.

Rory didn't seem to notice Chloe's distress. "I know you're not thrilled with me pursuing this," he said to her, "but you're an important part of Shelly's life, and I'd really like to get your opinion of how she ended up on the beach way back when."

Daria cringed at Rory's timing. He didn't realize how much Chloe resented his intrusion on their lives.

Chloe leaned across Daria to rest her hand on Rory's knee. She looked at him intently, her long lashes casting shadows on her cheeks. "Rory, it just doesn't matter how Shelly turned up on the beach," she said. "I know you don't understand. I know it doesn't fit in with your plans for your show. I know you want the answer to be something dramatic, something you can uncover and expose. But it just isn't important. Shelly was our gift from the sea. There's nothing more we need to know."

Chloe stood up. She squeezed Daria's shoulder. "Good night, you two," she said. She stepped onto the screened porch and disappeared inside the cottage.

"Ouch," Rory said once she had gone. "I don't think Chloe is very fond of me."

"It's not just you," Daria said. "It's true she's upset that you're probing into Shelly's life, but she seems withdrawn lately. I'm not certain what's going on with her."

"I'm sure I'm not helping," Rory said.

"Well, she thinks you're exploiting Shelly."

"Is that what you think, too?" Rory asked.

"I think your intentions are honorable," Daria said, "but I'm afraid your prying might do more harm than good."

Rory was quiet a moment, and when he finally spoke there was exasperation in his voice. "But Shelly, herself, wants me to—"

"Shelly has lousy judgment, Rory," Daria said. How many times did he have to hear that? She hesitated a moment, then the words slipped out of her mouth as though they had a will of their own. "Do you want to know why I'm not doing EMT work these days?" she asked. "Do you want to know the truth?"

He said nothing, just looked at her, puzzled and waiting, and Daria shivered. The thought of telling him was both frightening and seductive.

Drawing in a breath, she pressed her clammy palms together and began to speak.

"A few months ago, I was working on a construction job

at an old cottage near the beach, about half a mile from here," she said. "Pete was working with me, along with Andy Kramer, and this other guy, George. Andy and I were in the house, and Pete and George were outside. Pete suddenly came running into the house, yelling that there was a plane down in the water."

She remembered running to the front door of the house to look out toward the beach. From where she'd stood, she had not been able to see the downed plane, only a few people running across the sand. She'd taken off her tool belt and dropped it on the floor as she headed out the door, Andy and George close on her heels.

Daria wasn't able to see the plane until she reached the squat hill of sand marking the start of the beach. Even then, it had been hard to make out the plane's shape or size. The sun was low in the sky behind her, reflecting off the water in sharp beams of blinding light.

Pete, already halfway to the water, turned to wave at them. "It's an air pig!" he shouted.

Good, Daria thought as she ran after him. If the pontoons weren't damaged, they would keep the plane afloat. Otherwise, there was very little chance of recovering anyone alive.

People were gathering on the beach, most of them in street clothes, shivering as the evening air grew cooler. They pointed toward the plane, speaking to one another in excited voices. She and Andy pushed through the growing crowd. "Did anyone call 911?" Daria called out.

Several people shouted that they had.

"I called from my cell phone," a man standing near Daria said.

"How long ago?" she asked.

"Just a few minutes," the man said. "Right after the plane hit the water. It just dropped out of the sky. I thought—"

Daria didn't wait to hear more. She ran up to Pete, who was standing at the water's edge, squinting against the reflected sunlight as he stared at the plane.

"Ocean Rescue should be here in a few minutes," she said. Ocean Rescue would have a boat. Without a boat, there was little they could do.

"We can't wait a few minutes," Pete said as he stripped off his shirt. "It looks like one of the pontoons is damaged."

Daria looked again at the plane, and this time she could see it was listing to one side. Someone—she couldn't tell if it was a man or a woman—was pounding against one of the side windows, trying to get out.

"You can't go out there," Daria said, although she was thinking of going herself. The plane was not out that far, and she and Pete were both good swimmers. "What if there's fuel in the water?"

"I'm not going to stand here and watch—"

"Hey! We've got a boat!"

Daria turned to see two boys dragging a boat across the sand by a rope. The boat was little more than a dinghy, but it would have to do until something more substantial came along.

"Great!" Pete said. He ran up to the boys, grabbed the rope from their hands and began tugging the boat toward the water. The tattooed muscles in his arms did not even appear to strain with the effort.

Andy and Daria helped him drag the boat into the water, and Daria was about to climb in when she saw the look of longing in Andy's eyes. He wanted to help; he wanted to save lives.

"Come with us," she said. "We can use an extra pair of hands out there."

Andy climbed into the boat and picked up the oars. "I'll

row," he said, and he began pulling against the water. Although he was slender, he was strong, and the craft cut easily through the breakers, heading toward the plane.

Daria looked back toward the beach to see if any of the rescue vehicles had arrived, but she could see only the thickening crowd of people—and Shelly. Shelly stood out from everyone else because of her height, her distinctive blond hair and the assertive way she pushed through the throng toward the water. She was wearing her wraparound skirt, and Daria watched as she untied it and let it fall onto the sand, then walked into the water. She was going to swim out to them!

"Shelly!" Daria called to her. "Don't come out! It's too cold. There could be a fuel spill!"

She knew Shelly couldn't hear her; the crackling of the waves drowned out every word. Pete heard her, though, and he looked behind them to see why she was yelling.

"Shelly's in the water," Daria called to him.

"What's she doing out there?" Andy asked.

Pete glanced behind him toward the darkening water, then turned back to the front of the boat, but not before Daria had caught the look of disgust in his face. She knew what he was thinking.

It was a moment before she realized that another small boat was in the water, ten yards or so from them. Two men were in the boat, neither of whom she could recognize in the fading light, but she was relieved they were there. She glanced back to see Shelly only a short distance behind them, her smooth strokes propelling her through the water, and Daria felt a thrill of admiration at her sister's grace and energy—despite her questionable judgment at coming into the water at all. If any fuel had spilled from the plane, it could burn her, or worse yet, ignite. But if the water was clear, they might be able to use Shelly's help.

The two boats came together as they neared the plane.

"Ocean Rescue's tied up in the inlet," a man in the second boat said. "Capsized fishing vessel. Don't know when they'll get here."

The boats glided close to the plane, and the situation became instantly, painfully clear. There were two women in the back seat of the plane. One was unconscious, a cut on her temple, blood spilling over her ear. The other woman was screaming, pounding on the window, begging them to release her from the plane. The door next to the pilot had been ripped off by the force of the crash, and the pilot appeared to be unconscious. At first, Daria thought the pilot was a man. *All* of them did. A man who was twisted somehow in the front seat, his body contorted at an angle, his head bent forward, long dark hair covering his face. Daria was not sure he was alive.

Pete struggled with the pilot's seat belt. "He's got a pulse," he called over his shoulder to Daria and Andy. "But I can't get him out. Let's go for the passengers first."

If they'd had a tool, even a crowbar, extricating the passengers would have been easy, since the skin of the plane was thin and pliable. But they only had their bare hands and the oars to use, and although the sea was calm, the bobbing of the plane and boats made the work difficult.

Shelly suddenly appeared at the side of the boat, and Andy was first to spot her. "Shelly!" he said. "What are you doing out here, crazy woman?"

"Get in the boat, hon," Daria said to her sister. "You'll freeze."

"I'm all right," Shelly said. She was treading water, her hair flowing out from her head like pale sea grass. The water was dark, but Daria could see no skim of fuel on its surface. Shelly would be all right.

Pete barely seemed to register Shelly's arrival, and Daria thought it was probably just as well. He picked up an oar.

"Move your head back!" he shouted to one of the women in the back seat. "I'm going to break the window!"

The woman cowered beneath her arms, and Pete rammed the oar into the Plexiglas. It popped out in one piece, and the woman let out a scream, then started sobbing. With the window out, Daria could see that the interior of the plane was filling with water.

"We'll go around the other side," yelled a man in the second boat. They rowed to the far side of the plane and broke the window there. Pete was able to pull the woman nearest him through the window and into the boat, while the men on the other side of the plane did the same.

"This one's hurt bad," one of the men called out. "And the pontoon over here is shot. The one on that side is the only thing keeping this tin can up."

"Bring her over here," Daria shouted. She turned at the sound of sirens. An ambulance had pulled onto the beach, lights flashing. It looked very far away.

The woman in their boat seemed more shaken up than injured. "The pilot passed out, or something," she said. "We just started going down and she didn't do anything to stop it."

"She?" Daria asked. That's when she took another look at the pilot, contorted beneath the seat belt. Long hair, slim body. The pilot was indeed a woman.

The second boat had pulled next to them again, barely visible now because of the darkness.

"I should get in the other boat with the injured woman," Daria said to Pete.

"No, stay here," Pete said. "Help me with the pilot. The ambulance crew is on the beach now." He called to the men in the second boat. "You guys take these ladies in, okay?" he said.

"And bring us back a knife or something to cut this seat belt with."

Daria was usually crew chief, usually the one giving the orders, but this was not an official call, and she didn't balk at following Pete's instructions. She helped Pete and Andy transfer their terrified passenger into the second boat, and as the two men and the injured women sailed away, Daria and Pete turned their attention back to the pilot.

Daria reached into the plane and pressed her fingertips against the woman's throat, feeling for a pulse.

"Is she alive?" Shelly asked from the water.

"Yes." The pulse was very rapid, but strong. The woman suddenly rolled her head back against the seat and her brown eyes fluttered open. It was an instant before they registered alarm.

"Stay calm," Daria said. She was shocked to realize that the pilot was very young, no more than eighteen or nineteen, with long dark hair and a pronounced widow's peak that only added beauty to her heart-shaped face. Like the passenger, she also had a gash across her forehead, this one bleeding profusely. "We've just about got you out," Daria said as she took off her own T-shirt and pressed it against the woman's head. It was a lie, but a necessary one. The water was up to the woman's waist, and Pete's arms were submerged as he leaned over the side of the boat, struggling with her seat belt.

"The door frame's twisted somehow," he said under his breath to Daria. "The belt's caught in it. I can't see what I'm doing."

"I'm in the water, Pete," Shelly said. "Maybe I can do it from down here."

"You're just in the way, Shelly," Pete snapped, and for a brief moment, Daria felt hatred toward him. This was the man she planned to marry in a few months, and at that moment, she didn't even like him.

"She hardly looks old enough to have a pilot's license," Andy said.

"I don't think we can work on her from the boat," Daria said. She was losing her balance. Her hand holding the T-shirt kept slipping away from the woman's forehead.

"Yeah, and we can't extricate her this way, either," Pete added. "We'll have to get in the water."

The plane, Daria realized, was slowly sinking, seawater creeping up the pilot's body.

"Andy," Pete said, "you stay in the boat. Keep it close to the plane. Keep your eyes open for any fuel leaks, too." He unzipped his shorts, pulled them off and jumped into the water.

Daria took off her own shorts and followed him in. The water took her breath away, it was so cold. "I thought you said it wasn't cold?" she said to Shelly as she pulled herself closer to the plane.

"You'll get used to it," Shelly said, but her teeth were chattering.

"It's going down fast," Andy said from the boat.

"We need a knife out here, damn it," Pete said, and he dropped under the water to try to work the pilot's seat belt free. Daria felt the fruitlessness of his effort. He would be able to see nothing underwater in the darkness. She tried to keep pressure on the pilot's forehead as she let her body float out from the plane to make room for Pete to work. She wondered how long the pilot could survive being immersed in the cold water. How long could *any* of them survive?

"Shelly, Andy," Pete sputtered as he surfaced from the water. "This thing's sinking like an anchor. Y'all do what you can to keep it upright while Daria and I try to get her out."

"Okay." In the boat, Andy skirted the plane to reach the other side, and Shelly swam to the plane's submerged nose to do what she could to keep it afloat. Daria glanced over her shoulder at the beach, praying someone would bring tools out to help them.

The pilot's eyes were open now. Open wide. The young woman stared into Daria's eyes as Daria tried to stem the bleeding from her head wound. She dared to lift the T-shirt once, only to have blood gush down the frightened pilot's cheek. She didn't know how cognizant the pilot was of what was going on or of how much danger she was in. She was not uttering a word, yet her eyes were filled with fear.

"Don't worry," Daria said. "We're going to get you out. You'll be all right."

Pete surfaced from underwater again, tossing his wet black hair out of his face with a shake of his head. "Maybe I can get at her better from the other side," he said.

"I already tried the door over here," Andy called from his side of the plane. "It won't open." He sounded winded. Daria glanced at her sister to see how she was faring. Shelly was treading water directly in front of the plane's propeller, her hands submerged beneath the plane's nose. She appeared to be going strong.

A small yelp escaped from the pilot's lips. The water had reached her breasts, and Daria felt a flash of panic course through her own body. What if they couldn't get her out? It was beginning to look doubtful, and there was no way that Andy and Shelly would be able to keep the plane above water once it made up its mind to sink. Daria's legs ached from treading water. She struggled with her free hand to loosen the shoulder harness, trying at the same time to stay out of Pete's way. Her foot kept catching on the damaged pontoon, and it was tempting to rest it there to give herself a break from the relentless treading, but she knew that her weight would only pull the plane farther underwater.

Pete surfaced once again, gasping for breath this time. Daria saw fear mixed with the determination in his eyes. She wanted to talk to him, try to puzzle out the best course of action, but before she could say a word, he was underwater again.

"Please help." The pilot's voice was barely audible, and she reached out to grab Daria's wrist.

Daria gently extricated her arm from the woman's hand. "I need my hand to get you out," she said.

The water was rising more quickly now. It had reached the pilot's chin, and the young woman tilted her head back as though she could somehow prevent the water from climbing up her face. If only she could.

Pete came out of the water on Daria's right this time. He looked toward the beach, where a second ambulance had arrived. "Hey!" he shouted vainly against the sound of the sea. "Come on! We need help out here!"

The woman grasped Daria's wrist again, and this time Daria did not pull away. She watched in horror as the plane sank lower, pulling the pilot completely underwater, her terrified eyes still wide, staring hard at Daria.

"Oh, God," Daria said. "Pete! What can we do?"

Pete turned to Daria. He looked past her, though, and his face suddenly registered shock.

"Oh my God, Shelly," he shouted. "Move!"

Daria remembered that Shelly was near the plane's propellers, and she spun around in terror. But Shelly was safe and sound, treading water, still trying to hold up the plane and wearing a look of confusion at Pete's reprimand. Daria had no idea why Pete had yelled at her, but there was no time to find out. The plane was suddenly rising again. And another boat was coming toward them, this one motorized.

"Ocean Rescue's coming!" she said, then under her breath, "Hurry. Hurry."

The pilot's head rose out of the water, her hair slicked back from her face. Her eyes were still open, but she was not breathing. Floating on her stomach, Daria struggled to breathe into the woman's mouth as the rescue boat pulled alongside them. Pete got a knife from one of the men in the boat and, slipping beneath the surface of the water, finally freed the pilot.

"Get her into the boat!" Pete shouted, and he and Daria pulled the woman from the plane and passed her to the men in the rescue boat. The boat sped off, and Andy drew his small craft close to them again.

"Get Shelly in first," Daria said. "She's been in the water the longest."

Shelly was weak now, and Andy had to pull her into the boat.

Daria could barely climb into the boat herself. Her feet were numb and her entire body trembled from exertion and anxiety. Pete pushed her, while Andy pulled. Pete was winded and exhausted when he managed to crawl into the boat himself.

Andy rowed the boat toward shore, and the breakers caught them and carried them onto the beach. They could hear shouting and, in the distance, the whirring of a helicopter.

Too late, Daria thought. She shook with the cold, and her legs threatened to give out from under her as she climbed out of the boat. She was dressed only in her wet underwear, and she shivered as she staggered over to the cot where the medic was working on the pilot. The young woman was intubated, bagged and hooked up to an ECG. Daria peered over the medic's shoulder and saw the flat line on the ECG screen. The defibrillator paddles rested in the sand, obviously no longer needed. The pilot was dead, her brown eyes still open. Fighting tears, Daria turned away, but even with her own eyes shut, she could still see the pilot's pleading gaze.

"Sorry, Dar." Mike, who'd arrived with the ambulances,

handed her a blanket. "We'll take over from here. Do you need a form for your field notes?"

Paperwork. How could Mike even think of that right now? "I've got one in my car," she said. She tried to wrap the blanket around herself, but her fingers would not do what she wanted them to, and Mike had to help her.

"You're freezing," Mike said. "Go get warm." He walked back to the ambulance, and she turned away from the scene. She was dazed and dizzy. Where was Pete? Where were Shelly and Andy? Her breath was like fire moving in and out of her chest, and her throat was tight with the need to cry. She hugged the blanket tighter around her body, then spotted someone in the crowd handing Andy a stack of towels. Shelly was near him, and he passed a couple of them to her. She clutched the towels to her chest, and even with the sparse lights from the ambulances, Daria could see her violent shivering.

"Do you need a towel?" A woman walked up to Daria and pressed a couple of towels into her arms.

"Thanks," Daria mumbled. She turned around again, looking for Pete, and finally saw him several yards away, his back to her. By the way he was bending over the water, she knew he was sick. She walked toward him and put one of the towels over his shoulders. He was trembling uncontrollably and didn't even look at her as he took another towel from her arms and wiped his mouth with it.

She felt his need to be silent, to be asked no questions or receive no words of empty comfort. She rubbed his back through the towel as he stared at the ground, his breathing ragged.

Finally, he glanced at her, his gaze darting quickly to her face before turning out to sea. In the darkness, at least, it appeared the plane had disappeared. "Do you know what happened out there?" he asked.

She was confused by the question. "Do you mean…I don't understand what you're asking."

He looked at her directly now, and his eyes were cold. "Do you know why I yelled at Shelly when we were out there?"

She shook her head. "I have no idea."

"Your sister," he said slowly, deliberately, "was leaning on the propeller, trying to see inside the plane. That's what pulled the plane under. That's why the pilot is dead."

Daria was speechless. "But when I turned to look at her, she was just treading water. I think she was trying to buoy the plane up."

"*After* I yelled at her."

"Yes," Daria admitted. Horrified, the weight of his words sank in. "I can't believe it," she said. Surely Shelly would have known she was making matters worse by leaning on the propeller.

"Believe it," Pete said. "I was this close—" he held his thumb and forefinger apart by half an inch "—to freeing that woman—that *girl*—when the plane went under. Shelly has no common sense."

"Oh, my God, this is horrible." Daria thought of the report she would have to write on the accident and the debriefing that would occur the following day. What could she say happened? It would destroy Shelly to know her role in the pilot's death.

Pete seemed to soften at seeing Daria's distress. He put his arm around her. "Look," he said, his gaze toward the sea once again, his jaw tight. "No one else knows what happened out there. Just you and me. Shelly doesn't have a clue what she did. I doubt Andy realized what was going on, and there's a good chance the plane would have gone down, anyway," he conceded with a shrug. "And maybe the pilot would have died no matter what we did. I think we should just keep this to ourselves."

"I have to write a report," Daria protested.

"Then write it just as you would have without my input," Pete said. "Pretend I didn't tell you anything."

"It would kill Shelly if she…"

"I know," Pete said. "That's why…you should just forget about what I said."

She nodded woodenly. She had little choice, and what difference would it make now? The pilot was gone. Nothing would bring her back.

She spotted Shelly wandering among the thinning crowd, walked over to her and put an arm around her shivering shoulders. "Come on, hon," she said. "My car's at the cottage where I was working. I'll drive you home after I write my report."

They walked in silence to her car. Daria spotted Pete's truck a few cottages down the street and wondered how long he would stay at the scene. Wrapped in the blanket, she sat in the driver's seat and pulled the notebook containing her field-note forms from the back seat. She propped the notebook against her knees and started writing. The plane simply began sinking and the rescuers had been helpless to do anything about it, she wrote. She would have to recount the same story in her verbal debriefing the following day. This was the first time she had ever lied in the course of her job as an EMT, and she wondered if anything could ever ease the sick, guilty feeling in her gut.

When she finished the report and slipped it inside the notebook, she looked down the street to see that Pete's truck was gone. He would have had to walk right past her car to get to it, and he had not even bothered to say goodbye. She was worried about him, as worried as she was about herself.

Neither she nor Shelly said a word on the drive home. The only sound inside the car was that of Shelly's teeth chattering.

That night, after she and Shelly had eaten a quiet dinner in the kitchen of the Sea Shanty and fallen, exhausted, into bed,

Pete called. Daria pulled the phone from her nightstand onto her pillow.

"How are you doing?" Pete asked.

"Not so great," Daria said. Everything seemed wrong. She'd lied on a report, Shelly had unknowingly made a terrible mistake, a young woman had died a horrible death before her eyes. She stared at the darkened ceiling, the phone against her ear.

"I know," Pete said. "That was one ugly scene."

"Mmm."

She heard Pete draw in a breath. "I think we need to talk about Shelly," he said.

She stiffened. This would not be their first discussion about Shelly, but this time she knew he had the upper hand. "I don't want to," she said.

"We have to," Pete said. "Today was a clear indication that she needs more than you can give her, Daria. I know you don't want to hear that, but you have to face it. Her judgment is very poor. She needs a supervised living situation. You can see that now, can't you? Daria?"

Daria closed her eyes. "She's staying with me."

Pete sighed.

"I know why you want her to be placed somewhere," Daria said. "If she were in some…supervised-living situation, as you call it, then I'd be free to move to Raleigh with you." Pete had been offered an administrative position with a large construction company in Raleigh, a job he really wanted, and he'd been begging Daria to come with him. But when she'd agreed to marry him, she never thought it would mean leaving the Outer Banks. Leaving Shelly. She could not imagine Shelly ever being able to live on her own, but this supervised-living situation Pete kept pushing was out of the question. Those last few weeks, she'd been feeling torn down the middle between her sister and the man she wanted to marry. She could not move to Raleigh without Shelly, and Shelly would never leave the Outer Banks, the only place in the world she felt secure and safe.

"Well," Pete said, "that would be a bonus. But I'm really thinking about what's best for Shelly."

"So am I," Daria said.

Pete tried again. "So what would happen," he said, "if I agreed to have Shelly live with us, and—"

"She would never move to Raleigh."

"I know, I know," Pete said. "But speaking hypothetically, let's say I did agree to have her live with us and then you and I had children. After this incident today, I would never be comfortable leaving Shelly alone with our kids."

That was ridiculous, Daria thought. Shelly was no danger to anyone. Yet after what had happened that afternoon, how could she argue with him?

"Look, Daria," Pete said with another sigh. "I hadn't wanted to make this into an ultimatum, but the more I think about this, and especially after today, the more I feel the need to press the issue. I really want that job in Raleigh. And I really want to marry you. But if you won't move to Raleigh with me—and without Shelly—well, then, I don't see how this is going to work out."

She was quiet for a moment. "Are you saying…you'd end our relationship over this? After nearly six years of us being together?"

"I don't see what other option there is," Pete said. "The only choice you're offering me is to live in the Sea Shanty, or at least somewhere in the Outer Banks, with you and Shelly. I want to marry *you*, Daria. Not Shelly. And I need that job in Raleigh. I can't keep up this pace, physically, forever. I want that admin job."

When he put it that way, she felt unreasonable in her demands on him. Yet, unreasonable or not, she could not do what he wanted her to. For the second time that day, her throat felt tight with unshed tears.

"I love you," she said. "But I can't do what you're asking of me."

"Christ, Daria!" Pete suddenly exploded. "You live your life for Shelly," he said. "Her needs always—*always*—come first. You never put my needs—you never put your *own* needs—ahead of hers."

"Pete—"

"It's about time I faced that fact," he said. She heard the anger in his voice. "I wish you luck, Daria," he said. "Good luck with the rest of your life."

The line went dead, and it was a moment before Daria placed the receiver back in its cradle. She wondered why she didn't feel like crying now, why she felt this odd sense of relief. She was so, so tired of arguing with Pete over Shelly.

"Daria?" Shelly opened Daria's bedroom door a crack. "Are you awake?" she whispered.

"Come in," Daria said, sitting up.

"I can't sleep," Shelly said. She walked into the room, dressed in a nightshirt, her hair loose around her shoulders.

"Neither can I." Daria moved over to make room for her sister on the queen-size bed.

"Because of the pilot?" Shelly asked.

"Yes." Among other things.

"I keep thinking about how she died," Shelly said. "How horrible her death was."

"It was," Daria agreed.

"How old was she?" Shelly asked.

"I think I heard someone say she was eighteen," Daria said.

"Eighteen." Shelly blinked her eyes, and in the moonlight, Daria saw the glossy sheen of tears in them. "Three years younger than me. It's just not fair."

"I know," Daria said. "A lot of things in life aren't fair."

"I wish I could have traded places with her."

Daria felt some alarm. "What do you mean?"

"I don't mean that I want to die," she said quickly. "But I just feel so sorry for her, that she got three whole years less on earth than I've had."

Daria smiled and pulled her sister close to her. "You are such a sweetheart," she said, touched by Shelly's reasoning. She was glad that she'd lied on her EMT report. And she would lie in her debriefing tomorrow. How could Pete ever ask her to desert her sister?

Rory put his arm around Daria's shoulders. "What a horrendous experience," he said. "I assume you never told Shelly what really happened?"

"You haven't known Shelly very long," Daria said, "but I'm sure you know her well enough to realize she couldn't handle it." She leaned her head back against the screen door and looked up at the stars. Rory's arm was warm and comforting against her shoulders. "I still can't believe I filled out that fraudulent report," she said. "I *lied.*" She pounded her fist onto her knee. "I've never lied about anything so important, but I couldn't drag Shelly into that mess. Pete said the pilot might have died, anyway, but I don't know if that's the case."

"What a nightmare," Rory said.

"That's why I quit my EMT position," she said. "I just couldn't face another call. I couldn't stand to lose another victim, and I was...I still am...disgusted with myself for letting Shelly go out there and for covering up what she did. People here look up to me, and I feel like a fraud."

"I can't help but think you did the right thing in covering up Shelly's role in the accident," Rory said. "What good would it have done to point out her mistake to the world? It only would have hurt her, and it wouldn't have changed anything."

"I shouldn't have let her go out to the plane," Daria said.

"But you thought she could help," Rory said. "Had she ever given you a reason to think she was capable of making that sort of error?"

"No," she admitted. "That's why it was so shocking. It was so cold in the water. I keep using that as an excuse, that maybe her ability to reason was screwed up by the cold and confusion. We were all crazed. I doubt any of us were thinking straight."

"Was that the end of things between you and Pete?" Rory asked.

"Pete was so upset that he moved to Raleigh practically the next day," she said. "He quit being an EMT, probably for the same reason I did. I miss it so much, though." Her voice broke again.

Neither of them spoke for a moment. The crackling rush of the waves was the only sound.

"Why did you go tonight?" Rory asked finally. "Why did you go to the accident?"

"I was hoping I would find some strength inside myself that would allow me to help. They *are* short-staffed. I know that. When I got there, though, and saw how serious the accident was, I just froze. I can't handle someone else dying in my care. But I feel so selfish." She pounded her fist on her knee again. "Selfish. Guilty. Ashamed. Cowardly…"

"Shh." Rory hugged her tighter, closer, and she leaned her head against him.

"Sorry," she said, wiping the back of her hand across her wet cheek.

"What for?"

"Dumping on you. You're the only person I've told."

"Hey, I'm glad you could," he said softly. "Even though I know you told me about the accident to convince me that Shelly's judgment is poor. But there's a huge different between screwing up in the middle of a crisis and longing to know who your parents are. Don't you agree?"

Daria closed her eyes. Of course he was right. "I suppose so," she said weakly.

She felt him turn his head to look toward the beach road, and she followed his gaze with her own. Zack and Kara were walking into the cul-de-sac. They looked almost like one person, they were so close together, their arms wrapped around one another.

"They don't see us," Rory whispered.

Zack and Kara stopped in front of the Wheelers' cottage, turning to face each other, locking themselves in a long, intense embrace.

"Guess I'd better go make my presence known," Rory said. He squeezed her shoulders. "Are you going to be okay?" he asked, standing up.

"I'm fine." She smiled at him. "Thanks for listening."

"Anytime," he said, leaning over to kiss her cheek. "That's what friends are for."

19

DARIA HAD NO NIGHTMARES THAT NIGHT. INSTEAD, SHE dreamed that she and Rory were in Africa, riding together on the back of an elephant, crossing a golden plain so wide and flat that it looked as though it went on forever. Other people were there, riding elephants behind them. Shelly was there. Jill, from the cul-de-sac. Daria's mother. And people she didn't know, the line of elephants and riders streaming far behind her and Rory, curling toward the horizon. But she hadn't been interested in the other people. She was sitting behind Rory, her arms snug around his waist. The elephant's rhythmic walk, the bulk of his spine between her legs and the feeling of Rory's body beneath her hands excited her, and all she could think about was arriving at their destination. There, they would find a cabana, where she and Rory would have privacy.

She awakened before the chain of elephants reached the cabanas, and groaned with disappointment at finding herself in her blue and white, sea-air-filled bedroom. Her body was still charged from her erotic, surreal ride across the plain, and she allowed herself to relive it as she lay in bed awhile longer.

Finally, the scent of seaweed and coffee had grown so strong in her room that she had to face reality and get out of bed.

Downstairs, she found Chloe and Shelly already eating break-fast at the picnic table on the porch. She sat next to Shelly and busied herself pouring cereal, slicing a peach, struggling to let the dream go. She was still bursting with the physical sensa-tions of it, and her gaze was drawn again and again across the street to Poll-Rory.

If only she could confide her feelings for Rory to her sisters and get some sisterly advice, but that was impossible. She'd always avoided speaking to Chloe about love and desire. It didn't seem fair to talk to Chloe about that sort of thing, when Chloe, by virtue of her vow of chastity, could not experience those feelings for herself. And Shelly would make entirely too much of it. She might even say something inappropriate in front of Rory. Anyway, what advice would Shelly have to give?

Shelly was filling the porch with her chatter. She'd found a tiny, perfect starfish on the beach that morning, she said. And dozens of pieces of cobalt-blue glass.

Chloe was silent. Oddly silent. Finally, she interrupted her youngest sister.

"Shelly," she said gently, "can you tell us why you suddenly want to know who your real mother is? You never seemed to care before, and I don't understand why it's suddenly so im-portant to you."

The change in Shelly's features was abrupt. She looked into her bowl, dipping her spoon in and out of the milky cereal. There was a sheen of tears in her eyes that surprised Daria, and her own throat tightened as she waited for her younger sister to speak.

Shelly looked up at them. "I *always* wanted to know," she said. "I just never said anything about it. I didn't want to hurt Dad's feelings. But now that Dad is gone, I thought it was time for me to find out. You both know who your mother and father are. I loved Mom and Dad and I'm really glad they were my parents, but I need to know more." A tear spilled over her lower lashes and slipped down her cheek.

Chloe leaned forward to cover Shelly's hand with her own.

"I just don't want you to be disappointed," Chloe said. "I don't want you to get your hopes up and then have them shattered."

"I know," Shelly said. She wiped her nose with her napkin.

Daria's heart ached. They had accepted Shelly's good nature and ever-present cheer at face value. They'd never seen the pain behind that facade.

"Just know," Chloe said to Shelly, "that no matter what you learn or what you don't learn, we love you. Daria and I love you and adore you. Nothing you find out will ever change that."

Chloe looked across the table at Daria, who tried to read the message in her sister's eyes. For the first time, she wondered if Chloe might know what she knew about what had taken place that morning long ago. The thought sent a chill up her spine. Maybe it *was* time for Shelly to learn the truth, she thought. Maybe it was time for everyone to know what had happened on the beach that morning.

20

RORY INCREASED THE TENSION ON HIS EXERCISE BIKE AND glanced next to him, where Zack was pedaling furiously while reading the latest copy of *Sports Illustrated*. He was certain Zack had set his tension even higher than Rory's, yet he was still pedaling faster and barely working up a sweat. Rory could probably work just as hard, he tried to convince himself, but what was the point, really? This easy pace was fine. He planned to take Daria's advice about talking with Zack while involved in an activity, but he knew he wouldn't have the wind for a conversation unless he kept the tension low.

He was getting a little annoyed with himself about this new competitive streak he felt with Zack. He hoped that, at the age of thirty-six, he was not already slipping into a midlife crisis.

"Can you get your nose out of that magazine long enough to talk?" Rory asked.

Zack glanced over at him. "I'm working out," he said.

"But you'll only know you're at the proper level of exertion if you can carry on a conversation," Rory said.

"That's an old theory, Dad," Zack said.

It was? "Nevertheless," Rory countered, "I'd like to talk with you about Kara."

"What about her?" Zack shot him a wary look, and with good reason, Rory thought.

"Well, not about Kara specifically. But about you and Kara together. You and any girl." He was stumbling a bit on this.

Zack rolled his eyes. "Is this some kind of sex talk?" he asked.

Rory remembered when Zack was seven or eight and wanted to know how babies were created. He'd embraced the opportunity to talk with his son on the subject, and he'd been good at it, too, if he did say so himself. But that had been a piece of cake compared to this.

"Well, I just think it's time we had a man-to-man talk," Rory said.

"I have a feeling this isn't going to be man-to-man," Zack said. He was standing up on the pedals, pumping hard. "More like man-to-boy."

"Well, enough of the preamble," Rory said. "I'm just concerned that you and Kara are getting a little too...close. I have nothing against her. I like her." Rory still didn't know her well enough to know if he liked her or not. Kara was a closed book, as far as he could tell. "I just wanted to...talk with you a bit about it. I mean, I was your age once, and I know the temptation to go too far."

"You were fifteen in the Middle Ages," Zack said. "Things are different now."

"Oh, they're not as different as you think. Testosterone hasn't changed. What it can do to good judgment hasn't changed."

"Why don't you just say it and get it over with?" Zack asked. "Don't have sex. That's what you're getting at. I hear you. You've done the counseling thing. Thanks for the talk." He was speaking loudly. A young woman on the bike next to his glanced in their direction before returning her attention to the book she was reading.

"No, that's not all I want to say," Rory lowered his voice.

It certainly was his major point, but he knew it was not enough. Like spitting in the wind. He had indeed been fifteen once. "I just want to be sure that if you do end up…having sex, that you use protection."

"I know all about that, Dad."

"Well, you can know all about it, and still not use it," Rory argued. "Think about Shelly. She was an unwanted baby, left to die on the beach. Her mother was probably a kid Kara's age. If that boy had used protection, that girl wouldn't have gotten pregnant, and the baby wouldn't have been abandoned."

"So, you want me and Kara to break up."

Rory frowned. "No, that's not what I'm saying at all." It took him a moment to realize that Zack was being intentionally obtuse. "I think you know what I'm saying," he said.

"You and Grace are probably doing it every time I leave the cottage," Zack provoked him.

"For your information, Grace and I have barely held hands," he said, as though that noble restraint was his choice. "And besides, Grace and I are adults."

"What does that have to do with it?" Zack asked.

"You know the answer to that," Rory said.

Zack stopped pedaling. He lifted the towel from his neck and mopped his face with it. "Look, Dad. You dragged me to stupid North Carolina and I'm just trying to make the best of it, okay?" He got off the bike. "I'm going over to the cardio-kick-boxing class. I can walk home. You don't have to wait for me."

Rory watched him walk away. Cardio-kickboxing. Zack had gone to the one place in the gym where Rory could never hope to follow him. And he certainly knew it.

After leaving the gym, Rory drove to the cul-de-sac and parked his car in Poll-Rory's driveway, but didn't go inside. Linda's big female golden retriever, Melissa, was waiting for him on his front steps, and he decided to take that as a sign. It was time he picked Linda's brain about the summer of '77.

He walked down the cul-de-sac to the cottage nearest the beach road, Melissa at his side. The dog ran up the porch steps ahead of him, and Rory knocked on the screen door, instantly setting off a cacophony of barking from inside the cottage.

In a moment, a woman with chin-length red hair came to the door. A mass of gold fur swirled around her legs. Four dogs, at least. The woman looked at him just for a second before breaking into a smile.

"Hello, Rory Taylor," she said.

"Hi…Jackie, is it?"

"That's right." She opened the door just enough to reach out and shake his hand, then glanced down at Melissa, who hadn't budged from his side. "I heard Melissa's become your little groupie," she said. "She's our escape artist, I'm afraid."

"I've been enjoying her company," he said, scratching the top of Melissa's head.

"Are you looking for Linda?" Jackie asked.

"If she's not busy."

"She's been expecting you to stop by. I guess you've been talking to people who were here back when Shelly Cato was found, huh?"

"I'll talk to anybody who's willing to talk to me," he said.

"Stay there a second." Jackie disappeared inside the cottage, and in a moment Linda came onto the porch, three bottles of beer clasped between her hands and four dogs at her heels.

"Hey, Rory!" She offered him a broad, white grin. "Let's go up on the deck."

He was momentarily taken aback by the sheer force of her reception, although her greeting the day he'd met her on the beach had been equally as exuberant. The quiet, painfully shy girl from years ago no longer appeared to exist.

He followed Jackie and Linda and their large, blond retrievers up the winding wooden stairway to the small deck. Linda handed him one of the beers and motioned for him to sit on the lounge chair. The dogs sniffed and wagged around him, and Melissa rested her head on his thigh.

"So." Linda leaned forward, elbows on knees, the beer in her right hand. "You're trying to find out who deserted Shelly on the beach."

"That's right," Rory said. "I know it was a long time ago, but I thought I would see what you remembered."

"I've tried to forget those years, actually," Linda said, still smiling. "They were kind of rough for me."

He nodded his understanding. He had gay friends and knew that in many cases, their adolescent years had not been easy. "Well, you seem great now," he said. "What kind of work are you doing?"

"Besides raising too many dogs? Teaching. Jackie and I both teach at Duke."

"I'm math," Jackie said. "Linda's literature."

Rory grimaced at the combination. "And you two get along?" he asked.

"Most of the time." Linda laughed.

"So," Jackie said, crossing one leg over the other, "tell me what Linda was like when she was a kid."

Linda laughed again. "We're not talking about *me*, Jack. We're talking about all those rowdy kids who used to live on the cul-de-sac."

"Rowdy?" Rory asked. "I didn't think they were anything unusual."

"That's because you were one of them," Linda said. "I was sitting on the sidelines, watching the world go by."

"Then you're probably a good one to talk to," Rory said. "Maybe you can be more objective than anyone else."

"I bet it was no one we knew," Linda said. "I mean, I can certainly come up with some ideas for who it might have been, but the truth is, it was summertime and Kill Devil Hills was hoppin'. It could easily have been someone just down for the week. Or even the day."

"That's true," Rory said. "But I'm going to focus on the cul-de-sac for now. I'll branch out from there."

"Well, there was always Cindy Trump." Linda turned to Jackie. "They called her Cindy Tramp."

"Ah," Jackie said.

"She was unbelievable, wasn't she?" Linda asked Rory. "Honest to God. Those boobs. I remember she got them when she was, like, ten, or something. And she wore this bathing suit, this one-piece—she couldn't have been more than twelve—and when it got wet, it became sort of see-through. You could see her pubic hair through it, which really blew me away back then, 'cause I was only about nine and barely knew what I was looking at. You could see her nipples and everything."

Rory had to laugh. He could feel the heat of the memory on the back of his neck. "I'd forgotten about that bathing suit, although I can picture it now that you mention it. It was pink, right?"

"Lavender, I think. Close enough."

"And I remember the bathing suits she wore later on."

"God, yes." Linda groaned, and he knew that she'd had the same visceral reaction to Cindy and her voluptuous body that he'd had. "She'd wear these crocheted bikinis," Linda said to Jackie. "She was always real tan and she'd go prancing around on the beach leaving males lusting in her wake. And there I was, drooling from behind my book."

"I never knew, Linda," Rory said, shaking his head. "Never knew that you and I had so much in common back then."

Linda laughed.

"Chloe was pretty hot back then, too," Linda said. "She was…sultry, with that long thick hair and those eyelashes."

"*Sister* Chloe?" Jackie asked.

"Oh, yes," Linda said. "Chloe and her cousin, Ellen. You know Ellen, who comes down every once in a while with her husband? The heavyset woman?"

Jackie nodded.

"Yes, Chloe was hot," Rory agreed, "but she was always skinny as a rail. Except for…." He let his voice trail off. It felt odd to discuss Chloe's body with women, and odder still to discuss the body of a nun.

"I know what you mean." Linda finished the thought for him with a chuckle.

"Well, it sounds to me," Jackie said, "that it couldn't have been this Cindy Tramp person if she was always parading around in a bikini. How would she hide her pregnancy?"

"But that's the thing," Linda said. "Daria found Shelly right at the beginning of the summer, and the week before had been totally shitty weather. So nobody was parading around in any kind of bathing suit. We were all bundled up that week." Suddenly, she leaned toward Rory, a serious expression on her face. "Rory," she said, "I'm afraid to tell you who I really think Shelly's mother was."

He frowned. "Why?" he asked. "Who?"

"I always thought it was Polly." There was an apology in her voice.

"Who was Polly?" Jackie asked.

Rory sat back in his chair, sinking his fingers into the fur on Melissa's neck. "My sister," he said. Then to Linda, "Why would you think that?"

"It just seemed logical to me," Linda said. "I mean, hadn't you ever considered it?"

"No," he said vehemently, "not at all." He looked at Jackie. "My sister had Down's syndrome."

"And that's just it," Linda said. "It would have been easy for someone to take advantage of Polly, and if she'd gotten pregnant, she might not have had any idea what was happening to her body. She might not have known any better than to try to get rid of the baby."

Rory smiled tolerantly. "Even Polly would have known how cruel and inhumane that would be," he said. It disturbed him that Linda would think otherwise.

"Well," Linda said, sitting back in her chair. "I can assure you it *wasn't* me. And if it wasn't Polly, and if it *was* someone on the cul-de-sac, then you'd better try to track down Cindy Trump."

FROM THE LIVING-ROOM WINDOW IN HER SMALL APARTMENT above the garage, Grace could see her house. It was after ten in the morning; surely Eddie had gone to the café by now. She was avoiding her husband to the best of her ability. She had to see him when she went into work, of course, but even there, she limited conversation to those words that had to be said to keep the café and shop running smoothly.

She descended the outside apartment stairs and entered the house by the back door. Since moving above the garage, she only went into the house when she knew Eddie wouldn't be there, and the house always seemed too still and empty to her. Quiet as a tomb. Today, she had only one quick task to do there, and then she would head up to Kill Devil Hills.

She went upstairs and opened the door to the room she had been avoiding for months. Pamela's room. It gave her a jolt to see the bare mattress on the bed, the walls stripped of posters and photographs. Eddie must have cleaned out the room, and it angered her that he had not asked her permission. Had he cleaned out her closet, too?

She walked quickly across the room to the closet and slid open one of the doors. Pamela's clothes were indeed gone, but there were a few boxes of items left on the closet shelf, along with the large glass jar containing the shell collection. Grace reached up to pull the jar into her arms. Its lid was dusty, and she cleaned it off with a swipe of her hand as she walked out into the hallway. Shutting the door behind her, she realized she'd been holding her breath, and she stood still for a moment, trying to breathe normally again.

She was downstairs in the living room, nearly to the front door, when she was startled by the deep, very familiar voice of her husband.

"What are you doing with Pam's shell collection?" Eddie asked.

She nearly dropped the jar as she turned to face him. "How come you're not at work?" she asked.

"Sally opened for me," Eddie said, referring to one of the waitresses. "And I think I'm going to have to hire someone else, too. You've been...not too reliable recently."

"I know," she said. "I'm sorry."

"Where have you been lately, Grace?" he asked. "Why haven't you been at the café? I don't mind doing most of the work, but it would help if you could at least let me know when you're going to be there."

"I had a number of doctors' appointments," Grace lied, and immediately regretted it. A look of worry crossed Eddie's face as he took a step closer to her, but he seemed to know better than to touch her.

"Are you okay?" he asked gently, and her heart betrayed her by filling with love for him. He looked very tired. New gray streaks marbled his dark hair, and there were bags beneath his blue eyes. These past few months had been rough for him, too.

"I'm fine," she said, trying to shake off the feelings of warmth for him. "I'll be back at the café later this afternoon." With that, she clutched the jar closer to her chest and left the house, wondering if he'd noticed she was wearing the short seersucker robe she always wore over her bathing suit. She hardly looked as though she was on her way to a doctor's appointment.

She found Rory on the beach by the cul-de-sac.

"Hi!" he said when she set her beach chair in the sand next to his.

He looked pleased to see her, and that pleasure tugged at her guilt. She was not being very kind to the men in her life.

"Hello." She took off her robe, sat down and pulled a tube of sunscreen from her beach bag. "How are you?"

"Better, now." Rory said. "I didn't expect to see you today."

"Well, I had some time before I have to go in to work, so I thought I'd come up here for a while."

"Here." He leaned over to reach for the sunscreen. "Let me put that on your back for you."

She held the tube away from him. "I can do it," she said. She squeezed some of the lotion onto her hand and tried to transfer it to her back.

Rory laughed at her contortions. "Come on, don't be shy." He reached for the tube again, and this time she handed it to him. She leaned forward in her chair as he massaged the lotion into her back and shoulders.

This is a mistake, she thought. How should she handle things with Rory? She didn't want to lead him on, yet she knew of no other way to be able to spend time so close to Shelly. She knew she was giving him the wrong impression. He thought she was repeatedly driving round trip between Rodanthe and Kill Devil Hills just to see him.

She was relieved when he stopped rubbing her shoulders and was no longer touching her. She was not unaware of his attractiveness, but no man—not Rory, not her husband—

could pique her interest these days. "Thanks," she said, leaning back in her chair.

She chatted with him about the weather and a little about some attempted conversation he'd had the day before with Zack. Something about sex; she didn't want to get into *that*. She hoped he would mention Shelly, trying to wait an appropriate amount of time before delving into her favorite topic herself. Her gaze was on those people walking along the beach, hoping to see the tall, young, blond woman who was capturing her heart.

When a few minutes of silence had passed between them and it was apparent he was not going to mention Shelly, she could stand it no longer.

"Oh, before I forget," she said, forcing her voice to sound casual, "I have something for Shelly in my car."

"She's at work today," Rory said. "But I can give it to her, if you like."

"At work? You mean at the church?" Her heart sank at the realization that she had come all the way down here and Shelly was not even at the Sea Shanty.

"Right. St. Esther's." Rory shaded his eyes to look at her. "What do you have for her?"

"Oh, just an old jar of shells. It's been collecting dust at my house for ages, and I thought she might be able to put it to good use."

"I'm sure she will," Rory said. "Don't forget to leave it with me before you go."

"I might as well drop it off at St. Esther's myself," Grace said. "I have to go right past there on my way home."

Now that she knew Shelly was not around, she was anxious to get back on the road. But it would look odd to leave this soon, and besides, Rory still wanted to talk.

"I spoke with one of the neighbors today," he said. "A

woman who was here when Shelly was found. She was one of those kids who was very shy and quiet and faded into the woodwork, but I think it made her a keen observer of everything that was going on around her."

"And…so, what did she observe?" Grace held her breath, waiting for his answer.

"Oh, she's really playing a guessing game about who might have left Shelly on the beach. Same as everyone else. Only…" His voice trailed off.

"Only what?"

"She said she always thought it was my sister. My sister, Polly. She had Down's syndrome and was fifteen at the time Shelly was found. I think Linda's out of her mind, of course, but…the thought is still grating on me."

"Is there any chance she could be right?" Grace asked.

"No, no way." Rory shuddered. "At least I hope there was no way. Surely my mother would have known. But then…I'm starting to think crazy things. Like what if it *had* been Polly? And what if my mother knew and kept quiet about it to protect her? My mother was very protective of Polly, and I don't think that would've been totally out of the question."

Grace felt sorry for him. He was torturing himself with this, and she wanted to rescue him. "Yes, but if it had been Polly, don't you think you would have known something was going on with her? You lived in the same house."

"You're right," he said. "It's just that Linda planted that seed in my mind and it's been eating away at me ever since."

Grace looked down at her pale legs. "Well, as usual, I'm starting to burn," she said, although her legs looked just as white as they had when she arrived. "I'd better head back to Rodanthe."

"We can go in the cottage for a while," Rory suggested. "Or we can go somewhere for a drink or a cup of coffee."

She turned away from the hope in his eyes. "No, I can't, really. I just came down here for a little break, but I'd better get back to work."

Rory stood up and folded her chair for her. "You must love driving," he said, alluding to all the time she was spending in the car for a mere half hour on the beach. Especially when she had a beach a few blocks from her own home. He had to think she was either madly in love with him…or simply mad.

"I don't mind," she said.

"Are you sure you don't want me to give your shells to Shelly for you?" Rory asked.

"No," she said. "If I leave now, I'll have time to stop at the church."

Grace had never been to St. Esther's and was not certain if she should go into the church itself or the small building beside it. She opted for the building, and once inside, found herself in a wide, woodsy-smelling corridor. A man stepped into the hallway from one of the offices and walked toward her.

"Hello," he said. He was dressed in a short-sleeved, blue plaid shirt and khaki pants, and he was sandy-haired and handsome. He eyed the jar of shells in her arms, then looked at her quizzically.

"I'm looking for Shelly Cato," she said.

He motioned toward one of the wooden benches against the wall. "Have a seat," he said. "I'm Father Macy. I'll find her for you. I think she's working in Father Wayne's office right now."

"Thank you." Grace took a seat, the heavy jar on her lap, and watched the priest walk down the hall and disappear into one of the rooms.

In a moment, Shelly stepped into the hallway from the

same room. She smiled as she walked toward Grace, a small look of confusion on her face. "Hi, Grace," she said.

Grace stood up. Her heart did a dance in her chest, as it had every time she laid eyes on this young woman. "Rory said you were here, so I hope you don't mind that I stopped by," she said. She held out the jar in front of her. "I have this collection of shells that's been lying around my house forever, and I thought, rather than throwing them out, I'd see if you might be able to use any of them."

"Thanks." Shelly took the jar from her arms. She tilted her head to discern what might be behind the glass. "There's probably some in here I can use," she said.

Grace did not want to leave, but there seemed to be little else to say. Her throat began to tighten and ache. "Okay, then," she said. "I'll probably see you in the cul-de-sac next time I come up to see Rory."

"Okay," Shelly said. "Bye."

"Bye." Grace turned to leave, but Shelly stopped her.

"Grace?" she asked. "Are you and Rory just friends?"

"Oh. Yes, Shelly. We're just friends."

Shelly's smile broadened. "Good," she said. "Thanks for the shells."

Back in her car, Grace had to force herself to drive out of the church parking lot and away from Shelly. She was going to have to be very careful. Her heart was going to give her away if she didn't keep her emotions in check. She had not expected things to play out this way when she'd first gone to Kill Devil Hills. She'd only wanted to find out how much Rory had learned about the discovery of the newborn. She had not known then that the baby had lived.

Poor Rory was so far off the mark with his investigation. She was torn between being glad of that fact and wishing he knew about the nurse. Why had no one seen the nurse? She would love to have a word or two with that woman, although she wasn't at all certain she could control her actions if she were ever to find her. She almost felt sorry for Rory that he was barking so tenaciously up the wrong tree, but she would never help him. As a matter of fact, she would have to do all she could to lead him astray.

22

"MY CALVES ARE KILLING ME," KARA SAID AS SHE HUFFED UP Jockey's Ridge next to Daria.

Kara was a beautiful whiner. She was one of the prettiest girls Daria had ever seen, but she hadn't stopped complaining since she and Daria had turned onto the beach road from the cul-de-sac. She'd studied her nails in the car and seemed quite shy; if a complaint didn't come out of her mouth, nothing else did, either, despite Daria's attempts to get her talking.

Rory and Zack had invited them to watch their hang-gliding lesson, and although Daria figured her invitation came as a result of Grace being unavailable, she accepted it readily. It was a Thursday, which meant she'd had to take off early from work, leaving Andy to finish a project in one of the older homes in Southern Shores, but he had encouraged her to go.

It had been a while since she'd climbed the dunes at Jockey's Ridge. The last time had been a couple of years ago, when she'd come with Shelly and Chloe to watch the competition in which Sean Macy had prevailed. Strange how when you lived somewhere, you tended to take for granted the area's most interesting and easily available attractions.

"There they are." Kara pointed to a group of people surrounding a single hang glider at the crest of the dune.

Daria could pick out Rory and Zack, who stood side by side, their backs to her and Kara. They both shared that unmistakable broad-shouldered, narrow-hipped build.

"Let's get a little closer and sit down," she said.

They hiked higher, Kara complaining with every step about the hot sand burning her feet. Daria had advised her to wear shoes, but the warning had fallen on deaf ears.

They sat down near the group. Rory spotted them and waved, and Daria thought he was probably a bit nervous. She'd taken a lesson herself, years ago, but once had been enough. For all her athletic strength and usual fearlessness, she preferred to remain earthbound whenever she could.

It was fun, watching the class. Each student took several turns running down the side of the dune, the hang glider heavy on their backs until the air lifted them into a steady glide above the sand. Some students managed longer flights than others, some went fairly high while others stayed close to the ground, and a few never made it off the dune at all, the nose of the glider catching in the sand before they'd even had a chance to take off.

Rory's first flight was low, but the second took him high above the two instructors, who ran down the dunes beneath him.

"Go, Dad!" Zack yelled, his hands cupped to his mouth. "Whoo-hoo!"

Daria had to smile. For once, Zack didn't seem to think his father was such a loser. Indeed, Rory's body was in perfect alignment with the glider, and his flight was as smooth as satin. He was a quick learner.

Kara's gaze was fastened on Zack, though, not Rory, and she wore a perpetual smile on her lips. She was clearly enamored of him, and Daria could not blame her. Zack looked just like his father did at fifteen, with his tan, athletic body. He had Rory's green eyes and sun-streaked hair, covered right now by a helmet. She'd *thought* she was in love with Rory when he was Zack's age; she *knew* she was in love with him now. She'd seen many people fly hang gliders before, but this was the first time she'd been mesmerized by the pilot rather than the flight.

Okay, she thought, *so at least you have him for a friend.* She could talk easily to him, and he certainly was open with her, although she wished he would spare her his feelings about Grace. He was the first man she'd ever met who truly understood and respected the commitment she felt to Shelly. He was perhaps misguided and single-minded in his pursuit of Shelly's background, but at least he was being honest with Daria about it.

More honest than she was being with him.

23

THE DAY WAS PARTICULARLY HOT, THE SUN DAZZLING ON THE glassy waves of the ocean, and Shelly reveled in the feeling of the cool salt spray against her skin as she walked along the beach. She had a destination; she usually did, although Daria and Chloe and most everyone else thought her walks were aimless and without purpose. They didn't really know her. They thought she was one person, but she was actually another.

Although she was anxious to get where she was going, the young couple and their baby sitting on a blanket near the water were an irresistible lure. Shelly stopped next to their blanket and got down on her knees in the sand near the baby.

"She's adorable," Shelly said, studying the baby's blond ringlets. "She *is* a girl, isn't she?"

"Yes," the young woman said. "Her name is Anna."

"How old is she?" Shelly asked. The baby was banging a plastic shovel against a pail, and Shelly picked up a small plastic rake to help her in the game.

"Thirteen months," said the mother. The father said nothing. His gaze shifted from Shelly, out to sea, and back to Shelly again. A lot of men were shy like that when it came to talking about their children.

"Hi, Anna." Shelly ran her hand gently over the baby's fine blond curls. "My name's Shelly." She glanced up at the green and white umbrella above the blanket, then looked at the mother. "It's good you have this big umbrella for her, because her skin is very fair," she said.

"Yes, it is."

Shelly looked at the baby's perfect little hands and feet. "Did you worry when she was born that she wouldn't have all her fingers and toes?" she asked. "I know moms worry about that."

"Yes," the mother said. "But we were very lucky. She was perfect."

She touched one of the baby's toes, and leaned close to the little girl. "This little piggy went to market," she said. Then she looked at the mother again. "How long did it take you to have her? I know sometimes it can take a really long time."

"Oh, not that long." The woman glanced at her husband, who continued to sit in silence.

"Were you scared?"

"Scared?" the mother asked.

"About the pain, I mean," Shelly explained. "I think I'd be scared."

"A little," the woman said.

"Do you nurse her?" Shelly asked.

"I…at first." The woman glanced at her husband again, as if he might know the answer to these questions.

"How old was she when you stopped nursing her?" Shelly asked.

"I think we'd better get back to the house." The young man suddenly spoke to his wife.

"Good idea." There was a look of relief on the wife's face, and Shelly realized their abrupt departure was to get away from her. She had asked too many questions. Too many *personal* questions. It was a bad habit of hers.

"No, no." She jumped to her feet. "It's still a beautiful day. Still early. I think you all should stay here, but *I* should go." The man and woman stared up at her, not saying a word, no doubt surprised by her sudden exit. "Bye, now." Shelly waved. "Bye-bye, Anna." She walked away from them quickly, a bit embarrassed over her behavior. She'd made them nervous. They probably thought she was a crazy child abuser. They had it so wrong. She could never harm a child, especially not a baby as beautiful as Anna.

She felt again that aching inside her, that longing that had been with her for quite a while now. How she wanted a baby of her own! And with any luck, she would have one soon: her period was late.

24

RORY SAT ON HIS FRONT PORCH, WAITING FOR GRACE. THEY were going to an early movie, then out to dinner. He'd suggested he come down to Rodanthe for this outing, but as he might have predicted, she said she would prefer to drive up to Kill Devil Hills. He finally asked her why she never wanted him to come to Rodanthe, and she sounded surprised by the question. "I don't have anything against you coming down here," she said. "It's just that I love to get out. And I know you'd rather not be that far from Zack."

He'd spent the last couple of hours on the Internet, trying to find information on those two young women who'd disappeared from North Carolina and Virginia twenty-two years ago. He tracked down some old newspaper articles, but they didn't tell him anything he didn't already know.

"Hi, Rory!"

He looked next door to see Jill walking toward her car. He waved, and Jill changed direction, heading toward him. She climbed the steps to his porch and sat down.

"I heard you and Zack had a great time on the dunes," she said, slipping her sunglasses onto her head, where her thick, silver hair held them snugly in place.

"Yeah, we did." The afternoon had been, for want of a better term, a bonding experience. No doubt about it. Of course, there had been no time for heavy conversation, which had made life easier for Zack. Instead, there had been shared concentration on the task at hand and the pleasure of reliving every moment of the class afterward. "We might even do it again," he said to Jill.

"My son was on the phone to his dad last night, begging him to take him hang gliding," Jill said. "See what you started?"

Rory smiled, pleased. He'd finally done something right.

"So when are you going to talk to me about what I think happened the morning Shelly was born?" Jill asked.

"How about now?" he said. "I'm waiting for a friend, but we can talk until she shows up."

"Well, I don't know that I can add anything new to what you've already heard," Jill said. "I've always felt sure that Shelly was Cindy's baby. I think the only reason we don't know that for certain was that the police didn't have enough evidence to examine her. But I remembered seeing her a couple of days before Shelly was born and she was wearing a loose shirt over her shorts. That wasn't her style of dress, in case you don't remember."

"I remember," Rory said. "But—" this had been gnawing at him "—Cindy spent a lot of summers down here after Shelly was born. Don't you think it would have come out somehow? Wouldn't she have shown some special interest in her?"

"But she did," Jill said. "She always wanted to baby-sit for Shelly. Of course, she baby-sat for a lot of kids in the neighborhood—I think so she could have boys over, frankly. My brother was one of those boys. Do you remember Brian? He was pretty wild."

"Your twin, right?" Brian had slept with Cindy?

"Uh-huh. He slept with her the summer before Shelly was born, and he slept with her that summer, too. I never understood how he could do that, since everyone was so sure Cindy was Shelly's mother. But his hormones were stronger than his common sense, I guess."

"I had no idea Brian was seeing Cindy," Rory said, trying to think back. He could barely remember what Brian looked like.

"Well, I don't think what he was doing with her would be described as 'seeing her.' He was...well, screwing her." Jill shrugged. "That's about it. You were a few years younger than us, so what was going on probably went right over your head."

"True," he said. "I was only fourteen the summer Daria found Shelly." He saw Grace's car turn into the cul-de-sac, and Jill followed his gaze.

"Your friend is here," she said, standing up.

Rory was still thinking about Brian and Cindy. "Excuse the rudeness in this question," he said, "but if Brian slept with Cindy, is there any chance he was the baby's father?"

"I don't think so," Jill said. "I thought about that myself. But it would have meant that he'd been with Cindy nine months before Shelly was born. That would have been September, which was possible, but unlikely. Besides, Shelly doesn't look a thing like anyone in our family."

Grace had pulled her car to the side of the cul-de-sac in front of Poll-Rory. Rory walked with Jill down the front steps to greet her.

"So what is Brian up to these days?" he asked.

Jill laughed. "He's a juvenile-court judge," she said. "Is that ironic, or what? He's got three teenage girls, and he's the strictest parent I know."

Grace got out of her car, and Rory introduced the two

women, then he and Grace went back to his porch, where he had the newspaper with the movie listings. They were about to sit down to peruse them, when Grace pointed toward the beach.

"There's Shelly," she said.

Rory turned to see Shelly walking through the sea oats a little east of his cottage, coming up from the beach toward the cul-de-sac. He'd seen her set out for the beach many hours ago, just after lunch. Was this a different walk, or had she actually been out on the beach, walking, all afternoon?

Shelly smiled when she saw them. "Hi, Rory," she said. "Hi, Grace." She was wearing a pale blue tankini, cut high on her legs, the ever-present sack of shells strung loosely around her waist.

"Did you have a good walk?" Grace asked her.

"It's always good," Shelly said. She stopped near them. "I talked to Zack, Rory," she said. "I think it's so cool that you took him hang gliding."

"It was great," Rory said.

"We're going to a movie," Grace said. "Would you like to go with us?"

Rory was surprised by the invitation. He wouldn't mind having Shelly accompany them, but he never would have thought to invite her himself. This was supposed to be a *date*. At least, it was a date in his mind. Perhaps it was not in Grace's. The thing that irked him the most, though, was that if it had been Zack standing there, talking to them, Grace almost certainly wouldn't have invited him.

"Oh, no thanks," Shelly said. "I'm working on a necklace for Jackie. Only it's a surprise from Linda, so don't say anything."

"Oh, we won't," Grace reassured her. He did not think Grace even knew who Jackie was.

Rory looked at his watch. "We'd better get going, Grace," he said.

They said goodbye to Shelly, quickly scanned the movie listings and got into his car. Grace looked across the street at the Sea Shanty, where Shelly was sitting on the front steps, dusting the sand from her feet before going inside.

"She's so beautiful," Grace said. "She could be a model."

Rory backed the car into the cul-de-sac, then headed toward the beach road. "I've thought the same thing about you," he said, knowing it would be the first truly personal thing he had said to her.

"What do you mean?" Grace asked.

"That you could be a model. The way you...carry yourself. The way you walk. Not to mention that you're beautiful."

He thought he detected some color in Grace's cheeks.

"No one's told me that in quite a while," Grace said.

"Well, it's the truth." He was glad he had said it. It seemed like something she needed to hear. Maybe she'd been so reticent in this relationship because she was taking her cue from him. Maybe *she* was wondering when he was ever going to make a move.

In the theater, he was keenly aware of her presence in the seat next to him. She seemed to contain herself carefully in her chair, however, so that their arms did not touch, and she allowed him to have the armrest between their seats. Halfway through the movie, he dared to take her hand, and she allowed it. Her fingers were cold, and he tried to warm them with his own. The movie was a comedy, light head-candy, but Grace only laughed a couple of times during the entire hour and a half, and Rory thought their taste in comedy was not quite in sync.

"Did you enjoy that?" he asked when they were back in the car.

"Very much," Grace said, although she hadn't seemed to. She smiled, though, and her face was so beautiful in the lights from the parking lot that he wanted to kiss her. *Now.*

He leaned across the console, rested one hand against her cheek and kissed her lightly. She smiled uncertainly, then turned her head before he could kiss her again.

He drew away. "I think we need to talk," he said.

She looked down at her lap. "I'm sorry," she said.

"You don't need to be sorry," Rory said. "But I do need to understand why you pull away when I try to get close."

She looked out the window, drawing in a long breath. "I'm...not ready," she said. "It's just that I haven't been out of my marriage all that long. I'm confused about my feelings these days." She looked at him. "I'm sorry," she repeated.

"It's understandable," Rory said, although he felt the disappointment down to his toes. "I'd rather you be honest about your feelings than try to pretend that everything's okay." He remembered how he'd felt when Glorianne first left him. "Are you hoping to get back together with your husband?" he asked.

"No," she said firmly. "That's over."

"What happened?" He tried to sound sympathetic rather than curious.

She bit her lip. "Can't talk about it," she said. Even getting those four words out seemed an effort.

He squeezed her shoulder. "That's okay," he said, and he reached for the key in the ignition.

"Where shall we go to eat?" he asked as he pulled into the road. "What do you feel like?"

"I'm really not hungry, Rory," she said. "I think I just want to go home. I'm sorry to put a damper on your evening."

He was disappointed by the sudden change of plans, but he had the feeling she needed a good long cry and didn't want to

do that in front of him. Even Daria had cried in front of him
when she told him about the plane crash. Why was it so much
easier to talk about difficult topics with a friend than with a
potential lover?

"It's not a problem," he said.

They were both quiet on the drive to Poll-Rory, and he
had a sudden, jarring thought: *a mastectomy.* Maybe her illness
had been breast cancer. That would explain the high-necked
bathing suits she wore. It would explain her fear of intimacy.
He glanced at her as he drove. Her face was turned away from
him, toward the window, and he wished there was something
he could say to ease whatever fear and pain existed inside her.
But it would have to be her decision to confide in him. He
could think of nothing he could do to hasten that process.

Daria looked up from her seat on the rocker as Rory pulled
into his driveway. She and Chloe were sitting on the Sea
Shanty porch, reading, but now Daria's attention was fixed on
the car across the cul-de-sac. Rory got out of the driver's side
of the car, and Grace emerged from the passenger side. There
was a physical pain in Daria's chest—a twisting, wrenching
feeling. Rory rested his hand on Grace's back as they walked
toward her car at the curb. Grace got into her car, and Rory
leaned close to the open window to talk to her, or to kiss her—
Daria couldn't see. Rory stood up from the car and walked
into his cottage. The pain in Daria's chest sharpened, and she
knew her feelings for Rory were out of control.

"I'm worried about you."

Daria jumped at the sound of Chloe's voice, unaware that
her sister had been watching her.

"Why?" she asked.

Chloe rested her book upside down on her knees. "Because
of Rory," she said. "Because of the way you feel about him."

"It's that obvious, huh?"

"Yes, it is. And it's crazy, Daria. I understand. You're still reeling from Pete. You'd been with him for six years and you thought you would have married him by now. Of course you're vulnerable. But infatuation with Rory Taylor is *not* the answer. It's got to be taking a toll on you, pining for him every day."

"I'm not pining," Daria said.

"You are, too. And it's pretty obvious he's interested in Grace. I mean, he cares about you as a friend, same as he did back when you were kids. But his *romantic* interest is in Grace, Daria. You can see that, can't you?"

"Of course, I see that. That's what hurts."

"You don't really know him, Daria. He's not your type. Maybe he was your type when he was ten years old and you were seven. But now…he's Hollywood, Daria. He's glitzy."

"Glitzy?" Daria laughed, but the sound was weak. "That's not a word I'd use to describe him. He's very down-to-earth."

"You're seeing him here, in Kill Devil Hills, so, of course, he seems down-to-earth. But watch the reruns of *True Life Stories*. Tell me then that he's down-to-earth."

She *had* watched the summer reruns, just as she'd watched the original shows during the rest of the year, and he was the most down-to-earth the host of a TV show could be. But she could see no point in arguing that with Chloe.

"I really just want a friendship with him," Daria said, more to convince herself than Chloe.

"Bullshit," Chloe said in her sometimes-I-just-can't-sound-like-a-nun voice. "You're tied up in knots over him. And even if he did give you some hint that he might be interested in you that way, he's leaving at the end of the summer. He's a California boy."

Daria didn't answer. She didn't want to fight about this,

because she was afraid she would lose and that Chloe was right. She opened her book again, and Chloe did the same, but Daria's thoughts were still on the cottage across the cul-de-sac. She had tried not to think about the end of the summer. She couldn't bear the thought of Poll-Rory being home again to a string of weekend renters, then finally standing cold and vacant, while she and Shelly had the winter cul-de-sac entirely to themselves once more.

25

WHAT WAS SHE GOING TO DO ABOUT RORY?

Grace drove through the darkness toward Rodanthe, that one thought blocking all others from her mind. She had never treated anyone this way before. Never used another person for her own gain. It had gotten out of hand, and she didn't know how to fix it. She was driven to see him…but only because it put her so close to Shelly.

Shelly was stunning! She had been an ethereal vision, walking through those sea oats, golden in the early-evening light. She looked so healthy, and Grace clung to that reassuring fact. But Pamela had looked healthy, too. She wished Shelly was not constantly taking those solo walks on the beach. How quickly did she walk? How strenuously?

Shelly was tall and lithe, just like Grace had been at that age. She had the body and the presence of a model. She remembered what Rory had said: Grace looked like a model, too.

Oh, Rory, she thought, *if only you knew.*

She'd first heard those words when she was sixteen years old. She'd been walking alone through the shopping center where she and her best friend, Bonnie, had after-school jobs, when a man suddenly stepped in front of her. She'd had to stop short to avoid running into him. He was probably her mother's age, maybe a little older. He had silver hair, but his face was relatively unlined and his blue eyes smiled at her. For someone his age, he was very handsome.

He apologized for disturbing her, then told her his name was Brad Chappelle and he ran a modeling agency. "I'm walking through the shopping center today, looking for girls who might be model material," he said. "And I have to tell you that you are the most beautiful girl I've stumbled across in my search so far this year."

Already shy, Grace could think of nothing to say in response to such an effusive compliment, and the man continued talking.

"You'll have to get some photographs taken for a portfolio," he said, "and then you'll have to go through the training program at my agency. It will cost you some money, but you'll easily make ten times that in your first year as a model. I can practically guarantee it."

He wanted money. Was that what this was about? Some sort of scam?

"I really don't have any money," she said.

He studied her for a moment. "Well, in your case, if you can spring for the photographs, I'll cover the training program for you," he said. "I think you'll be a good investment."

He told her she would need her mother's permission to take classes at the agency, and Grace thought that would be a major stumbling block. Her mother always seemed to view Grace as more of a liability than an asset, and she was indeed resistant to the idea—at first. Once Brad talked to her about Grace's earning potential, though, she readily gave her permission.

Getting pictures taken for her initial portfolio turned out to be one of the most awkward afternoons of Grace's life as she tried unsuccessfully to relax in front of the camera. The photographer was nice about it, telling her how much more confident she would feel after taking Brad's modeling course.

She loved the classes at the agency right from the start. Since grade school, she had been teased about her height and her thin form. Now, her height, her slender body, her high cheekbones were the envy of other girls, and she found herself walking tall. She knew she was Brad's favorite among his students, and she felt his eyes on her as she moved through the class. Admiration was in his face, and after the fourth or fifth class, he told her that she had a natural ability in addition to her beauty. Grace overheard one of the more experienced models say that Brad was grooming her for the big time.

Her first real assignment came that summer, at a fashion show at Beck's, a local department store. Brad invited her mother as his special guest, which told everyone who hadn't already figured it out that Grace was his pet. It was the first time her mother had seen her model, and the show went spectacularly well. Grace's mother could not mask her pride at seeing her daughter, a changed young woman, on the runway. Grace was no longer painfully shy; she no longer walked hunched over to mask her height.

After that show, Grace's mother began buying fashion magazines. She'd point to pictures in the magazine and hold them out in front of Grace. "Maybe you should have your hair cut like this girl's," she would say. Or, "If you'd do those leg lifts, you'd get a better rear end for those clothes you have to wear." Grace's mother and Brad conspired to persuade her to quit high school and focus entirely on her career, but Grace refused. She loved modeling, but she was beginning to envy her classmates' normal lives as they entered their senior year. Bonnie was still her best friend, but things had changed. Bonnie had met a boy over the summer, and she usually had a date on Saturday nights. Grace often worked on Saturdays and was too tired to go out when evening rolled around. Not that anyone was asking her out, anyway.

As she was drawn deeper into her modeling career and became aware of the life-style Brad's more experienced models were living, Grace grew uncomfortable. Most of the other models were older and out of school. Drugs were rampant, and although she didn't think Brad used drugs himself, he turned a blind eye to whatever his girls were doing to get themselves through their grueling schedules. There were more and more fashion shows out of town, and Grace had little choice but to skip school in order to take those jobs.

Her relationship with Brad was gradually changing. While the other models might be driven to shows in Washington or Philadelphia in a specially equipped van, Brad often asked Grace to ride with him in his car. At first, she thought this was because he knew she didn't fit in with the other girls and that she felt awkward with them. But she began to realize that he no longer thought of her as simply one of his blossoming models. She would catch him staring at her when she was doing nothing more than putting on her makeup or eating her dinner of fish and vegetables. He hugged her often. He hugged the other girls, as well, but she knew there was something different in the way he touched her.

One night, while driving back from a fashion show in Washington, he was uncharacteristically quiet in the car. She was tired, so she didn't mind. Resting her head against the car window, she had nearly dozed off when his voice broke the silence.

"I know this is crazy," he said, his gaze fixed out the front window of the car, "and I have no idea how you'll react to this, but…I've wanted to tell you something for a while now."

She turned her head in his direction, waiting.

He glanced at her, and for the first time since she'd known

him, he looked unsure of himself. "I've fallen in love with you," he said.

The words stunned her. She opened her mouth to speak, but nothing came out. She had no idea how to respond.

"I know, I know," he said hurriedly. "I'm old enough to be your father. And believe me, I've been fighting the feelings. But I can't help myself. I've been attracted to you from the very beginning, and you've just become more…appealing to me as you've matured and grown as a model. You project this…savvy innocence. It's irresistible, Grace."

She couldn't help being flattered that a man like Brad Chappelle was interested in her, but she still felt shocked by his admission.

"Say something, Grace," he said. His voice was almost pleading.

"I'm very grateful for what you've done for me," she said slowly. "And…I do love you, Brad." She did. He was the dearest man she'd ever known. He'd become like a father to her, and more. But she knew that would not be the best thing to say right now. "I'm not *in* love with you, though. I've never thought of you that way." She had to be honest with him. He was handsome, kind and generous, but nothing could change his age.

Brad sighed. "See what I mean?" he asked. "Any of the other girls would have said, 'oh, I love you, too, Brad,' just to stay on my good side. But not you. I knew I could trust you to tell me how you're really feeling. I certainly won't push you, Grace. But I want you to know how I feel, in case that makes a difference to you. In case you might just possibly start looking at me…'that way,' as you say."

When she got home that night, she called Bonnie, even though it was quite late. She lay on her bed and told Bonnie, in perfect detail, what Brad had said to her.

"I'm in shock," Bonnie said when Grace had finished her story.

"And I'm mixed up," Grace said.

"I think it's neat that he's interested in you," Bonnie said. "He's really cute, don't you think?"

No, she didn't think Brad was "cute." Bonnie's seventeen-year-old boyfriend, Curt, was "cute." Grace longed for Bonnie's normal, teenage-girl life.

"Can you picture going to bed with him?" Bonnie asked.

"No," Grace said, although she had never even kissed a boy, so it was difficult to imagine actually sleeping with one. And Brad was no boy.

There was a knock on her bedroom door.

"Grace?" Her mother opened the door and poked her head inside. "Hang up," she said. "I want to talk to you."

Something in her mother's voice told her not to argue.

"I have to go, Bonnie," she said. She hung up the phone and waited as her mother sat down on the edge of the bed.

"I happened to overhear your conversation with Bonnie," her mother began. "And I heard what you said about Brad."

Grace had been in her bedroom with the door closed while talking with Bonnie. Her mother must have had her ear pressed against the door, eavesdropping. Either that, or she'd been listening on the extension. Grace swallowed her rage; it would do no good to express it. "I was talking to Bonnie," she said, "not you."

"I think it's wonderful." Her mother ignored the barb. "Do you realize how lucky you are? Do you know how many women would give their right arm for a man like Brad Chappelle? He has money. He has power."

"But I'm not in love with him," Grace said, shocked that her mother would want her involved with a man as old as Brad.

"Love can come later. Love can grow," her mother philosophized. "You just have to be willing to allow it to happen."

"He's too old for me," Grace said.

Her mother leaned toward her, clutching Grace's arm in her hand. "You owe him a great deal, Grace," she said. "Have you thought about that? About how much he's done for you? You need to keep him happy."

"You sound like you're more concerned about Brad's happiness than you are about mine," Grace said, freeing her arm from her mother's grasp.

"I don't think you know yet *what* will make you happy," her mother said, standing up. "I want you to think seriously about this, all right? You need to give Brad a chance."

Grace lay back on her bed after her mother left the room. She shut her eyes, remembering Brad's kind, open face as he admitted his feelings for her. She was afraid. Afraid of needing Brad's approval so much that she'd hurt him to get it.

She never realized that she was the one who would end up being hurt.

26

THE PILOT'S EYES WERE BROWN. BROWN AND HUGE AND terrified as her face slipped into the black water. Daria clung to her arm, trying to hold her above the water's surface, but the plane was going down. She turned to see Shelly hanging by her hands from the propeller, dragging the plane and the pilot under. She screamed at Shelly to let go, but Shelly hung on.

"You don't really want me to let go," she called out to Daria. And the plane slipped under, taking the pilot with it, dragging Daria beneath the water's surface as she tried vainly to pull the pilot up again.

Daria sat up in bed, gasping for air as if she had in fact been underwater for far too long. Her sheets were soaked with sweat, and it took her a moment to get her bearings. She was in her bedroom at the Sea Shanty, and the room was dark and eerily still. She could barely hear the waves breaking on the beach.

Relief washed over her at finding herself on dry land, but it was relief tainted with sorrow: it had been a dream, yes, but a dream too rooted in reality.

Sleep would never come now, she knew, and she didn't dare close her eyes again for fear of the pilot's return. Getting out of bed, she pulled on her robe, then walked barefoot downstairs and out onto the front steps of the Sea Shanty. The night was warm and balmy, the sort of Outer Banks summer night she had treasured all of her life, but the soft air and rhythmic lapping of the ocean on the shore didn't soothe her the way it usually did. She leaned back against the porch door and looked up at the stars.

Poll-Rory's porch door squeaked open, and in a moment Rory was walking across the cul-de-sac toward her. She sat up straight.

"What are you doing up?" His voice was quiet, as though he didn't want to wake anyone. He sat down next to her on the steps.

"I could ask you the same question," she said.

"I'm a night person," Rory said simply. "What's your excuse?"

She rested her head on her arms. "Nightmare," she said. "That plane crash. The pilot drowned in front of my eyes one more miserable time."

He put his hand on the back of her neck, massaging lightly, and she closed her eyes, willing him to keep it there.

"You can't get away from that night, can you?" he said.

"Shelly was a bitch in this one," Daria said, shuddering at the memory of her sister's belligerence. "She wouldn't let go of the propeller. She said I didn't want her to. What the heck does that mean?"

Rory's fingers dug a little deeper, slipping beneath her hair. "I'm not much of a believer in the deep meaning of dreams," he said. "I think you still have some unfinished business regarding that night. That's all."

He was right. "I keep wondering about the pilot's family," she said. Her cheek rested on her knee, and the words slipped slowly from her mouth. "I don't know anything about her life. I don't know how she came to be a pilot at eighteen. I don't know if she had sisters and brothers, or a boyfriend who thinks he can't live without her. I don't even know her name, although I probably knew it at the time of the accident. I wish I'd made an attempt to get in touch with her family. I was the last person with her. If I'd lost someone close to me, I'd want to know what their last minutes had been like. Although, in this case, it sure wouldn't be comforting information. And I couldn't tell them what really happened, just like I haven't told anyone else."

"Except me," Rory said.

She opened her eyes and raised her head to smile at him. "Except you," she agreed.

He dropped his hand from her neck to his lap. "Well, it isn't too late, is it?" he asked. "Don't you think they'd appreciate hearing from you, even after all this time? If I were in their shoes, it would make me feel good that the EMT still cared so much about what happened. And maybe it would help you, Daria. Maybe you'd stop being haunted by it all."

"I hadn't really thought of doing that," Daria said. "I guess I'm afraid to, since I'd have to lie about what happened."

"But wouldn't you feel better to see that they've been able to go on with their lives? Assuming, of course, that they *have* been able to go on," he said. "I guess that would be the risk you'd take by getting in touch with them. But no matter what you found out, at least you'd be dealing with reality instead of your fantasy. I bet it would put an end to your nightmares."

"Maybe I will," Daria said, and the idea gave her some relief. Rory was right. It would be good to know, in concrete terms, exactly how the pilot's family was faring.

They both started at the sound of a bark and turned toward the beach to see Linda and three of her dogs crossing the dune to the cul-de-sac. Linda waved when she saw them and continued walking toward her cottage, the panting of the dogs loud and harsh in the still air.

"Someone else is having trouble sleeping tonight," Rory said.

27

RORY HAD PLANNED TO CALL FATHER MACY TO SPEAK with him about Shelly's adoption, but the priest beat him to it. He called Rory and invited him in to "have a talk," as he put it. Rory gave Shelly a ride to the church the morning of his appointment, since she was to start work at the same time. She was her usual, bubbly self in his car, chatting mostly about Zack, as if realizing his son was one of Rory's favorite topics.

"He's a terrific volleyball player," Shelly said as Rory turned the car onto Route 158. "Not as good as me, but still pretty good."

Rory had to laugh. "You're just like your sister, you know that?" he asked. "She could beat me at anything. And she wasn't too modest about it, either."

"You turn right in there." Shelly pointed to the parking lot as they approached St. Esther's. "You can park in any space you like."

The lot was nearly empty, and he pulled into a parking space near the small office building. He wondered if Shelly understood the reason for his visit with the priest. If she did, she'd said nothing about it.

The front door to the office building was open, and they

walked into a wide corridor. Sunlight spilled onto the hardwood floors from the skylights and the large window at the far end of the hallway and the clean, open, sunny feeling of the building made him even more optimistic about a comfortable, amiable visit with the priest.

"Come on." Shelly grabbed his hand and drew him down the hall. "I'll introduce you to Father Sean."

The door to the priest's office was open, and Rory saw Father Macy sitting at his desk, his back to the door. He was sandy-haired and wearing a blue plaid shirt.

"Father?" Shelly rapped lightly on the open door.

The priest turned in his swivel chair to face them. He stood up when he saw Rory.

"This is Rory, Father," Shelly said.

The priest walked across the room, holding his hand out to Rory. "Good to meet you, Mr. Taylor," he said.

Rory shook his hand. "My pleasure," he said.

"I'm going to get the vacuum," Shelly said to Father Macy. "I'll start out here in the hallway so I don't make too much noise for you and Rory, okay?"

Father Macy touched her arm. "Good idea," he said, then to Rory, "Come in and have a seat."

Rory followed him into the room and sat down on the couch, while the priest sat once again at his desk, turning his chair to face him. He looked younger than Rory had expected. The corners of his eyes were creased with laugh lines, but he was not laughing now. Not even smiling, and Rory's vision of a cordial visit evaporated.

"I understand you're trying to find out who Shelly's mother is," the priest began.

"Well, yes. Shelly wrote to me to ask for my help in finding out who her parents are," Rory said. "But I'm also trying to create a complete picture of the situation. Not just the *who*, but the *why,* as well. Why it happened, the human drama of it, how the woman has dealt with her actions since that time, etcetera. Also, I want to focus on how Shelly has thrived with the Cato family."

The priest leaned forward. "And you would pursue this even knowing that Sister Chloe and Daria strongly object to your interference?"

The priest made him sound like a villain. "Shelly's twenty-two years old," he said, wondering how many more times he would have to offer this argument. "And she, herself, asked me to pursue this."

"Shelly has never known what is best for her."

"I keep hearing that," Rory said in frustration, "but I don't see any evidence of it."

Father Macy scowled. "I know Shelly very, very well," he said. "I see her at least several times a week, and I know she's a vulnerable young woman with a need for stability in her life, which she's been given by the Catos, especially Daria. Digging up the past can only harm her fragile hold on that sense of security."

"With all due respect, Father, I think you're being melo-dramatic."

"And I think you are being stubborn," the priest said. "You don't want to hear any argument that will interfere with the production of your program. You're in this for monetary gain, with no concern about the lives involved."

It wasn't the first time he'd been accused of callous disre-gard for people's feelings in his pursuit of material for *True Life Stories.* But the priest was wrong this time. He would not do anything that might hurt Shelly. Everyone was exaggerating the potential fallout from his research…or were they? His skin crawled with a sudden thought. The protestations of Daria, Chloe and the priest were so extreme, so vehement. Perhaps there was more behind them than simple concern for Shelly's well-being. Perhaps they all knew something they did not want him to uncover.

Rory leaned forward. "What's going on here, Father?" he asked. "What is everyone afraid I'll find out?"

The priest looked surprised by the question. "The only thing we're afraid of is that Shelly might be hurt by what you find. Or, even by what you *won't* find. Her hopes are up so high, that the fall itself would damage her."

"I care very much about Shelly," Rory said. "I promise that if I uncover something that I feel would be truly damaging to her, I'll back off."

"I don't particularly trust your judgment about what would damage her and what wouldn't," Father Macy said.

Rory stood up. This meeting, short and bitter, was over. "I assume it's hopeless asking for your cooperation on this," he said. "I would have liked to hear your memories about Shelly's adoption and how you went to bat to make that happen."

The priest didn't bother standing up. "You're right. It's hopeless," he said. "Daria found Shelly that morning, and I believe that was God's plan. It was God's plan that Shelly become part of a pious family. A true miracle. As far as I'm concerned, Shelly has no other parents, and no other family."

"All right." Rory nodded. "I appreciate your time."

He walked across the room, opened the door and left the office. Shelly was vacuuming the hallway, but when she saw him, she turned off the vacuum and came over to him.

"Isn't he nice?" she asked.

"Yes," he lied. "Very." He glanced at the vacuum in the corner of the hall. "Do you need a ride home later?" he asked.

"Oh, no, I'll walk," she said. "I like to walk."

"I'll see you later at the cul-de-sac, then," he said. He walked through the hallway to the open door, leaving Shelly alone with one of her many guardians.

★ ★ ★

Sean Macy's office window looked out across the salt marsh toward the sound, and for a long time after Rory left, the priest simply sat and stared at an egret standing in the water and weeds. The brief encounter with Rory had exhausted him, but he knew that was only one facet of his misery. He had never before felt so low, and prayer no longer brought him comfort or answers.

"Father?"

He turned away from the window at the sound of Shelly's voice. She stood in the doorway, the pretty, blond custodian of St. Esther's, and he couldn't help but smile at her.

"Can I come in to vacuum now?" she asked. "Or will it disturb you?"

"You can come in," he said. He studied her as she rolled the upright vacuum into his office. She turned on the machine and began vacuuming in the corner of the room. Her long blond hair was pulled into a ponytail, and she looked much younger than her twenty-two years.

Shelly.

He knew so much about her. More than anyone else, perhaps. He turned back to the window. A sailboat was out in the sound, far beyond the marsh, leaning almost parallel to the water.

Suddenly, the noise from the vacuum stopped, and he turned to see Shelly staring at him. She looked worried.

"You seem unhappy again," she said.

Sean looked down at the papers on his desk. He truly didn't want to burden her with his problems. He never did. But right now he felt driven to tell her, his own personal confessor, what was troubling him.

28

THE MEETING WITH THE PRIEST CERTAINLY HAD NOT GONE according to plan, Rory thought as he drove home from the church. He wouldn't be able to get information on Shelly's adoption from Father Macy, that much was certain. Sure, he could get the facts from public records, but he had wanted the priest's angle on the emotions involved. Without either of the elder Catos still living, it was impossible to understand exactly why and how they had longed to adopt the foundling.

He was waiting at a stoplight when his eyes were drawn to the roof of a house across the street. Construction workers were on the roof, building a deck, and one of the workers was obviously a woman. Her back was to him, and she was leaning over, hammering, her khaki shorts defining her shape. Her narrow waist curved into trim, shapely hips, and he felt an instant, visceral attraction. Was this the sort of work Daria did, balancing on the side of a roof, wielding a hammer? His gaze drifted to one of the other workers, a man whose blond hair was tied back in a ponytail, and he realized the man was Andy Kramer, Daria's co-worker. Rory jerked his gaze back to the woman. She stood up from her task, and he saw the wild black hair. *Daria.* A grin broke out across his face. He was filled with warmth at seeing her up there on the roof, and he was surprised, and a little shaken, by his unexpected physical attraction to her. It was a bit like being attracted to your sister. Except that Daria was not his sister.

The driver behind him honked, and Rory quickly looked at the traffic light to discover it was green. He pressed on the gas, wondering how long he had been sitting there in a daze.

Later that evening, he and Zack were batting the volleyball across the net on the beach, when Kara showed up. She was dressed in a green halter top and tiny shorts that displayed the gold hoop in her navel. Leaning against the post that supported the net, she watched the two of them, and Rory was aware of the vibrations passing between his son and the girl. No doubt, they wished he would disappear. He was superfluous now that Kara had arrived.

He happened to glance toward the Sea Shanty and spotted Daria standing on the widow's walk, watching them.

"Hey, Daria." He waved to her. "Come join us so we can have two teams."

He was pleased when Daria called back that she was coming down, and in a moment she was on the beach. She was still wearing the tank top and khaki shorts she'd had on when he spotted her on the roof. "How do you want to divide up?" she asked.

"Kara and me against you guys," Zack said quickly, and Kara walked onto his side of the net. "This is going to be too easy," Zack said to Kara. "I don't know about Daria, but my dad's an old guy with a screwed-up knee."

Rory rolled his eyes at Daria. She was laughing.

The game began. Daria was one mean volleyball player. She could spike the ball over the net with unstoppable speed, and when she jumped for a shot, it was as though she had springs on her feet.

Rory positioned her on the court. He knew that touching her was unnecessary, yet his hand seemed drawn to her. This was crazy. A few hours ago, he'd thought of her as his little playmate. Grown-up now, yes, but still essentially that spirited, sexless child. One glimpse of her up on that roof and suddenly, her body beneath his hand was the body of a woman.

He and Daria won the game. They were both sweaty and winded, and his knee throbbed, but they savored the victory, celebrating with a hug. Zack muttered something about having let the old folks win and refused to play again, which was a secret relief to Rory, who doubted his knee could handle a second game.

He collapsed on the sand, and Daria sat down next to him to watch Zack and Kara play one-on-one. Daria's thick hair was loose and blew around her face in the ocean breeze.

"I saw you at work today," Rory said. "You were up on a roof, working on a deck."

"Oh, yeah," she said. "Where were you? Driving by?"

"Uh-huh." He still remembered how she looked up there. "I was driving back from St. Esther's. I had an appointment with Father Macy."

She shifted on the sand to look at him. "You did?" There was unmasked disapproval in her voice.

"He called me," Rory defended himself.

"Oh," she said. "Well, how'd it go?"

Rory sighed. "That man does not like me," he said.

"What makes you think that?"

"Well, he's sure not going to give me any information about Shelly's adoption."

"He cares very deeply for Shelly," Daria said, brushing her hair back from her cheek. "He's trying to protect her."

"Yeah, yeah. That same old song and dance," Rory said tiredly. "Nobody wants me to pursue this, except Shelly herself."

"And Shelly doesn't—"

"Doesn't know what's good for her," Rory finished the sentence. "I know that's the party line. I just don't buy it. I started wondering today if you know more than you're letting on. If you're trying to protect someone."

"I'm trying to protect Shelly," Daria said. "She's the only one I care about." She shut up then. Zack and Kara were batting the volleyball back and forth in an easy rhythm, and Rory grew uncomfortable with the silence between Daria and himself. She was first to break it.

"I'm going to Rodanthe tomorrow," she said suddenly.

"Rodanthe?" He thought of Grace. "Why?"

"That's where the pilot lived," Daria said. "I got the name and address for her parents, and I'm going to pay them a visit."

"You move fast," he said. "Have you spoken to them yet?"

"No, I thought of calling them first, but I think a face-to-face meeting would be better." She was staring toward the ocean, stoic determination in her eyes.

"It's going to be hard," he said.

"Yes," she agreed, "but so is not knowing how they're doing." She looked at him. "I'm glad you pushed me to do this, Rory," she said. "At least, I'm glad right now. We'll see how I'm feeling tomorrow night after I've seen them."

"Well, while you're down in Rodanthe, say hi to Grace for me. My mystery woman." He lifted a handful of sand from the beach and watched it flow through his fingers. "She doesn't know what she wants. I was wondering about that illness she had. Maybe it was breast cancer. Maybe she had a mastectomy."

"You mean…you… Wouldn't you know by now?"

He was confused for a moment, then realized what she meant and laughed ruefully. "No, I wouldn't know. I told you, she keeps me at arm's length."

Daria's eyes widened in surprise. "Still?"

"Still. She seems to want to be with me, but she shies away from physical contact. I don't know if she's still got a thing for her husband, or what."

"It must have something to do with her illness," Daria said. "It's time you asked her, don't you think?"

He dug his feet into the sand, shaking his head. "She's not like you," he said. "You don't seem to have a problem talking about anything. Grace is very…closed."

"When do you see her again?"

"Saturday. She's coming to watch the hang-gliding competition with me. Are you going?"

"I plan to. I haven't been for a couple of years, but I want to root for my favorite priest."

"Father Macy's in the competition?" Rory asked. He'd forgotten that the priest was a hang-glider pilot.

"He wouldn't miss it," Daria said.

Suddenly, Daria jumped to her feet and ran onto Kara's side of the net. "Kara, girl," she said, "you need to learn how to rush the net."

Rory watched as Daria gave Kara a few tips, helping her jump higher, helping her place the ball where Zack didn't stand a chance.

"No fair!" Zack complained after missing several of Kara's shots. "Show me how to do that."

Daria stepped over to his side of the net to offer him the same training.

Rory leaned back on his elbows in the sand. He remembered the other night, when he'd sat with Daria on her porch steps, acutely aware of the unrelenting anguish the plane crash had brought her. He'd had his hand on the back of her neck, and he wished he'd somehow been able to absorb her pain through his fingertips to free her from it. He hoped her trip to Rodanthe served that purpose, that it eased her guilt and brought an end to her nightmares.

Kara pounded the ball across the net, and both Zack and Daria ran for it. They collided in midair and fell to the sand, laughing. Rory laughed with them, and he knew in his heart that he was watching *two* people he loved.

29

THE DAY WAS BLISTERING HOT AS DARIA DROVE SOUTH TO Rodanthe, and the heat rose from the road in shimmering waves. She'd barely slept the night before, rehearsing what she would say to the pilot's parents, but with the meeting looming in front of her, she found she couldn't think about it. Instead, her mind slipped back to the evening before, when she'd played volleyball with Rory, when he'd touched her on the court. The last thing she'd needed was his help; she was now and always had been a superior volleyball player to him. But she *had* needed that touch. She'd hoped for it, even moving herself into positions where she thought she might find his hands on her body. And he had read her need and touched her. It had felt like a dance, but she had to remind herself she was dancing alone.

So, he and Grace still were not lovers. She kept him at arm's length. A smile formed on her lips at the thought. He was most likely right about Grace: she'd probably had breast cancer, maybe a mastectomy. She always wore those high-necked bathing suits. Naturally, she was struggling with intimacy, and Daria was a grade-A bitch for taking any pleasure in that fact.

She drove across the bridge above the Oregon Inlet and

through the green, undeveloped stretch of land that formed the Pea Island Wildlife Refuge. A short time later, she was in Rodanthe, the northernmost town on Hatteras Island. The houses were fewer here on this narrow strip of land, and the sense of commercialism that permeated Kill Devil Hills was missing.

Rodanthe was so small that she found the street she was looking for with little trouble. She turned onto it, toward Pamlico Sound, and parked in front of the address she'd been given. The house was older, small and yellow, fronted by a tidy landscaped yard. There were no cars in the driveway, but there might have been one in the small garage at the rear of the property. She hadn't thought about what she would do if no one was home. Maybe she *should* have called first.

She knocked on the door and waited.

"They're not home."

She turned to see a woman getting out of a car in front of the house next door, grocery bags in her arms.

"Do you know where I can find them?" Daria asked.

"Probably at their store," the woman said. "It's called Beachside Café and Sundries. It's straight down that way." She pointed toward the sound. "Make a left at the fork."

Back in her car, Daria followed the woman's directions to the Beachside Café. She parked on the street and sat in her car for a moment, debating what she should do. She didn't want to interrupt them at work with something this weighty. Maybe she could just tell them who she was and ask if there would be a more convenient time for her to speak with them.

With that plan in mind, she got out of the car and walked inside the café.

The café was small and crowded and smelled strongly of coffee. All the tables by the windows overlooking the sound were full, and a couple of women stood near the counter, waiting for their orders, Daria supposed. A very young woman—too young to be the pilot's mother—carried a tray of sandwiches to the diners at one of the tables. Standing behind the counter, a dark-haired man worked the espresso machine. He glanced up as Daria approached.

"What can I do for you?" he asked, his attention already back on the coffee machine.

"I'm sorry to disturb you," she said, "I'm looking for Edward Fuller."

He dried his hands on a towel. "I'm Eddie," he said. He handed two cups of coffee to the women waiting at the counter, and they carried them over to the crowded tables.

"I'm so sorry to disturb you at work, Mr. Fuller," she said again.

"Eddie," he repeated.

"Eddie. My name is Daria Cato. I was one of the EMTs on the scene of the plane accident where your daughter, Pamela, was—" she glanced toward the tables by the windows and lowered her voice "—where your daughter was killed. I was wondering if there was a time I might be able to talk with you and your wife."

He stared at her for a moment, then nodded. "Sally?" he called to the waitress.

The young woman turned from the table she was serving to look at him.

"Can you handle things out here for a few minutes?" he asked.

"No problem," Sally said, and Eddie Fuller led Daria into a room at the back of the café. The room was minuscule and made smaller by two large desks set against adjacent walls.

"Please—" the man pointed toward one of the desk chairs "—have a seat."

Daria sat down. "Is your wife here?" she asked. "I was hoping to talk with both of you."

"No, I'm afraid she's not here right now. But I'd really like to hear what you have to say. You were there, on the scene?"

"Yes, I was. And although it's been months, I still think about her—your daughter. I just needed to make contact with you and your wife to be sure you're doing okay and to belatedly convey my condolences."

With a heavy sigh, Eddie sat down himself, and Daria was distressed by the tears in his eyes. "Well, to be truthful, we're not doing okay at all. It's hell to bury a child," he said, his gaze out the window. "It's even worse when you blame yourself for her death."

"Why would you do that?" Daria asked, surprised. "How could you possibly be at fault?"

He waved away the question. "Can you tell me what it was like?" he asked. "The accident, I mean? They told us she died almost instantly. She didn't suffer much, did she?"

Daria chose her words carefully. "It all happened very quickly," she said. "And I guess you know that the passengers reported she'd lost consciousness before the accident, so I don't think she was all that aware of what was going on." The lie slipped awkwardly from her mouth, but the look of relief on Eddie Fuller's face made her glad she had told it.

"The autopsy said she'd had a seizure," Eddie said. "That's why the plane went down. I'm just thankful the two passengers were all right."

"A seizure?" Daria hadn't known that. "Did she have a history of seizures?" She thought of Shelly. Shelly was not even allowed to drive, much less fly a plane.

"No, that was her first, as far as I know. I never would've let her fly if I'd known she was prone to them. She had a condition called Marfan's syndrome, although she never really had any symptoms of it. But apparently one of the symptoms is seizures." He was quiet for a moment. When he spoke again, it seemed to take great effort. "I always wanted to fly," he said. "It was a dream of mine from the time I was very small. But I couldn't, because of high blood pressure. So, I pushed my daughter to be a pilot. I gave her model planes when she was little. A friend had a Cessna, and he took us up and would let her operate the controls." Eddie played with the corner of his apron, rubbing it between his thumb and forefinger. "Pam was bitten by the bug. I'd made sure that she was. She got her license the day she turned seventeen. She loved it, and I loved that she loved it."

"Is that why you blame yourself?" Daria asked.

His nod was almost imperceptible.

"You could never have predicted what happened." She hurt for the man. "You and she probably had a special relationship because of your shared love of flying. That sounds wonderful to me."

"I was selfish, living vicariously through Pam," he said. "My wife never wanted her to fly. She was always afraid something awful would happen. And she was right. She still hasn't forgiven me for it, either." He looked down at the apron, smoothed it across the denim covering his thigh. "She and I... We're not doing too well."

"I don't mean to be intrusive," Daria said, "but it sounds to me like both you and your wife loved your daughter deeply, and that maybe you haven't really been able to grieve together because...because your wife is spending her energy being angry with you, and you're spending your energy being angry with yourself, and so neither one of you is able to heal."

"You hit the nail right on the head," he said.

"What about counseling?" Daria said. "Maybe that would help the two of you."

"We went once, but then my wife had to have surgery and she was..." His voice trailed off as he looked out the window again. He shook his head. "She's just had too much to deal with. So, we haven't been back to the counselor, and Grace wouldn't go, anyhow. She's too angry with me."

Daria caught her breath. *Grace?* From Rodanthe? But Rory's Grace was named Grace Martin, and Grace was not all that rare a name. Besides, Rory's Grace was separated from her husband. Surely this couldn't be… She looked around the room and found exactly what she was searching for on one of the cluttered desks: a photograph of Eddie, Pamela—and Grace Martin. Her mind raced as she tried to put two and two together.

"Um…" Her voice had a tremor in it. "Your wife. Grace? How is she coping?"

"You'd have to ask her that question," Eddie said. He did not sound bitter, only confused. "I don't know where she is half the time," he said. "She won't talk to me. She won't tell me what she's thinking or feeling. We're both pretty alone in this…not grieving together, like you said."

He hadn't mentioned a thing about a separation, and she needed to know. "Have you and your wife…separated over this?" she asked.

He looked surprised, as well he should, since he had said nothing to make her think that. "No, and I sure hope it doesn't come to that. Though right now we may as well be. She's staying in an apartment above our garage. I'm just hoping some time to herself is going to make a difference."

"I hope so," she said absently. No wonder Grace never wanted Rory to come to Rodanthe to see her.

Daria stood up. "I'd better let you get back to work," she said. "I'm so sorry for your loss."

"I'm glad you came," Eddie said, standing himself. "It makes me feel like Pamela had the best chance possible, knowing somebody like you was there. Somebody who really cared."

Daria wrote her phone number on a pad lying on the desk.

"Please call me if you need to talk again." *Or if your wife needs to talk,* she should add. But of course, she could not.

Outside the café, Daria sat in her car, turning on the ignition only long enough to lower all the windows, not yet ready to drive. What the hell was going on with Grace? Was that why she was so pathologically attentive to Shelly? Was she trying to replace the daughter she'd lost? With a horrified jolt, she wondered if Grace might somehow know about Shelly's role in Pamela's death. She tried to follow that thought to its logical conclusion: Grace had somehow found out what Shelly had done at the scene of the accident. Then she plotted to meet Shelly, and now, perhaps, was planning to harm her in some way as retribution. "That's crazy," she said out loud. Her imagination was running away with her. But what else was she to think? One thing she knew for certain was that Grace Martin—Grace *Fuller*—was a liar. Should she tell Rory? She had to. She couldn't keep this from him. For all she knew, Grace was simply using Rory to get close to Shelly.

Driving home in a daze, glad the route was a straight shot and required little of her attention, she tried to puzzle out, not only what Grace was up to, but what she could do about it.

She pulled into the driveway of the Sea Shanty just as Shelly walked into the yard from the beach, and all of Daria's protective instincts kicked into gear at the sight of her. *Grace better not harm a hair on her head,* she thought.

"Hi, Shell," she said as she got out of the car.

Shelly mumbled a greeting and reached for the door, and Daria could see that her face was red.

"Shelly?" Daria started walking toward the house. "What's wrong?"

Shelly froze, her hand on the knob of the screen door. "Nothing," she said.

Daria caught up to her. Shelly had definitely been crying. "Oh, sweetie." She put an arm around her sister's shoulders. "What's got you so upset?"

Shelly hesitated, then sat down heavily on the front steps. Daria sat down with her, her arm still around her shoulders.

"I'm afraid," Shelly said.

"Of what?" Daria asked.

Shelly frowned. She looked down in her lap, where she was pressing her fingers together so firmly that the knuckles were white. "That Father Sean is going to kill himself."

Daria almost laughed. Where had Shelly come up with this one? "Why would you think that, honey?" she asked.

Shelly shook her head. "I don't know," she said. "I know it sounds silly. I just started thinking it while I was out walking."

"Well, sometimes our imaginations can run away with us, huh?" she asked.

"Yeah. I guess."

It was unlike Shelly to be this distressed unless she was facing a trip away from the Outer Banks. "You know Father Macy would never do anything like that, don't you?" Daria asked.

Shelly shrugged, her gaze still glued to her fingers.

"He's a Catholic priest, for heaven's sake, Shelly. He's the last person you would expect to commit suicide."

Shelly pressed her lips together. She looked up at Daria and forced a weak smile. "I guess you're right," she said.

Daria studied her sister's face. Her eyes were truly red, her nose a bit swollen. "You don't usually have unpleasant fantasies like that," she said.

"I know," Shelly said. "But I think I'm over it now."

Daria laughed. "That was quick," she said. This was just another of Shelly's peculiar, wayward thoughts. "Tomorrow, we'll go watch the hang-gliding competition, and maybe Father Macy will win. Wouldn't that be great?"

The weak smile again. "Yeah," Shelly agreed, and Daria was not at all certain her sister was "over it," as she'd said.

She looked across the street at Poll–Rory. "I need to go have a chat with Rory."

"He's not home," Shelly said, and Daria realized the blue SUV was not in the driveway.

"Do you know where he is?" she asked.

"Yeah," Shelly said. "I talked to Jill earlier today, and she said that she and Rory were taking Zack and Jason out to dinner and a movie."

Dinner and a movie. What time would he be home? She was anxious to tell him what she'd learned in Rodanthe.

30

DARIA SHADED HER EYES AND LOOKED UP TOWARD THE crest of the tallest dune on Jockey's Ridge. The dune was covered by a sea of spectators, and above their heads, a hang glider dipped and turned in the air.

"How are we ever going to find them?" Andy said as they stopped climbing to survey the scene.

"I told them I'd meet them as close to the crest as I could get, so they should be watching for me," she said.

The hang-gliding competition was about an hour into its run, and Daria had planned to meet Shelly, Chloe, Ellen and Ted when she got off work. Even though it was Saturday, she and Andy had put in a couple of hours this morning. When she was ready to leave the job, Andy asked if he could go with her to the dunes. She'd readily agreed. Andy always seemed a bit lonely to her. He had friends on the crew, but he didn't seem to socialize much with them outside of work.

"Daria!"

Daria looked up to see Rory standing near the crest of the dune, waving at her. She spotted Shelly and Chloe with him, and as she and Andy made their way through the crowd, she saw that Ellen and Ted were there as well. Zack and Kara sat a short distance away, so close to one another, that at first, Daria thought they were one person. It was a minute before she noticed Grace sitting next to Rory. *Damn.* She would have no chance to tell Rory what she'd learned in Rodanthe the day before. She wondered if Grace's husband had spoken to her about Daria's visit. Did Grace now realize that Daria had been at the plane crash? Or, she thought with a shiver, had she known it all along?

They'd saved just enough room on the sand for Daria, but Andy managed to squeeze in between her and Shelly. Daria introduced him to Grace, the only person in their party he didn't know, and Grace smiled warmly at him. Her husband hadn't told her, Daria thought. If he had, surely she could not sit here looking so innocent. Grace was wearing long white pants, a long-sleeved white shirt, white visor and blue sunglasses. She wasn't taking any chances on getting too much sun.

"I was afraid you were going to miss Father Sean." Shelly leaned across Andy to speak to Daria.

"When does he go up?" Daria asked.

"I think there's a couple more before him," Shelly said.

The day was beautiful. There was a gentle breeze off the ocean, just enough to give the gliders the lift they needed as they performed their intricate maneuvers to the delight of the crowd. But Daria had trouble concentrating. She was aware of Grace speaking to Shelly, although she couldn't hear what was being said.

Leave my sister alone, Daria thought. There was something creepy about Grace's attentiveness to Shelly now that Daria knew the truth about her. And she knew Grace annoyed Shelly with her incessant questions. She wished she were sitting next her sister, so she could save her.

"There's Sean." Chloe pointed to the highest ridge on the dune, where a man was attaching his harness to a glider. They were quite a distance from him, and Daria marveled at the fact that Chloe was able to identify him. Sean adjusted his helmet, tugged at his harness, and most of the crowd turned in his direction to watch him prepare for his takeoff. Grace turned away from the priest to say something to Shelly. The breeze lifted her bangs from her forehead for a few seconds, and Daria saw the unmistakable widow's peak—the same widow's peak that had marked her daughter, Pamela.

Father Macy took a few awkward steps backward with his glider. Then he ran toward the edge of the dune, the glider above his shoulders, and took off, lifting gently into the sky to the "oohs" and "aahs" of the crowd. "Go for the gold, Father M!" someone shouted. The priest was the undisputed favorite of the locals in the crowd.

Daria felt the sun on her face as she watched the priest and his glider slip effortlessly into the sky, flying higher than any of the other gliders had flown since her arrival on the dunes. A burst of applause swept over the dunes, and people waited in anticipation for his first maneuver. But then, suddenly, his glider appeared to stall. It hung motionless in the air, as still as the sun in the sky above them. Was this part of his performance?

"What's he doing?" Andy asked, but before anyone could answer, the colorful triangle of fabric pitched forward, soaring toward the ground in a nosedive. Daria jumped to her feet, horrified, as the glider and priest crashed headfirst into the sand at the bottom of the dunes.

Screams and gasps erupted from the crowd, and Daria hesitated only a moment before pushing her way through the throng, running down the dune toward the priest. She was vaguely aware of Chloe on one side of her, Andy on the other. Were there other EMTs in the crowd? There had to be. *Please, let there be someone here to help me.*

People were huddled in a circle around the priest. "Don't move him!" she called out as she slid the rest of the way down the dune on the seat of her shorts. The sand burned the backs of her thighs.

"It's Daria Cato," someone said. "Get out of her way."

Daria broke through the circle of people to reach the injured priest. She dropped to her knees next him, but knew in an instant that moving him would not make a difference, either to help or to harm. His head was twisted at a sharp angle to his shoulders. She pressed her fingers against his throat, in what she knew was a futile effort to locate a pulse. Behind her, a child began to cry.

Chloe fell to her knees on the other side of the priest, then looked at her sister. "Is there anything you can do?" she asked.

Daria shook her head. "His neck is broken." Her mouth was dry; the words came out in a hoarse whisper.

Chloe lifted the priest's hand and held it between her own. Although she made no sound of weeping, tears flowed freely over her cheeks, and she prayed quietly over the fallen priest, as the wail of sirens filled the air.

31

SHELLY SAT NEXT TO DARIA IN THE HUSHED STILLNESS OF St. Esther's Church as people took turns standing in front of the pulpit to speak in soft voices, paying tribute to Father Sean. The speakers' faces were colored blue or green or pink by the sunlight streaming through the stained-glass windows. Chloe was one of the speakers, and her face had looked beautiful in the rose-colored light. She sat in the front pew of the church with the other speakers, while Shelly and Daria sat a few pews back. Chloe had already spoken, dry-eyed, about the important role Father Sean had played in the lives of the Cato family since coming to St. Esther's twenty-four years ago. The fact that Chloe was able to say all she did without crying was pretty amazing, but it didn't surprise Shelly. Ever since the accident on the dunes, when Chloe had wept her heart out, she had been walking around in a daze, no emotion at all on her face. Daria said she was in shock.

Old Father Wayne was standing at the front of the church now, green light on his face, telling some anecdote about Father Sean that was obviously supposed to be funny. Some people chuckled, but Shelly had trouble concentrating on what the priest was saying. She was remembering Father Sean in her own way. She remembered that during the cooler months of the year, Father Sean was full of life and laughter. He would tell her jokes—clean ones, of course. There was always a smile on his face. And then, summer would come, and he would lose his smile. It happened every year. Shelly had come to expect it, to feel the arrival of summer with a certain dread. As joyful as it made her, she did not like the torment that the hot, sunny weather brought to the priest. She knew some people suffered from a kind of depression that came over them in the winter months. That was common. Father Sean had the opposite problem. And she was one of the few people who understood why.

Daria pulled a tissue from her purse and blew her nose, and Shelly rested her cheek against her sister's shoulder and patted her hand. "It's all right, Dai," she said, wanting to comfort her sister. For some reason, Daria's suffering felt worst to her than her own. *That's the way it is when you love someone,* Father Sean had said to her once. The worst time was after Pete broke up with Daria. Shelly had never particularly liked Pete. He was too wrapped up in himself, too selfish to deserve someone as good as Daria, and he had those stupid tattoos that made Shelly embarrassed to be seen with him in public. But Daria had loved him, so Shelly could not help but feel anger at him when he ended that relationship. How dare he hurt Daria? Daria had been so devastated that she'd even quit being an EMT. It was as though she'd quit living altogether, at least until Rory showed up.

Everyone in the church suddenly moved forward to kneel on the padded benches, and Shelly joined them. She wasn't paying attention to where they were in the service, but now that she was on her knees, she began to pray.

She prayed that Daria and Rory might somehow get together.

She prayed that she was indeed pregnant—although the thought of breaking that news to Daria was truly frightening.

When she'd finished with those prayers, she focused all her concentration on the most important prayer of all: *Dear Lord, please forgive Father Sean.* She repeated this over and over again, praying very hard, because she was carrying the burden of that prayer alone. Everyone else thought that Father Sean's death was an accident.

She, alone, knew better.

32

DARIA FOUND RORY AFTER THE FUNERAL. HE'D SAT NEAR the rear of the church and waited for her outside afterward. His feelings about the priest were mixed, and Daria was pleased he had come at all. He knew how much Sean Macy meant to their family.

Silently, Rory put one arm around her, the other around Shelly, and led them away from the church toward the parking lot. For some reason, the light, warm weight of his arm across her shoulders threatened to make her cry all over again. She breathed through her mouth to keep the tears in check.

The events of the past few days had squelched her enthusiasm for telling him about Grace, yet she knew she still needed to fill him in on what she'd learned. Shelly was with them, though; once again, the timing wasn't right. But Shelly was intuitive.

"I feel like walking home," she said, somehow picking up on Daria's need for time alone with Rory.

"Are you sure?" Daria asked. She didn't think Shelly had yet come to terms with Father Macy's death, and she was concerned about her.

"I'm sure," Shelly said. "I'm fine. I'll see you at the Sea Shanty."

Daria watched her walk away from them, then turned to Rory. "Do you have your car here?"

"Uh-huh. Do you?"

"Yes. But…" She looked into his green eyes. He appeared to be studying her. "I need to talk with you," she said. "Can we take my car and go somewhere? I can bring you back here after."

"Is this about Shelly again? About me researching—"

"No," she interrupted him. "No. This is something else."

"Okay," he said. "Where are you parked?"

She drove across the island to the sound, and they walked onto the pier where they had crabbed together a few weeks earlier. There were children on the pier this afternoon, crabbing, fishing, and threatening to push one another into the water. Daria and Rory walked past them to the pier's end, where they took off their shoes and sat down in their good funeral clothes to dangle their legs above the water.

Daria was not sure how to begin. "I never got to tell you how my visit went with the parents of the pilot," she said.

"I wondered about that," Rory said. "But with Father Macy and everything, we haven't really had a chance to talk."

She looked into the green-brown water. A crab swam just below the surface, slipping sideways through the water.

"So?" Rory prompted. "How did it go?"

She glanced at him, then looked back at the water. "There's no easy way to say this," she said, trying to warn him about what was coming. "Only the pilot's father was there. I met with him at a little café he and his wife own. And as I talked with him, I realized that his wife—that the mother of the pilot— is Grace."

For a moment, Rory's face was impassive. Then he suddenly seemed to understand what she was saying and turned toward her. "Grace?" he asked. "Grace Martin?"

"That was my reaction, too," Daria said. "I still don't understand. I still don't quite know what's going on. She may go by the name Martin, but her husband's name is Fuller. Eddie Fuller."

"Her *ex*-husband, you mean," Rory said.

She shook her head. "He referred to his wife as Grace, and then I saw a picture of her on his desk. I didn't let on that I knew her. I asked if he and his wife were separated, and he said no. They aren't getting along, though. She blames him for—"

"Wait a minute," Rory said. "Slow down, will you, please? Grace is separated. Maybe he just didn't want to admit that to you."

One of the roughhousing young boys on the pier ran into them, and Rory told him to knock it off. It was the first sign of impatience she'd seen in him, and she knew how disturbed he was by what she was telling him.

"That's possible," she said. "But I think he was telling me the truth. He said she's living in the apartment above their garage, because she's angry with him about their daughter's—"

"The Grace I know doesn't even have any children," Rory interrupted her again.

Daria felt exasperated. "Rory, I'm sorry, but I'm telling you, this is the same woman. He even said she had surgery not too long ago, although I didn't ask what she'd had surgery for. And she did have at least one child. A daughter named Pamela, who was the pilot in the plane crash. And the reason she's so angry with her husband is that he was the one who had encouraged Pamela to become a pilot. Grace never wanted her to—"

"Wait a minute," Rory said again. "Assuming you're right, and Grace Fuller is Grace Martin, isn't that a bit of a coincidence that I would end up meeting her when you had been so intimately involved in her daughter's—in trying to save her daughter?"

"Yes, huge coincidence," Daria agreed. "And, I'm sorry, Rory, but it's made me wonder if maybe it wasn't a coincidence at all."

"What are you saying?"

"I'm not sure what I'm saying," Daria said. A windsurfer sailed so close to the pier that she could see the cleft in his chin. "I haven't been able to figure this out," she said, "but it's made me wonder about Grace's interest in Shelly. Maybe it *was* a coincidence and now she's just interested in Shelly because Shelly is…a substitute daughter, in a way. But let's say it wasn't a coincidence. That somehow she knows what Shelly did when we were trying to save her daughter, and she's planning to get…I don't know, revenge or something." She knew it was an outlandish suggestion and heard the doubt in her own voice as she explained it to him. "Though, how she would know, when only Pete and I knew about it, is beyond me."

"Well, I vote for the coincidence theory," Rory said. "The way I met her…on the beach…she'd been bitten by a fly…I just don't see how that could be some sort of setup or plot on her part. But obviously, she lied to me about being separated, unless she considers living above the garage a separation. And she lied about not having kids." He shook his head. "No wonder she never wanted me to come down to Rodanthe."

"Can you try to find out what's going on?" she asked. "I mean, can you make sure that she's not…well, nuts? That she doesn't have some wacko plot to hurt Shelly?"

"If anything, she seems to adore Shelly."

"Everyone adores Shelly," Daria said. "But not everyone pummels her with personal questions and brings her jars of shells."

Rory drew in a long breath, then nodded. "I'm seeing her again tomorrow night," he said. "I'll talk to her then."

33

IN AN AREA WHERE A HUGE PERCENTAGE OF THE RESIDENTS were tourists, it was amazing how quickly rumors flew among the locals. Daria first heard the rumblings on one of her construction jobs, the day after Father Macy's funeral. She and Andy were installing kitchen cabinets when she overheard George and Billy talking about the investigation. His brother was a cop, so he was privy to information others might not know.

"It was such a weird sort of accident," George said from his perch on one of the ladders. "I mean, does it make any sense to you guys? Here, Sean Macy's been hang-gliding for a dozen years, maybe, and suddenly he crashes."

"It was probably just a lapse in his concentration," Daria said. She held the base cabinet tight against the wall, while Andy screwed it to a stud.

"That's not what my brother thinks," George said. He left Billy holding up the ceiling fan as he ticked off the facts on his fingertips. "First of all, it was a competition, not some everyday flight. If there's any time Sean would have been paying attention to what he was doing, it would be then. Second, the weather was perfect. I mean, he would have to go out of his way to crash in that kind of weather."

"So, what are you saying?" Billy asked. "You think someone wanted to off him?"

"They considered that," George said, helping Billy with the fan again. "Maybe somebody didn't like the penance Sean gave them after confession or something, and so they tampered with his hang glider. But the police have gone over the hang glider with a fine-tooth comb, and it was in perfect working order."

"What do they think happened, then?" Andy asked as he backed out of the base cabinet.

"That maybe he took that nosedive into the sand on purpose," George said. He waited for the drama of his words to sink in.

"That's nuts," Andy said.

"Well, there's more." With the fan secure, George climbed down from the ladder. "My brother and a couple of other cops have been talking to some witnesses—experienced pilots who were there. It looked to them like an intentional stall."

"Maybe it was part of his performance," Andy said. "Maybe he was going to—"

George interrupted him. "That other priest at St. Esther's. The old guy, Father Wayne? He told my brother he'd been worried about Sean lately. He said Father Macy had been withdrawn and upset. He thought Sean might have been screwing... Excuse me. There's a lady present. He thought Sean might have broken his vow of celibacy."

Daria was incensed. How far had this rumor spread? The man had been dead only a few days, and already his memory was tarnished. "That's all just speculation," she said. "And it really bothers me to hear it. Why does everyone always have to look for the dirt? Sean Macy was a really good man and a good priest. He wouldn't have—" She suddenly remembered Shelly's prediction that the priest would kill himself, and an eerie sense of dread filled her chest.

"He wouldn't have what?" George prompted her to finish her statement.

"I just wish you wouldn't spread this kind of thing around until you have some facts to back it up."

"Don't listen, then, Miss Priss."

George continued talking about Sean Macy and what the cops had or had not been able to uncover, but as Daria resumed her work on the cabinets, her thoughts were on Shelly. Shelly had always been unusual in her ability to see things others could not, but she'd never before displayed psychic powers. If Sean Macy had indeed killed himself, how had Shelly predicted it?

That night, Daria sat at the picnic table on the Sea Shanty porch with Chloe and Shelly, eating cold roasted chicken and potato salad for dinner. No one was talking much; neither Chloe nor Shelly was finished with her grieving. And although Daria knew the timing was poor, she had to bring the subject up.

"There's a rumor going around that Father Macy might have killed himself," she said halfway through the meal.

Chloe looked up from the chicken breast she had barely touched. "I've heard some rumblings to that effect," she said, her voice flat.

Daria looked at Shelly, who kept her gaze fastened on her plate.

"Shelly?" Daria prompted.

Shelly looked up. "What?"

"I know you thought that might happen. That Father Macy might commit suicide."

Chloe looked surprised. "You did?" she asked Shelly. "What would make you think that?"

Shelly shrugged and poked at her potato salad with her fork.

Daria looked at Chloe. "About a week ago, Shelly was

upset, and she told me she thought Father Macy might kill himself," Daria explained. "I thought she was...I thought she'd misinterpreted something he'd said. Now I'm not so sure."

Shelly began to cry. She pushed her plate away and pressed her napkin to her eyes. "I knew he was going to do it," she said. "I should have done something about it."

Daria leaned forward, her elbows on the table. "Why on earth did you think he was going to do that?" she asked.

Shelly sat back on the bench, her nose already red from crying. "He said he was upset with himself," she said. "He said he was a...sinner."

"A sinner?" Daria repeated. "What did he mean by that? Did he say why he thought he was a sinner?"

Shelly shook her head. "He always talked like a puzzle to me. I was never sure what he meant about things." She picked up her fork again and poked it into the potato salad. "He asked me if I thought it was wrong to kill yourself, and I said that I thought it was. And *he* said, that he thought God would forgive a suicide if it was done to save somebody else."

Daria and Chloe exchanged looks of confusion on their side of the table. "Who would he be saving?" Daria asked. "I think you must have misunderstood him."

Chloe slipped off her side of the bench and moved around the table to sit next to Shelly. She rested her hand on her younger sister's arm, and Daria saw tears brimming in Chloe's eyes.

"I think Daria's right, honey, and you misunderstood what Father Sean was saying," she said. "So, I think that what you just told us has to stay between the three of us. Understand? It doesn't make a lot of sense, and if you were to spread it around, I'm afraid it would just fuel the fire right now." Chloe pressed her lips together, her glistening eyes fixed on the picnic table. "The thing we need to keep in mind is that Sean was a good man. Maybe he *did* do something that would make him a sinner in the eyes of the Church, but not in the eyes of God, and that's what counts. God could never think of such a person as a sinner. So, maybe you got confused in what you heard, or maybe Sean himself was confused by what he was thinking or feeling. Either way, we need to keep what he told you in this house. Okay?"

Shelly nodded, and Daria could see that she was relieved to have told them what she knew and that she'd been comforted by Chloe's words. Chloe stood up, leaning over to give Shelly a hug.

All three of them looked up at the sound of a car door slamming. Across the cul-de-sac, Grace was walking from her car toward the front door of Poll-Rory. Daria wondered if she had a clue what was waiting for her inside that cottage. She fervently hoped Rory could get to the bottom of the game she was playing.

Chloe looked down at Daria, who had not yet told her what she knew about Grace.

"And how about you, sweetheart?" Chloe said to her, nodding in the direction of Rory's cottage. "Are you okay?"

"I'm fine now," she said. At Chloe's disbelieving look, she repeated to herself with a smile. "Really, Chloe," she said. "I'm fine."

Rory let Grace into the cottage. He'd been both dreading and looking forward to this moment since his talk with Daria the day before. Grace greeted him with a smile, obviously unaware that she had been unmasked. What truly lay beneath that mask, he couldn't say, but he planned to find out in the next few minutes.

She stood inside the cottage door, and she must have seen the seriousness in his face, because her smile quickly faded.

"What's wrong?" she asked.

"You and I need to have a talk," he said.

The apprehension in her eyes was instantaneous. "What about?" she asked.

He walked into the living room, and she followed him, but remained standing when he sat down in a chair.

"I know you're not really separated," he began, "and I know you had a child who was killed in a plane crash in April."

Grace let out her breath. Shutting her eyes briefly, she sat down on the sofa. "How do you know all that?"

"Did you know that Daria was one of the EMTs involved in trying to rescue your daughter?" he asked.

The color drained from her face so quickly that he was certain she had not known. She probably knew nothing about Shelly's involvement, then, either. "I had no idea," she said.

"Well, she was," Rory said. "And the fact that she wasn't able to save your daughter really distressed her. It got bad enough that she quit being an EMT, and she was so upset about it, that she decided to track down your daughter's family to speak with them about it. So, she went to Rodanthe and talked to your…husband."

"Oh my God…"

"And I guess your husband mentioned you, and Daria put two and two together and realized that you and the pilot's mother were one and the same person."

Grace lowered her head to her hands. "Oh, Rory, I'm so sorry. This must all seem insane to you. I had no idea Daria was involved in that accident. That's just a crazy coincidence. I lied about not having children because I didn't want to talk about Pamela. It's too painful to talk about. She was my baby." Grace began to cry in earnest, and Rory felt the hard edges of his heart begin to soften. "And I only partly lied about being separated," she said.

"Daria said you live on the same property as your husband."

Grace nodded. "I live above the garage," she said. "I'd live somewhere else, if I could afford to. But right now, I can't. If Eddie doesn't know we're separated, then he's in denial."

Her lower lip trembled, and Rory knew that Daria was mistaken about Grace's ulterior motives. This was a woman who had recently lost a child, and she obviously did not have support from her husband in grieving for that child. Plus, she'd recently had a serious illness. He could only imagine the emotional pain she'd been suffering. So she'd gone a little crazy. He'd been crazy after his separation, and that had not been coupled with the loss of a child. His throat tightened at the thought of losing Zack.

He moved to the sofa, sitting down next to her, close to her. "I have one more question I need an answer to," he said.

She pressed her lips together and nodded, waiting.

"What kind of illness did you have?" It was time he knew. He was tired of her secrets and evasiveness.

She swallowed hard and a look of panic came into her eyes. "I think I'm going to be sick." She stood up, swaying, and he stood, too, holding her arm to steady her. "I'll be right back," she said, and she walked unsteadily toward the bathroom.

He waited what seemed like a long time, and was about to check on her when she emerged from the bathroom, holding a wet washcloth to her throat. He stood up. "Are you all right?" he asked.

She offered a wry laugh. "Oh, I'm just great," she said, taking her seat again.

He held her hand on his knee, not caring whether she wanted him to, not caring if she had a husband, or if she had lied to him. Her palm was clammy and cool. She pressed the washcloth to her forehead with her other hand, then lowered it to her lap.

"I had heart surgery just before Pamela died," she said, drawing away a bit to look at him. "I have a condition called Marfan's syndrome. It's hereditary and can sometimes affect the heart. Pamela had it, too. She'd just been diagnosed with it, although she hadn't had any obvious symptoms—until the seizure she had on the plane. That's why the plane went down. My husband always pushed her to fly." She suddenly looked angry. "If it hadn't been for him, she would have taken up some normal hobby, like softball or…a musical instrument, or something. And she'd still be alive." She closed her eyes tightly, and the tears started again. "I'm sorry, Rory," she said. "When I lied to you that first day on the beach, I didn't know I was going to become friends with you. Or that I'd even see you again. And once the lie was out…"

"Shh." He put his arms around her and pulled her close to him, and she did not resist. She wept against his chest, tangled up in her lies and grief. He was not certain what impact all those lies would have on their relationship. All he knew was that, right now, she needed a friend. He was more than willing to play that role.

34

DARIA AND CHLOE ARRIVED HOME FROM WORK AT THE SAME time, when the sky above the ocean was pewter-colored and cloudless and there was no hint of menacing weather.

"Did you hear about the hurricane headed this way?" Daria asked as she and Chloe walked onto the Sea Shanty's porch.

"No," Chloe said. "That's just what we need."

"It's a big one," Daria said. In the living room, she clicked on the TV to wait for the weather report. "It's still pretty far out," she said, "so maybe it'll weaken as it nears shore. Or it might even turn out to sea. You never know, at this stage."

"You'd better not say anything to Shelly about it." Chloe looked at her watch. "I just came home to change," she said. "I have to go back to the church to help Father Wayne with a meeting tonight."

Chloe would be working longer hours for a while, taking on extra duties at St. Esther's in Father Macy's absence. Daria sat down in front of the TV as Chloe went upstairs to change.

All day, while she and Andy had been paneling a condo in Duck, she'd been wondering how Rory's talk with Grace had gone. As soon as Chloe left, she'd go over to Poll-Rory to find out.

But, as the meteorologist was giving his uncertain report about Hurricane Bernadette, Rory knocked on the porch door.

"Daria?" he called.

"Come in," she said, looking up as he walked into the living room. "I was going to come over a little later."

Rory sat down on the other end of the sofa. "Is that Bernadette?" he asked, eyeing the perfect white doughnut of clouds on the weather map.

"Uh-huh. She's a monster."

"When do they predict it will hit us?"

"They're not sure it will."

Chloe came downstairs and into the room, wearing a skirt and blouse in place of the shorts and T-shirt she'd had on earlier.

"Hello, Rory," she said, her voice so cool that Daria felt irritated with her.

"Hi, Chloe." Rory turned on the sofa to face her, his arms folded across his chest. "You know, I've been hearing some rumors."

"About?" Chloe asked, and Daria cringed, fearing she knew the rumors Rory was alluding to. He would not win any points with Chloe by bringing them up.

"Some people are saying that Father Macy's accident might actually have been a suicide," he said. "Had either of you heard anything like that?"

Chloe rolled her eyes.

"Where did you hear that?" Daria asked.

"Zack said he heard some kids talking about it," Rory said.

"It's ridiculous, Rory," Chloe said. "And it's not helpful to give any credence to that sort of gossip."

"I don't know," Rory said. "I think it's kind of suspicious. I mean, he died just a few days after I spoke with him, and he'd been very upset during his conversation with me. Maybe he knew something about Shelly's background, and that's why he killed himself. He wanted to take that information with him to the grave."

Daria noticed that the tops of Chloe's ears were red, a sure sign of anger that she had not seen in her sister in many, many years.

"I'm certain your conversation with him had nothing whatsoever to do with it," Chloe said coldly. Her hands were on her hips, her eyes blazing. "You think everything revolves around you and your damn TV program. Probably now you'll decide to do one of your shows on this new mystery, huh? 'The Secret Agony of Sean Macy.'" She turned abruptly to Daria. "I need to get over to the church," she said. "I hope none of the parishioners has heard any of this slander."

Turning on her heel, Chloe marched out the front door, slamming it shut behind her.

"Whoa," Rory said. "Why do I get the feeling she's not pleased with me?"

Daria sighed, leaning against the back of the sofa. "We had a conversation with Shelly last night about the same thing," Daria said. "I think hearing about the rumors again was just too much for her."

"Maybe I should go after her," Rory said, looking toward the front door. "Apologize."

"I'd leave her alone right now." Chloe's anger was so out of character that Daria could not predict how her sister would react to Rory's apology. "Maybe in a few days, when the wounds aren't so fresh, she'll be more receptive. Right now, though, I want to hear about your visit with Grace last night." She drew her bare feet onto the sofa and turned to face him.

"Well," Rory began, "she's screwed up, I'll grant you that, but I don't think she had a clue about Shelly being involved in her daughter's death." He went on to tell Daria about his conversation with Grace, and Daria listened quietly. She didn't feel as trusting of Grace as he did.

"I felt really sorry for her," Rory said. "I think she just got caught up in the lies about the separation and having no kids. She told me those things the first time I met her, and she didn't know that we were going to end up having a relationship. Once we did, I guess she figured it was easier to stick with her original story. She didn't have a mastectomy, like we thought. She had heart surgery. She has a disease called Marfan's syndrome."

"Pamela—the pilot—had that."

"Yeah, Grace said it's hereditary. She's in a lot of pain over her daughter. I think that's why she's drawn to Shelly. Shelly's close in age to her daughter. I don't think it's any more complicated than that."

"I hope you're right," Daria said. "It still seems like a pretty amazing coincidence that she stumbled into our little cul-de-sac." She heard the callous tone of her words and wished she could take them back. It was obvious that Rory felt sympathy for Grace. She had not wanted that, or expected it. Why couldn't he see that, for whatever reason, Grace was manipulating him?

"If you could have seen her last night, I think you would stop worrying about it," Rory said.

"So," Daria said, "where do things stand now with the two of you?"

Rory laughed. "Funny you should ask," he said. "I was thinking to myself that I was an adulterer for having had an affair with a married woman. But there *was* no affair. Grace had made sure of that. It was only an affair in my fantasies. So, to answer your question, I don't know." He locked his hands together and stretched his arms out in front of him. "I still want to see her. I'm not angry with her. I just—"

A sudden noise came from upstairs, and Daria cocked her head to listen. "I didn't think Shelly was home," she said in a near whisper, her heart beating a little faster.

There was a thud, followed by the sound of voices. One of them was a man's, and Daria was instantly alarmed. "It's coming from Shelly's room," she said. "Who could be with her?"

Rory looked toward the stairs. "Does she have any male friends?" he asked.

Daria shook her head. "None that she should have in her bedroom," she said. "God, Rory, what if it's someone she picked up? Some stranger? She befriends everyone. What if it's some psychopath?"

"Calm down," Rory said. "The likelihood of that is pretty slim. But…maybe you should go check on her, anyway."

"I don't want to humiliate her," she said, looking toward the stairs, "but I'd never forgive myself if somebody was hurting her."

"I'd say her safety is more important than her pride right now," Rory said.

Daria stood up. "Call the cops if I start screaming," she said, walking toward the stairs.

In the upstairs hallway, she knocked on Shelly's door. "Shelly?"

There was an ominous silence from behind the door, then hushed voices and the rustling of sheets.

"Shelly, are you all right?"

She heard footsteps, and the bedroom door was opened a few inches…by Zack. Daria could see Kara in Shelly's bed, the sheets pulled up to her chin, and she was too surprised to speak.

"I'm not Shelly," Zack said with a sheepish grin. "Shelly said we could use her room while she was out on a walk."

Daria heard Rory's footsteps on the stairs. It sounded as

though he was taking them two at a time, and Zack's grin faded. "Is my dad here?" he asked, eyes wide, and Daria nodded.

"Zack?" Rory called as he neared the top of the stairs.

"Oh, shit." Zack started to shut the door, but Rory had already reached the hallway. He pushed past Daria to hold the door open with his hand.

"What do you think you're doing?" he said to his son, the question so idiotic and unanswerable that Daria almost laughed. She remembered having asked the same thing of Shelly years earlier, when she'd caught her in bed with one of the sleazy guys she used to see.

"Shelly said we could use her room," Zack said weakly.

"Well, I think you two better get dressed and get out of here," Rory said. "I'll see you at home in a few minutes." He pulled the door shut, ran his hands through his hair, then looked at Daria. "Yikes," he whispered, and she stifled a laugh.

She followed him down the stairs. "I apologize for my sister's lousy judgment," she said.

Rory opened the living-room door and looked up at the ceiling. "What do I do now?" he asked, although he didn't sound as though he actually expected an answer.

"Be understanding," Daria said. "Be kind. Be all the things I wasn't when I caught Shelly doing the same thing."

Rory smiled. "I'll try," he said. He turned and left the Sea Shanty.

Treat Zack with the same kind of sympathy you so easily lavish on Grace, she thought as she watched him walk across the cul-de-sac and into Poll-Rory, where he'd wait to have it out with his son.

35

IT WAS NEARLY FORTY-FIVE MINUTES BEFORE ZACK DARED TO come home, and Rory was waiting for him in the living room, still not sure what he was going to say.

"I don't want to talk about it, Dad," Zack said as he walked past him toward the bedrooms.

"Well, I do."

Zack stopped walking and turned around, a look of resignation on his face, and Rory noticed for the first time that his son was nearly as tall as he was. When had that happened?

"Did you at least use a condom?" Something told him that was not the best way to start this conversation, but the words slipped out before he could stop them.

"Kara's on the Pill," Zack said.

"A fifteen-year-old girl on the Pill?" Rory asked. "That says something about her right there, doesn't it?"

"Yeah," Zack said. "It says she's smart and careful."

"What it says to me is that she's probably had a number of partners, which opens her up to all sorts of diseases. AIDS and a dozen others. You should have used a condom, anyway. What if she's lying to you? What if she's not on the Pill at all and is just trying to trap you? And, damn it, you're too young for this, anyhow." *Whew.* He sounded judgmental. Irrational. Hysterical. But he couldn't seem to shut up.

Zack simply stared at him. "What's the problem, Dad?" he asked. "Are you telling me you did it for the first time on your wedding night, or what?"

Be understanding, Daria had said. *Be kind.* With a heavy sigh, he sat down on the sofa.

"I know I'm not doing a good job of this, Zack," he admitted. "I'm sorry. I just worry about you, that's all."

"Well, you don't have to," Zack said.

"Yeah, I do," he said. "I was fifteen once, too, hard though that may be for you to believe. And I know how you can be drawn into things without thinking through the consequences."

"I'm thinking things through, Dad. Have a little faith in me, all right?" Zack turned to leave the room.

"I think it's time I had a talk with Kara's grandparents. The Wheelers," Rory said.

Zack spun around. *"What?"*

"Not to tell them about what happened tonight," he said quickly. "Don't worry about that. I just think I should get to know them a bit better, since you and Kara are seeing each other."

"That is *really* not necessary."

"I'd like to talk with them, anyway," Rory said. He'd had a few short conversations with the couple this summer, reminiscing about old times on the cul-de-sac, but he hadn't yet spoken with them about Shelly. "Now is as good a time as any."

"What a coincidence," Zack said. "You decide to talk to them right after you find Kara and me…"

"I told you, I won't say anything about that," Rory said. "That's a promise."

"I'm going to bed," Zack said.

"It's still early."

Zack looked at him suspiciously. "You mean, you'd let me go out?"

"Of course."

"If I go out, I'm going to see Kara." It sounded like a threat.

"I'm sure you will," he said. "I know there isn't anything I can do about that, Zack. Just…use good judgment, please. That's all I ask."

The Wheelers' cottage was swarming with grandchildren of all ages the following day, but the older couple invited Rory onto their screened deck, away from the noise and clutter. Rory remembered the Wheelers fondly from his childhood. Every evening, they would stroll arm in arm on the beach together, and he'd thought of them as a kind old couple, although they must only have been in their fifties then. Now, in their mid-seventies, Mr. Wheeler was tall and lean and looked fit, while Mrs. Wheeler had grown quite heavy and walked with a cane. He did not know their first names; they would probably always be Mr. and Mrs. Wheeler to him.

"We watch you every week on *True Life Stories,*" Mrs. Wheeler said as she poured him a glass of iced tea from a plastic, childproof pitcher. She handed the tea to him, then lowered herself into a deck chair.

"Well, thanks," Rory said. "I'm sorry I haven't stopped by yet this summer. I guess you've seen my son more than you have me."

"He's a sweet boy," Mrs. Wheeler said.

"Thanks. He's a good kid." Rory took a sip of tea. It was overly sweet. "I do worry that he and Kara might be getting a bit too serious, though," he said.

Mrs. Wheeler raised her eyebrows. "Do you?" Rory had the feeling she knew exactly what was concerning him.

"Oh," Mr. Wheeler said, "it's just a little summer romance. Nothing to get upset about."

"Well, I just wanted to make sure you don't mind how much Zack is around," Rory said. "How much the two of them are together."

"He's about the nicest boy she's gone out with," Mrs. Wheeler said. "So, no, we don't mind a bit."

For a moment, Rory worried about what the other boys Kara had dated had been like—and what diseases they might carry—but he put those thoughts aside.

"I'll tell you the girl we need to worry about," Mr. Wheeler said. "That Bernadette. They say she's heading straight for the Outer Banks now."

"I didn't know that," Rory said. He hadn't listened to the weather report yet that day.

"There's still a chance she'll veer off course," Mr. Wheeler said. "I just hope we don't have to evacuate. Remember doing that when you were a kid?"

"I think we only had to do it once or twice," Rory said. "I don't remember where we went." He supposed he and Zack would go to a hotel on the mainland somewhere, if they needed to evacuate.

"Oh, we usually end up in one of the shelters," Mr. Wheeler said. "Cheaper than a motel, with our crew, and the kids wind up having a lot of fun."

Rory took another swallow of tea. "Well," he began, "I guess you know why I'm here this summer."

Mrs. Wheeler nodded. "Shelly," she said.

"That's right. I've been talking to people on the cul-de-sac about what they remember. Do you two have any thoughts on who left Shelly on the beach that morning?"

"I always figured it was that Cindy girl who lived at the end of the street," Mr. Wheeler said.

"Oh, it wasn't Cindy," Mrs. Wheeler said. "She was too thin. Remember? We talked about it back then. She was a skinny minnie."

"Well, you were skinny back in your baby-having days, yourself," Mr. Wheeler said, and his wife made a sound of mock annoyance.

"Cindy preserved her figure a heck of a lot better than I ever did," Mrs. Wheeler said. "We see her every once in a while when we go up to Smokey's restaurant in Corolla for the sweet-potato fries. She's always so nice."

Rory leaned forward. "You've seen Cindy Trump recently?" he asked. "Does she live around here?"

"Oh, yes," Mrs. Wheeler said. "She and her husband and kids own one of them huge houses in Corolla. Her last name is Delaney now."

Rory made a mental note of the name, unable to believe his good fortune. He would be able to talk with Cindy after all.

"You know," Mrs. Wheeler said, "I'd like to think of Shelly the way Sue—her mother—did—as a gift from the sea, with no parents other than the Catos. Shelly is such a sweet girl, and she gave Mrs. Cato such happiness in her last years. And Daria's been a saint to take care of her."

"Maybe it was that retarded girl," Mr. Wheeler said suddenly. "Maybe she was Shelly's mother."

"Hush," his wife said sharply. "That was Rory's sister."

Rory smiled. "I'm quite certain Polly had nothing to do with Shelly," he said, although he was beginning to wonder why he was so sure of that fact. The thought of Polly having been taken advantage of sexually, the thought of her being confused about being pregnant and delivering a baby by herself, was too horrifying to ponder.

"Rory…" Mrs. Wheeler sounded hesitant. "Did you ever

consider that your own mother might have been Shelly's mother?" she asked.

Rory masked the shock in his face. "No, I'd have to say my mother would be last on my list of suspects," he said.

"Oh, I know," Mrs. Wheeler said hurriedly. "And you're probably right. But your mother and I had a lot of conversations back in the old days. She was very upset that she'd had a Mongoloid child and she'd been terribly worried when she got pregnant with you. She was afraid you might turn out to be slow, too, especially since she was even older when you were born than when your sister came. She told me how relieved she was when you were born normal." Mrs. Wheeler ran her fingertip over the sweaty handle of the pitcher. "I always wondered if maybe she had gotten pregnant again. Maybe she was so afraid that she'd have another retarded child that she—" Mrs. Wheeler shrugged "—left the baby to the sea, thinking that was the best and kindest thing to do."

"Do you really think that was a possibility?" Rory was incredulous.

"I guess I thought she was just as likely as anybody else on the street."

Why not his mother? he thought. He'd considered nearly every other woman on the cul-de-sac. But this was one direction his thinking refused to take him.

He took a last swallow of the too-sweet tea. "Well," he said, standing up, "I should get back to Poll-Rory."

"Watch out for Bernadette," Mr. Wheeler said.

"Cindy's last name was Delaney, you said?" Rory asked.

Mr. and Mrs. Wheeler got to their feet as well. "That's right," Mrs. Wheeler said. "And wait till you see her. She hasn't changed a bit."

36

"I THINK EVACUATION IS INEVITABLE," DARIA SAID. SHE WAS sitting next to Rory on the widow's walk. "They said there's a high-pressure system that's going to pull Bernadette straight toward us."

"It's hard to believe there's a storm out there," Rory said.

They were both sitting on the west side of the widow's walk, facing the sea, and the water was calm, the glassy waves rolling toward shore with an easy, uniform rhythm. Daria had seen enough storms on the Outer Banks to know that this tranquillity was deceptive. It was difficult to worry when the air and the sea were this quiet, and she could understand how someone not familiar with the area could convince themselves the storm would veer off course and miss them. But she didn't need the weather to tell her what was coming. She felt it in her gut, that churning apprehension she always had when a storm was heading their way. It *could* miss them. They might receive no more than a few sprinkles and some harmless wind. Or, the water could cover Kill Devil Hills, destroying the beaches and pulling the cottages out to sea. It was the not knowing that made her stomach churn. She needed to prepare for the worst scenario. She needed to think about lowering the storm windows, closing the storm shutters, bringing the tools up from the workshop, and most important, keeping Shelly as calm and occupied as she could.

"I can already feel Shelly tensing up," Daria said. "I don't think she's eaten anything all day."

"Did you give her a hard time about letting Zack and Kara use her room?" Rory asked.

"Not too hard," Daria said. "By the time she got home last night, she was already getting nervous about the storm. I didn't have the heart to upset her more."

"Where do we go if we have to evacuate?" Rory asked. "Where do *you* usually go?"

"We'll go to a motel in Greenville," Daria said. "As a matter of fact, I'd better make reservations now, just in case we need them. Would you like me to make reservations for you and Zack, too?" She hoped he said yes. She wanted him close by.

"That would be great," he said. "I guess I should get some plywood, huh? I've never done this before. I remember my father nailing wood over the windows, though."

"Yes, you should. And take down the Poll-Rory sign so it doesn't blow away. Move the porch and deck furniture inside." She looked across the cul-de-sac at his cottage. "Put your garbage can inside, too, and anything else that might turn into a missile in the wind."

"You're starting to make *me* nervous now," Rory said.

"I know." She laughed. "My stomach hurts just thinking about it."

They were quiet for a few minutes. She could see Zack and some of the other kids playing volleyball on the beach. Rory finally broke the silence.

"I had a talk with the Wheelers today," he said.

"Oh. About Kara?"

"Well, I skirted the issue of Kara and Zack," he said. "They think my son is a great guy. I'd best leave it at that."

"He *is* a great guy," Daria said. Then she realized what he had spoken to the Wheelers about. "Shelly," she said. "You talked to them about Shelly."

"Uh-huh." Rory slouched down on the bench, his hands locked behind his head. "You'll be pleased to know that they weren't much help. As a matter of fact, all they succeeded in doing was rattling me."

"What do you mean?"

"Well, Mr. Wheeler thinks Shelly's mother was Polly," Rory said. "And guess who Mrs. Wheeler thinks is Shelly's mother?"

Daria felt momentarily unnerved. What did Mrs. Wheeler know? "Who?" she asked.

"*My* mother."

Daria laughed. The thought was bizarre. "You're kidding. Why would she think that?"

Rory shrugged. "Well, she made a good point. My mother, I'm sure, was afraid of having any more children after Polly and I were born, fearing that another child might have Down's syndrome. Mom would have been in her late forties by then, so if she had been pregnant, that would have been a realistic concern. Mrs. Wheeler suggested that my mother might have gotten pregnant and decided that leaving the baby on the beach was the way to go."

"I don't remember your mother all that well, but I can't imagine her doing something like that," Daria said.

"I don't know," Rory said. He unlocked his hands from behind his head, and leaned his elbows on his knees, looking out to sea. "It's been bothering me all day," he said. "She *did* have some psychological problems later on in her life. I didn't think she had them then, but maybe they were already brewing. I mean, *someone* did it. *Someone* was a little crazy that night. I guess it could have been my mother as well as anyone else."

He sounded despondent, and Daria rested her hand lightly on his back. The gesture felt awkward and alien to her, but it was the sort of thing *he* would do, and she knew how good it felt to be comforted that way. It was the least she could do for him—or the least she was willing to do, at any rate. She had the ability to put his doubts to rest, completely and forever, but there was no way she could tell him what she knew.

"What would you do if you found out that it *was* Polly or your mother?" she asked. "Would you still do the story?"

"Are you kidding?" He turned his head to look at her. "No way."

"Then I'm asking you," she said gently, "to remember that the woman you're trying to expose might also be someone else's sister or someone else's mother, and people can be hurt by the information you uncover."

Rory studied his bare feet. She could not see his face.

"Most likely it was Cindy," she continued, "and she probably has a family who would be devastated by learning about Shelly. You need to—"

"Oh," Rory interrupted her, sitting up straight again. "I found out where Cindy is."

"You did?" This was news Daria did not want to hear.

"Right. The Wheelers said she lives up in Corolla with her husband and kids."

"I didn't know that." Daria had no idea Cindy still lived in the Outer Banks. "Are you going to talk with her?"

"Absolutely," Rory said. "I'd get on it right now, if it weren't for the storm coming up. But I figure I'd better spend tomorrow battening down the hatches."

"Good idea," Daria said, still shaken by the news about

Cindy. It had been easy to pin the blame on Cindy when she was little more than a hazy figure from the past. Knowing that she was a living, breathing woman just up the coast a few miles was something else again.

37

THE LUMBERYARD SMELLED OF WOOD AND WORRY AS RORY and Zack fought their way through the crowd. Everyone was buying sheets of plywood to cover the windows of their vulnerable homes, and Rory overheard many of them grumbling about ruined vacations, lost revenue from their rental properties and how long it was going to take to drive over the bridge to escape the Barrier Islands.

He and Zack tied the plywood to the top of the Cruiser, then headed back to the cul-de-sac. The sky was still clear, the sea still calm, when they reached Poll-Rory. Across the street, Daria and Chloe were closing the storm shutters on the Sea Shanty, and Rory waved to them as he and Zack unloaded the plywood. They rested it against the side of the cottage facing the ocean, near the windows most in need of protection, then Rory went into the cottage to get a couple of hammers and some nails.

The phone rang as he was pulling the toolbox from the storage closet. He'd left a phone message for Cindy Trump about the possibility of getting together in a couple of days, and he figured she was returning his call. He picked up the receiver.

"Rory?" It was Grace. He had not spoken to her since the other night, when he'd confronted her with her lies. He was glad to hear her voice.

"Hi, Grace," he said. "Are you getting ready to evacuate down there?"

She hesitated. "That's why I was calling," she said. "Eddie—my husband—and I usually go to a hotel on the mainland, but I can't go with him. I just can't." Her voice quivered.

"Maybe it would be good," Rory said, although he would rather she were with him. "Maybe the two of you need some enforced time together."

"I don't want to be anywhere near him," she said. She hesitated a moment. "I wanted to find out where you were going to be," she added.

"Zack and I are getting a room in a motel in Greenville," he said. "We're leaving early tomorrow morning."

"Is that…is that where Daria will be, too?"

"Yes. And Chloe and Shelly."

"Do you think it's too late for me to get a room there? Would you mind if I'm there?"

Maybe she was ready to talk with Daria about her daughter's death, he thought. Maybe that's why she'd asked if Daria was going to be there. He didn't want to deprive her of that opportunity.

"Of course not," he said. "But it's so far for you to—"

"I want to, Rory."

"All right." He heard hammering on the side of the cottage and was surprised that Zack would start covering the windows without him. He gave her the name and phone number of the motel. "I'll see you there," he said.

Daria handed her hammer to Zack, and while she and Chloe held the sheet of plywood in place, Zack pounded nails into the woodwork. Rory walked out of the cottage, and she saw the surprise in his face at finding her and Chloe there.

"Hey, thanks," he said, helping her lift another sheet of wood in place. He looked toward the ocean, and she followed his gaze. The sea was glassy and calm, and the blue sky was reflected in the water. It was still hard to imagine that something foreboding lurked beyond the horizon.

Rory shook his head. "Are you sure we're not wasting our time with this?" he asked her.

"Unfortunately, I'm sure," she said.

"The storm is picking up speed as it heads this way," Chloe said. Chloe was merely being neighborly, coming over to help Rory with the windows. Daria knew the gesture changed nothing about her ill feelings toward him.

"I just can't believe the ocean could get up as far as our cottage," Zack said.

The sheet of plywood in place, Daria lowered her arms to her sides and faced Zack. "When your dad and I were little, there was a cottage right there." She pointed to the sea-oat-covered sand where Cindy Trump's cottage had once stood. "A storm swept it away. It could make our cottages disappear just as easily."

"Scary," Zack said.

"Yes, indeed," Daria said. Her stomach still had that unsettled, agitated feeling that always dogged her when a storm was heading to Kill Devil Hills, but she knew her anxiety was nothing compared to Shelly's. Backing away from the windows for a moment, she stood at the edge of Poll-Rory's porch, looking north and south along the beach. Shelly was out there somewhere, walking. She'd grown very quiet and pensive over the last twenty-four hours, and Daria knew it was not the storm itself that terrified her; it was the prospect of leaving her beloved Outer Banks.

"Does everybody have to leave?" Zack asked as he helped

Chloe lift another sheet of plywood against the cottage. "Is that what they mean by 'mandatory'?"

"They always say 'mandatory,'" Chloe said. "But what it really means is, if you stay behind, you're on your own. There might be no services available to help you in an emergency."

"Does anyone stay?" Zack asked.

"There are always people who think they're being brave to stay behind," Chloe said, "but they're really being foolish. Some of the emergency workers will still be here, but even they—the sheriff's department and the ambulances—aren't allowed on the streets once the wind hits sixty miles per hour. It's too dangerous."

Daria and Rory hammered the plywood into place, and when they stood back from their work, Rory looked at her.

"Grace is planning to meet us at the motel," he said.

She wondered if her disappointment showed on her face. "Why would she come all the way to Greenville?" she asked.

"Well—" Rory stepped back from the window to admire their work "—two reasons, I think. One, she doesn't want to be with her husband. And two, I think she wants to talk with you. She asked me specifically if you would be there."

Great, Daria thought. Once on the mainland, she would have to worry not only about the fate of the Sea Shanty and the well-being of her anxious, phobic sister, but she would have to answer Grace's questions about an accident she could not honestly discuss.

Rory must have picked up her dismay. "Maybe I should have told her not to come," he said.

"It'll be all right," Daria said, and she helped Zack lift the next sheet of plywood into place.

That night they packed their suitcases, carried Daria's tools into the cottage from the first-story workroom and brought the porch furniture inside. Shelly threw up half the night, and Daria felt nearly as sick.

Early the following morning, she sat up in bed and looked out the window toward the ocean. The waves were distinctly swollen and frothy, the sea oats blew nearly parallel to the sand, and the sky was low and thick with bloated gray clouds. Even in her room, Daria felt that shift in the atmosphere that was so hard to describe but so clearly an indicator that the storm was well on its way. The air seemed to lack oxygen; it was hard to breathe.

She dressed quickly and went downstairs, where Chloe was making a fruit salad for breakfast.

"Where's Shelly?" Daria asked. Shelly was usually first up in the morning and her absence sent an instant chill up Daria's spine.

"I haven't seen her," Chloe said. "I told her last night that she should be ready to leave by eight this morning."

It was already seven-thirty.

"I have a bad feeling about this," Daria said.

Chloe looked up from the peach she was slicing. "Maybe she's on the beach," she suggested. "One last chance to gather shells before the storm."

"I'm going upstairs to see if she's at least packed." With a mounting sense of dread, Daria climbed the stairs. Her knock on Shelly's door was not answered, and she went into the room. Shelly's bed was neatly made, but there was no sign of a suitcase. Maybe she hadn't packed yet. Then Daria spotted the note taped to the mirror above Shelly's dresser. She moved closer to read it.

Go on without me, it read. *I'll be all right.*

38

DARIA AND CHLOE SET OFF IN ONE DIRECTION ON THE BEACH, while Rory and Zack headed in the other. "If Shelly's out here, we'll find her," Rory had reassured her. Daria had alerted them to Shelly's disappearance after combing the Sea Shanty from top to bottom. She'd looked in the workroom, the closets and under the beds, but Shelly was nowhere to be found. Pete had been right, she thought. Shelly's judgment was atrocious. She needed more supervision than Daria was able to give her.

There were still a few hearty souls on the beach, dressed in windbreakers, their hair whipping around their heads as they stared out to sea to watch the sky darken and the water churn. Daria and Chloe didn't speak as they walked. It was too difficult; the wind threw their words back in their faces. Even walking itself was a chore, and it distressed Daria to think that Shelly might be out here somewhere, expecting to weather the storm alone on the beach. But by the time she and Chloe had thoroughly scoured the beach to the south, and Rory and Zack to the north, Daria was convinced her sister was not on the beach, after all. Those few people who had been out to watch the storm's approach had disappeared as well by then, wisely heeding the warnings to leave the Outer Banks.

She searched the Sea Shanty once again, checking the nooks and crannies, peering inside her car and Chloe's car and Rory's Cruiser. It was close to noon, and Jill and her family, Linda, Jackie and the dogs had long since left the cul-de-sac. Only the Wheelers remained, and they were packing up their minivan and station wagon, filling them with suitcases and kids.

Daria stood on the bare porch with Rory, a well of frustration in her chest. Her hair was thick and woolly as it blew around her face, and she tightened her windbreaker across her chest. "You and Zack need to get out of here," she said to Rory.

"What are you going to do?" Rory asked.

"I'm not leaving until I find her," Daria said. She felt the quivering of her chin, betraying her worry, and Rory reached out to squeeze her arm.

"I'm not going, either, then." He glanced down the cul-de-sac toward the Wheelers' cottage. "Let me see if Zack can go with them. It would thrill him, I'm sure. Then I can stay behind."

"You really should go," she said, although she desperately wanted him to stay. "We might not be able to get out of here, and it could get dangerous. And won't Grace be expecting you to show up at the motel?"

"Yes, but at least she'll be safe. I can't leave without knowing that Shelly is, too." He looked toward the Wheelers' cottage again. "I'll be right back," he said.

She watched him walk down the cul-de-sac to the Wheelers' cottage, where he spoke with Ruth Wheeler. Tears burned Daria's eyes; she wanted him to stay so badly. After a minute, he walked back to Poll-Rory, and she guessed he was asking Zack if he would mind going with the Wheelers. She was still standing on the porch when Zack emerged from the cottage, carrying a duffel bag. He waved to Daria as he started walking toward the Wheelers', and Rory rejoined her on the porch. "Okay," he said. "I'm yours as long as you need me."

Chloe stepped out of the cottage onto the porch. "I bet she's holed up in one of the abandoned cottages," she said. "She could be right across the street, for all we know. I think we should go door-to-door."

Chloe could be right. Shelly had done exactly that during a storm a few years earlier. She knew enough to get inside somewhere. Would she know enough to select a cottage as far from the beach as possible? It was anyone's guess. She could be anywhere. "If she *is* in a cottage somewhere, and we knock on the door, she won't answer it," she said.

"We won't knock, then," Chloe said. "We'll just snoop around the cottages and see if we can spot her."

"I'll start with Jill's," Rory said. "Then let's split up to cover the streets on the other side of the beach road."

"Look for a light on," Daria said as she walked into the cul-de-sac with them. She pulled up the hood of her windbreaker, holding it closed with a hand beneath her chin. It had grown so dark outside that she could barely see the expressions on the faces of Rory and her sister. Shelly was not crazy about the dark. She would turn on a light if she had sequestered herself in someone's cottage.

Only, there were no lights on. They searched Jill's and Linda's cottages, then separately covered six streets west of the beach road. Every single cottage was dark. It might as well be the dead of winter, Daria thought. There was no one around. Not even any cars. The wind literally blew her off her feet from time to time and made her eyes tear. A few shingles flew past her as she walked, along with a child's plastic pail and the lid of a garbage can, projectiles being flung through the darkening air.

The rain had started, and it felt like darts against her face as she fought her way back to the Sea Shanty. Rory and Chloe were already on the porch, and any hope she'd had that one of them had found Shelly vanished when she saw the look of defeat on their faces. She started to cry, and was surprised when Rory put his arms around her.

"I'm sure she's all right," he said. "Chloe and I thought she might be at St. Esther's."

Daria suddenly drew away from him. St. Esther's!

"I was just about to call over there," Chloe said. "I'll be back in a minute."

Chloe went into the cottage to make the call, and Daria pictured Shelly hiding out in the church, where she would no doubt feel secure. Of course that's where she was! She even had a key. The thought of her safe inside the church was an enormous comfort.

A car turned into the cul-de-sac, and Daria walked out to meet it, hoping that Shelly might somehow be inside. She had to plant her feet wide apart to avoid being blown away as the car pulled in front of the Sea Shanty. She recognized the sheriff's-office insignia on the side of the car, and Don Tibble, one of the deputies, struggled to open the car door against the wind. He was alone, and she knew he was most likely driving around to make sure Kill Devil Hills was evacuated.

"Daria?" he asked. "Is that you?"

The hood of her windbreaker nearly masked her face. "It's me," she said. "Have you seen Shelly anywhere?"

Don leaned against the car, the wind tearing at his uniform. "Don't tell me she's gone missing again," he said.

"Yes, and this time we can't find her."

"Golly, that girl," Don said. "Well, you know you've got to get out of here now, Daria. The wind is just about too high to get over the bridge as it is. You've got maybe a half hour left."

"I can't leave without her, Don," she said.

Don put his hands on his hips and looked past her into the Sea Shanty. "Is Sister Chloe with you?" he asked.

"Yes. And Rory Taylor."

"Well, you at least have to move to a higher spot," he said.

"I want to be here in case Shelly comes back," Daria said. "I know the risks."

"I know you do," Don said. "Look, I'll keep my eye out for her, okay? And I'll alert the other deputies to do the same."

"Thanks, Don."

He glanced at the two cars in the driveway. "At least get your cars to higher ground."

She hadn't even thought of that, a sure sign her brain was not functioning as it should. "Okay," she said.

Chloe stepped onto the porch. "Hi, Don," she said.

"Hey, Sister," the deputy replied. "I was telling Daria here you folks really need to leave."

"Was anyone at the church?" Daria asked her sister.

"No answer."

Daria turned to Don. "Is there a chance you could check St. Esther's Church?" she asked. "We thought Shelly might be there. She'd probably be hiding from anyone trying to find her, though."

"Bruce is patrolling that area," Don said. "I'll radio him to check it out."

After Don drove away, Daria, Chloe and Rory moved their cars west of the deserted beach road. They plowed headfirst into the wind and rain as they walked back to the Sea Shanty, and it took both Rory and Daria to get the porch door open. Daria knew that once they were inside, they wouldn't be going anywhere—and that the likelihood of Shelly being returned to them that night was slim. She could only hope that her younger sister was safe, sleeping peacefully on a pew in St. Esther's.

They cracked the Sea Shanty windows open an inch or so, then gathered candles and a hurricane lantern in case the lights went out. Sitting together in the living room, they watched the progress of the storm on television. The weather reporter was drenched and windblown, even though he was now stationed on the mainland, having evacuated himself and his camera crew from the Outer Banks. The eye of the storm was headed for Hatteras, the reporter said. At least Kill Devil Hills would not get the full brunt of it. Still, the swirling vortex of clouds on the weather map was spinning directly over them.

It was only the clock that told them when it was time for dinner. None of them was very hungry, and there was little food in the cottage, but Daria found some cheese and a couple of cans of soup in one of the cupboards.

"I have some bread over at Poll-Rory," Rory offered.

"You can't go out there." Daria looked toward the window, where the storm shutter prevented her from seeing outside. Even so, she knew the night was black as pitch, and the sounds of the wind and the sea were ferocious. "You'll blow away."

"I think there are some rolls in the freezer," Chloe said.

They put together a dinner of cheese sandwiches and lentil soup and ate it at the kitchen table.

"We're nuts to be here," Daria said. She was thinking ahead. How would they know if the sea came up too high? Should they stay upstairs, just in case? She had faith in the Sea Shanty's construction and foundation, yet she could still remember how the Trumps' cottage had looked as it floated out to sea. That had been a winter storm, she kidded herself. This summer hurricane could simply not be that bad.

They had just finished washing and drying the dishes, when the lights flickered twice, then went off, plunging them into darkness.

Daria felt around on the counter until her hands landed on the flashlight, and she turned it on.

"Wherever Shelly is, she's going to be terrified," she said.

"Well, then maybe the next time she won't be this foolish." Chloe's words sounded harsher than the tone of her voice. Daria knew she was as worried about Shelly as she was.

"Where did you put the lantern?" Rory asked.

"In the living room," Daria said. "Let's all go in there. That's where the radio is."

In the living room, they lit the lantern and a couple of candles. Chloe sat on the couch, and Rory took a seat in the chair next to the radio, but Daria stood by one of the windows, trying to see outside through the cracks in the storm shutters. She wished they had heard something from Don about finding Shelly at St. Esther's. No news was bad news.

"Sit down, Daria," Chloe said. "There's nothing we can do to help Shelly at this point."

Daria sat down in a chair. Chloe was right. Worrying was not going to help.

Thunder began rumbling above the cottage, and flashes of lightning pierced the cracks in the shutters. They listened to the radio for a while through the static, but it soon seemed pointless. They were closer to the hurricane than any of the newscasters, and they turned off the radio and simply sat, listening to the storm.

The atmosphere inside the Sea Shanty grew strange. Despite the angry sounds outside the cottage, the breathless warmth inside was rare and, somehow, wonderful. Flames from the candles pierced the darkness, and despite her concern for Shelly, Daria felt her body begin to uncoil and relax.

"I'm thinking about leaving my order," Chloe said suddenly.

Her voice sounded alien and disembodied in the peculiar air of the living room, and Daria didn't understand.

"You mean…you'd join another order?" she asked.

"No, I wouldn't go anywhere else," Chloe said slowly. "I'm saying, I would no longer be a nun. I'd ask to be dispensed from my vows."

"Chloe." Daria was stunned. "I thought you loved what you do. I thought you loved being a nun."

"Oh, I have. I truly have. But…I don't think I can continue this way."

"*What* way?" Daria asked.

Chloe studied the glow of the lantern, as if mesmerized. "Sean…" She hesitated, then started again. "Sean took his life in a misguided attempt to try to save me from temptation."

"I don't understand." Daria wasn't certain she *wanted* to understand.

"I've always had difficulty with my vow of chastity," Chloe said bluntly. "Poverty was no problem. Obedience was no problem." She shook her head. "But I've always had a hard time denying that part of myself. That sensual, sexual part. When I was in the convent, in my early days as a sister, I'd sometimes wake up in the morning and realize that I'd had an orgasm in my sleep, during a dream, perhaps, and I'd berate myself over it. What was wrong with me, I thought, that even though my days were filled with pure thoughts, that wretched…*carnal* part of me still came out at night, when I couldn't control it. I'd beat myself up over it. But then—" Chloe looked at Daria "—then I began to think that my distress over feeling that way was ridiculous. I had done nothing wrong. What I was feeling stemmed from a normal, natural God-given part of myself, a part I was trying to deny existed. But it *did* exist. And I couldn't make myself believe any longer that there was something wrong with that."

Daria couldn't speak. She had never heard Chloe talk so openly about sexual feelings. About *anyone's* sexual feelings, much less her own. She'd thought that Chloe simply did not have those longings, that she was above them somehow. She'd been wrong. Chloe was nearly forty, and had denied that part of herself all these years. The realization brought tears to Daria's eyes, and she could feel her sister's pain from across the room.

"What did you mean when you said that Sean was trying to save you from temptation?" Rory had the courage to ask.

Chloe stared at the lantern. The thunder had receded into the distance, and only her voice filled the darkness.

"He killed himself to save me," she said. "No one knows this, but it's time I said it out loud." She let out a long sigh. Her hands were folded in her lap. "Sean and I were lovers," she said.

"Oh, Chloe," Daria said.

"It started years ago," Chloe said. "I would see him when I came here in the summer, and in those early years, I talked to him about what it was like for me, being a nun. We talked about our vows of celibacy and chastity and how hard it was to honor them. He had as much trouble with them as I did, and that reassured me. But the more we talked about it, the more we were drawn to each other."

Chloe's voice suddenly broke, and Daria moved to the sofa and put her hand over her sister's.

"I'd reached the point where I felt it was not so terrible to break that vow," Chloe continued. "I felt angry with the Church for imposing it so rigidly. It was a law made by man, not by God. I was able to rationalize that someone could be devoted to religious life and still be able to give and receive love with a partner at the same time. I *still* believe that. Completely. And so I felt comfortable about what we were doing. But for Sean, it wasn't that simple, and so a few years ago, we stopped the physical part of our relationship. He had been in turmoil over it, and I didn't want him to suffer any longer." Chloe's voice broke again, and this time she withdrew her hands from beneath Daria's to bury her head in them. Daria stroked her back. She looked across the room at Rory, whose face was somber in the light from the lantern.

Chloe raised her head again. "I was careful not to push him," she said. "I tried to be…sexless, around him. And it worked, at least until this summer. I don't think it was anything I did, in particular, but we were drawn to each other, very strongly, and then the intimacy started up again." Chloe wept openly now. "Sean was torturing himself," she said. "He called himself a sinner—I hate that word!—and he thought he was tempting me into joining him in that sin. He thought he was responsible for my downfall. That's what he called it, although I don't agree. I tried to dissuade him from thinking that way, but obviously I wasn't successful." Chloe's shoulders trembled with her tears, and Daria tightened her arm around her.

"I miss him so much," Chloe said.

"I'm so sorry, Chloe," Daria said. "And I'm sorry you've had to keep this all to yourself." She was worried about Chloe, not just because of what she'd revealed, but because she feared that her sister would come to regret having spoken so openly. She knew Chloe's confession would never have been given without the protection of darkness and the peculiar atmosphere of the night.

Chloe drew a deep breath, then seemed to pull herself together. "I have a lot of soul-searching to do in the next few weeks," she said. "A lot of praying to do. I can't bear the thought of no longer being a nun, but at the same time, I can't live with the restrictions…and I can't live with what those restrictions did to Sean."

"How can I help?" Daria asked.

Chloe nearly smiled. "Just be patient with my… preoccupation," she said. Then she suddenly pressed her hands to her temples. "I can't believe I told you all of this," she said. She looked embarrassed. "I'm sorry I dumped so much on the two of you."

"I'm glad you could, Chloe," Rory said, and Daria was touched by the tenderness in his voice.

Chloe looked at Rory. "I apologize for blowing up at you the other day when you suggested Sean's death might have something to do with your conversation with him," she said. "I was in a lot of pain then. I shouldn't have taken it out on you."

"And I shouldn't have talked to you about it right after he died," Rory said. "I knew you were grieving. I just didn't realize to what extent."

"I want to go upstairs," Chloe said, suddenly hugging her arms across her chest. "I just want to sleep through the rest of the storm. I want to wake up in the morning and find Shelly…" Her voice broke yet again. "I want to find her home and safe."

"I know," Daria said, squeezing her shoulder. "We'll find her in the morning, once the storm has passed."

Chloe got to her feet, and Daria handed her one of the flashlights. "Take this with you," she said.

She and Rory were quiet as Chloe climbed the stairs. It was a few minutes more before Daria found her voice. "I'm in shock," she said in a near whisper.

"It's very sad," Rory said.

They were quiet for another minute, still trying to absorb all they had heard, when a sudden loud crack of thunder made them both jump.

Daria drew her feet into the couch and wrapped her arms tightly around her legs. "God, Rory," she said. "Where is Shelly?"

39

RAIN POUNDED AGAINST THE ROOF AND BATTERED THE plywood covering the windows. It was scary to be in a stilt house right on the bay with this storm raging outside, but Shelly was safe in Andy's arms. He'd promised her his house could endure anything the weather threw at them, and she believed him. She always believed him.

They had made love in the pitch-black darkness, the thunder cracking through the sky outside, and now they were nestled together beneath the coverlet on Andy's bed. They were nearly alone on the bay. Andy's foolhardy next-door neighbors had refused to evacuate as well, but she guessed that these two houses were probably the only ones occupied on this stretch of water.

Andy kissed her temple. "You know we'll have to tell Daria soon," he said.

Shelly stiffened against him. She had taken the pregnancy test just that morning, and the results were positive. It was no surprise to her, but now she had to face reality. "I'm afraid to tell her," she said.

"I know, but we have to," Andy said. "We really should have told her long ago."

"She'll try to break us up," Shelly said. "That's what she's always done before."

"Well, this time is different. First of all, she likes me and she didn't like those other guys you were seeing. Second of all, this time there's a baby involved."

"She'll probably make me have an abortion."

"She can't make you do anything."

Shelly snuggled closer to Andy. It felt so good to know he would stick by her. She would not be battling Daria alone.

"Daria is the best, most wonderful sister in the world, but she's never let me live my own life."

"She's never let herself live her own life, either," Andy said.

Shelly raised her head to look at him, but it was too dark to see his face. "What do you mean?"

"I mean, she's always had to look out for your welfare. She's always put you first."

Shelly shut her eyes and let her head fall to Andy's shoulder again. She knew that was the truth, but it hurt to think about it, to think about the sacrifices Daria had made for her. Even right this minute, she was causing problems for Daria. She knew that Daria had not evacuated the Outer Banks when she should have. She'd made Andy drive by the cul-de-sac to see if Daria and Chloe had left, and she was upset to learn they had not. It was because of her. They'd been all set to leave, but they'd stayed behind for her, even though she'd left that note telling them to go.

"I'm always messing up Daria's life," she said. "But I just couldn't leave."

"I know," Andy said. He'd been more than willing to ride out the storm with her. Andy was like that. He would do anything for her.

"Did you hear that?" Andy asked. He raised his head to listen. All Shelly could hear was the sound of the hurricane battering the house. Then suddenly she heard someone yelling. Pounding on Andy's back door, calling Andy's name.

Andy got out of bed and pulled on his shorts. He ran into the kitchen as Shelly dressed. By the time she got into the kitchen, Andy was pulling open the back door, and his neighbor, Jim, nearly fell into the room.

"We need help!" Jim said. He wore a yellow slicker, and water poured from it onto Andy's kitchen floor. "They're stuck! They're trapped."

"Slow down," Andy said. "What do you mean? Who's—"

"The boat turned over," Jim said. He tried to look through Andy's kitchen window, but plywood blocked his view. "I'd tied it to the pier," he said, "but when the water rose and the wind picked up, it looked like it was coming loose. So me and Julie went out there to tie it tighter, and we didn't realize Jack was right behind us. The boat flipped onto the pier, and Jack and Julie are underneath it."

"Oh, God." Shelly covered her mouth with her hand, picturing Jim and Julie's adorable five-year-old son trapped beneath the boat. She started toward the door, but Andy grabbed her arm.

"Get the slicker out of the front closet first," he said. "I'll meet you out there."

Shelly did as she was told, then ran outside to the pier, the wind nearly blowing her off her feet. The boat was barely visible, a great, beached whale on the pier, but she could hear the screams of the little boy beneath it. There was no sound, though, from Julie, at least none that could be heard above the howling of the wind.

"Help us, Shelly," Andy said.

She could barely see the shapes of Andy and Jim standing at either end of the boat, trying to lift it off its victims. She ran to the side of the boat and tried to slip her hands beneath the rim. She could not budge it, not an inch, and her hands slipped off the wet fiberglass again and again. From beneath the boat, she heard Jack's screams turn to whimpers, and she started to cry herself.

Andy ran toward her, grabbing her arm again. "Go into the house and call 911," he shouted. "My cell's on the counter. I'm going to get Daria."

Then Daria will know, she thought, but they had no choice. They needed help, and they needed it right away. She fought against the wind and rain into the house as Andy ran up the road toward his van, where he'd parked it away from the threat of the sound.

In the kitchen, Shelly found Andy's phone and began to dial. Her fingers shook so violently that she could barely press the numbers, and it wasn't until she'd tried dialing them for the third time that she realized why her call wasn't going through: the cell towers were down.

40

"WHAT'S THAT?" DARIA STARTED AT THE THUMPING SOUND. She and Rory were still talking in the Sea Shanty living room, but the sudden pounding from the front porch had interrupted them. Standing up, she walked toward the door.

"Maybe one of the shutters came loose," Rory suggested, following her.

Daria saw someone open the screen door and step onto the porch. She thought it might be Don Tibble with news about Shelly, and her heart picked up its pace. Only when the man burst through the living-room door did she realize it was Andy. He was shirtless; his long hair was loose and soaking wet, and water streamed over his face.

"Andy!" she said, alarmed by the sight of him. "What are you doing here? Why didn't you evacuate?"

"I need you and Rory." Andy was winded, gasping for air. "There was an accident next door to my house. My neighbor's boat flipped over on the pier and his little boy and wife are trapped beneath it."

Daria froze. *I'm not an EMT anymore,* she wanted to say, but knew there was no time for her to surrender to her fears. She ran back into the living room to get her sneakers, crouching to tie them on her feet. "Did you call 911?" she asked.

Andy nodded. "It's taken care of," he said.

"Then let's go." She grabbed two flashlights, handing one to Rory, then clipped her cell phone to her waistband.

Stepping off the porch was like walking into a wind tunnel. "What's the wind speed, do you know?" she asked Andy as they battled their way to his van. He didn't hear her; the question was swept away by the wind. If the wind was over sixty miles per hour, they would be on their own. Emergency Medical Services wouldn't send an ambulance into wind that high.

They piled into Andy's old van, and the wind buffeted the vehicle as he drove out of the cul-de-sac.

"I think the wind is too high for them to send out a rig," Daria said. "Do you know what the wind speed—"

"Listen, Daria," Andy interrupted her. "You need to know that Shelly is at my house."

What? For a moment, Daria couldn't speak. Shelly was safe. But how had she ended up at Andy's? "She's at *your* house?" she asked. "Why would she go there?"

"Is she all right?" Rory asked.

"She's fine," Andy said. "I left her there to call 911 while I came over here."

"I don't understand why Shelly would go to your house," Daria said. "I'm sorry she put you in the position of having to…hide her, Andy."

Andy glanced at her, then returned his gaze quickly to the road. "It's not like that," he said.

"What do you mean?" Daria asked.

She felt Rory's hand on her shoulder. "We can talk about that later," he said. "The important thing right now is that Shelly is safe." Daria had the feeling that Rory understood something she was not ready—or willing—to understand herself.

They pulled into Andy's driveway, and Daria looked toward the pier. Something was going on out there, she could see the light from a flashlight, but other than that she couldn't tell where the pier ended and the sound began.

"Can you pull your car closer to the pier?" Rory asked Andy. "Shine your lights on it?"

Andy drove over the packed sand that formed his yard, until his headlights illuminated the pier and they could see the drama playing out on its surface. The boat was upside down and fully on the pier. Two people stood next to the boat, waving frantically at them, and although she could not see them clearly, Daria guessed one of them was Shelly.

She and Rory followed Andy out to the pier, trying to run, although it was like running through mud. It wasn't just the wind that made Daria's legs feel like lead; it was fear. She was afraid of what she would find on the pier. She used to meet emergencies with courage, confidence and a rush of adrenaline. The adrenaline was still there, but she'd left the courage and confidence at the scene of that April plane crash.

"The phone was dead," Shelly screamed the words at Andy. "I couldn't call 911."

Daria pulled her cell phone from her waistband and pressed it into Shelly's hand. "Go in the house and call," she instructed her, trying to make her voice heard over the wind. "Tell them we need to extricate two people from beneath a twenty-two-footer." She knew they would be lucky to get anyone to respond to this call, much less the equipment they might need to extricate the victims.

"No, don't go!" Andy's neighbor yelled at Shelly. "We need all of us to lift the boat."

Daria gave her sister a little shove. "Go, Shelly," she said. Then she turned to the neighbor, whose dark hair was plastered to his head, his face creased with fear and worry. "We can't lift the boat until I assess their injuries," she said. "We could make things worse." She shined her flashlight into the water. It was lower than normal. "Is the sound on its way down or up?" she asked Andy. She knew that during the first hours of hurricane, the sound could nearly empty itself, only to come back with a ferocious roar and serious flooding.

"Up," Andy said.

"That's what flipped the boat," the man said.

The rising tide could be either good or bad, Daria thought. The higher water might lift the boat from the pier and free its captives, but it could also make their work far more difficult.

She dropped to her knees, shining her flashlight beneath the boat. The tiny boy, pinned beneath the center of the boat, let out a wail when the light hit his eyes, and he reached toward Daria with his one free hand. She slipped her fingers into his. "Where do you hurt?" she asked him.

The boy only cried in response to her question. It looked as though the frame of the short, angled front windows was across his chest, probably breaking some of his ribs, and she could see a gash on his thigh. A small amount of blood had pooled on the pier beneath his leg. She squeezed the boy's hand. "I'll be right back, honey," she said. "I want to check on your mommy."

She crawled on her stomach toward the stern of the boat where the woman was pinned. She could not quite reach her, but managed to get her arm under the boat far enough to touch her fingers to the woman's throat, where she felt for a pulse. Beneath her fingertips, the pulse was faint and irregular, but at least the woman was still alive. How she was pinned, though, Daria couldn't determine. If her legs were crushed and they raised the boat from her body, she could die within seconds. But they had little choice at this point. They had to lift this boat, or both the woman and her son would perish beneath it.

"They're both alive," she shouted as she slipped from beneath the boat and raised herself to her knees. Rain whipped against her face, and when she spoke, the three men leaned close to hear her. "You guys try to lift the boat enough for me to pull them out, okay?" She saw Shelly running from the house toward them. "What did they say?" Daria called to her.

"It's too windy, they said. If it dies down, they'll send an ambulance."

"What do they mean, it's too windy?" Andy's neighbor said. "They've *got* to send one!"

"Right now," Daria said to the man, "put your energy and your anger and your fear into lifting this boat. Come on, Shelly. You can help, too."

She had seen it before, even in herself, that superhuman strength that coursed through otherwise normal men and women in the moment of crisis, so she wasn't surprised when the three men and Shelly were able to lift the boat by a few inches. Daria dived beneath it, grabbing the little boy and pulling him clear of the boat. "Can you hold it up another minute?" she asked as she scrambled toward the stern for the woman.

"It's coming down!" Andy yelled. "Get out, Daria. Get out!"

Daria quickly retreated from beneath the boat just as it rocked back onto the pier. It caught her right index finger, and she stifled a scream. Her finger would be badly swollen and bruised within minutes, but that injury was nothing compared to what this boy and his mother were enduring.

She felt torn between attending to the boy and trying to extricate the mother, but the light of her flashlight on the boy's pale face told her how desperately he needed her attention. The pressure of the boat must have been serving as a tourniquet of sorts, and now the blood gushed freely from his leg.

"Shelly!" She tore off her windbreaker. "Come here and press this against his leg."

Shelly knelt next to the boy, her hands over the windbreaker.

"Press hard," Daria said. "Really hard. It's the only way to stop the bleeding." She turned back to the boat and positioned herself near the stern.

Rory grabbed her shoulder. "You can't go under there again," he said. "It's too hard for us to hold the boat up. You nearly got crushed last time."

"You just have to hold it up longer." She dropped to her knees and realized she was kneeling in several inches of water. Panic coursed through her. The sound was rising far too quickly for comfort.

"On the count of three!" Rory shouted. "One...two... three." Daria saw the hull of the boat rise up in front of her. She dived beneath it, grasping the woman's clothing with her hands and tugging backward, but suddenly the water poured over the woman's face, trapping her. *Drowning* her. Daria found herself in the middle of one of her nightmares. She could not truly see the woman's face, could not see brown eyes or a widow's peak, but in her mind the woman became the young, dying pilot. Thrashing with her arms beneath the boat, she reached for the woman's clothing once more. Water splashed into her own face just as she was taking a breath, and she had to let go, choking and coughing. Someone's hands were on her, pulling her out from beneath the boat, and she gagged as she struggled to catch her breath. In an instant, a wall of water swept onto the pier, lifting the boat, and Daria saw Rory plow beneath the stern, pulling the unconscious woman to safety before she was dragged into the sound.

"Get them off the pier!" Andy said, and Daria saw that Shelly was already doing that, carrying the little boy in her arms, through the rising water on the pier, to the driveway and away from the sound. Daria struggled to get to her feet, and could only do so with Andy's help. Rory or the husband, she wasn't sure who, carried the woman to the driveway. Daria ran after them, moving as quickly as she could through the water on tremulous legs. She knelt down next to the woman, feeling again for a pulse.

"There's blood everywhere, Daria," Shelly called to her from the side of the little boy. "I'm pressing hard, but it's not stopping."

The woman had no pulse, nor was she breathing. "I know CPR," Rory said. He was suddenly kneeling on the other side of the woman. "You take care of the boy."

Daria called to Andy. "Do the compressions, Andy," she said. Andy had never been put to the test, but she knew he could do it; she'd taught his CPR class. "Rory can do the breathing."

She ran over to the boy, who was unconscious, but breathing. Shelly's hands were covered with his blood, and Daria said a quick prayer that the boy had no blood-borne diseases. "We need to get them to the ER," she said. She was wondering exactly how they were going to do that when she heard the sweet call of a siren somewhere on the other side of the wind. "Thank God," she said out loud.

"I hear a siren!" Andy's neighbor said. He was sitting near the boy, looking dazed and helpless.

Within a minute, the ambulance pulled into the driveway. It was staffed by only one paramedic—Mike—and an EMT, who was driving. But it didn't take long before they had the woman intubated and the boy bandaged, and both of them placed in the ambulance.

"Rory and I will go with them in the rig," Daria said to Andy. "You take Shelly back to the Sea Shanty, please."

"No," Shelly said. "I'm staying with Andy."

Daria turned to Andy. "What's going on?" she asked.

"There's no time to talk about it now," Andy said. He was pushing her toward the ambulance, but Daria held her ground. "Tell me," she said.

"Shelly and I have been together for a couple of years," Andy said. "I'm sorry I didn't tell you. She was afraid you'd try to break us up if you knew. Okay? Now get in the ambulance."

Daria backed away from Andy, stunned.

"Daria?" Mike called from inside the rig. "Let's go!"

With one more glance at her sister, she turned and ran toward the ambulance.

41

DARIA WALKED OUT OF THE TREATMENT ROOM IN THE NEARLY empty ER. Rory, who had been waiting on one of the chairs in the hallway, stood when he saw her.

"They're going to be all right," Daria said, walking toward him.

"Both of them?" Rory asked.

Daria nodded. The woman had not looked good in the ambulance, but after two hours in the treatment room she was breathing on her own and alert enough to ask about her son.

"Thank God," Rory said, and he drew her into a hug. Daria closed her eyes, resting her cheek against his shoulder for a moment before pulling away.

"You're soaking wet." She brushed her hand over the damp front of his shirt.

"How can you tell?" he asked. "So are you."

Her wet clothes clung to her body, but she had not given them a thought until this moment. Suddenly, she felt cold.

"There's nothing more we can do here," she said. "Woody—the EMT—said he can give us a ride home."

She sat in the passenger seat of Woody's car, barely noticing how the wind pushed them around on the deserted roads. Shingles and twigs flew against the car's windows, and she didn't even blink when they hit the glass in front of her face. Woody and Rory were talking, about the storm or the hospital; Daria didn't know or care. She felt shaky and strange. She still hadn't absorbed all that Chloe had told them earlier that evening—that conversation seemed like a bad dream from weeks ago. And then there was the revelation about Shelly and Andy. She did not truly know either of her sisters.

Woody let them out in front of the Sea Shanty. At least two of the porch screens were torn, flapping wildly in the wind like a trapped bird.

Rory leaned close to her ear. "I should check on Poll-Rory while I'm out here," he said.

Daria stared at the front door of the dark Sea Shanty, not wanting to go inside, not ready to explain the past few hours to Chloe, if she happened to be up. "I'll go with you," she said, shouting above the wind.

Rory nodded. He put his arm around her and they plowed their way across the cul-de-sac.

Inside Poll-Rory, the darkness was disorienting, and the wind groaned and whistled. Daria stood in the living room, feeling lost and cold. The storm had brought frigid air with it, and she shivered in her wet clothes. Her sore finger throbbed. Rory tried the switch for the overhead light, but the power was, of course, still out.

He shined his flashlight toward a cupboard at the rear of the room. "I have a lantern in that closet," he said. "And matches in the drawer in the kitchen. Why don't you take care of that, and I'll find us some dry clothes to change into."

He disappeared into one of the bedrooms, and, by the weak, yellow beam of her own flashlight, Daria found the lantern, checked the oil and lit the wick. In a moment, Rory reappeared. He handed her a bundle of soft fabric and pointed toward another bedroom. "Why don't you change in there. There are towels in the bathroom."

The wet clothes stuck to her body like a thin layer of cold plaster. She peeled them off, underwear and all, and hung them over the shower rod in the bathroom. Rory had given her one of his sweatshirts, either navy blue or black, she couldn't tell which in the fading glow from her flashlight, along with gray sweatpants that were way too large for her. She put the clothes on over her bare skin, tried unsuccessfully to run her fingers through her wet hair and walked into the living room.

Rory, too, was in sweatpants and sweatshirt, standing in the middle of the room, holding the lantern. He smiled at her. "Feel better?" he asked.

"Physically," she said, sitting down on the sofa. "But I'm...still pretty shaken up by everything that happened tonight."

"How about something to drink?" he asked. "Power's out, so I can't make anything hot. There's iced tea. Wine. Beer."

"Wine." She rested her head against the back of the sofa and closed her eyes while he carried the lantern into the kitchen. A moment later, he handed her a glass of wine, and she took several sips from it before placing it on the coffee table.

Setting the hurricane lantern next to her glass, Rory sat down near Daria on the sofa. He looked toward the boarded windows, which rattled in the wind. "I have a feeling there's still more to come," he said. "I wonder what part of the storm is over us now?"

"We've been spared, so far," Daria said. "Let's hope it continues that way. I wish Shelly weren't right there on the sound, though." She looked at Rory. "Why have my sisters kept their lives secret from me?" she asked, hoping Rory didn't hear the catch in her voice. "I thought I knew both of them so well.

I thought I knew everything about them, that they loved me and trusted me and knew I'd be there for them, no matter what. I failed them somehow. And I feel…betrayed and hurt and just plain confused."

Rory rested his arm across the back of the sofa and touched her shoulder with his fingertips. "Well, Chloe could hardly tell anyone what was going on with her and Sean Macy," he said. "And Shelly…" He looked away from her, toward the dark ceiling, as if this was difficult for him to say. "I remember you telling me that you were pleased she wasn't involved with anyone. And you told me you put an end to a couple of relationships she'd had. So, I don't think it's surprising that she would keep this relationship from you."

Daria lowered her head. She wasn't certain what she would have done had she known about Shelly and Andy. While she didn't think she would have tried to end their relationship, she no doubt would have intervened to make sure that Andy treated her sister well. "I thought Shelly was content with her life," she said. "I thought she wanted nothing more than long walks on the beach and stringing shells for her necklaces." How could she have wanted so little for her sister? "I thought I was giving her everything she needed. I didn't know she needed more than what I could provide. I bet she was actually seeing Andy some of those times she told me she was out walking."

"Well," Rory said, "from the little I saw of them together tonight, it seems that Andy is taking good care of her."

Images from the pier suddenly flashed into her mind: the little boy reaching for her hand from beneath the boat; the woman's face as the water threatened to pull her under. "I'm glad you went with me tonight," she said. "That mother and son wouldn't have survived without your help. I think, somehow, we were meant not to evacuate. If we had, they would be dead."

"Whew," Rory said with a shudder. "I hadn't thought of that." His fingers touched her shoulder again, lingering there a moment, and she wanted to move closer to him to receive more. "I thought you were incredible," he said. "I know you must have been afraid, since you haven't worked as an EMT for a while, but you sure didn't let it show. I couldn't believe the way you just dived under that boat to get the little boy. You weren't even thinking about yourself. *I* was more afraid for you than you were for yourself, I think. Then when the water washed over the woman…" He shook his head. "I thought it was going to drag all of us out into the sound."

Daria smoothed a tear away from her cheek with her fingertips, and Rory must have known she was crying, because he moved closer, putting his arm around her shoulders.

"Did it remind you of…Grace's daughter?" he asked. "Seeing the woman go underwater like that, when she was trapped by the boat?"

It touched her deeply that he was thinking of that, that he understood so well. Lowering her face to her hands, she let the tears come.

Rory stroked her hair, letting her cry for a minute, then pulled her into his arms. She felt his warmth and strength, the seductive comfort of his embrace. They were quiet for a moment and, as her tears abated, she became aware of the pressure of his arm against the side of her breast, bare beneath the sweatshirt. The sensation was delicious and provocative, and before she had time to think, she lifted her head from his shoulder and found his mouth with her lips. She felt his surprise; for a second, his body stiffened. Then he reached between their faces with his fingers, drawing back from her to look into her eyes, to touch her lips. In a moment, he was kissing her again, this time with a fever she had not expected. Impulsively, she straddled him, catching her breath when she felt his erection, already hard, already teasing her, from beneath the layers of soft fabric that separated them. His hands stroked her back through the sweatshirt, and she was the one to pull the shirt over her head and drop it to the floor. But he needed no more invitation than that to take over—to lay her down on the sofa, finish undressing her, cover her body with heated kisses. He slipped inside her and rocked with her in the lantern-lit darkness, until her body burned and the howling of the wind was forgotten.

She lay next to him, naked, afterward, and he reached over her to lift pieces of their clothing from the floor and lay them across their bodies, rubbing her arms and back through the fabric to warm her. Brimming with love for him, she turned her head to press her lips against the warm, quick pulse in his neck.

"Do you realize how long we've known each other?" Rory asked. "I think I've known you longer than anyone else, outside my family."

Daria smiled. "Who would have guessed back when we were kids, pulling crabs out of the bay, that we'd be lying here like this right now?" she said.

"I admired you back then, just like I admire you now. You were so strong and self-confident. I always felt as though I was in competition with you, even though you were younger than me. You were the best at everything. You caught more crabs, you could cast your fishing line the farthest, you could wallop anybody at volleyball and build the highest sand castle on the beach. You were something else." He gave her a squeeze. "You still are."

She felt his lips press against her temple. "I had an agonizing crush on you back then," she said.

Rory laughed. "You did?" he asked. "I had no idea. *I* had a crush on Chloe."

"Chloe?" Daria repeated in astonishment. "She was so much older than you."

"Yeah, well, I had big dreams," Rory said. "And now she's a nun."

Daria laughed.

"I have to admit, she was never really my type," he said. "She was just such a...knockout. It was the yearning of an adolescent male for the best-looking girl on the beach."

Daria was quiet, thinking that some things never changed. Rory was still attracted to the best-looking girl on the beach: Grace. But she didn't want to think about Grace just then. Surely what Rory now knew about Grace, not to mention what had just passed between him and Daria, had changed his feelings.

Rory suddenly squeezed her tight, letting out a long sigh. "I hope what we just did wasn't a mistake," he said.

The comfortable warmth she'd been feeling turned suddenly to ice. What did he mean? It was anything but a mistake to her.

"I'm sorry," he said. "I'm not sure what got into me."

"I kissed you first," Daria said. "Remember?"

"Well, I'm sure that we were both just responding to what an emotional night it's been. Let's not let it harm our friendship. Okay?"

The pain she felt was physical, in her throat, in her chest. He didn't have a clue what this had meant to her. He could rationalize it all away. She sat up and pulled on the sweatshirt and pants, feeling his eyes on her, his hand on her back, and she wondered if he felt the icy tension coursing through her muscles.

"Well, Rory," she said, standing up. "This may have been nothing more than a response to an emotional evening for *you,* but for me it was something much more. I'm in *love* with you.

Haven't you figured that out yet?" Without waiting for his response, she turned and left the cottage, running as fast as the wind would let her across the cul-de-sac to the Sea Shanty.

42

GRACE STARED OUT THE MOTEL WINDOW, AND HER EYES ACHED from trying to pierce the darkness and the rain. Where was Rory? Where was *Shelly?* She was certain she'd heard Rory correctly when he'd told her the name of the motel where they were planning to wait out the storm. She'd checked and rechecked the name and number. Every time a new car pulled into the motel parking lot, she followed it with her eyes, hoping, hoping. She wondered if somehow she had missed them, and they were in the motel, after all, maybe just down the hall from her. She would have loved to call the front desk and ask if Rory Taylor had kept his reservation, but she couldn't. She wasn't alone in the room.

"Do you want any of this?" Eddie's voice came from behind her, where he was sitting on the bed. She glanced over her shoulder at him. He was eating chow mein from a carton.

"No, thanks." She returned her gaze to the window, although by now she knew her vigilance was futile. For one reason or another, they weren't coming. *Dear God, let Shelly be all right.*

Eddie finished the chow mein and put the empty carton on the nightstand.

"Grace," he said, "you've been standing at that window all night. Who are you waiting for?" He spoke so softly that she barely heard him above the sound of the storm. There was no accusation in his voice, only the gentle question.

"No one." She walked over to the chair at the side of the room and sat down, giving up. "Just watching the storm," she said. It had shocked her to discover that Eddie had followed her all the way from Rodanthe. She'd been angry at first to find him at her motel-room door, but now that she realized Shelly and Rory weren't coming, she was glad she was not alone. Eddie had said nothing about why she had picked a motel so far from Rodanthe, and she'd offered no explanation. Now he shifted his position on the bed, and she knew that he wanted to talk.

He leaned toward her. "I love you, Grace," he said. "And I need to know what's going on. I'm worried about you. If it's another medical problem, we'll work it out. Please let me in on what's troubling you." He was pleading with her, and she felt cruel. "It's more than Pam," Eddie said. "It *has* to be. Why are you so secretive these days? Where are you spending so much of your time?"

Most men might guess that a woman so preoccupied, so absent from home, was having an affair; but Eddie knew better. He knew she had nothing to give anyone right now.

"I'm all right, Eddie," she said. "I don't want to talk about…me, or about anything, really. I just want to go to sleep. And I can't sleep with you." Her voice broke on the last word. The thought of lying next to her husband in bed was unbearable. Because she hated him. And because she loved him.

"I'll ask them to bring in a cot," he said, reaching for the phone.

After a silence-filled half hour, a housekeeper rolled a cot into the room. Grace undressed in the bathroom, and when she returned to the room, Eddie was already beneath the covers on the cot and had turned out the light.

"I love you," he said once she'd gotten into bed, and Grace squeezed her eyes shut, pretending the clamor of the storm had swallowed his words before she'd had a chance to hear them.

She tried not to think about anything—not about Shelly or the storm or about Eddie lying nearby. Yet her mind would not cooperate, and the memory of the modeling job in Maui came to her, quick, sharp and unbidden.

She remembered every miserable detail, even the sunburn. In the mirror above the marble-topped vanity, her shoulders glowed a fiery red. It was a good thing that day had been the final shoot, because her skin would not hold up to another day of Hawaii's burning sun. But that was not the only reason she was anxious for this job to be over.

She had made great strides in her modeling career, garnering enough attention and positive commentary at the age of seventeen that she'd been hired for this photo shoot in Hawaii, along with three other models from Brad's agency. It was her big chance, and she'd been thrilled with the opportunity. Right from the start of the trip, though, she knew she was in trouble.

She'd sat with Brad on the plane. It was always that way. The other models would hang out together, while she would be with Brad. The girls were jealous of her relationship with the head of the modeling agency, and they treated her coolly. She'd learned to stick close to the only person who cared about her—Brad. He was kind and tender, and although he told her repeatedly that he was in love with her, he never pressed her for anything more intimate then a warm embrace. Although his restraint confused her, she was grateful for it. She didn't know how she would refuse someone who had done so much for her.

They had flown first class, of course, and the other models sat near them in the plane. The girls had bantered among themselves, talking openly and loudly about binging on sweets and throwing up, about sex and drugs. But the thing that had disturbed Grace most was that Brad had joined in the conversation. She was shocked to realize that he, too, used cocaine and popped pills. Somehow, he had kept that sickening fact hidden from her, but it was obvious that with these three more experienced models, all of whom seemed to know him well, he felt comfortable showing that side of himself. She'd felt small, scared and alone on the plane, and that feeling had only worsened during the five days in Maui. The only time she'd felt comfortable and confident was in front of the camera's lens.

She slathered moisturizer over her sunburn and slipped into a short black dress with spaghetti straps for the party Brad was throwing in his suite that evening. She would have preferred to stay in her sumptuous hotel room and read for her last night in Maui, but she knew that part of her success as a model was dependent on her making an appearance at events like this one. She would cut out first chance she got.

By the time she got to Brad's suite, it seemed that everyone was already high on something, and she felt nearly overcome by her social awkwardness.

"There she is!" Brad said as he moved through the crowd toward her. He held her by the shoulders and kissed her cheek, and she smelled the alcohol on his breath, although she guessed that alcohol was not all he had ingested.

She plastered a smile on her face as Brad moved her through the crowd, his arm around her waist. He introduced her to people and poured her a drink she knew she wouldn't touch. She interpreted the gaze of the other models as envy and disdain and the stares of the photographers and makeup artists as critical. The suite was smoke-filled; the music was too loud. She wondered how long she would have to stay.

"Come here," Brad said, guiding her over to the side of the room. Joey, one of the photographers, was there.

"How's my favorite model?" Joey asked. His eyes were glassy.

"Okay," Grace said. She had thought that Joey was kind of cute. He had long, curly blond hair and pale blue eyes, and she'd felt some attraction to him the day before when he'd taken pictures of her on the beach. But now the glassy-eyed look, the small white speck of chip dip at the corner of his lips, turned her off.

Brad suddenly flattened his hand against her stomach. The pressure was not intense, but the gesture was intimate and took her off guard. She tried to gently remove his hand, but he only laced his fingers between hers and pressed closer to her, kissing her cheek.

"Brad," she said, feigning a laugh as she tried to pull away. She couldn't budge, though, because Joey was pressing against her from the other side. He leaned over to nuzzle her neck, his blond hair tickling her chin. She was sandwiched between them, unsure how to extricate herself.

"Guys." She managed another weak laugh, as though amused by their attention. The truth was, she felt trapped. She was pinned against the wall by two men who were slobbering on her. Her head throbbed with the loud music and her throat burned from the smoke. She felt betrayed by Brad, who until this moment, had treated her with nothing but respect, but she tolerated their antics until Joey raised his hand to her breast. Instinctively, she flailed against their arms and stepped away from the wall.

Brad quickly took her hand. "I'm sorry, I'm sorry," he said, slipping his arm around her waist again. "Come here," he said. "Come with me."

He walked with her into his bedroom, which was shut off from the party, and she pulled in a breath of clean air.

"It's better in here, huh?" he asked. "I'm so out of it tonight, I didn't realize how bad it was out there." He took both her hands in his and looked into her eyes. "Grace," he said, "you know I love you, don't you?" The scent of alcohol on his breath was nauseating.

"Yes, I know." It came out as a whisper. She had a terrible feeling that he was finally going to ask her to sleep with him.

"Listen to what I'm going to tell you. Please. I'm on some medication, for a condition I have," he said. "And it makes me...impotent. Do you know what that means?"

"You can't have sex," she said.

"That's right." His jaw was tight. "One of the shitty cards life dealt me. So this might sound kind of...kinky to you, but the way I get off is..." He winced, and she thought he looked embarrassed. "What I'm trying to say is, I want you to have sex with Jocy and let me watch."

She gasped. *"No,"* she said. "You're crazy." She started to walk away from him, but he caught her arm.

"I'm begging you, Grace," he said.

"I barely know Joey," she said. "And even if I was in love with him, I still wouldn't let someone watch."

"I know, I know. I know you're not that kind of girl." He smoothed his hand over her hair. "Sweet Grace," he said, and she thought she saw tears in his eyes. "Please, Grace. I haven't asked much of you, have I?"

He hadn't. Up until now, he'd been nothing but generous and loving toward her.

"And I've done a lot for you, Grace," he said. "I'm asking you to do just this one thing for me."

She tried to remember how cute Joey had looked on the beach the day before, with the sun in his hair, and the way he'd grin when she'd strike just the right pose. She closed her eyes, blocking her most recent image of him: the glassy eyes, the sloppy mouth. She was seventeen. Practically no one her age was still a virgin. Even Bonnie had done it a few times. What could it hurt?

She opened her eyes and looked at Brad. "All right," she said. "But…the lights have to be really dim."

Brad smiled. "You're a good egg," he said. "Wait here."

She sat down on the bed. Her hands were damp and clammy, and she pressed them against her dress to dry them. What was she doing? She thought of all Brad had done for her. He'd paid for her classes. He'd charmed her mother into accepting her modeling. This was not such a huge favor. It was time she knew what it was like to make love to a man, anyhow. This just wasn't the place—or the way—she'd expected to do it.

In a few minutes, Brad and Joey walked into the room. Neither of them said a word to her. Brad flipped off the lights, leaving just one dresser lamp burning, then sat in a chair in the corner. Joey instantly began unbuttoning his shirt, walking toward her.

She stood up and reached behind her back to unzip her dress, but Joey turned her around with a hand on her shoulder.

"I'll do that," he said. He lowered the zipper, then slipped the spaghetti straps from her shoulders. As her dress fell to the floor, Joey pulled back the covers on Brad's bed. Then he reached behind her back to unfasten her bra, glancing briefly at her bare breasts before lowering her panties.

"Hop in," he said.

She did as she was told, glad to be covered over. Joey unbuckled his belt, unzipped his pants and lowered them to the floor, along with his shorts. She caught a glimpse of his penis, which looked impossibly huge, as he climbed into the bed next to her. When he kissed her, she shut her eyes, wondering if that speck of dip was still in the corner of his lips.

It lasted only a few minutes. Joey was not rough or mean, but he was mechanical and she felt nothing except fear and humiliation. She yelped when he entered her and gritted her teeth against the pain, praying that he would be quick. He was. When he was finished, he raised himself above her, smiling to the air, not to her. He climbed off her and out of the bed and dressed in silence. As he walked out of the room, Grace turned to look at the chair where Brad had been sitting. It was empty.

She dressed quickly and escaped from the suite without seeing Brad, without even looking for him. Once back in her own room, she took a long bath, too numb even to cry. She was in her robe, ready to get into bed, when someone knocked on her door. She froze.

"Grace?" It was Lucy, one of the other models. Not Brad. Not Joey. Breathing a sigh of relief, she opened the door a crack, and was surprised by the look of concern on Lucy's face. "Are you all right?" Lucy asked.

Why would she ask her that? Did she know what had happened? Grace felt her cheeks burn. "I'm fine," she said.

Lucy folded her arms across her chest. "You know, you're one of us now," she said.

"What do you mean?"

"This is the way Brad pays off his debts," she said.

"His debts?"

"He owed Joey for the coke. You were the payment."

"I...don't understand," she said, although she was afraid she did.

"Yes, you do, honey," Lucy said. "And you'd better get used to it."

Humiliated and enraged, Grace quit the agency the moment she returned home. Facing her mother with that decision was almost worse than facing Brad. Her mother was furious, and Grace did not dare tell her what had prompted her leaving. Both her mother and Brad tried to coerce her into sticking with her fledgling career, but she ignored their pleas.

Within a few months, she knew she was pregnant with the photographer's child. Bonnie was the only person she told. She began to dress in loose, sloppy clothes, and everyone wondered what had happened to the beautiful, stylish model. But Grace no longer cared about her modeling career. She had something better: the child who was growing inside her. Finally, someone to love who would love her back, for herself, and who would not want anything more from her than that.

43

DARIA PRIED THE MOLDING FROM AROUND ONE OF THE screens, while Chloe mopped seawater from the porch floor. They had not spoken yet that morning, not about anything important at any rate, as though they both knew they still needed time to shift from the emotions of the night before into this bright, new day. Their energy went into the physical work of cleaning away debris from around the Sea Shanty and opening the storm shutters. Daria had told Chloe about the rescue the night before at Andy's cottage, and she'd told her that Shelly was there and safe. But she'd said no more about it—and she'd said nothing about her time with Rory.

Across the street, she could see Rory removing the sheets of plywood from his windows. He waved. She waved back, a tightness in her throat.

Chloe finished her mopping. She set the mop in the bucket and put her hands on her hips. "How about a break?" she said to Daria. They had been working nonstop since dawn.

"Good idea," Daria said. "You want some lemonade?"

Chloe nodded, and Daria walked into the kitchen for the drinks. She was going to have to tell Chloe about Shelly. Now.

They moved the picnic table back onto the porch, and

Daria set the glasses of lemonade down on it and took a seat. She was surprised when Chloe sat next to her and put an arm around her shoulders.

"You're as troubled as I am this morning, sis," Chloe said, giving her a squeeze. "I'm hoping it's not because of everything I told you last night. Maybe I shouldn't have burdened you with all of that."

Daria's heart broke for her sister, and she turned to embrace her. "I'm glad you could tell me," she said, "and so sorry for all you've been through." She pulled away, and moved to the end of the bench so that she could look squarely into Chloe's eyes. "But to be honest, Chloe, that's only part of what has me upset this morning."

Chloe reached forward and held Daria's hand in her own. "What is it, then?" she asked.

"A couple of things," Daria said. She looked quizzically at her sister. "Don't you think it's strange that Shelly was at Andy's last night?"

Chloe nodded. "Yes, but I suppose she somehow knew he was still in the Outer Banks and figured he'd be a safe person to stay with."

"It's more than that," Daria said. "They've apparently been seeing each other for a couple of years."

Chloe's eyes were wide. "Andy and Shelly?" she asked. "A couple of years? Didn't you ever pick up on anything between them?"

"Not at all," Daria said. "You've seen them together. They act as if they barely know each other. Now I realize their behavior was calculated to keep us from suspecting anything."

"Do you think he's taking advantage of her?" Chloe asked.

Daria shook her head. "That was my first thought, but Andy's not like that." She shrugged. "Although, right now I'm not sure I know either of them. But I think Andy's a good person with good values, and I have to admit that, from the little I saw of them together last night, there seems to be a mutual caring between them. I'm just upset that they've kept it from me all this time. Andy and I work together nearly every day, and he never said a word."

"They're afraid you'd break them up, don't you think?" Chloe asked.

Daria sighed. "I didn't know I was considered such a shrew," she said.

"You're not a shrew," Chloe said. "You're just one of those women who loves too much."

"There's something else." Daria couldn't believe she was going to tell this to her sister.

"Spit it out," Chloe said.

"I...Rory and I made love last night."

Chloe winced. "Oh, Daria, why did you do that to yourself?"

"It was an emotional night, and..." No use offering excuses. "I just wanted him," she said. "I still do."

Chloe looked through the now-screenless porch windows toward Poll-Rory. They could hear Rory working on his cottage windows, but he was around the side and invisible from the porch. After a moment, Chloe turned her gaze back to Daria. "Well," she said with a rueful smile, "who am I to cast stones?" Her gaze suddenly shifted toward the beach road. "Is that Andy's van?" she asked.

Daria saw the van turn into the cul-de-sac. She stood up as Andy drove into the Sea Shanty driveway. He walked around the car and opened the passenger-side door for Shelly, and Daria was moved by his chivalry. Shelly got out of the car, and for the first time, Daria realized how perfectly matched they were, physically at least, with their long blond hair and tall, slender bodies. She held the door open for them as they walked onto the porch.

"Julie and her little boy are at the hospital in Elizabeth City," Andy said. "Jim says they're going to be okay. Thanks for coming over, Daria."

"I'm relieved to hear that," Daria said. She glanced at Chloe. "Why don't you two have a seat?" She motioned toward one of the picnic-table benches. "I explained to Chloe that you've been seeing each other, but I think we'd both like to…have a better understanding of what's going on."

Andy and Shelly sat down as a unit on the bench, holding hands. Shelly looked nervous, and Daria felt sorry for her. Still, she was angry with both of them for their dishonesty.

"It's just like I told you last night," Andy said. "Shelly and I have been seeing each other for two and a half years. I apologize for not telling you, Daria. I tried a few times, but you always started talking about how Shelly needed to be protected from men, and I was afraid of what you'd say. Or what you'd do."

Chloe had brought two rockers onto the porch, and Daria lowered herself into one of them. Her mind raced back over the previous two years, hunting for clues she might have missed. She could remember a few conversations with Andy in which he'd talked to her about Shelly's need for more freedom. She'd told Andy he didn't know Shelly well enough to understand.

"I'm really angry with you, Andy," she said, leaning forward. "You lied to me."

"No, I never lied," he said. "I just never said anything about what was going on."

"Shelly is…she's vulnerable," Daria said. "Do you know what that means?" She was not sure either of them understood the meaning of the word. "She needs to be protected."

"Not as much as you think," Andy said.

"I can take perfectly good care of myself," Shelly finally spoke up. "You worry too much about me, Daria."

"Besides," Andy added. "I wouldn't let anything bad happen to her. I love her. I—"

"If you'd known about me and Andy, you would have tried to ruin it," Shelly interrupted him. "You ruined things with my other boyfriends."

"That was different," Daria said. "No matter what you think, Shelly, those guys were going to hurt you." Was that true? she suddenly wondered. Had she really known those two young men well enough to know that about them?

"There's something else you need to know," Andy said. He glanced at Shelly. "Shelly is pregnant, and we're going to get married."

Chloe groaned, and Daria felt her patience snap. "I thought you weren't going to let anything bad happen to her," she said, unable to mask the sarcasm in her voice.

"It's not a bad thing," Shelly said. "I'm happy about it. I want to have a baby. And I want to marry Andy."

"You can't have a baby," Daria said. "Shelly, sweetheart, I'm sorry. You're just not able to take care of a baby. You'll have to…consider options." She would have suggested an abortion, but found she couldn't with Chloe sitting right there. Chloe might be a rebel where the Church was concerned, but Daria knew she was still passionately opposed to the idea of abortion.

"Let's not get ahead of ourselves, here," Chloe said. "How far along are you, Shelly?"

"Not very," Shelly said.

"She's only missed one period," Andy said. "But she's not having an abortion."

"Well, we have time, then," Chloe said. "Time to look at your options and figure out what's best for both of you *and* the baby."

Chloe continued talking, impressing Daria with her calm, supportive approach. Daria knew enough to stay out of the conversation, because right now she was not thinking clearly. Her mind was torn between what was going on here on this porch, and the sound of Rory working on the windows across the street. How did Rory feel this morning? What was *he* thinking?

Soon Zack would return with the Wheelers, and soon Grace would swoop down again on Poll-Rory. Her one sister was grieving an illicit affair and facing the end of her life as a nun. Her other sister was pregnant with a child she couldn't possibly raise herself. And neither sister had seen fit to confide in her.

And she felt, suddenly, very much alone.

44

THE MUSCLES IN HIS ARMS ACHED WHEN RORY WENT INSIDE the cottage after taking the plywood off the windows. He could have waited to do it until Zack came home and could help him, but he'd been anxious to get some sunlight back into Poll-Rory. The cottage had sustained very little damage in the storm, and he knew he'd been lucky. There were some bare patches on the roof where he would need to reshingle, and a piece of driftwood blown up from the beach had torn a chunk from the siding, but other than that, Poll-Rory was relatively unscathed.

The answering machine blinked from its perch on the kitchen counter. The phones must be working again; the electricity had come on sometime before he'd gotten out of bed that morning. There were two messages, the first from Zack, telling him he would be returning to Kill Devil Hills that afternoon. The second message was from Cindy Trump.

"Are we still on for today, Rory?" she asked. "I don't know if you're back yet—I assume you evacuated. But I'm around, if you still want to get together. You don't need to call. Just show up when you can. I'll be here all day, mopping up."

He'd forgotten his appointment with Cindy, but he was pleased by the reminder and the fact that she was able to meet.

Just as he clicked off the answering machine, the phone rang. He picked up the receiver.

"Rory?"

"*Grace,*" he said. "I'm sorry if you went to the motel and I wasn't there. We ended up not evacuating."

"I wondered what happened," Grace said. "I was just hoping all of you were all right."

"We're fine," he said. "It seemed like a horrendous storm when it was over our heads, but at least here on the cul-de-sac, it didn't do too much damage. Are you in Rodanthe? How is it down there?"

"Some of the cottages close to the water really took a beating," Grace said. "But our…my house is fine. So, why didn't you leave?"

"It's a long story." It seemed as though all that had occurred the night before had taken days to transpire, not mere hours. "Shelly was afraid to leave the Outer Banks," he said. "So when it came time to evacuate, we couldn't find her."

"Oh my God," Grace said. "Where was she? Is she okay?"

"We searched everywhere, looking in abandoned cottages and all over the beach. We finally had to give up. Daria was really upset."

"I can imagine."

"The power went out and the phones weren't working." He remembered listening to Chloe's confessions in the darkness. He would skip over that part. "Then Daria's co-worker, Andy, suddenly showed up to tell us that his neighbor's boat had flipped up on the pier, and a woman and little boy were trapped beneath it. So, Daria and I went over there to help." The image of Daria throwing herself beneath the boat to save the child was still fresh in his mind. "And that's where Shelly was. It turns out she and Andy have been involved for a while."

Grace was silent for a minute, probably trying to absorb all he had just said.

"Involved?" she asked. "You mean, dating?"

"I don't know if *dating* is the right word," Rory said. "But they've obviously been more than friends. We didn't get to talk about it much because things were too crazy over there, trying to extract the people from under the boat and getting them to the ER."

"Are they all right?" she asked.

"They were, last I heard," Rory said.

"Rory…could we get together tomorrow? Up there?"

For the first time, he didn't feel enthusiastic about seeing her. His mind was still on Daria. He winced when he remembered her telling him she was in love with him. Those words had taken him by surprise, and he'd felt guilty, as though he'd used her by making love to her. He'd thought Daria was the type of woman who could not be used, who would never do something she did not have completely under her control. She seemed invulnerable—so independent and strong and self-sufficient—that he hadn't seen the need in her for anyone, much less for him. His body had responded with instant arousal when she'd kissed him, and he had not considered stopping himself. He'd treated it almost like one more activity with his old friend, like crabbing or fishing. He hadn't realized that, for her, it meant much more than that. He shouldn't have let it happen. Yet, it had been so damned *good*. And he knew he would rather spend tomorrow afternoon pulling crabs out of the bay with Daria than spending time with Grace.

"Why don't we talk again tomorrow," he said. "See how our schedules pan out."

She hesitated once more. "All right," she said. "But I really would like to come up there."

"We'll talk then," he said. "And I'm sorry again about standing you up at the motel."

He hung up the phone, and stared at the receiver for a minute before getting up and walking to the front door. There was one more woman he needed to apologize to this afternoon.

Chloe was on the front steps of the Sea Shanty, sweeping away the eelgrass that the storm had brought to their door.

"Looks like you lost some screens," he said.

Chloe barely glanced at him. "Yes," she said. "But that's about the worst damage that was done, fortunately. To the cottage, anyway." She darted her eyes in his direction again, and he had the feeling she knew what had happened between him and Daria the night before. Maybe, though, it was just his imagination—or his guilt—at work. Maybe she was simply alluding to the trauma suffered by Andy's neighbors. Or more probably, to the embarrassment she herself had suffered when she'd admitted to him and Daria about her affair with Sean Macy.

"Is Daria in?" he asked.

"She's up in her room," Chloe said.

"Would it be all right if I went up?"

"Why not?" Chloe said. "I guess there's not much mystery left between the two of you, huh?"

Ouch. "Chloe…" he began, not sure what more he could say.

Chloe sighed and leaned on the broom. "Don't listen to me, Rory," she said. "It's just that my sisters are getting jerked around right now, and it's upsetting me."

"I'm not jerking Daria around," he said.

"What would you call it?" she asked. "In spite of the fact that you're involved with someone else, you have sex with a woman who loves you dearly, who would do anything for you. I'm not excusing Daria's behavior, but at least her motivation was noble. She did it because she's crazy about you."

He didn't know what to say, so he said nothing, just walked past her into the cottage and up the stairs.

The door to Daria's room was open. She was sitting cross-legged on her bed, architect's drawings spread out in front of her. He knocked on the open door, and she looked up.

"Hi," he said.

"Hi."

"I thought I'd come see how you're doing," he said.

She bit her lip and lowered her eyes to the drawings, pushing them around with the tips of her fingers. He walked across the room and sat down on the edge of the bed, rescuing her hand from its futile wandering across the drawings and holding it on his knee.

"I'm sorry, Daria," he said. "I didn't mean to hurt you."

"It wasn't your fault," she said. "I started it. I shouldn't have done that if I wasn't prepared to accept the consequences."

"You know I care about you, don't you?" he asked.

She uttered a small laugh, and he knew his words sounded pale, meaningless and, he feared, patronizing.

"I didn't know how you felt," he said. "And…it caught me off guard when you told me." There was more he wanted to say. He wanted to tell her he needed time to sort out his feelings for her, to figure out why, if she were to kiss him at that moment, he would do it all over again. But he knew it wouldn't be fair to say that to her right now. It would only ease his burden and add to hers.

She looked at him squarely. "Shelly's pregnant," she said. And then she began to cry, drawing her knees up to her chest and burying her head against them.

"Oh, no." He wanted to pull her into his arms to comfort

her, but remembered that was how things had gotten out of control the night before. Instead, he held her hand tighter. "What is she going to do?"

"I don't know," she said. "She wants to marry Andy and have the baby. I just can't see it."

"How...pregnant is she?" He thought of Shelly's slim figure. "She must not be very far along."

"Only a matter of weeks," she said.

"So there's time to—"

"Yes." She sighed, as though tired of the discussion. "There's time."

He hesitated. "Look," he said. "I'm on my way up to Corolla to see Cindy Trump. Why don't you come with me?"

She shook her head. Tears still streamed down her cheeks, and he reached up to smooth them away with the back of his fingers before standing up.

"I'll see you later," he said. "Take care."

The beach road was littered with shingles and shutters and the branches of small trees. Water pooled in spots, and traffic was thick with people returning to their homes and vacations. The landscape of Corolla was washed clean, its huge houses sprawling from the road to the sea. These were true houses up here, not cottages. Many of them could be considered near-mansions.

He followed the directions Cindy had left on his machine, and found her house on, of all things, a cul-de-sac. He parked in the driveway, and had to skirt an uprooted tree as he walked to her front door. Before he had a chance to knock, the door was opened, and there stood Cindy Trump in an orange bikini, looking very much as she had twenty years ago.

"Rory!" She stepped back to let him in and gave him a hug. "I can't believe it," she said. "You look even better than you do on TV."

"Thanks," he said. "And you haven't changed a bit." The trite words were the truth. Of all the people he'd met from the cul-de-sac that summer, Cindy had changed the least. She was tan, slender, blond and still did a bikini justice. She reminded him of some of the women he knew in Hollywood, and wondered if she'd paid a visit or two to a plastic surgeon or if she'd just been lucky with her genes.

She led him out to the stone patio behind her house and handed him a glass of iced tea.

"Sorry about the noise," she said, pointing to the house in the lot behind her, where workers were repairing storm damage on the roof. "It's usually very quiet here."

Rory looked at the house under repair and was reminded of the day he saw Daria working on the roof. All of these workers were men, but in his mind's eye, he was seeing Daria up there, and he felt that same rush of desire that had gotten him into trouble the night before.

"Did you evacuate?" he asked as they sat down at a glass-topped table.

"No," she said. "We're back so far from the beach, and nothing's going to blow this house away."

He was glad she didn't ask him if *he* had left the Outer Banks. He didn't feel like recounting last night's events yet again.

Cindy was a chatterbox. She told him about her husband, who sold real estate, and her two boys, who were just entering their teens. They commiserated for a few minutes about teenage boys, while Rory explored her face for hints of Shelly. There were none. The blond hair, he had to admit, was about it.

He explained the reason for his visit: he was researching Shelly's past, trying to uncover her parentage. "So," he said, "who do *you* think Shelly's mother might have been?"

Cindy laughed, crossing one long brown leg over the other. "Why, me, of course," she said. "Isn't that what everyone thought?"

He smiled. "Well, you were the right age and your cottage was nearest to where she was found," he said, as if those were the only reasons she'd been under suspicion.

"You're being very kind, Rory," she said. "Cindy Tramp. Wasn't that what the kids called me?"

"Perhaps some of them," he said diplomatically, but he could tell from Cindy's smile that her skin was quite thick.

"Well, I can assure you that I was not Shelly Cato's mother. I have to admit, though, it was probably pure luck that it *wasn't* me. I look back now and shudder over the kind of girl I was. I'm glad my kids are boys instead of girls. I would lock the girls up."

"I'm tempted to lock Zack up myself, sometimes," he said.

"It was probably just a tourist, Rory," she said. "That's why the police never came up with a suspect. Although…" She wrinkled her nose, looking out toward the ocean.

"Although?" he prompted her.

"I've always had a nagging suspicion," she said. "I really hesitate to say this. I hate to speak ill of another woman. I know how it feels."

Rory leaned forward, thinking that Cindy had truly not changed: she was still a tease. "You can't tell me that much and not tell me what you're talking about," he said.

"I always thought it was Ellen," she said. "You remember Ellen? The Catos' niece?"

He nodded.

"Well, I don't know how well you remember her, but she was pretty loose with the boys." Cindy shrugged. "Not as loose as me, I admit, but still… She could be nasty. Do you remember that?"

He remembered it very well. He'd been exposed to it only a few weeks ago.

"There was something mean about her. One time, my aunt and uncle were visiting us. They had two little kids, my cousins, and my brother and I were going somewhere, so they hired Ellen to baby-sit for them. Well, she smacked one of the kids around pretty viciously. The little girl had a couple of bruises on her arm. I know my aunt and uncle spoke to Mr. and Mrs. Cato about it, and probably to Ellen's mother, as well. That was the end of it, as far as I know. But I think about that incident from time to time. There was no denying that Ellen had been abusive. I could see her leaving a baby on the beach and not giving it another thought."

Now that she said it, so could he. "Ellen doesn't look anything like Shelly, though," he said.

"Well, I haven't seen Shelly since she was tiny," Cindy said. "But I remember she had brown eyes. Very light hair, but big brown eyes, like Ellen's." Cindy suddenly sat up straight in her chair and looked toward the sky. "Don't go by what I'm telling you, Rory," she said. "It's a big stretch from hitting a child she was baby-sitting to leaving a newborn to die on the beach." He sensed her trying to backpedal and knew that speaking her hunch out loud had made her uncomfortable. "I was probably right with my first guess. It was most likely a tourist. Maybe if you do a show about it, that person or someone who knew her will come forward with the truth."

"Maybe," he admitted, but he was still thinking about Ellen, about how she was always trying to interfere in Daria's parenting of Shelly.

"How is your sister?" Cindy changed the subject. "Polly? I remember her so well. She was the first mentally retarded person I ever really got to know. I liked her a lot."

Her words touched him. "She died a few years ago," he said.

"Oh, I'm sorry, Rory. How unfair. You know, my strongest memory of you was of your devotion to her."

"She was special to me."

"It wasn't just Polly," Cindy said. "You were always so nice to everyone. Remember that boy who couldn't catch any fish, and you—"

"Yes, yes." His claim to sainthood.

"That was unusual for a boy, to be so sensitive to other people. If I'd had to predict what you would have become, I would have guessed a social worker."

"A social worker!"

"Yeah, think about it. That's really what you do on *True Life Stories*, isn't it?" she asked. "I always get the feeling your heart breaks for the people whose stories you tell on your show. I bet some viewers think it's an act, but anybody who knew you when you were a kid would know that you've always been a sucker for people in need."

He thought suddenly of Grace. He'd been a sucker, all right, seduced by her neediness. Was that why he'd been drawn to her?

It had been the same with Glorianne. He remembered what his ex-wife had been like when he first met her, how unsure of herself she'd been, how desperate to find someone to lean on.

And then there was Daria, who didn't seem to need anyone at all. He'd been so smitten by Grace's beauty, so seduced by her need for him, that he'd failed to see the loving woman standing right in front of him.

"Cindy," he said, abruptly standing up, anxious now to get back to Kill Devil Hills. "I have a feeling you just did me a big favor."

45

DARIA CAME HOME FROM TEACHING HER EMT CLASS THAT night to find Rory waiting for her on the Sea Shanty steps.

"Isn't it a beautiful night?" he asked as he got to his feet.

She hadn't noticed. She'd gone through her class in a fog. Everyone had wanted to talk about the hurricane and the real-life drama that had played out on Andy's pier, easily the most exciting rescue of the night. She'd tried to shift the discussion to the need for emergency readiness during the heart of a storm, but no one was interested. Instead, they wanted to know how she'd gotten two people from beneath an overturned boat, with the sound rising and whirling around her feet. Supergirl, they thought, was back.

Now she looked up at the sky and saw that it was filled with stars.

"Come out to the beach with me," Rory said. He was carrying a blanket. "There's a meteor shower tonight. We can watch the sky."

Her heart was saying yes, her head, no. "I don't think so, Rory," she said.

"Come on," he pleaded. "Just for a while."

Against her better judgment, she walked with him out to

the dark beach and helped him spread the blanket on the sand. She lay next to him, and the instant her head touched the blanket, three stars sailed across the sky.

"I told you it would be worth it," he said.

How did he think she could simply lie there with him after what had happened the night before?

"How was your visit with Cindy?" she asked.

"Interesting," he said. "She looks just like she did back in the old days. Even had on a bikini."

"Did she shed any light on your story?"

"Oh, she has her theories, just like everyone else."

"What are they?"

"She has kind of a crazy one," he said. "Don't laugh. Her primary suspect is your cousin Ellen."

Another white diamond, this one with a tail, shot across the sky, but Daria barely registered its existence. She was too stunned by what Rory had just said. "What makes her think that?" she asked.

"Well, first of all, I got the sense that Cindy couldn't stand Ellen, so this probably needs to be taken with a grain of salt. She said that Ellen once baby-sat for Cindy's cousins, and she apparently hit one of the kids a few times. That made Cindy think that Ellen was capable of dumping a baby on the beach. Seemed kind of a stretch to me."

Daria shut her eyes. This was it. Time for the truth. "Cindy's very perceptive," she said.

"What do you mean?" he asked.

"I mean she's right. Ellen is Shelly's mother."

Rory sat up abruptly, turning to look at her, and she could barely see his face in the darkness. "Do you know this for certain?" he asked. "Have you known all along?"

"Shelly wasn't the only thing I found on the beach that morning," she admitted. "I also found a pukka-shell necklace that I knew belonged to Ellen. It was lying on the beach right next to the baby."

"My God, Daria. Did you ever tell anyone?" he asked.

"No one," she said. "I was horrified to realize that Ellen could have done such a thing, but she was family, and she was also one of the older kids. I wouldn't dare say anything to anyone about her."

"Did you ever talk to Ellen herself about it? Does she know that you know?"

She turned her head to look at him. "I've never said a word to anyone, until now. Ellen doesn't have a clue that I know. It's one of the reasons why I have such a hard time tolerating her. She's always trying to tell me what to do with Shelly, and she makes me feel as though everything I've done with her has been wrong. But I don't believe she really cares about Shelly; sometimes she's even cruel to her. And she's a rotten mother to her own two daughters, as far as I'm concerned."

Rory stared out at the ocean, his arm resting on his knee, and she could only imagine how he felt about her having kept this from him. Reaching up, she touched his shoulder.

"I'm sorry I didn't tell you sooner," she said. "I simply didn't want you to find out. I didn't want anyone to know."

Rory lay down again and let out a sigh. "No one will know, Daria," he said. "Revealing the fact that Ellen is Shelly's mother can bring no good to anyone, least of all Shelly. I'll just have to be satisfied that the mystery is solved for me, personally."

Daria's eyes burned with relief. "Thank you for understanding," she said.

"Come here," he said, slipping his arm beneath her shoulders and pulling her closer.

"No, Rory," she resisted. "I can't go through that again."

Rolling over, he propped himself on his elbows and looked

at her. "Remember when I told you that I saw you working on a roof?" he asked.

She nodded.

"Well, I didn't realize it was you at first," he said. "All I knew was that I wanted the woman who was up there. I wanted her *bad*. When I realized it was you, I was sort of shocked that I could have those feelings for you. I'd always thought of you more like a kid sister."

"I know you did," she said.

"This has been a wonderful summer, even without getting a story for my show," he said, "because I've gotten to know you again." He smiled at her, and she couldn't resist reaching up to touch the tips of her fingers to his lips. He turned his head instantly to kiss her hand, then looked at her again. "Our old pal Cindy and I had a little chat this afternoon that opened my eyes," he said. "You were right about me being a caretaker. Glorianne needed that. Grace did, too. You don't. And I think it's time I broke out of that role. Time I had an equal partner. I'm not quite sure how to run a relationship with someone as strong, if not stronger, than I am," he said, "but I'd like to try. If you're willing, that is."

That made her smile.

"I love you, too, Daria," he said. "The feelings snuck up on me when I wasn't looking. I'm sorry I was so blind." He pulled her close to him, and this time, she gave no thought to resisting.

46

GRACE FOUND RORY AT HIS COTTAGE, WHERE HE WAS repairing some of the siding that had been damaged by the storm. She had come without calling, afraid that if she'd called first, he might have told her he was busy, and then she would have no opportunity to see Shelly. It had been too long since she'd seen her.

Rory spotted her as she walked toward him. "Hi." He stood up, and she knew she'd surprised him.

"I was out all morning and didn't have a chance to call," she said, "so I hope you don't mind that I just stopped by."

"No," he said. "I'm just about finished up here. Why don't you wait for me on the porch?"

"Okay." She turned and walked around the cottage to the front steps. From Poll-Rory's porch, she studied the Sea Shanty. There were no cars in the driveway; Daria and Chloe were probably at work. Shelly might be at work, as well. She hoped not; she had no good reason to stop by St. Esther's today.

After a few minutes, Rory walked up the steps and sat near her on the porch. "I'm glad you're here, actually," he said. "I wanted to talk with you."

His voice was so serious that her heartbeat quickened. *There's no way he could know,* she told herself. *No way.* Unless maybe… Could he have somehow found the nurse?

"What about?" she asked.

"Well, it's a bit awkward," he said. "I need to tell you that, over the past few days, I've come to realize that I care about Daria as more than a friend."

It took her a moment to understand. "You mean… you're in love with her?" she asked.

"Yes."

She could not help but smile, despite the implications of that news for herself. Daria and Rory. She had certainly never thought of them as a couple, but it made very good sense. They were a team. "I'm glad for you," she said.

He leaned over to take her hand. "Thank you," he said. "I wasn't sure how you'd feel about it."

"I can't blame you for that," she said. "I haven't exactly been an open book with you, have I?"

"No," he admitted. "You haven't."

"Well, I've enjoyed the time you and I spent together, but I think it's really good that you and Daria found each other." She kept the smile on her face, but inside, her heart was twisting. She no longer had an excuse to come to Kill Devil Hills—or to see Shelly. She'd hoped that somehow she and Shelly could have developed a bond that would transcend her need for a relationship with Rory, but that had not happened. And now, she'd run out of time.

"I guess I won't be seeing you again, then, huh?" she asked.

"You don't need to be a stranger," Rory said, although he had to know as well as she did that there was no point in her visiting Kill Devil Hills again.

She struggled to find a way to shift the conversation to Shelly. "It must make Shelly happy, that you and Daria are together," she said. Not exactly a seamless transition, but it was the best she could do.

"I don't know if she knows yet," he said. "Daria and I just came to this conclusion last night, and I think Shelly was at Andy's."

"Oh, yes, what's that all about?" she asked.

"Apparently, they've been seeing each other for a couple of years. And Shelly is pregnant. They want to get married, but Daria's worried about—"

"She's *pregnant?*" Grace leaned forward. The rapid heartbeat again. Her doctor would have a fit if he knew the stress she was putting herself under. "How far along?"

"Not far," Rory said. "You've seen her in her bathing suit."

"She should probably have some prenatal testing, shouldn't she?" Grace proposed. "I mean, given her...you know, her...the brain damage."

"But brain damage isn't inherited," he said. "There's no reason to think her baby wouldn't be perfectly normal."

He probably thought she was an idiot. "Oh." She smiled, trying to make herself look sheepish. "Right."

"No, the real question is whether she should have this baby at all. And if she does, can she take care of it."

The baby's grandmother could help her, Grace thought, and she felt tears rush to her eyes. She quickly lifted her sunglasses from her lap and slipped them onto her face. "Well," she said, standing up. "I think it's time I was on my way. Thanks for putting up with me, Rory."

He stood up to give her a dispassionate hug. "Keep in touch," he said. "I hope things work out for you."

"Thanks," she said. She left the porch and walked across the sand to her car, not daring to look back at Rory—or across the street at the Sea Shanty.

★ ★ ★

Eddie was waiting for her in the above-garage apartment. Grace stopped short when she saw him there, and he launched into an obviously rehearsed speech.

"Look," he said, "I know I was wrong to do this, but please believe me, I did it because I'm worried about you."

"What are you talking about?"

"I followed you when you left today," he said. "I followed you all the way to Kill Devil Hills, and I saw you go to the cottage where Rory Taylor is staying. I didn't know whose cottage it was, but I asked someone and they told me. I guess…I guess that's where you've been going, huh? To see him? Was that who you were watching for outside the motel window in Greenville?"

Grace felt trapped and weary. She wished Eddie would at least yell at her, express some anger, so that she could get angry back. But that was not Eddie's style. She sat down on the sofa. "It's not what you think," she said. The line sounded as tired as she felt.

"I'm in a state of shock," Eddie said, taking a seat on the other side of the room. "The last thing I expected was another man. I didn't think you had the energy or interest for that. I didn't think that was what you wanted."

There were tears in Eddie's eyes, and she couldn't bear to look at them. "You're right," she said. "That's not what I wanted."

"Then why have you been seeing him? I don't understand, Grace. Do you want a divorce? Is that what would make you happy? I want to help you, and I don't know how."

Grace closed her eyes and felt her body sink lower into the sofa. It was all too much. Shelly was pregnant. Rory had chosen Daria over her. She might never see Shelly again. She wished she could simply crawl into bed and bury her head under the pillow. But Eddie was questioning her, begging her for answers, and somehow she had to find a way to explain to him her behavior of the past few months.

She could think of no way other than to tell him the truth.

★ ★ ★

"Great beach weather," Bonnie said sarcastically as she stood by the cottage window and stared out at the street. It was not raining, not yet, anyhow, but the clouds were thick, and there was a chill in the air. It had been this way for three days, the first three days of their week-long postgraduation vacation in Kill Devil Hills. The cottage was two blocks from the beach, a one-bedroom with a view of the street. It was the best they could afford.

Grace looked up from the book she was reading. "Maybe tomorrow will be better," she said, although she didn't personally care one way or another. She was just relieved to be away from her mother and Charlottesville, where she'd had to mask her pregnancy. Here, for the first time, she was wearing actual maternity shorts and a top that ballooned over her abdomen. She was nearly eight months along, although she knew she didn't look it, maternity clothes or not. A few of her classmates might have suspected something, but her mother attributed her weight gain to nothing more than her obstinacy. Her mother rarely spoke with her, anyway; she had not forgiven her for quitting Brad's modeling agency and for letting herself "go to pot," as she put it.

This week at the beach was not simply an idle getaway for her and Bonnie, though. They were supposed to use this time to figure out what Grace should do. The only thing she knew for certain was that she was keeping the baby. She already loved it. She'd loved it from the moment she knew it existed. Her maternal instincts were very strong—strong enough that she'd gone to a neighboring town for prenatal care, not wanting to take any chances with the health of her baby. The doctor there had tried to persuade her to put the baby up for adoption, but Grace was firm in her resolve. Her mother would have a fit, of course, and would most likely kick her out. But Grace was determined to find a way to take care of herself and her child, and Bonnie had promised to help in any way she could.

Bonnie flopped down in one of the ratty-looking chairs and put her feet up on the coffee table. "I've already run out of books to read," she said.

"You can borrow some of mine," Grace offered.

"No offense, but I'm not very interested in reading baby books," Bonnie said.

There was a sudden knock at the door, and Grace jumped. She couldn't shake the fear that somehow her mother would find out she was pregnant and show up in Kill Devil Hills to drag her home. She stiffened as Bonnie got up and walked to the door.

A woman stood on the front steps. "Hi," she said with a smile. She was probably in her late twenties. "I'm Nancy. My husband and I are staying in the cottage next door, and we don't have a TV or radio. But we heard some talk that a storm was on its way in the next few days, and we were wondering if maybe you knew what was going on. Do you have a TV in your cottage?"

"Yes, a little one," Bonnie said. "We haven't had it on much, though. I don't know what the weather report is."

Grace stood up and walked to the door. "You're welcome to come over later when the news is on," she said.

"Thanks, I'll stop by around five, if you don't mind," Nancy said. "We may leave if it's going to be like this all week. We've been planning this vacation for so long, and I can't believe how crummy the weather's been." Her gaze was on Grace's belly as she spoke, and Grace felt torn between self-consciousness and pride.

"We'll be here," Bonnie said. "There's not much else to do."

At exactly five, Nancy and her husband returned to Bonnie and Grace's cottage, and the four of them sat in the living room watching the news on the small black-and-white television.

The husband's name was Nathan, and he was an engineer with short, jet-black hair, dark eyes behind thick, wire-rimmed glasses and a bushy beard. He was very quiet, lying on the cottage floor, his back propped up against the sofa, as he focused on the TV. Nancy, though, was talkative.

"Where are you girls from?" she asked.

"Charlottesville," Bonnie said. "We just graduated from high school. This week at the beach is our present to ourselves."

"High school?" Nancy asked. Again, her gaze moved to Grace's stomach, and this time Grace felt distinct discomfort. "You're not married, then, I take it?" Nancy asked.

"No," Grace said.

"Wow," Nancy said. "When are you due?"

"Another month," Grace said.

"Do you… Excuse me for asking such personal questions, but I'm a nurse. Do you have a boyfriend?"

"No," Grace said. For some reason, she didn't mind Nancy's probing. The woman's questions were personal, but gently asked.

"Are you keeping the baby?"

"Yes, though I haven't figured out yet how I'm going to support it and me," she said.

"Won't your parents help?"

Grace laughed. "I just have a mother," she said. "And she doesn't know."

"She doesn't know?" Nancy asked, incredulous. "Is she blind?"

"I've hidden it," she said. "She just thinks I'm fat."

"Wow," Nancy said again. "What will she do when she finds out?"

"Have a heart attack." Grace laughed. "Right after she kills me."

"Why didn't you have an abortion?" Nancy asked.

"I didn't want one," Grace said simply.

"It must be scary not to know how you'll support the baby," Nancy said. "You're wise to be concerned about that. You're only eighteen, right?"

"Not quite," Grace admitted.

"Gee, honey, I think you should give some serious thought to adoption."

"No, I'll figure out a way to make it work."

Nathan yawned from his station on the floor.

"It's just that there are so many couples out there who can't have a baby of their own for one reason or another," Nancy said. "They would be able to give your baby a good home, with two parents and lots of love."

Nancy was tapping into the one misgiving that gnawed at her: she was not being fair to this baby by depriving it of two parents and the material goods it deserved to have.

"I couldn't give it away," she said.

"I understand," Nancy said. "I don't think I could, either. But you still have a month to think through that decision."

"I've thought it through," Grace said.

"Well, how has your pregnancy been?" Nancy asked.

"Easy," Grace said. "I was never even sick. Although now…I'm getting kind of nervous. I've been reading books about labor and everything. It scares me."

"You'll be fine," Nancy said.

"What kind of nurse are you?" Grace asked. "Have you ever helped at a delivery?"

"When I was a student, yes, I sure did. Right now, though, I'm an oncology nurse."

"What's that?" Bonnie asked.

"I work with cancer patients in a hospital in Elizabeth City."

"That must be hard," Grace said.

"Hard, but rewarding," Nancy said.

"So," Grace began, hungry for information, "when you were a student, what was the longest labor you ever saw?"

Nancy laughed. "You're worrying yourself into a tizzy, aren't you?" she asked. "It's not worth getting worked up about, I can promise you that. It'll all be over before you know it, and then you'll have your beautiful baby in your arms."

Grace didn't feel particularly comforted. She knew no one else she could discuss this with. "But why do women scream?" she asked. "I mean, I fell and broke my arm once, and I didn't scream even though the pain was truly unbearable. So I figure, the pain of having a baby must be thousands of times worse."

She thought there was sympathy in Nancy's eyes. "I've never gone through it myself," she said, "so I'm afraid I can't tell you anything from personal experience."

Grace thought Nathan glanced at his wife when she said that, but she couldn't be sure. His glasses were so thick it was hard to tell just what his eyes were doing.

"But every woman I've ever known has been just fine with it," Nancy continued. "Yes, they might scream, but in a couple of years they turn around and do it all over again. It's worth it to them. Really, Grace, you don't want to spend this whole last month of your pregnancy worrying about that."

Grace let her head fall back against the chair, suddenly overwhelmed by everything she had to worry about. "Worry is my middle name, lately," she said. "I don't know what I'm going to do. How do I tell my mother? Where will I live? I only have a little bit of money in my savings. At first, I can nurse the baby, right? I won't have to pay for food?"

Nancy stared at her hard for a moment before answering. "You're not prepared for this," she said, her voice now low and serious. "You need to get help from an agency. You're in Charlottesville, you said? Write down your name and phone number for me and when I get back to Elizabeth City, I'll do some research and find out where you can go to get help. Okay?"

"Thanks," Grace said. She suddenly felt less alone. Bonnie was a good friend and a loyal supporter, but she knew just as little about birth and babies as Grace did.

"And," Nancy continued, "I think the first thing you need to do when you get back to Charlottesville is to tell your mother what's going on."

She shook her head vigorously. "You don't know my mother," she said. "As a matter of fact, I don't think I can go back to the house at all. I'm getting too big. She'll know. Bonnie and I have to figure out where I can lie low during the next month."

Nancy sighed, and Grace read disapproval in her face. "This is no way to live, Grace," she said. "I'll get you that information on agencies that can help you, but I want you to promise me one thing."

"What?"

"That after this baby is born, you'll go on the Pill. You can't let this happen again. This baby you're carrying should never have been conceived."

Grace wanted to say it wasn't her fault. She wanted to pour out the story of what had happened in Hawaii. But she could have said no to Brad; she could have said no to Joey. No one had raped her. It *was* her fault.

"I know," she said. "Believe me, it won't ever happen again. Not this way, anyhow."

There were brief intervals of sunshine over the next few days, enough to encourage Nancy and Nathan to remain in Kill Devil Hills for the rest of their vacation, and enough to keep Bonnie from complaining too much. The promised storm hit on Saturday. It was not a hurricane, although there had been talk of it becoming one. It was considered a tropical storm, and evacuation was not required, although most vacationers left the Outer Banks that Saturday morning, knowing what was coming. Grace and Bonnie did not leave, however. Their lease was up the following day; they were due to be out by one in the afternoon, but Grace was not ready to let go of her time away from home. She still didn't know where she was going to go. She'd given Nancy her phone number so that the nurse could call her as soon as she had information about an agency that might be able to help her. She wished it were winter instead of summer, so she could cover her body more easily with heavy clothing. Maybe she could simply avoid her mother.

As darkness fell, the wind was wild and whistling, and the cottage shuddered violently, as though it might collapse around them. For the first time that week, Grace and Bonnie were glad they had not been able to afford a house on the ocean. Surely they would be washed away.

They had very little food left, and it was too nasty to go out for more, so for dinner, they made do with peanut butter and jelly sandwiches. The power went out shortly after dinner, taking their lights and their TV. There was one hurricane lantern in the cottage, and they lit it and set it on the coffee table. Sitting on the sofa, they watched the flame lick at the inside of the glass chimney. And that's when Grace's cramping started.

"Can peanut butter and jelly go bad?" she asked Bonnie.

"I don't think so. We just bought it a few days ago, anyway. Why?"

"I have a stomachache."

"Oh," teased Bonnie, "you're probably going into labor."

"Very funny," Grace said. But she feared that Bonnie might be right. This was not a typical stomachache. More like men-

strual cramps that came and went. But they were mild, ig-
norable, certainly not like labor would be. And she was only
eight months pregnant.

"We might as well go to bed," Bonnie said.

"Oh, God, Bonnie." Grace couldn't bear the thought of
going to bed. When she woke up, she would only have a few
hours left of her freedom. She would finally have to face the
uncertainty of her future, and that of her baby. "I don't want
to go home tomorrow."

"I do," Bonnie said. "No offense. But I want to see Curt.
And I bet the weather has been better in Charlottesville than
it's been here."

"You don't have to hide a bowling ball under your shirt
when you go home, though," Grace said.

"My mother would have known a long time ago," Bonnie
said. "She pays way too much attention to me."

Grace glanced away from her friend. Bonnie's words were
spoken as a complaint, but she didn't appreciate how good she
had it. Grace shifted on the couch, trying to find a position
that would make her stomach more comfortable. Maybe lying
down would help.

"Okay," she said, getting to her feet. "Let's go to bed."

Her sleep was fitful. She'd closed her bedroom window
against the rain, but the glass rattled in its frame, and despite
the storm raging outside, the room was hot, her sheets damp
with perspiration. Even while asleep, she was aware of the pain.
She dreamed she was in the hospital room, having the baby,
and she was screaming. She screamed herself awake, and knew
at once that she was truly in labor. This pain was not a dream.

Bonnie rushed to her side. "Grace? What's the matter?"

The room was pitch-black. Bonnie's voice cut through the
darkness, but Grace had no idea which direction it had come
from. "I think the baby's coming." She managed to get the

words out between explosions of pain. She let herself scream, throwing all of her breath and energy behind the sound, understanding now why women in labor felt that compulsion. No other sound would do.

"It can't be coming," Bonnie said, and Grace heard the panic in her voice.

Grace could not respond with words, only with gasping breaths and yet another howl of pain.

"I'll get the lantern," Bonnie said. "Wait here." Then she laughed. "Like, where else would you go?"

In a moment, she returned to the room with the burning lantern, which she set on the old dresser, and Grace could see how frightened she was. She imagined her own face held that same look of terror.

"I don't know what to do, Grace," Bonnie said, waving her hands feebly in the air. "Tell me what to do."

Grace felt helpless. What was happening to her had a life of its own, and she was completely unable to stop it. She looked at Bonnie, wordlessly pleading with her to take over.

"The nurse!" Bonnie said suddenly. "Nancy!" Bonnie ran out of the room, ignoring Grace's plea not to leave her.

She screamed in Bonnie's absence, screamed and screamed just to keep her mind off the raging pain in her body and the fact that she was alone. She was still screaming when Nancy and Bonnie rushed back into the room.

Nancy gave Bonnie instructions Grace could not make out, and Bonnie left the room. Nancy uttered words of comfort as she moved around, as if nothing unusual were occurring, and Grace suddenly felt enveloped by the nurse's calming presence. She was only vaguely aware of Nancy rearranging the bedclothes and holding the lantern between Grace's legs as she examined her. Nancy's movements, her entire demeanor, were confident and unhurried.

Placing the lantern back on the dresser, Nancy sat down on the edge of the bed. "I'm going to tell you how to breathe," she said to Grace, her voice soft and even. "It will help with the pain." Grace was aware that Bonnie was in the room again, and she glanced at her friend's face only long enough to know that she was crying. Fear always induced tears in Bonnie. Grace had seen it happen before.

She struggled to follow Nancy's instructions to breathe, calmly and slowly one moment, panting the next.

"Squeeze my hand when you have to," Nancy said, slipping her hand into Grace's. Grace clutched at her fingers.

"Now listen to me, Grace," Nancy said, leaning close to her. "Surely you now realize you can't keep this baby. You know that, right? You're simply too young to raise a baby by yourself, especially without the support of the baby's father or your own mother. You don't even know where you're going to live. You'll have to leave here tomorrow morning with a newborn baby in your arms and no diapers, no clothing, no formula and no knowledge of how to take care of it. Be honest with me, can you take this baby home to your mother?"

Grace let out a wail at the thought.

"She can't," Bonnie agreed. "You don't know her mother."

"I know you've had a fantasy of keeping this baby," Nancy said. "But it was a fantasy, just that. I can help you, though. Let *me* take the baby. Let me take it to the hospital where I work. I'll get the baby checked out and make sure it's healthy and then I'll arrange to have it adopted by a good family. That way, no one, not even your mother, will ever have to know that you were pregnant. You, me, Bonnie and Nathan. We're the only ones to know. And it can stay that way."

"She's right," Bonnie said. "I'm scared, Grace. I mean, it was one thing when you were just pregnant. But any minute there is going to be a baby here. Another life! You've got to let Nancy take it."

A boulder of pain pressed down on her stomach, and Grace screamed again. Her mind filled with jagged shards of thought. She could see her mother's face, yelling at her, forcing her to tell her how this pregnancy had happened. She could see Bonnie and herself tomorrow, struggling to keep a newborn alive. Oh, God, what if her selfishness caused the baby harm? Suddenly, through the veil of pain and terror, her idea to have the baby and keep it seemed unspeakably selfish, almost cruel.

She squeezed Nancy's hand with both of hers. "Would you call me? If you take the baby, would you let me know that it's all right? That it's been adopted...by somebody wonderful? Promise me you'd only let it go to somebody wonderful who could give it everything." Her voice broke and she clutched Nancy's hand even harder.

"Absolutely, Grace," Nancy said. "I'd do all of that. You wouldn't have to worry about anything. Just turn the baby over to me and I'll take care of it."

"This is like a miracle, isn't it, Grace?" Bonnie asked. "I mean, you happened to go into labor a whole month early, but a nurse just happens to live next door, and she knows exactly what to do and she can find a good home for the baby. You have to do it, Grace. This is obviously the way it's supposed to be."

She writhed on the bed with a fresh wave of pain. The storm pummeled the window above her head. Thunder cracked in her ears and lightning lit up the room with an eerie, unearthly pulse of flight. *Let me out of this nightmare.* She'd wanted this baby so badly, now she just wanted to be free of it. Get it out of her body. Make the pain stop. Let Nancy take it away, safe and unharmed with a future better than any she could hope to give it.

"*Yes,*" she wailed. "Please take it, Nancy. Please make this be over!"

★ ★ ★

The baby girl was born at four-fifteen in the morning, when the ferocity of the storm had dissipated, and Grace had reached the end of her own strength and will to fight. Through a fog, she heard the cries of her baby, and she stretched out her arms into the darkness toward the sound.

"Let me see her, Nancy," she said weakly.

"No, no," Nancy said. "Trust me, Grace. It will be easier for you if you don't see her."

"She's right," Bonnie's voice came from somewhere beside her. "It might be harder for you to give it up…give *her* up…if you see her."

She was too tired to fight, and she let herself be lulled into sleep by the release from pain and the peace and quiet that had finally come to settle outside her window.

It was nine-thirty when Grace opened her eyes the following morning, and the night came back to her like a bad dream. She felt the dampness on the bed beneath her bottom, and reached down to touch the towel Nancy, or perhaps Bonnie, had folded beneath her. She'd had her baby. She'd given it to Nancy. That had been the right thing to do; Nancy could take good care of the baby. But there was no reason why Nancy had to find it a permanent home. The baby could stay in a foster home! As soon as Grace got up on her feet again, as soon as she had a place to live and a job, she could take the baby back. All her desperate fears of the night before seemed out of proportion to the situation now.

"Bonnie?" she called out.

Bonnie came into the room, deep bags under her blue eyes. "You're awake!" she said. "How are you feeling? Are you terribly sore?"

Grace raised herself to her elbows. "I want to see my baby," she said.

"You can't, Grace," Bonnie said. "Remember what Nancy said? It'll just make it harder for you if you see it."

"Not *it*," Grace said. "Her. And I've thought about what I said last night. What I agreed to. I don't want her to have the baby adopted out. I was feeling crazy last night. If Nancy could find a foster home or something until I can figure out what to do, then I can take the baby."

"Oh, Grace, you're still not thinking clearly." Bonnie sat down on the bed. "You have to do what's best for the baby. And also, what's best for *you*. You haven't even ever had a boyfriend, Grace. You haven't even gotten to live. I've always thought it was crazy that you were going to tie yourself down with a baby, but I knew that was what you wanted, so I went along with it. But this is such a perfect solution. The baby will be fine. She'll have a better life than she would have with you—you have to admit it. And then you can get on with your own life."

It bothered her that Bonnie could not understand. "You weren't pregnant with this baby for eight months," she said, starting to cry. "You didn't carry her around right beneath your heart. You didn't feel her moving around inside you. You talk about the baby like she's some…nuisance, or something. She's my *child*. I may not be able to give her every single toy she sees or dress her in perfect, matching little outfits, but I'm going to give her so much love and attention that she's never going to feel deprived of anything."

Bonnie sighed tiredly. "What do you want me to do?" she asked.

"Go next door and ask Nancy to bring the baby over so I can finally see her, and then I can talk to her about how I can get the baby into foster care while I'm getting on my feet."

"All right," her friend said, standing up. "Remember, we have to get out of here by one. And we don't have a thing to eat, so after I get Nancy, I'm going to go to the store and get some bread and some sanitary napkins for you. Nancy said you'd need them."

"Okay, but bring the baby over first, please?"

"Okay."

Grace got out of bed, slowly, after Bonnie left the cottage. She cleaned herself up in the bathroom, and she was horrified to see several bloodied towels in the wastebasket. They would have to remember to get rid of them before they left. She improvised a sanitary pad for herself out of a washcloth and got dressed. She couldn't wait to see her baby.

She walked out of the bathroom to find Bonnie in the doorway of the bedroom. Her face was white.

"They're gone," Bonnie said.

"Who?" Grace asked, although she was afraid she knew the answer.

"Nancy and Nathan," Bonnie said. "The cottage is deserted. Their car and suitcases and everything are gone."

Struck instantly by an overwhelming grief, Grace sat down on the bed. Her mind raced. "I don't even know their last name. Do you?" she asked.

Bonnie shook her head. "I don't think they ever told us," she said.

"Oh, God, Bonnie. My *baby*. They took my baby." She began to cry, and Bonnie moved to the bed and put her arms around her.

"I know. I'm sorry. But she'll be all right. I'm sure they left early so they could get to the hospital to make sure the baby was fine and healthy. Nancy seems like a really good nurse to me. She's going to make sure everything's perfect for your baby."

"But I'll never get to see her!"

Bonnie was crying, too. "I shouldn't have agreed with Nancy last night," she said. "I didn't realize you'd change your mind, though. It seemed to make such good sense."

Grace cried for a long time in Bonnie's arms. Then, finally, she looked down at the pillow on her bed. It was inviting. She lay down, facing the wall, and pulled the covers over her head. She felt Bonnie's hand on her back and closed her eyes.

"I'm going to the store," Bonnie said. "I'll get you the pads. Is there anything else you want? Soup or anything?"

Grace didn't bother to answer. She'd barely heard the question.

47

"My God, Grace," Eddie said. He was sitting next to her on the sofa, having moved there sometime while she was speaking. "Why didn't you ever tell me about this?"

"It was something I was trying to forget," Grace said.

"So…I'm trying to understand. Was it Pam's death that made you start thinking about this other baby? Realizing that somewhere out there you had a child living with her adoptive parents? And I still don't get it—the part about Rory Taylor. What's going on between the two of you?"

So many questions, so much he still didn't know. "I haven't told you everything yet," Grace said. God, she hated saying all of this out loud. She'd gone over it in her own mind too many times to count, and, of course, she and Bonnie had revisited the experience over the years, but to recite it this way gave it a terrible credibility. "Bonnie went to the store that morning," she said, "and when she came back, she was very quiet. I thought maybe she just felt guilty about her role in getting me to give the baby to Nancy. She tried to get me to eat something, but I just couldn't. I'd never felt so despondent. I wanted to die." She looked at Eddie. "It was the same as I felt after Pamela died."

Eddie covered her hand with his, and she didn't pull away. "Me, too," he said. The two words cut through her. She had given him no comfort, no sympathy after Pamela died. Only blame and recriminations.

"Bonnie finally started talking," she said. "She told me that when she was in the little market, everyone was talking about a newborn baby girl that had been found on the beach very early that morning."

"Oh no." Eddie tightened his grip on her hand.

"The store clerk told Bonnie the baby had been found dead. When Bonnie told me that—" Grace shut her eyes at the memory "— I was torn apart, Eddie. I'd wanted that baby. I'd been willing to turn my life inside out for her. But I thought the nurse might be right, and I'd trusted her. And she went and left my baby on the beach to be washed away like a piece of driftwood."

"Oh, Grace," Eddie said. "How awful."

"So, Bonnie called me early this summer and said that she'd found out that Rory Taylor wanted to do an episode on his *True Life Stories* show about that baby. He was going to look into how she came to be on the beach that morning."

"So, you contacted him and told him you thought you were the mother?" Eddie asked.

"No," Grace said, horrified by the thought. "I didn't dare do that. I…manipulated a meeting with him to try to find out what he knew. And what I found out was…the baby had not died. A little girl found her, and her family adopted her. And now she lives in the house right across from the house where Rory Taylor is staying. She lives with her sister. She had some brain damage from that night. It's mild, but she really does need someone to look out for her. Her sister seems to have done a good job of that."

Eddie stood up and began to pace, something he always did

when he was upset. "This is unbelievable," he said. "Who knows that the girl is your daughter? Have you gotten to meet her? Talk with her? Have you told—"

She held up a hand to interrupt him. "I don't know, with one hundred percent certainty, that she *is* my daughter. It seems crazy that in the middle of a storm, the nurse would take her out to the beach, but—"

"How many babies could have been born that night in Kill Devil Hills?" Eddie asked.

"I know, I know. I just can't make myself tell her, though, Eddie. What if I'm wrong?"

"Does she look like you?"

"Not really. She's very blond, but then, so was her father." She said the word *father* as though it tasted bad in her mouth. It did. "But she's tall and slender, just like me. Just like Pamela was. And she has seizures, Eddie."

"Marfan."

"That's what I'm afraid of. And to make matters worse, now she's pregnant. She's pregnant, she doesn't know she has Marfan's syndrome, her child might have it, it might go undiagnosed, and—"

"You're being tortured by this." Eddie sat next to her and took her hand again. He touched her cheek. "I wish you could have told me what was going on with you this summer. I would have been there for you, Grace."

"I know," Grace said. "I was too angry with you."

"I loved Pamela, too, you know."

"I know you did," she admitted. "As much as I did. And you didn't know she was sick, just like I didn't know it. She loved flying—I can't deny that. You might have encouraged her to do it more than I would have liked, but it was her choice. You only gave her that choice."

Eddie lowered his head, and she knew he was struggling for

composure. "Thanks for saying that," he said. He leaned back against the sofa. "The girl," he said. "What's her name?"

"Shelly."

"Shelly. If you truly believe Shelly is your daughter, and if she and her unborn baby are…at risk, then you have to tell her. Or, at least tell her sister so she can get her evaluated and started on any treatment she might need. You have to do that, Grace."

"But what if she's *not* my child?" Grace asked. "She's a bit fragile. I don't want to confuse her."

"Does Shelly have a widow's peak?" Eddie asked.

Grace shook her head.

"Don't all the women in your family have one?"

"Most, but not all."

"Did you ever try to find the nurse?" Eddie asked. "It seems that she's the missing link in all of this."

"There's no way to find her," Grace said. "All I remember about her was that her name was Nancy and she worked in the oncology department of a hospital in Elizabeth City, twenty-two years ago. That's not much to go on." Grace was suddenly overwhelmed by the hopelessness of the situation. "I was using a…friendship with Rory Taylor to stay close to Shelly," she admitted. "I can't believe I did that, but I did. But now he's involved with Shelly's sister, so I have no reason to go up there anymore. I want to see Shelly again. I miss her already."

"Let me help you with this," Eddie said. "Let me take on some of the burden you've been carrying around all summer, okay?"

She didn't know what he could do to help, but she was far too tired to fight on her own anymore.

"Okay," she said.

He gently pulled her closer, lowering her head to his shoulder, and for the first time since before Pamela's accident, she let her body relax against his.

48

DARIA ROLLED ONTO HER BACK, STILL TRYING TO CATCH HER breath. She stared at the ceiling of her room, while Rory traced her profile with the tip of his finger.

She had cried out. That was a first. No one had ever elicited that from her—surely not Pete—and she'd wondered if that sort of intensity ever truly happened for women outside of books and movies. Now she knew. She had never thought of lovemaking as a talent before, but Rory certainly had it, and she was glad no one else had been home at the Sea Shanty when he'd revealed it to her.

"Well," Rory said, the tip of his finger circling her lips, "I think Zack is on to us."

"You mean…that we're lovers?" Zack certainly knew she and Rory had been seeing each other for the past two weeks, but Rory had been careful about concealing the physical side of their relationship from his son.

"Uh-huh. This morning he asked me if I'd been sure to use a condom when I was out with you last night."

She laughed. "Touché, huh? What did you say?"

"I said I'm an adult in an adult relationship and that it wasn't appropriate for him to ask me a question like that. Then he called me a hypocrite and went out to the beach. Not sure I handled it the right way."

"I think you did," she said. "He needs to know there are some boundaries between you and him."

The past two weeks had been a mixture of joy and worry. Being with Rory, being able to openly acknowledge her feelings for him, had been glorious. Everyone on the cul-de-sac knew about them and approved. Shelly was delighted. Only Chloe seemed less than enthusiastic. "He'll be leaving in a few weeks," she'd say to Daria. "Don't throw yourself into this so freely." Chloe was only trying to protect her from being hurt, Daria told herself. Yet she felt as though there was something less noble in Chloe's admonitions, and she wondered at times if Chloe was simply jealous. After all, Chloe's lover was dead, her life in a serious state of disarray.

And that's where the worry came in. Chloe's silence and irritability were evidence of the war going on inside her, and although Daria could think of no way to ease her sister's suffering, that didn't stop her from worrying about her. Then there was Shelly, who grew more attached to her unborn baby with each passing minute. Daria would never be able to persuade her to have an abortion, that much was clear, so some other arrangements would have to be made. She felt no rush to do that. Right now, she wanted to focus her time and attention on Rory. With her sisters' turmoil swirling around her, she had found a safe harbor in his arms.

"So, when do Ellen and Ted get here?" Rory asked her.

She rolled onto her side, resting her head against his shoulder. "Early tomorrow morning," she said, then added sarcastically, "I can hardly wait. They hadn't planned to be here this weekend, but when I stupidly mentioned that the bonfire was scheduled for tomorrow night, they changed their minds."

"I'm not going to be able to look at Ellen the same way now," Rory said.

"Well, I don't think she was one of your favorite people to begin with."

"Shelly was really lucky that you were the one to raise her, and not Ellen."

"I've thought of that," Daria said. "And I was lucky, too. I can't imagine my life without Shelly."

"She hasn't asked me if I've uncovered any more information about who left her on the beach," Rory said.

"How have you explained to Zack or the neighbors why you suddenly stopped researching Shelly's background?" she asked.

"No one's asked me yet," he said. "When and if they do, I'll tell them I wasn't able to come up with enough information to make it worthwhile. The person I worry about telling that I failed in my research is Shelly."

"I know."

"Have you thought about whether Shelly should know the truth?" Rory asked. "I think I would want to know the truth if I were in her shoes, no matter how hard it might be to hear."

Daria smoothed her hand across his chest. "Well," she said, "I'd have to confront Ellen with it first, and I have no desire to do that. I hoped that someday she would come forward herself, but that's never going to happen. It's not Ellen's style. Ellen has one person on her mind, and that's Ellen. I sometimes think she's in denial about Shelly being her daughter. In a different sort of world with a different sort of mother, I would say that Shelly should be told the truth. But Ellen is such a bitch to her, that I can't see how it would do Shelly any good to know."

"Maybe Ellen is a bitch to her, as you say, because she resents her. Shelly was unwanted. The pregnancy got in Ellen's way."

"I don't know, Rory," Daria said. "I've tried analyzing Ellen over the years, and I've never come up with any very charitable perspective on her. I try to remind myself that she was only fifteen. If something like that had happened to me when I was fifteen, I might have done the same thing."

"I doubt that very much." Rory rolled over and leaned on his elbows. He smiled down at her. "Not my Daria," he said. "You would have been too smart to get pregnant in the first place. But if you did, you would have probably delivered the baby yourself, cut the cord with your teeth and breast-fed her while saving three swimmers caught in an undertow."

She laughed. "I think you have me on a bit of a pedestal," she said.

He was quiet a moment. "You haven't talked about your EMT position," he said finally. "After the incident on Andy's pier, I thought you might want to get back into it."

She drew in a long breath. "I feel less afraid," she admitted. "I haven't had a nightmare about the pilot in a few weeks. But I still lied, Rory. I was involved in a cover-up, and I just can't get past that."

"What would happen if you admitted what you did?" he asked.

"I've thought about it. You know, plead temporary insanity and beg for mercy. But the system doesn't work that way. There would have to be an investigation. This sort of thing is taken very seriously, and it should be. I did it to protect my sister, and you and I both know she had no idea what she was doing and that she truly needed that protection. But if *I* can get away with doing that, then someone else should be able to protect his brother for having done something else, and maybe that something else wasn't quite so innocent. So, it can't simply be erased and forgotten. At some point, I'll have to deal with it, because I truly do want to be an EMT again. For the rest of the summer, though, I just want to forget about it and have steamy sex with you. Okay?"

He laughed. "Glad I can help with your escape from reality," he said.

Finished with that topic, she flipped onto her back again. "I have to buy the ingredients for my baked beans today," she said. "What are you bringing to the bonfire?" Everyone on the cul-de-sac was expected to bring food to share.

"Jill suggested I bring the paper plates and napkins and plastic silverware," he said. "I guess she figures I don't look like much of a cook."

Daria could already imagine the smell of the bonfire. Once the daytime crowd had left the beach, Jill and her husband and children would set up two fire rings, one for the adults, a second for the teenagers. Everyone from the cul-de-sac would slowly make their way to the fires, to eat and talk and bemoan the fact that summer was nearly over. The bonfire was always the prelude to summer's end.

Rory glanced at the clock on her night table. "Well, I guess I'd better get back to Poll-Rory," he said. "Time to face more of my son's probing questions about my love life."

He sat on the side of the bed as he dressed, and Daria ran her hand across the warm empty space on the bed where his body had been.

The bonfire. The end of summer.

"Rory?"

"Uh-huh."

"I haven't asked you this, because I've been afraid of the answer," she said. "But when exactly are you going back to California?"

He looked at her over his shoulder, hesitating for a moment before answering. "Let's not talk about it now," he said.

She accepted his answer willingly, not truly wanting to know.

49

"Mmm," Shelly said as she walked in the back door of the Sea Shanty. "You're making the beans."

Daria looked up from the stove, where she was adding brown sugar to the pot of beans. "How was work?"

"Okay. Where are Ellen and Ted?" she asked.

Daria turned the heat down under the beans. "Ted managed to talk Ellen into going fishing with him today," she said, and she was tempted to add, *Isn't that great?* It was a true pleasure not having Ellen at the cottage all day. She knew Shelly felt the same way, although neither of them would say it.

Shelly sat down at the kitchen table. "I don't like working at St. Esther's as much without Father Sean there. Nobody else talks to me like he did. I liked talking to him."

Daria leaned against the counter. "Did Father Macy know about you and Andy?" she asked.

"He knew everything about me," Shelly said bluntly.

Daria wiped a spot of molasses from the counter with a sponge. So, Sean Macy had known about Shelly's relationship with Andy and had said nothing about it to her or Chloe. She was momentarily angry with the priest, but knew that wasn't fair. Shelly had not felt able to talk with her sisters about Andy; it was good she'd at least been able to confide in the priest. No wonder Father Macy's death had been such a loss for her.

Setting down the sponge, Daria walked over to the table and gave her sister a quick hug. "You must really miss him," she said.

"Tons."

Daria looked at her watch, then lifted her purse from the table and rooted around inside it for her car keys. "Could you keep an eye on the beans for a few minutes while I run some errands?" she asked, keys in hand.

"Sure."

"I just have to go to the drugstore and the drive-through at the bank," Daria said. "You got paid today, right? If you want, I can deposit your check for you."

"Oh, I don't have it anymore."

"What do you mean?"

"When I was walking home from the church, I met this girl," Shelly said. "She's only fifteen, and she doesn't have any family."

Daria felt her shoulders stiffen. She had a terrible feeling where this was going; they'd been down this road before. "How do you know she doesn't have a family?" she asked.

"Well, actually she *does* have one." Shelly's large brown eyes were filled with concern. "She has a mother and a stepfather, but they treat her terrible. So, she's in the Outer Banks all by herself. And she didn't have any money, Daria. No money at all! She hadn't had anything to eat all day today and no dinner last night. So, there was a bank right there, and I cashed my check and gave her the money."

Daria dropped her purse onto the table. "Shelly, you can't do things like that!" she said. "First of all, the girl could have been lying to you. Maybe she's using your money right now to buy drugs."

"No, I don't think so," Shelly said. "She was really skinny. I believe that she hasn't eaten in—"

"Even if she *hadn't* eaten, even if she needed a few bucks for a meal, you didn't have to give her your whole check."

"Daria, I wish you could've seen her. You would've given her your whole check, too. She's poor. We're not poor. She needed that money a whole lot more than I did."

"We're not as wealthy as you seem to think," Daria said, although that was hardly the issue. "And now you're expecting a baby. And babies cost money."

Shelly looked stricken. "I won't give any more money away, then," she said quickly. "But really, Daria, she said her stepfather beat her and everything. You wouldn't want her to go back to that kind of home, would you?"

"No, of course not. But there are other ways of handling a situation like that and getting her help." Daria looked toward the ceiling in frustration. "We've been through this so many times, Shelly. You can't save the world, honey."

"I know that. I just wanted to help this one single girl. I don't think that was so wrong."

"It was really...foolish." She had started to say "stupid," but caught herself in time. Tears were already brimming in Shelly's eyes. "This is why I worry about you, Shelly," she said. "This is why I don't believe you're mature enough to have a baby. Your judgment is not always good. I know it's hard to hear that. I know you don't really understand it. But there is no way you're ready to get married and have a child."

Shelly didn't respond. Her eyes suddenly went blank in an expression Daria knew all too well, but hadn't seen in a while. She rushed to her sister's side just as her body stiffened and dropped to the floor.

Shelly began to writhe with convulsions. Daria quickly turned her onto her side, then pulled a cushion from one of the kitchen chairs and slipped it beneath Shelly's head. As she held on to her sister, waiting for the convulsions to run their course, she wondered if the seizure could hurt the baby. If it did, if the baby suffered damage, would Shelly then agree to an abortion? Daria squeezed her eyes shut, horrified with herself for even entertaining the thought.

"Daria?"

She glanced up to see Rory standing in the doorway between the kitchen and living room.

"I think it's almost over," she said, looking down at Shelly, whose body no longer twitched and jerked. She shifted Shelly's head slightly on the pillow to be sure she could breathe easily.

Rory walked across the room and knelt down by Shelly's head. Moaning, Shelly curled herself into a fetal position and slipped her thumb into her mouth. Rory smoothed his hand over her silky blond hair, and Daria fell even more deeply in love with him.

"Could the seizure hurt her baby?" Rory asked.

"It's possible, but this one was very short," Daria said. "I doubt it did any damage."

"Is this the first one she's had all summer?"

"The first in about six months, actually," Daria said. "And I'm afraid I might have brought it on. I yelled at her." She leaned over and kissed Shelly's temple. "I'm sorry, sweetheart."

Rolling onto her back, Shelly opened her eyes. She pulled her thumb from her mouth. "Seizure...?" she asked.

"Uh-huh." Daria nodded. "How do you feel?"

"Did I hurt my baby?"

"No. I don't think so."

Shelly rolled back onto her side and closed her eyes again. "Tired," she said.

"You can't sleep here on the kitchen floor," Daria said. "Stay awake just another minute, honey, so Rory and I can get you to the couch in the living room."

They managed to raise Shelly to her feet, and with their help, she stumbled through the house to the sofa in the living room. She lay down, her thumb back in her mouth.

"Let's go out on the porch," Daria whispered to Rory.

They sat down in two of the rockers, side by side. Rory reached out to hold her hand. "Are you okay?" he asked.

She smiled at him. "I am now," she said.

Shelly had never felt this tired, yet she was awake. Awake enough to hear voices coming through the open window above the sofa. Her eyes were still closed, her head heavy, and it took her a few minutes to recognize the voices as those of Daria and Rory. They were speaking softly. Daria was telling Rory about what she'd done with her paycheck. It seemed like days ago that she'd given the money to that girl. It had seemed like the right thing to do at the time. Had she been foolish? Would Andy have been angry with her, too?

"Sometimes lately," Daria was saying, "I think Pete might have been right about Shelly needing more supervision than she's been getting."

Shelly frowned, concentrating on the words coming from the porch. She needed to listen, especially if the words were about her. But she must have slipped into sleep again, because the next thing she heard was the sound of the ocean, the backdrop for Rory's voice.

"Yeah, I'm down," he said.

"Why?" Daria asked.

"Well, last night you asked me when I was going back to California, and I put you off. I just didn't want to think about it. But I know I have to."

"So…when?" Daria asked, and Shelly knew she was having trouble getting the question out. "When do you go back?"

"September third," he said. "Less than two weeks from now. I have to get Zack back for school. I could kick myself for wasting so much of the summer without you when we could have been together."

"That wouldn't make your leaving any easier," Daria said.

"I know."

For a minute, neither of them said a word. Shelly heard some kids yelling out on the beach. Then Rory spoke again.

"I'm pretty sure I know how you feel, Daria, although I guess I need to hear it, anyway. But I can tell you that *I* don't want this to be the end. I have to go back—that's where my life and job and my son are. But I don't want that to mean we can't still be together."

Daria started to say something Shelly couldn't hear, but he stopped her and kept on talking.

"I know long-distance relationships are for the birds," he said, "and I know our relationship is very new. But in some ways, it's one of the oldest and most enduring relationships I've had. I have to ask you this. I'm sure of your answer, but selfishly, I just have to ask it. Is there any chance…any chance at all that you would move to California? With Shelly, I mean, even though I know it would be hard for her to leave the Outer Banks."

Shelly's heartbeat quickened at the thought, and Rory rushed on, without waiting for Daria to answer him.

"I know there's the baby to take into consideration now," he said. "But I just don't want to lose you now that I found you. We could move closer to the beach in California. Maybe that would make it easier for Shelly to live there."

Shelly held her breath, waiting for Daria's answer. What about Andy? Plus, there were earthquakes in California. And she wouldn't be able to breathe there. She couldn't even breathe in Greenville.

Daria's answer was a very long time coming. "It's impossible," she said finally, and Shelly's body literally shook with relief. "There's no way Shelly could ever move to California, with its earthquakes and its…. It's just not the Outer Banks."

"Leaving Shelly out of this for just a minute," Rory said. "What do *you* want?"

Again, it took Daria a long time to answer, and Shelly heard tears in her sister's voice. "I want to be with *you*," Daria said. "But I love Shelly. I love her so much, and she's my first concern. I was the one who found her and saved her life, and I'm the one responsible for taking care of her. And now there's going to be a baby to take care of, as well. She's never going to give it up, and she can't possibly be expected to take care of it herself. And…I don't see a way of doing that…of taking care of Shelly, and being with you at the same time. It's the same as it was with Pete."

Shelly turned her head toward the window. What did she mean, "The same as it was with Pete"?

"Only Pete didn't want Shelly to come with you to Raleigh," Rory said. "I'd want Shelly with us. That's the difference."

"Yes, that's one of many differences between you and Pete," Daria said. "But the end result is still the same: Shelly can't leave here, so neither can I."

"There's one other difference," Rory said. "Pete broke up with you because you wouldn't leave. I don't have any intention of doing that. I'll find a way to make this work. If I have to choose between having a long-distance relationship with you and no relationship with you, well, that's a no-brainer."

"I'm glad to hear you say that," Daria said.

"Daria," Rory said slowly, "I don't mean to push you on this.

But maybe Shelly is more capable than you give her credit for. Maybe she would be able to take care of a baby with Andy's help."

"You don't know Andy well enough," Daria said. "He is nearly as…unreliable as she is. He's a great carpenter, but he wants to be an EMT and there's no way he'll ever pass the test. And do I have to remind you of the accident with the pilot? Grace's daughter? If it hadn't been for Shelly's lapse in judgment during that rescue, Grace's daughter might still be alive. How can I be sure she'd use any better judgment in taking care of a child?"

What? Shelly raised herself to her elbows to hear better. What was Daria talking about? The pilot was Grace's daughter? What had she done to cause her death? She searched her memory, racing back over those frantic minutes in the cold water. *What had she done?* And what was she doing to Daria? Daria was crying on the other side of the window because of her. She'd been the cause of Pete breaking up with her. She'd had no idea. She'd just gone merrily on her way, thinking Daria was just as happy as she was in the Outer Banks. And now she was standing in the way of her relationship with Rory, as well. But there was no way she could leave the Outer Banks. No way. No way. No way.

If Daria had never found Shelly on the beach, the pilot would still be alive.

Somehow she'd killed the pilot. And she was slowly killing her sister, as well.

50

RORY WAS BEGINNING TO GET WORRIED. HE'D BEEN ON THE beach nearly an hour, and there was still no sign of Daria or Shelly. He'd helped Jill and her husband build the fires and carry the picnic table from their house to the beach. People had arrived, including Chloe, who was carrying Daria's baked beans, and Ellen and Ted, sunburned from their day on the fishing pier. Daria would be over soon, they told him; she was with Shelly, who was still a little groggy from her seizure that afternoon. Now he was wondering if he should go to the Sea Shanty to make sure everything was okay.

As darkness fell, Zack and the other teenagers loaded their plates and went off to their own bonfire, away from the adults and the Wheelers' two youngest granddaughters, who at eight and nine, were caught between the older kids and the grown-ups and not very happy in either camp.

The adults started eating once the teens had moved away from the food-laden table, but Rory held off, still waiting for Daria. Coppery sparks rose into the sky from the bonfire, and he sat on a beach chair, talking to Linda and Jackie, their dog Melissa lying at his feet. He kept glancing toward the Sea Shanty, and finally spotted Daria walking toward him. He excused himself from Linda and Jackie and went to meet her. Only when he was next to her, did he see that Shelly was with her.

"Hi, Shelly," he said.

Shelly gave him a halfhearted wave before walking away from them, toward the teenagers.

Putting his arm around Daria's shoulders, he guided her to the picnic table, covered now with half-empty bowls and trays of food.

"I was getting worried about you," he said.

"I didn't want to leave Shelly," Daria said, looking over her shoulder toward the group of teenagers. "She hasn't pulled out of her post-seizure fog the way she usually does."

"She doesn't seem like her usual perky self," he admitted, remembering the weak wave she'd offered him.

"She's not. She's very…subdued. And she's not talking to me. She's angry with me for blowing up at her, I guess. I still feel bad about it."

"Isn't she going to eat?" Rory asked.

"I doubt it. She said she's not hungry."

"What is she usually like after a seizure?" he asked.

"Tired. She usually sleeps for a while, and then she rallies. Not this time, though."

"Could her pregnancy have something to do with it? Either physically or psychologically?"

"I wondered that myself," Daria said. "I'll have to do some research into seizures during pregnancy."

Rory handed her a plate. "The food is different than it was when we were kids," he said, spooning some of her beans onto his own plate. "Everything's low-fat now. It's all salads and couscous and tabouli. What happened to the burgers and the barbecue?"

Daria smiled, and he was glad to see it. "I didn't realize it, but you're right," she said. "I come to the bonfire every year, so the changes have been gradual for me. But compared to when we were kids, this is completely different fare."

"Except for your beans," he said. "They're the only good, down-home cooking on the table. Your mother used to make these, too, didn't she?" He ate a forkful of the beans before moving on to the next offering.

"Uh-huh."

"I remember, because I wouldn't eat them," he said with a laugh. "I thought it was weird that they had all these different-colored beans in them. Didn't look like the canned kind I was used to." He took another bite. "Didn't know what I was missing."

He couldn't believe he was talking to her about beans and food, when his insides were still churning from their conversation that afternoon. In less than two weeks, the country would divide them. She felt the same way, he could tell by the way she looked at him as they sat down on the beach chairs near the fire. It was a look of resignation and sorrow that made him reach out to touch her arm. He wished they had the beach to themselves rather than having to share it with their neighbors from the cul-de-sac.

Daria suddenly looked over her shoulder in the direction of the cul-de-sac. "There's Grace," she said.

Rory turned around. Sure enough, Grace had crossed through the sea oats and was walking toward them, a large bowl in her arms. "What's she doing here?" he said under his breath to Daria. He hadn't seen Grace, hadn't even heard from her, since the day he'd told her that he and Daria were together. He stood up and took a step away from the circle to greet her.

"Hi, Rory. Hi, Daria," Grace said, an uncertain smile on her face. "I hope you don't mind my stopping by. I brought some fruit salad."

Daria rested her plate on the fire ring and stood up to take the bowl from Grace's arms. "We've got the food over here," she said, walking toward the picnic table.

Grace must have caught Rory's look of confusion as they followed Daria to the table. "I know you weren't expecting to see me here," she said. "And, Daria, I want you to know how really pleased I am that you and Rory are…you know, seeing each other."

Daria gave her a half smile. "Thanks," she said.

"I think you two are really good together," Grace continued. "But when I remembered that tonight was the bonfire, I decided to come over. I hope that's all right. It's just that I knew everyone from the cul-de-sac would be here, and there's something I need to talk about. To everyone."

Why? he wanted to ask. Grace had perplexed him from the moment he'd met her. He wasn't sure what she was up to this time, but he didn't feel like making her his responsibility.

"Okay," he said. "Help yourself and come sit by the fire."

He and Daria waited while she took a couple of spoonfuls of food onto her plate, then the three of them moved to the fire. Rory found an empty beach chair and set it in the sand next to Daria for Grace. Better next to her than him, he thought. Chloe, who was sitting on the other side of the fire near Ellen and Ted, greeted Grace by name, but the other neighbors merely nodded and smiled in her direction.

Chloe stood up and moved to the empty beach chair next to Rory, leaning across him to speak to Daria.

"How's Shelly?" she asked. "Isn't she eating?"

"She said she's not hungry," Daria said.

"What's wrong with Shelly?" Grace asked. "Where is she?"

"She had a seizure today," Daria said. "I think she's still feeling a little tired from it."

"Is she at the Sea Shanty?" Grace glanced over her shoulder, where the widow's walk was barely visible in the darkness.

"No, she's down there with the kids." Daria pointed toward the second fire.

Melissa lifted her head to sniff Rory's food, then leaned against his legs. He scratched her behind her ears.

"My guys are going to miss you when summer's over," Linda said to Rory from her seat on the other side of the fire. She had her arm around Jackie.

"Yeah, I was thinking I might have to get me one of these when I get home." Rory looked down at Melissa's kind eyes.

"When do you leave?" Ted asked.

"September third."

"I'm sorry to see you go," Ted said. "It's great seeing you and Daria together."

Ellen rested her empty plate on the edge of the fire ring. "So, was this just an end-of-the-summer fling for the two of you?" she asked bluntly. "What happens next?"

Rory took Daria's hand again. "No," he said calmly. "It's not a summer fling. We'll have to figure out how to keep things going. I'd like to have Daria and Shelly move to California, but Daria doesn't think that would work out."

"Shelly would never survive in California," Daria said. "And she needs me too much for me to just pick up and move three thousand miles away."

"Oh, for Pete's sake," Ellen said. "When are you going to start living your own life, Daria?"

Rory felt Daria bristle next to him, and Ellen continued. "It's like you're married to her," she said.

"Ellen, that's really not fair," Rory said. He wondered how Ellen could talk that way to Daria, when Daria had been the one to so lovingly raise the child Ellen had abandoned.

"Daria's done the best job possible with Shelly," Chloe said to Ellen.

"I agree," Grace said firmly. "From what I've seen, Daria's been fantastic for Shelly."

"Give me a break," Ellen said. "If anything, she's ruined Shelly."

The atmosphere around the bonfire was suddenly thick with tension. Mrs. Wheeler told her granddaughters to "go over to the picnic table and get some dessert." Jill studied her fingernails, and Jackie studiously began petting one of the dogs.

"I'm sorry, Daria," Ellen continued, "but it's the truth, and it's time somebody told you. You've made Shelly so dependent on you and on this tiny little corner of the world, that living anywhere else is going to be a major hurdle for her. But it's a hurdle she has to jump over one of these days, and you need to let her."

"Don't you dare give me advice about Shelly." Daria's voice was even, *too* even, and in the firelight, Rory saw the rigid set of her jaw. "You see her for a couple of days at a time, then you go back to your own, self-absorbed life and complain about what I've done with her. That doesn't help, Ellen. As a matter of fact, you've done nothing to help with Shelly, have you?"

Chloe reached across Rory to wrap her hand around Daria's arm. "Daria," she said softly. "Not here, sis."

"You wouldn't have accepted my help even if I'd offered it," Ellen said. "You resented any suggestions I've ever made. In my opinion, you should move to California and be with Rory. Leave Shelly here, if this is where she wants to be. She's an adult now. She'll survive somehow."

Daria wrenched her arm free of Chloe's hand. "Is that what you thought when you left her on the beach twenty-two years ago?" she snapped. "That she'd survive somehow?"

The bonfire crackled, waves broke and hissed to shore, and the teenagers laughed. But no one around the bonfire uttered a word. People looked from Daria to Ellen and back again. Ellen's mouth dropped open in what Rory guessed to be a pretense of shock.

"What the hell are you talking about?" Ellen bit off each word as it came out of her mouth.

"I've had it with your insensitivity to Shelly," Daria said.

Rory stroked his hand down Daria's back, wishing there was something he could do to change the direction of her anger. This was not the place or time for a personal confrontation. But Daria seemed completely unaware that her neighbors were even present, much less paying attention to every word.

"Shelly has special needs," Daria continued. "And she probably *wouldn't* have them if you'd… If she'd been born in a hospital to a mother willing to take responsibility for her, she'd probably be fine. You've even been a lousy mother to the two daughters you acknowledge as yours."

Ted leaned forward. "Daria, you're off your rocker," he said. "If you've got a bone to pick with—"

"Are you accusing me of being Shelly's mother?" Ellen interrupted her husband. "Is that what you're saying?"

"That's exactly what I'm saying," Daria said.

"You are losing it, Daria," Ellen said. "I didn't have anything to do with Shelly being dumped on the beach."

Daria started to stand up, but Rory caught her arm. She looked at him and must have seen the plea in his eyes, because she dropped into the chair again. When she spoke, her voice was calmer.

"I know this isn't the time for this," Daria said. "I'm sorry I spilled it out this way. But it's the truth, Ellen, and it's time you admitted it. I found your pukka-shell necklace lying right next to the baby. I've known all along. I didn't say anything back then because I didn't want to get you in trouble. But it's twenty-two years later, and it's time to own up to the fact that Shelly was yours."

Rory's gaze was suddenly drawn to Grace. She looked truly ill, her face more ashen than usual. Even the golden flames from the fire brought no color to her cheeks. She opened her mouth as if to say something, but Chloe spoke first.

"I took Ellen's necklace that night," Chloe said.

All heads turned in her direction. Sitting right next to her, Rory could see the resolve in Chloe's face.

"I borrowed it without her permission," Chloe continued. "I never knew what happened to it. I guess it fell off while I was…" Her voice trailed off. She stared into the fire, then looked up again, her eyes glassy and apologetic as she turned to Daria. "Shelly's mine," she said.

"Chloe." Mrs. Wheeler breathed the word in disbelief.

Rory's mind raced. *Sean Macy.* The priest had been involved with Chloe for many years, had even managed to help her parents adopt Shelly. No wonder he had killed himself when Rory was trying to uncover Shelly's parentage. He rested his hand lightly on Chloe's arm. "Yours and Sean's," he said softly, not wanting anyone else to hear.

"No," she said in a whisper. The piercing look in her eyes was meant just for him, and it sent a chill down his back. "Not Sean's," she said.

Rory went numb as he realized what she was telling him.

"Chloe," Daria said. "I don't understand." And Rory knew she understood even less than she thought.

"Where's Shelly?" The voice came from the beach, and Rory turned to see Andy approaching the bonfire.

For a moment, no one said a word; Chloe's admission had stolen their voices. "She's down there with the youngsters." Mr. Wheeler pointed toward the second bonfire.

"No, she's not," Andy said. "I was just down there. She *was* with them, but Zack said she went in for a swim. He thought she might have come out of the water up here to be with you guys."

"A swim in the dark?" Daria got to her feet. "She knows better than that."

Rory stood up. "Zack!" he called, waving toward the huddled group down the beach.

"What?" Zack called back.

"Come here!" Rory said.

Zack must have heard the urgency in his voice, because he came over to the adults' bonfire at a jog.

"When did Shelly go into the water?" Daria asked.

"I don't know." Zack shrugged. "Maybe five or ten minutes ago? I thought she was just taking a dip and planned to come out up here by you. She was saying some strange things."

"Like what?" Daria asked.

"She told me...she said she wanted you to be able to go to California with Dad. She said you wouldn't have to worry about her anymore, or something like that. I wasn't sure if that was something you were actually thinking about doing or if she was just, you know, like fantasizing or something. Because then she said she was sorry about the pilot. I don't know what pilot she's talking about. I wasn't paying much attention to her. She—"

"She overheard us." Daria pressed her fist to her mouth and looked at Rory. "Our conversation on the porch. I thought she was asleep."

Rory thought back to that conversation, imagining how it had sounded to Shelly's sensitive ears.

"I'm sure she planned to swim up here to you guys, because she said goodbye to us," Zack said. "I mean, like a real goodbye, like she was leaving us for the night."

"Or forever." Rory grabbed his son's arm. "Come on," he said, running toward the ocean. "Show me where she went in."

Running away from the bonfire, he was vaguely aware of the shouting behind him. He heard Daria yell for someone to call 911. Someone else said they would check the Sea Shanty to see if Shelly might have gone back there. And he knew that several people were running after him, as beams from their flashlights darted off the sand ahead of him.

"I think it was here, Dad," Zack said, pointing into the black ocean. "I think she went straight out from our bonfire."

Rory tore off his shirt and plunged into the water. "Give me light!" he called over his shoulder, and the flashlights instantly illuminated the water around him. Swimming through the breaking waves, searching the water with his eyes, he realized how fruitless his quest was. He had no idea how far out Shelly had gone, or where she had been when she let herself go under—surely that had been her plan. Sean Macy had said it was all right to kill yourself if you were doing so to save someone else, and Shelly must have thought she was saving Daria. She had no idea that her death would have exactly the opposite effect on the sister who adored her.

Rory felt disoriented in the water. The sky and water and air all around him were black, and he thought about how easy it would be to die out here. To simply slip beneath the surface into more blackness. He heard splashing as other people came into the water. One of the beams of light illuminated Daria as she fought her way through the waves.

"Daria!" he called. "How did she usually swim out here? Would she swim straight out, or parallel to the beach, or—"

"Depends on her purpose!" Daria shouted back to him. "I'm afraid…I'm afraid straight out, this time."

She knew as well as he did what Shelly's purpose had been.

He oriented himself to the teenagers' bonfire, then turned and began swimming farther into the opaque sea. He had gone only a few strokes when he felt something soft brush against his leg. Seaweed, he thought. He almost didn't bother to reach down to touch it, but he did, and his fingers slipped into the silky, undulating tangle of Shelly's hair. Diving beneath the surface of the water, he grasped her arms and lifted her up to the air. She was a heavy weight against him, heavy and silent, and he knew she was not breathing.

"I have her!" he called. The beams of light darted around him, finally focusing directly on him as he swam, Shelly's body still beneath his arm.

"Is she alive?" someone called from the beach. It sounded like Grace's voice.

"Is she okay?" someone else shouted.

He was winded as he neared the shore, and Daria and Andy pulled Shelly from him, dragging her through the breaking water and laying her down on the beach. In the light from the flashlights, Shelly's skin was already waxy and blue, and he felt a cry rising up his throat. He managed to swallow it back down as he fell to his knees next to her.

"I'll do the compressions," Daria said to him. "You breathe."

He had his mouth on Shelly's, her nose pinched closed by his fingers, before Daria had even finished her sentence. The sound of sirens wailed far in the distance as he blew air into Shelly's lungs, breathing for her in a fury, trying his best to save his daughter's life.

51

RORY WAS COLD. SOMEONE—HE HAD NO IDEA WHO—HAD given him a sweatshirt to put on, but his shorts were still damp and the air-conditioning in the hospital was bone-chilling.

Daria put her arm around him, trying to warm him, but her effort was futile. She was equally as cold, and her body shivered next to his. They were sitting on a vinyl-covered couch in a tiny waiting room in the ER, across the hall from the treatment room where doctors were working on Shelly. Chloe, Andy and Zack were with them. He thought that Grace and Ellen and some of the neighbors were in the larger, general waiting room, but he wasn't sure. He wasn't sure of much. Not even how long they'd been sitting there, waiting for word on Shelly's condition.

Not one of them had spoken since they'd been ushered into the room. There was so much that needed to be said, but no one knew exactly where to begin. Andy sat on one of the hard plastic chairs in the room, his eyes downcast. The only sign that he was alive was the too-rapid rise and fall of his chest. Zack sat next to Rory, on the other side of him from Daria, and Rory rubbed his son's back. Zack had cried openly on the drive to the hospital. "It's my fault," he said over and over again. "I should have realized something was radically wrong with her by how weird she was acting."

Rory had told him it was not his fault. It was no one person's fault. To himself, he thought that everyone shared a bit of the blame.

He looked across the small room at Chloe, where she sat alone on the vinyl love seat. Her eyes were closed, the dark lashes long and flat against her cheeks, and he guessed she was praying. Suddenly, she looked up, and her gaze met his.

"I need to talk." Her voice splintered the silence in the room.

The others turned their heads toward her in slow motion, as though not quite certain they'd heard her.

Chloe looked at Daria. "I'm so sorry, Daria," she said. "I'm sorry I never told you."

"I thought it was Ellen," Daria said. "All these years, I thought it was her. I could imagine her doing something like that. I couldn't imagine you doing it."

Chloe nodded. "It's hard for me to imagine it myself," she said. "Something happened to me back then. I snapped. That's my only excuse. You remember what I was like, Daria. I was a pretty good kid. I attended church every Sunday. I was obedient." She laughed. "I even prayed the rosary every night, I wanted so much to be good and pure and holy. But I was always fascinated by sex. I knew that having sex prior to marriage was a sin, but I was drawn to it. I was drawn to boys."

"I remember that," Daria said.

"In high school, I had sex with a few different boys," Chloe said. "I'd come home afterward and pray to God to forgive me. I promised myself that it would never happen again, but, of course, it always did. Then, when I was seventeen, I became pregnant."

Daria removed her arm from around Rory's shoulders to

lean toward her sister. "Who was it?" she asked. "Who is Shelly's father?"

Rory held his breath. Chloe didn't so much as glance in his direction, and he knew she wasn't going to give him away.

"It doesn't matter. He was just a boy." Chloe gnawed at her upper lip. "I was terrified," she continued. "There was no way I could tell Mom and Dad, and there was no way I could ever have an abortion. I was away from home, in my freshman year of college, but I didn't really have very many friends. I was younger than most of the other kids, both chronologically and socially, but I pretended that I had this great social life and that's why I didn't come home for holidays. I was just afraid Mom would figure out I was pregnant if I went home." Chloe scratched her cheek. "I really don't know what I thought I was going to do when I came to the Sea Shanty that summer. I was wearing oversize clothing, but I knew I couldn't do that for the whole summer. I remember being glad that the weather was so bad that first week, and it didn't seem too strange to be wearing sweatshirts and whatever. I hadn't gotten any prenatal care. I had no idea how far along I was. In retrospect, I know I was about eight months pregnant."

She glanced at him now, but quickly shifted her gaze to a spot on the floor, and Rory wished he didn't have to hear this. Yet, he only had to *hear* it, he thought. Chloe'd had to *live* it.

"One night, I woke up in bed and I was in labor," Chloe continued. "I was terrified. I didn't know what to do. I couldn't go into Mom and Dad's bedroom and say, 'Guess what, Mom, I'm having a baby.' I know this sounds crazy—" she looked at Daria "—but I don't think I ever really believed it. Not even then, when I was in so much pain. You hear about teenage girls delivering babies when they didn't even know they were pregnant, and it sounds so crazy. But I can under-stand it. I had somehow managed to ignore what was happening to me. So, even that night, I felt detached through it all. It's hard to explain. I knew I had to get away from the house, though, so I went out on the beach." Chloe lowered her head. She was breathing through her mouth. Her nose was red, and when she looked up again, her eyes were overflowing with tears. Rory had the urge to move next to her, to take her in his arms and tell her he was sorry for all she'd been through— and for his role in it. Instead, he stood up, plucked a tissue from the box on one of the end tables and handed it to her before taking his own seat again next to Daria. "It was horrible," Chloe said, blotting her eyes with the tissue.

Daria moved across the room to sit next to her sister. She put her hand on Chloe's back. "It must have been so frightening," she said.

Andy stared at both women, and Rory had the feeling he didn't care about Chloe's trauma. He just wanted Shelly to be all right.

"I thought I was going to die," Chloe said. "I thought I deserved to die, and there was no way I could turn to anyone for help. I just lay there on the beach, crying and terrified. And then…it was the strangest thing. The baby just came out of me. I wasn't even sure it was alive. It was so dark out there, and the baby didn't cry. I was certain it was dead. And to be completely honest, I was relieved. If it was dead, no one ever had to know. I washed myself off in the water. I didn't even look at what had come out of me—that's how I thought of it. Not as a baby, but as something foreign that had been inside of me and, to my relief, no longer was. I went back in the house, went to bed and fell asleep, and I slept until the next morning, when you found Shelly." She looked at Daria. "I can't describe how I felt when I heard you had found the baby and that she was alive. I was in so much denial, that I actually convinced myself that maybe it wasn't *my* baby that you'd found. Some other baby had somehow gotten out there on the beach, but I knew in my heart she was mine. I felt such relief that she was alive, but terribly guilty that I had left her out there to fend for herself. And, of course, I still couldn't admit to Mom and Dad or anyone else that the baby was mine. Except for Sean. I went to see him that afternoon. He was still Father Macy to me then. Still a priest and not a man I loved."

Rory wondered how that sounded to Zack. He had known nothing of Chloe's relationship with Sean Macy. Zack was sitting very still on the couch, not moving, barely breathing.

"I cried and berated myself," Chloe said, "and Sean told me that God loved the truly repentant sinner. We talked for a long time, and I knew I could trust him. He made me feel forgiven and safe. I knew right then that I wanted to be a part of the Church forever. I hoped that taking a vow of chastity would somehow erase my sexual side. Of course, that had been an unrealistic expectation, but I was young. I didn't know."

She blew her nose, then sat hunched over her lap, Daria's hand on her back, and Rory knew he had to speak. Chloe had gone through that pregnancy alone. He wasn't going to let her carry this burden by herself, as well.

"Chloe's left out one important fact," he said slowly.

Chloe raised her head sharply to look at him.

"This is hard to say." He looked at Daria, squarely, trying not to flinch. "I believe I'm Shelly's father."

No one said a word. Daria looked at him hard, a crease between her eyebrows.

"What?" Andy finally broke the silence.

"You don't have to do this, Rory," Chloe said gently.

"Yes, I do," Rory said. "It's time for the truth."

"You're…" Daria shook her head with a frown. "Have you known this all along?" she asked.

"No," he said. "I had no idea. Not until the bonfire tonight.

When Chloe said that she was Shelly's mother, I could tell...
She gave me an unspoken message..." He looked at Chloe,
and she nearly smiled at him. "And I knew," he said.

"But she was seventeen," Daria said. "You would have
only been..."

"Fourteen," he volunteered. He wondered how to say
anything more without painting a worse picture of Chloe
than she had already painted for herself. "I was fourteen," he
repeated, "and anxious to experience anything I could." He
still remembered that night vividly. The dunes at Jockey's
Ridge had been chilly, the sand downright cold. It was
October, Columbus Day weekend, when most of the home-
owners of the cul-de-sac came to the beach for a three-day
getaway. He'd been naive, but willing—no, *eager*—to learn, and
Chloe had been an excellent teacher.

Rory smiled weakly at his son. "I owe you an apology,
Zack," he said. "I came down on you pretty hard this summer
for your relationship with Kara." He had even used Shelly's
birth and desertion as an example of one young couple's poor
judgment and irresponsible behavior. He waited for Zack to
rub his nose in it.

But Zack surprised him. "It's okay, Dad." His voice was
husky, and he put an awkward arm around Rory's shoulders.
"Everybody makes mistakes."

"Daria." Chloe turned to her sister, taking both Daria's
hands in her own. "I'm so sorry you had to take such complete
responsibility for Shelly. When Mom died, I probably should
have taken over, but it would have meant leaving my order,
and you never seemed to mind being in the position of caretaker."

"I never did mind," Daria said. She sounded flat, and Rory
had no idea how she was handling the revelations filling this
tiny room. She had to feel betrayed by both Chloe and himself.

But he guessed that right now, her mind was on Shelly. Nothing else—no confessions, no disclosures—could eclipse that primary concern.

"If Shelly lives…" Chloe pressed the tissue to her eyes, and it was a moment before she could continue. "If she lives," she said, "I'll take care of her, Daria. I'll stay in Kill Devil Hills with her. It's time you were able to live your own life. Move to California with Rory, if that's what you want."

Daria said nothing. She avoided Rory's gaze, and he could hardly blame her.

Andy suddenly spoke up again. "What did you mean at the bonfire, Daria, when you said that Shelly overheard you and Rory on the porch?"

Daria pressed her fingers to her forehead, rubbing her temples. "I think Shelly must have heard us talking about how Pete broke up with me because of her. And she heard us talking about…" Daria's voice trailed off. "Do you remember the plane accident back in April, Andy?" she asked.

Andy nodded.

"Remember how Shelly swam out to help us? The pilot was this young, eighteen-year-old girl," she explained to Chloe and Zack. "It turns out she was Grace's daughter, but none of us knew that at the time."

"Grace's *daughter?*" Andy asked. "Why didn't you tell me?"

"It's not important now," Daria said. "What *is* important is that Pete was trying to free the pilot. She was trapped in her seat, twisted around in her seat belt, somehow. Pete kept having to go underwater to try to get to her belt. And then, suddenly, he started yelling at Shelly. Shelly was supposed to be keeping the plane afloat, but she was leaning on the propeller instead, actually dragging the plane down. She was—"

"What?" Andy interrupted her. "Is that what Pete told you?"

Daria stared at him. "Yes," she said. "He—"

"Son of a bitch." Andy stood up, fire in his eyes. "Shelly didn't do anything wrong. How stupid do you think she is? It was *Pete* who dragged the plane down. I saw the whole thing. He didn't mean to, I know that, but he was standing on the pontoon for a minute, and that pulled the plane and the pilot under. When Pete figured out what he was doing, he started yelling at Shelly. I didn't get why he was yelling at her. She was just treading water; she didn't have a clue what he was yelling at her about. Pete is a frigging coward. He wanted to find a way to get you to lock Shelly up so you could go with him to Raleigh."

"My God, Andy." Daria's face was ashen, and Rory knew she believed every word Andy had said. "I wish you'd told me sooner."

"If I'd known he was pinning the blame on Shelly, I would have."

"Poor Shelly," Daria said. "She probably overheard—" She turned at the sound of the door opening, and the woman physician who had been treating Shelly walked into the room. Rory stood up, and the others followed his lead, as they waited to hear what their futures would hold.

52

THE SUN WAS A CREAMY ORANGE GLOBE HANGING LOW over the ocean as Grace drove to Rodanthe in the morning. She was exhausted and numb, confused and dazed. Shelly was not hers; that much was clear. Yet she had come to love her, and as she drove, she prayed. Prayed and cried.

She pulled into her driveway and went into the house. She'd been living there with Eddie ever since the day he'd followed her to Rory's house. It was Eddie who'd persuaded her to go to the bonfire the night before. It was time she told everyone the truth, he'd said. She needed to do it to be sure Shelly was evaluated for Marfan's syndrome. Chloe, though, had beaten her at the truth-telling game. How Grace's heart had survived that revelation, she had no idea.

She'd called Eddie from the hospital late last night to tell him all that had happened, and now she found him waiting for her in the living room. He handed her a cup of coffee, gave her a hug.

"How is Shelly?" he asked.

"She's in critical condition," she said, sitting down on the sofa. "They only give her a fifty percent chance of pulling through. And if she does make it, she may have even more brain damage."

"That's terrible." Eddie shook his head. "What a shame."

"I'm still in shock." She lifted the coffee to her lips, but lowered the cup again without taking a sip. "I just can't believe she's not mine, Eddie."

"I can," he said.

"Why do you say that?"

"Because," he said, "I found the nurse."

"What?" She set the cup on the coffee table. "How did you—"

"That doesn't matter," he said.

"Does she know what happened to my daughter? Does she know who adopted her?"

He nodded. "Yes, she knows. But she didn't want to get into it on the phone. She asked that I bring you to her. She said it was the sort of thing she should talk to you about face-to-face."

Grace looked at her watch. "Can we go today? Is it too early to go now?" She was ready to race out the door.

Eddie smiled. "Let me give her a call first," he said. "But I think it will be okay."

He made the call to the nurse, Grace dissecting his every word as she tried to imagine what Nancy was saying on the other end of the line. *Nurse Nancy.* How Grace had hated her all these years!

Then Eddie called Sally to tell her they wouldn't make it into the café today and to ask her to take over for them. Finally, they were ready to leave.

They were both quiet in the car as they drove up the Barrier Islands and across the bridge to the mainland. Grace kneaded her hands together in her lap, anxiously wondering what sort of people had adopted her child. And would her daughter want to see her? She had to be prepared for the fact that she might not.

She read the directions to Eddie as they entered Elizabeth

City. They drove through a beautiful old neighborhood, with tree-lined streets and old-fashioned streetlights, finally coming to stop in front of a large brick house. Nancy and Nathan had obviously moved up in the world since Shelly was born, Grace thought, when they'd only been able to afford that raunchy little cottage for their vacation.

Eddie looked at her across the seat. "Ready?" he asked.

She nodded, pressed her clammy palms together and got out of the car.

They walked hand in hand up the slate walk to the front door. Eddie rang the bell, and Grace waited for Nancy to appear. Instead, though, the door was opened by a young woman Shelly's age. She was tall and slender, with dark hair, an uncertain smile and a deep and definite widow's peak.

Epilogue

ONLY AS THE AMBULANCE RACED TOWARD THE BEACH NEAR milepost 6, did the irony of the situation strike Daria full force. Here she was, one year almost to the day after the plane crash, heading for another water emergency on the beach. This time, it was an early-morning surfing accident that needed her attention.

Daria was once again a full-fledged EMT, having battled her demons over the death of the pilot, and she felt no trepidation as the ambulance parked at the end of the street. She and Mike jumped out and ran toward the small crowd that had formed around the fallen surfer. People drew back to let them through, and only then did Daria see that the surfer was a woman. Dressed in a wet suit, she lay on the cold sand, while a male surfer pressed a towel to her head.

Daria and Mike dropped to their knees next to the woman. She was conscious, even laughing a bit at something her surfing partner had said to her.

"Her board hit her in the head," the man said. "She lost consciousness for a minute or two, but seems all right now."

Daria took the woman's vital signs, while Mike tended to the laceration on her head. They were strapping her onto a backboard when Daria happened to look up to see Shelly standing near the center of the crowd, baby Mattie in a sack against her chest. Daria waved, and Shelly waved back. She remembered that Shelly planned to make dinner for everyone that night.

In a matter of hours, Rory would be in Kill Devil Hills. He was bicoastal these days, spending Monday through Thursday in California and living at the Sea Shanty the rest of the time. Zack came with him every once in a while. Their presence made the Sea Shanty a wonderfully full house, since Andy, Shelly and the baby were living there, as well. Daria needed to be certain that Andy and Shelly could handle child care without her help, although she had few doubts at this point. Both Shelly and Andy were attentive, careful parents.

During the week, when Rory was not with her, Daria watched him on *True Life Stories.* It was strange to see him on television and know that he was hers—and that they'd been brought together by the one true life story he would never talk about in public.

The crowd dispersed after the surfer had been taken away in the ambulance, and Shelly began strolling toward the Sea Shanty, talking to Mattie as she walked. This last month, she'd come to understand Daria's overprotectiveness, because she now experienced the feeling herself. She could not get enough of her month-old daughter. She studied the way Mattie clenched and unclenched her tiny fists and the expression on her face that was beginning to resemble a smile, and she prayed that the baby was all right. She had deprived Mattie of oxygen when she was underwater; no one really knew how long she and her baby had gone without air. She herself had no memory of that night at all.

She'd had to deliver Mattie at a special maternity ward in a hospital in Elizabeth City, because her doctor was afraid the baby would not be okay. Mattie had surprised everyone, though. She was born healthy, and she still seemed healthy. But Shelly had seemed healthy when she was a baby, too. It would only be later, when Mattie tried to learn how to tie her shoes or add two plus two that they would know what the time without oxygen had done to her.

If she let herself think about it too long, Shelly could still cry over this. Chloe helped her with the guilt, though; Chloe knew all about guilt. She called Shelly several times a week from Georgia, where she was still teaching, but no longer a nun, and she talked about how sorry she was about the poor start she'd given Shelly in life. But Shelly felt no anger toward her. No one ever talked about this, but Shelly knew that Chloe was one of those women who wasn't cut out to be a mother. Chloe loved her, Shelly was certain of that, but it was a sisterly kind of love, not the motherly kind. She got plenty of that, though, from Daria.

In the last eight months or so, Shelly had undergone a metamorphosis. That was the word Zack had used to describe her transformation the last time he visited Kill Devil Hills, and she liked the way it felt in her mouth. She was definitely a stronger person. She'd been seeing a therapist, and he'd helped her feel less afraid about leaving the Outer Banks. He even drove her onto the mainland every couple of weeks during her session, taking her farther and farther away from Kill Devil Hills each time, and she no longer trembled at the thought of leaving the Barrier Islands. The therapist, of course, thought it was his fine work with her that had led to that result, but it was actually the baby. Mattie could do what no one else had been able to do: make Shelly less afraid. It was impossible, Shelly discovered, to focus on her own fears when she was concentrating on Mattie and her needs. Last week, she and Andy had driven the baby all the way to Greenville to be checked out by a specialist, and Shelly hadn't realized the magnitude of what she had done until they were in the car coming home. Andy was proud of her, and she was proud of herself.

Her family had grown quite complicated. She had a father—an *excellent* father. She started calling Rory "Dad" just a couple of months ago. It had felt funny at first, and made them both laugh whenever she said it, but now it felt natural. Just a few weeks ago, he and Daria and Shelly and Andy had gone out to dinner together and discussed how confusing the Cato family tree had become. Rory and Daria planned to get married that summer. Once they did, Rory pointed out, Daria would be Shelly's sister and stepmother, as well as Mattie's aunt, great-aunt and grandmother. Plus, Rory said, Shelly had a new half brother—Zack—in addition to her two sisters, one who was actually her mother, the other, her aunt. Andy had laughed and said what a crazy family he'd married into.

Someday, she and Andy and Mattie would leave the Outer Banks. Even though everything she could possibly need was there on that long narrow strip of land, Shelly wanted more for Mattie than Kill Devil Hills could offer. Andy talked about how much he would like to live in California, and Shelly was beginning to think she might be able to actually go there someday. No matter where she lived, though, she was looking forward to the day when she would bring an older Mattie back to the Outer Banks. She would walk with her on the beach in the morning and teach her the names of the shells, and she'd stay with her daughter in Kill Devil Hills long enough to make the scent of the sea part of Mattie's soul. It would be a time with family, when she, Andy and Mattie, Daria, Chloe, Rory and Zack were all at the Sea Shanty. And she would tell Mattie the story of the girl who kicked over a horseshoe-crab shell on the beach and gave all of them a chance at life.

Acknowledgments

I would like to thank the following people for their input into the creation of the fictional world in *Summer's Child*:

Caitlin Heagy Campbell was instrumental in helping me add another layer to my story, and Cindy Schacte enthusiastically aided and abetted me during the plotting process.

Skeeter Sawyer provided information about the Dare County Emergency Medical Services. Any mistakes in applying that information to my story are mine alone.

Joann Scanlon and Priscilla McPherson gave me excellent feedback on my outline.

My former editor at MIRA Books, Amy Moore-Benson, and my former agent, Ginger Barber, helped in countless ways to make this a better book.

Finally, I'd like to thank the many people who shared with me their love and knowledge of North Carolina's beautiful Outer Banks.

A riveting new novel from acclaimed author

DIANE CHAMBERLAIN

Secrets She Left Behind

One afternoon, single mother Sara Weston
says that she's going to the store—and
never returns. She leaves her teenage
son alone with his damaged past
and a legacy of secrets.

Keith Weston nearly lost his
life in an act of arson. He
survived—but with devastating
physical and emotional scars.
Without his mother, he has no one
to help him heal, no money, nothing
to live for but the medications that
numb his pain. Isolated and angry,
he has one tight focus for his hatred:
his half sister, Maggie Lockwood.

Now the person Keith despises
most is the closest thing he has to
family—until Sara returns.
If Sara returns…

Available now,
wherever books
are sold.

MIRA®

A riveting novel by acclaimed author

DIANE CHAMBERLAIN

Laurel lost her son once through neglect. She's spent the rest of her life determined to make up for her mistakes. Still, she loosens her grip just enough to let Andy attend a local church social—a decision that terrifies her when the church is consumed by fire. But Andy survives...and saves other children. Laurel watches as Andy basks in the role of unlikely hero and the world finally sees her Andy.

But when the suspicion of arson is cast upon Andy, Laurel must ask herself how well she really knows her son....

BEFORE *the* STORM

"Chamberlain skillfully...
plumbs the nature of crimes of the heart."
—*Publishers Weekly* on *The Bay at Midnight*

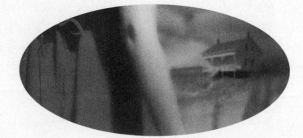

Available wherever books are sold.

MIRA®

MDC2541TRR